Churchill's In

A tale of escape from the Russian Civil War. 1919 – 1920.

Andy Stuart

Inspired by stories from my Grandad, Arthur Walton.

A portrait photo of Arthur taken some time in the 1930's.

Cover Picture: Churchill and Lloyd-George.

For my wife Diane.
Children, Olivia, Tom and Sam.
And their partners, Steve and Ashley.

In memory of my Dad,
Roderick Royal Stuart 1938 – 2024.
Always encouraging, always enthusiastic.

Table of Contents.

A Short Review   Tales From The   1
           Great War I and II

Prologue   Kovno, Lithuania 3
           1871

Part One
1. Loughborough   Thursday 30th July 4
           1914

2. Martin's Pharmacy I   9
3. David Saffer   14
4. 17 Clarence Street   17
5. Alice Baker   Saturday 1st August 21
6. Syphilis Ointment Monday 3rd August 23
7. Tynte House   29
8. Departure   Tuesday 4th August 38
9. Martin's Pharmacy II   41
10. Enlistment   Trafalgar Square, 4th 44
           August 1914.

Part Two
1. Demobilisation,   21st March 1919 50
Grantham.
2. Churchill's Call   April 1919   55
3. North Russian Relief 13th May 1919   59
Force
4. Russia's War and   63
Revolution
5. The Trial   May 1919   67
6. Archangel Docks June 1919   76
7. Dyer's Battalion   85
8. Topsa and Troitsa   93
9. Dyer's Battalion   7th July 1919   100
Mutiny
10. Bolshevik Captivity July – September 105
11. Cossacks.   September 1919 116
12. Freedom from   Early October 1919 136
'Custody'

13. Vyatka Railway Station	7th October 1919	146
14. Czech Mates.		155
15. Comrade Krupskaya	22nd October 1919	164
16. Onwards from Omsk	November 1919	171
17. Imperial Gold	December 1919	179
18. Buryat Bandits	January 1920	184
19. Amelia's Genius		193

Part Three

1. Vladivostok	11th January 1920	201
2. Star Gazer's	19th January	207
3. Hong Kong Bankers	20th January	214
4. "Promise you will Frank"	21st January	225
5. Return to Britain	February - April	230
6. Walton Gaol, Liverpool	21st April	241
7. 'B' Wing	22nd April	247
8. Amelia's Quest, London	April	252
9. Kowalski Returns	22nd April	260
10. Garrard's Jewellers		264
11. Churchill's Intervention		268
12. Release	23rd April	274

Epilogue

Tynte House, Loughborough	20th June 1920	279

Notes   281

A short review of Books I and II

Book I.   A Journey From Boy to Soldier. 1914-1916

On the 4th of August 1914, Arthur (Wally) Walton, a sixteen year old boy from Loughborough took a train to London, walked to Trafalgar Square and enlisted in the Royal Artillery. War was declared at 11pm. that night. The inevitability of Britain in a pan-European conflict had been guaranteed by the international treaties in place across Europe.

He left behind friends and family, including David Saffer, with whom he'd worked in the stockroom of a town chemist and Alice Baker, who, over time became his sweetheart with regular letters throughout the war. And his mum, Betty, who's letters were shared with Eric 'Aims' Amos, the taciturn Scot with a tough upbringing in a brutal orphanage near Glasgow.

The cohort of men enlisting that day came from a wide range of trades, professions and backgrounds. Some were highly educated. Others, like Eric, could barely read. There were office clerks, hotel staff, draymen and railway workers, a Hackney cab driver and an Eton schoolboy. Their different backgrounds became increasingly irrelevant through training as they were forged into gun crews. They arrived in France in late May 1915 to populate 63 Brigade, Royal Field Artillery.

The battery was staffed with experienced sergeants and bombardiers who'd been serving before the war. Some had been on the north-west frontier in India and others had fought in the Boer War at the turn of the century. The young officers had passed through the Woolwich Officer Training Academy in the few years before the war.

The brigade were in action at the Battle of Loos in September 1915, the first time the British used gas. They became 'Movie Stars', being filmed on the gun position by Sam Weeks, a young officer from the Royal Engineers. Inspired by a Punch and Judy show, Arthur and another battery marksman, Bob Hewitt, created a new technique to deal with a problem sniper. Petty rivalries and prejudices emerged in the early training days continued at the front.

A period of 'Rest and Recuperation', closed with Arthur being selected to man a firing squad. At close hand guarding a prisoner of war camp he witnessed the arrogance and inhumanity of the German officer class. He picks up the unlikely nickname 'cosher'. After action at The Somme, Arthur and a diminutive Indian of the 59th Scinde Rifles rescue a drunk British driver from a burning truck about to explode. A close knit group including Eric Amos and Frank Abraham sample fine Indian cuisine. The Indians entertain the gunners with games of chess and carrom.

In the autumn of 1916 Arthur was eighteen years old. His presence at the front was now legal. His transition from boy to soldier was complete.

Book II.   Is this Forever? 1916-1919

As the war and stalemate grinds on, the soldiers ask this question. They have no choice but to continue.

Arthur's gun crew compose a submission for 'The Wiper's Times'. The unit scrounger, Bombardier Lowles creates 'Dugout Gin' and gets caught by an ineffectual battery commander. There's no snow on Christmas Day, but the London Press report there is and a long-planned betting scam succeeds. Arthur gets home to see his dying father one last time.

There is grief at a freak incident as they work on a 'toy' rail track. At Arras in April 1916, Arthur works with the infantry laying communication cable. He saves a young Sussex boy's life to the singing of the Highland Light Infantry and gets blown up after a successful action firing a German gun – back at them. Remarkable twins get him fixed up.

Constant letters from home, from his mum, Alice and David help morale. On the road to Cambrai, what looks like certain death becomes a miracle of survival. At the battle, as part of an observation section, Arthur contributes to a VC action – without knowing.

In 1918 they meet the fit and highly motivated Americans where Lowles takes advantage of naivety – all in a good cause. Arthur gets a short break in London where David Saffer arranges a surprise guest.

The war draws to a close with a popular young officer not getting through. After the Armistice, French and Russian prisoners of war emerge from the forest as Arthur leads a patrol exercising horses. Amongst them a giant Silesian Legionnaire who proves taller than Captain Cook the unit commander.

The cohort of Trafalgar Square veterans celebrate in a hidden chateau wine store. In Calais, January 1919, Arthur is part of a trio trying to keep out of a mutiny.

The war is over, but for some the future seems more difficult.

Prologue

Kovno, Lithuania 1871.

Heavy banging on the wooden door. Shouting and screams could be heard from somewhere else in the village on the edge of the Lithuanian town of Kovno.

"Ezra, Ezra, it's started."

Shouted the familiar voice of his near neighbour, Gershon Rappoport.

"Wake up, wake up! Get Miriam and the boys away now."

Ezra, a tailor and his wife were prepared. Their bags packed and their three very young boys, Adam, Samuel and Solly had been told that they would soon be on a long journey. Other villages had been attacked in the area; Ezra had decided it was time to take his boys to start a new life in another country.

They had to hitch the mule to the cart, load the four suitcases with clothes and his tailoring tools and slip away on the track heading north from the village. After a couple of days, if the mule made it, they would reach Klaipeda, a port city on the Baltic Sea coast. From there, somewhere else.

Miriam was rushing about raising the boys and within ten minutes they were ready. As they loaded the cases onto the cart Sarah Rappoport appeared with a small, blue cotton bag.

"Ezra, take this. The boy made it. Take it. Look after it for us. We can't leave here while he's away. He won't know where to find us."

Ezra was reluctant to take the bag.

"But Sarah, what shall I do with it?"

"Look after it. We'll find you and collect it. It's a small world Ezra. We'll find you."

She forced the bag into his hands.

"Go now, go! Take care of your family. Go!"

The two wheeled cart pulled away with some others. Miriam stared back at their home. A bit further away she could see the flames rising, hear the sounds of crackling fires destroying other houses and the shouts and screams of men, women and children.

Part One

1. Loughborough, England.
Thursday 30th July 1914.

Tap, tap.

The loud rap on the first-floor, bedroom window of the worker's terraced cottage jolted Arthur Walton out of his fuzzy state. It was already light outside. 'Tap', the knocker-upper with his twelve-foot whippy stick was on his second round of morning knocks. No-one knew his real name. But with his thick white beard, bald head and florid outdoor face, no-one in the streets of tight terraced houses surrounding the Britannia Iron Foundry and Paget's Hosiery Factory knew a time when he wasn't the local "wake-up!" rap on the windows.

There were no twittering birds in this part of Loughborough to sooth people awake. Rasping industrial coughs, hob-nailed boots and wooden clogs pounding on Clarence Street's cobbles might do it in an hour's time.

However, today's clog-clatter, chest-hacker noises would be too late for Arthur. Work started early to finish the stock-take that he and the other stockroom boy, David Saffer, had started on Monday.

He had to crawl over his older brother Wilfred; Fred to friends and family, lying next to him in the three-quarter sized bed, now completely inadequate for two big lads. It only just fitted into the small room. Tap's early knock on the window never bothered Fred. Arthur always tried but failed not to wake him when getting up. The outcome was typically a few foul words and an attempted punch that Arthur had become adept at avoiding. With Fred working the late shift at the iron works with the fires on day and night, he was rarely home before midnight, resulting in Arthur always sleeping on the inside against the wall.

It was already warm and the large bed sheet that covered them both had been kicked off during the night. In the cold of winter, in a worker's house with no morning fires and frozen condensation on the insides of the windows, they needed good blankets and mutual body heat. Something that one day Arthur would dream of and take great comfort from the dreams. But not today.

Clambering over the big lump to a few groans and expletives, he managed to move quickly enough to avoid the sudden outstretched arm with the clenched fist. Fred's physical job had bulked him out over the last couple of years, and now at the age of twenty he'd grown well into his six-foot frame. When a punch landed, it hurt. They were now the same height, with Arthur more beanpole than oak at the age of sixteen.

4

His work clothes were in the scullery. The landing floor with its deep-blue, foot-worn, runner rug creaked under his bare feet. As he passed his parent's bedroom at the back of the house he could hear the start of his dad's coughing routine turning his lungs inside out. He was also called Arthur. The early morning phlegm clearance was due to over thirty years inhaling fluff and other fibrous matter in the textile mills and clothing factories across town. The old-fashioned clay pipe he smoked probably didn't help much either. The hacking would settle down after ten minutes. By then Arthur's mum Elizabeth, just known as Betty, would be up as she couldn't bear the throaty racket.

Despite the well-paid work in the textile factories, Arthur senior was adamant that his boys would not work in the cloth industry. Factory injuries and long-term breathing conditions afflicted the workforce to a much greater extent than other jobs. It was near impossible to get the mill owners to accept responsibility or pay compensation for injury and ill-health, although there were some exceptions. Nor were many keen to improve conditions despite growing Trade Union power. The boys would not follow the proud lacemakers, warpers and stocking-stitchers of previous generations. Arthur and Fred found good jobs away from the fluff, deafening noise and bone crushing machinery, although other dangers existed for Fred in the foundry.

Paper wrapped bread and a pot of jam sat on the fancy Nottingham lace cloth covering the table, left out last night by his ever-thoughtful mum. Also, a copy of *"Labour Leader"*, with the latest 'political news for working men'. Guaranteed to be discussed at length over the weekend by the whole family. Often leading to loud and angry disagreements between Fred and his dad, both politically well-informed. He avoided saying too much when the noise started as he felt he didn't know enough about the radical revolutionary socialism that Fred touted and Arthur senior's completely different and far more moderate ideas for the working class.

Despite these heated exchanges, they understood the rules of a weekend debate – no matter what had been said, they all sat down to a Sunday dinner and reconciled their different opinions. Generally with humour and laughter, accepting they agreed to differ. It was the way Arthur senior encouraged the lads to explore and discuss the many new ideas emerging in a rapidly changing 20th century world. After Sunday dinner, a family walk, and no more political discussion until the following weekend…. when it would all kick-off again. Arthur ignored the socialist paper; he would read it later. He knew he needed to educate himself on politics if it was able to incite such intense emotions.

Now to get the cooking range on. A chore avoided if possible as it meant the dirty process of scooping out the ashes and getting rid of them in the metal bin in the tiny walled-in back yard. With a warm sunny dawn this morning he didn't mind doing this in his loose pyjamas and bare feet on the cool, black and white checked linoleum covering the floor. Once done, he ran cold water from the scullery tap into a large china jug knowing the wash bowl was already outside in the privy where Fred will have left it the night before.

He lit the black enameled range with its metal chimney enclosed in an alcove with a red tiled floor. It took several minutes to get going with the bellows. He placed the copper kettle on the iron plate above the growing heat from the kindling and coal below. It would be boiling by the time his mum came down and greatly appreciated for her first morning tea.

With cold water in the bowl outside he took his cut-throat razor with its ivory handle from the scullery windowsill where the three men's razors lived in the summer months. He pulled up the leather strop hung on a hook, added a pinch of abrasive, red iron-oxide powder and ran the razor up and down to hone a fine cutting edge. Already adept at this; he'd been shaving for a couple of years having started bristling early. Until recently he'd been able to get away with every other day, but no longer. Now he was expected to show up for work looking smart and clean shaven.

He peered into a small mirror hung on a rusting nail knocked into the top of the window frame. Looking back at him was a young adult's face with fresh, alert blue eyes covered with thickening brown brows. Visible, but not prominent cheekbones lined up with a straight featureless nose underlined by a semi-permanent smile. He liked to find humour where he could, reflecting his positive, optimistic approach to life.

Arthur bowed forward a little to inspect the hairline which already seemed a half-inch higher than a year ago, now with a visible peak in the centre of his short-cut hair. His smile dropped a little, he wasn't so positive about this particular physical feature. Arthur senior was completely bald, Fred's already rapidly receding. Early hair loss was a family trait. He'd reconciled himself to losing most of his brown hair within a few years.

He lathered his face with the rabbit haired shaving brush, under his chin and the top of his neck. With a number of careful strokes, pulling his facial skin taught with his left hand, he removed the stubble from neck, cheeks, chin, and finally top lip. He might soon be able to grow a fashionable moustache. Splashing the chilly water to remove the remaining soap he dried himself off. No nicks or blood today, a good result.

Black trousers, white shirt and navy blue tie, even for a stockroom boy. Smartly dressed as he worked at 'A.B. Martin's, established 1803'. As he was regularly told by the present Mr. Martin, 'the premium chemist in the centre of town'. The white lab-coat was left at the shop, brought home on a Saturday to be washed.

Fifteen minutes' walk to the centre of town. At this early time there was little road traffic, just some of the new double decker motor buses with open top-decks. Some of these carried a familiar advertising banner; *"Martin's, for all your Dispensary needs"* run along the length of the top deck. They were used by people from the outskirts of town who could afford them, but never by Arthur for work. Also some commercial vehicles, mainly horse-drawn, delivering fresh produce to the greengrocers, butchers, fishmongers, and florists in the centre of town.

In the opposite direction milk floats and baker's wagons delivering dairy products, bread and cakes to inns and cafes. Noticeable too at this time were the very young children, often less than ten years old carrying trays of meat, bread, pies, and other goods to some of the smarter houses with wealthy residents close to the centre of town. The kids were from poverty-stricken families who led a daily hand-to-mouth existence and had to work to contribute to the family pot, getting paid with a pie or loaf. The dad had an unskilled, insecure job paid at a piece or day-rate, often at less than six or seven pence an hour. Mum might take in sewing, work at a communal laundry or have casual cleaning jobs.

On this particular morning Arthur saw two hand carts being pulled by some poorly dressed skinny, urchin-looking lads wearing threadbare tattered shirts and trousers held up with string. A common early morning sight. The carts were overloaded with ladders, wooden planks, metal pails, brooms, brushes, and tins of paint. Rattling over the cobbled streets, they were hauling them like donkeys to a house decorating job. The boys were paid pennies to deliver the kit. The men working there were paid hourly and were hired and fired on a daily basis making life very precarious. They could be seen in all weathers at this time in the Market Place standing opposite Martins hoping to be picked up and exploited by one of the town's building, decorating or labouring companies.

He also saw two early-shift street sweepers collecting the horse waste that would otherwise get ground into the road leaving a terrible earthy stink, especially in high summer. All very normal daily activity for a large East Midlands industrial and market town.

As Arthur got to the bottom of Baxter Gate, he could see David just approaching the shop front from the opposite direction having walked up Market Place. He lived with his family on the south side of town where some of the smarter houses were. Arthur knew the Saffer's were involved in a textile and clothing business and were somehow linked to Mr. Martin.

They were well-off but it wasn't obvious from David. Easy to work with, laughed a lot, was over-enthusiastic in his constant movement and active behaviour. With his smart appearance, good looks and confident manner he was able to attract the attention of the shopgirls, younger female customers and the maids and who came in to collect treatments and other products for the families they were employed by. For young Arthur, there were some benefits to an association with David.

Average height, narrow, sharp features with attentive, night-black eyes, David's defining physical feature went unnoticed by most people most of the time. When he was sixteen, he'd lost his middle and ring finger from his left hand when cleaning a knitting machine at Paget's mill where he was informally 'apprenticed'. Fortunately, he was right-handed. Not that he was at the mill by choice, he was there as directed by his father to learn about fabric manufacture that would be used when he went to work in the family business. David's irrepressible humour meant that the lost fingers provided a rich source of shocking practical jokes to inflict on unsuspecting victims, including Arthur when they first met.

With his one and a half good hands, he jokingly called himself the "Stock Room Assistant Manager" because at eighteen he was two years older than Arthur and had worked for Mr. Martin for about six months longer. With not much seniority to speak of, David's elevated, self-styled position was stated only by himself when out of earshot of all except Arthur and any young women he was trying to impress at the time. And never in the presence of Mr. Martin or old 'Dippy' Diplock, the actual Stock Room Manager.

The shop girls chatter, heard by Arthur, but not directed at him indicated that David got the job at Martin's because of a family connection. Or business connections, or political links; as David's dad and Mr. Martin both sat on the Town Council as Liberals and were big supporters of Sir Maurice Levy, the local MP who frequently came into the shop. Or it might have been Freemason, or Jewish associations, neither of which meant much to Arthur who had no idea who Freemasons were or why being "Jewish" might help to get you a job. These last possibilities were usually whispered conspiratorially, as if they were something underhand.

Arthur didn't care how David got the job that he clearly needed after his accident. He was of no use in the mill and his dad, Adam Saffer's work ethos was that family members needed to bring new knowledge or skills to the family business. Hence, after the two-finger disaster, this job would teach David about the use of compounds, dyes, and chemicals. The knackered hand was no hindrance to the way he worked. Highly energetic, he raced around the stock room at twice the speed the narrow aisles should allow. Dippy repeatedly pulled him up on this without effect. His work-rate was an attempt to compensate for his occasional inability to pick up some of the heavier items. He was a clever lad and had quickly acquired the skill of knowing exactly where stuff was and its alternative, usually Latin name.

2. Martins Pharmacy Market Place.
Loughborough, England.

The shop was in four parts. From front to back, retail unit, stockroom, the laboratory where Mr. Martin, his son Peter and Dippy prepared the ointments, lotions, and potions for retail customers, local doctors and the infirmary when they'd run out. At the back of the lab was a partition wall that closed off a toilet and room for the staff to use on breaks.

David unlocked the alley door with its opaque, mint green Muranese glass window. It let them into the side of the stockroom. Jackets off and David swapped his straight away for the white coat hung up on a stand. Arthur initially left his lab-coat off, as his first job for the second time today, would be to get the iron range located in the laboratory fired up again. This was easier than the one at home as it was always fed with coke or coal and closed up when the store was locked the night before. The morning embers would need a poke with some kindling and a shovel of coal. He left his white working coat off to avoid marks when rebuilding the fire. He filled a copper kettle from the large butlers sink in the lab and set it on the top-plate of the range. As well as for heating water, the range was used for heating, drying and crystallizing chemicals that were required in the preparation of various medicines throughout the day. On with the coat, he was now ready to continue the stock take.

The stockroom was laid out with three rows of floor to ceiling wooden built shelves running from front to back. This left four narrow aisles between the shelving and outer walls. Each lane was numbered, the alley door aisle number one, the opposite wall, aisle four. Running along the centre of each aisle was a single metal track that a wooden ladder was anchored into. The ladders could be flipped from one side of the lane to the other to enable the boys to get access to the higher shelves on both sides. There was space at either end to allow for access around and into the next aisle, and to get to the wall mounted, mainly glass cabinets on the four outer walls. To the right of the alley door was a locked glass fronted cabinet containing controlled, expensive, and dangerous substances in bottles and jars, shaped or coloured to indicate poisonous and noxious acids, alkalines and various volatile metals such as Sodium, Magnesium and Mercury. Mr. Martin and Dippy both had keys. David and Arthur were rarely asked to get anything from here.

David already had the stock book, which meant Arthur was up the ladder counting the bottles, jars, and packages. He didn't mind, apart from when the ladder needed moving to the next section. David thought it funny to shove it with a small jolt every time, so Arthur had to make sure he was holding on tightly. On day four he wasn't seeing it in quite the same hilarious way as David. They worked well as a team to count and record what was stored on the shelves against the stockroom ledger. Any discrepancies were noted with a red pencil and would be seen by Dippy when they'd finished. There were very few.

At this point in the week, they had half an aisle to do, where the shelves contained various sized jars, bottles and pots of traditional herbal creams and treatments. They needed to complete the job and became absorbed in the rhythm of David's call of what there should be according to the stock book, and Arthur's response of what was actually there. They were also becoming increasingly familiar with the Latin wording on the containers.

David, "Ceratum Calaminae, six."

Arthur, "Ceratum Calaminae, six." A tick in the book.

David, "Ceratum Camphorae, four."

Arthur, "Ceratum Camphorae, four." Another tick.

David, "Ceratum Crotonis, three."

Arthur, "Ceratum Crotonis three."

David, "Ceratum Plumbing Suba-something, five."

Arthur corrected "Ceratum Plumbi scuba-diver, five."

David laughed, "Not sure what it says Wally, but it's not scuba diver!"

"It'll do for now; at least we know what we're talking about. There's five of them anyway." Came the response from the top of the ladder.

Today, David, being David, and knowing the stock check would be completed within the hour, would occasionally call out an incorrect number. This only seemed to be if the actual number was ten or more, therefore requiring a more diligent count by Arthur. Time wasting yes, but this was the joking way their relationship had developed. They came from different parts of town, obviously different classes in a highly class conscious society, and different educational backgrounds, but that meant nothing to the two young, affable men starting out in the world.

*

In the next hour other members of staff started arriving. The shop manageress, the busy Mrs. Sheldon, now in her fifties. She'd started there as a fourteen-year-old. There were also six shopgirls, ranging in age from late teens to early thirties. They worked a variety of shifts in a random schedule that no-one quite understood except Mrs. Sheldon

Mr. Martin seemed to believe that his customers were better served and were more trusting of women. He'd never employed a man in the shop front. He'd trained his 'girls' to advise customers on newly arrived products, or additional, more expensive medicines that might help a snotty five-year-old or howling baby. The girls were not quite patent medicine, snake-oil sellers, but perhaps not far off it.

Peter Martin was the lab technician. Mr. Martin's son and heir, and the next shop manager. Quiet, studious, and difficult to engage with, Peter gave the impression he didn't want to be there and carried a constant superior and resentful air. This troubled the girls who found him snappy and unapproachable. They handed prescription slips that couldn't be fulfilled immediately to the stockroom boys to pass to Peter. After attending the prestigious and expensive Loughborough Grammar School, he went to college in Nottingham to study chemistry.

As David said of him one day, "With all that Latin learning, he certainly knows his 'ulna' from his 'anus'."

David knew some Latin as he'd also been to the local Grammar, one of the oldest schools in England, founded in 1495. His older brother, Ben, contemptuously described Peter as difficult and "shop-trade." An apparent social rung down from "wholesale trade" where the Saffer's were. Being Jewish though often meant that professional social standing was completely subsumed by being identified as; 'just being Jewish.' Even in supposedly polite circles and at smart schools. Ben's knew this which made his comment particularly ironic, and he knew it.

The laboratory as run by Dippy suited Peter Martin's humourless, organised personality. Apart from the cooking range and the butler's sink, there was a large workbench covered with equipment. At one end empty jars, test-tubes held in wooden racks, glass flasks, and beakers carefully arranged as if on a military parade. In the middle pestles of various sizes, each with their own mortar waiting to grind the next ingredient; some larger mixing bowls, a few crucibles to heat mixes to extremely high temperatures, some evaporating dishes, and a Bunsen burner. At the other end was a range of medieval torture implements. These shiny metal tools included test-tube gripping tongs, spatulas, clamps, scalpels, syringes, pipettes, and glass stirring rods. Under the bench were gas bottles for the burner. Next to the workbench was a smaller square table, in the centre a microscope with its base screwed firmly into the wooden tabletop.

The shop retail area was dramatic and intimidating when entered from the street. It rose like a three-tiered terrace from front to back. Across the width of the shop like a barrier, was a twelve foot-wide, waist high, glass cabinet split into four sections with a concave glass pane sloping away from the front. Each section contained a range of associated items that might be in demand on a daily basis, lint dressings, gauze bandages, plasters, anti-septic creams and ointments for wound treatment. The other sections had various creams, tonics, disinfectants, powders, scents and cosmetics all carefully arranged and easily accessed from the back.

Everything here was appealingly presented and packaged, some in bright coloured boxes and bottles, such as *"Higgin's German Laundry Soap"* and *"Mrs. Stewarts Liquid Bluing."* Others with questionable claims: *"Bile Beans"*, a laxative and tonic claiming to keep you *"Healthy, Happy and Slim"* with a picture of a stylish, pencil-thin looking women. *"Zam-Buk: Soon clears away skin trouble"* – a faultlessly smooth face of a young lady smiling back at you. Or the best-selling tonic, Mr. Ponderevo's Tono-Bungay promising *"Health, Beauty and Strength."* These coloured bottles and pictured labels were designed to catch the eye and lighten the purse of a steady stream of customers.

Behind the counter was the next tier on the terrace. The same width as the glass cabinet, was a five-foot-high dark-oak drawer rack with an open shelf on top. There were rows of square drawers, some six inches high and wide, others twelve by twelve for flexible storage. Every drawer had shiny brass pull handle and an engraved plate describing the contents of powders, oils, syrups, and resins.

Behind this second tier was another hidden aisle not visible from the sales area. Behind this the rear wall providing the backdrop to the whole terraced appearance. Here the shelves stretched to the ceiling containing more glass jars and ribbed bottles that had been grouped in vertical colour-coded sections. Running from left to right, blue, green, clear and red. Whether deliberately or not, they gave the impression of a flag with vertical stripes. Not quite French, not quite Italian, but visually grand and patriotically evocative to the right person.

Between the rear shelves and wooden drawer rack was Mr. Martin's working space. A long work top with a sink in the centre and large drawers underneath. Strewn across this surface were sets of dispensing scales, beam balances, and other measuring devices, a couple of pill-rolling machines, several box grinders and a small wooden rack of graduated medicine spoons. In complete contrast to the lab, this was an untidy mess, but it couldn't be touched or tidied as Mr. Martin knew where every item was. He took full responsibility for cleaning and sterilising everything he used. He would explode if he thought anything had been moved.

*

With the stock-check completed David returned the last of the four aisle books to Dippy's administration desk. Arthur grabbed the copper kettle from the range to take it to the staff room where he would make tea for the pair of them. He could already hear the chattering noise of urgent conversation from the back.

"Good morning Wally"

Said Mrs. Sheldon being more familiar than usual, and similar greetings from Martha and Rose, the two girls blessed with today's morning shift. Another girl would come after lunch as they were typically busier in the afternoon.

Mrs. Sheldon followed with.

"Do you know anything about this war that everyone says we'll be having with Germany?"

"All I know Mrs. Sheldon is that Germany, Austria and all the nonsense seems to be a long way from here. My dad reckons that England's wars are all to do with The Empire, Africa and India, and nothing to do with Archdukes or Kaisers."

Concern about the future was in everyone's thoughts. It was inter-generational with younger women being fearful for husbands, brothers and suitors, older women for sons and nephews. In general, the men were more stoical about the uncertainty, but there had been a marked rise in anti-German and patriotic British articles in most of the national newspapers. However, Arthur had seen the *"Labour Leader's"* position was that any future war was not the business of the working class, it would be the extension of a pan-European Royal Family and aristocratic feud. It believed working class lives should not be sacrificed to polish the bruised ego of Kaiser Bill or The Sailor Prince as King George was disparagingly referred to.

Dippy and Peter usually arrived around 9 am. and Mr. Martin arrived in the middle of the morning. Customers knew this so anything needing his attention was afternoon business. With regular access to doctors beyond the budget for most people, the chemists and pharmacies were the first places to go for those needing medical advice. Mr. Martin had a kind soul despite his focus on sales and profits and sometime sharp temper. He allowed Mrs. Sheldon to manage instalment payments when she thought they had a customer with a financial problem. He frequently wrote off outstanding debts for those in straightened circumstances. He also charged nothing in the most difficult situations of need and poverty.

An average shop where Arthur was starting his working life. Steady, structured and reliable, with a mix of people employed in a socially important business.

3. David Saffer

It was a regular, pedestrian Thursday at the chemists. Apart from the early start, a day receiving deliveries from suppliers; checking the contents were correct and matched up to what was ordered by Dippy; locating and storing the items, mainly in the stockroom or laboratory, but occasionally in the shop which gave them some exposure to the store environment, a brief conversation with the girls and sometimes a customer who happened to be there and known to them. One of the boys might also use the shop bike to deliver a prescription.

Martins didn't close for lunch. For some the middle of the day was the only opportunity they could get there. So lunch breaks were staggered with half an hour to withdraw to the staff room to eat something they'd brought in, or to nip out to one of the bakers on Swan Street or Church Gate, both a couple of minutes' walk.

Arthur knew he was lucky to have this job. His mum heard there was a vacancy, dressed him up in his only suit and tie, charitably bought from a poverty-stricken neighbour whose husband had died in a barge accident on The Grand Union canal. Normally reserved for special occasions, Mr. Martin was suitably impressed with the smart suit, tailor made for someone else, and took him on. Although unworldly, Arthur was impressively turned out, keen, curious, and presented himself as a confident young man.

Many shop days were routine but passed easily as there was always something to be done, bike errands to be run and new Latin names to be learnt of the many items sold and used as ingredients for pharmaceutical compounds. The dynamics between David and Arthur made work less of a chore for both.

In quiet moments David told stories passed down to him about the Saffer family and his Grandad, Ezra 'The Tailor', who'd come to England many year ago from somewhere in the Russian Empire. Social changes were freeing peasants from the land meaning people found work in the towns and cities, taking over traditional Jewish occupations. There were many trades the Jews had been excluded from and these jobs were becoming vulnerable. There'd been attacks on communities with houses, shops and whole villages burnt down. 'Pogroms' was the word used for these violent events. Arthur learnt this had been a regular occurrence over time in many parts of Europe and even in England. The family were then called Schaffer, Schlaffer or Schlieffer. It was never clear what, but Ezra changed the name to "Saffer". It sounded easier in his newly adopted country.

The stories were compelling. Arthur had heard nothing like this in his school history classes about the fantastic British Empire which ruled much of the world. Ezra, Miriam and their three sons arrived in Liverpool with nothing. They found refuge within the Yiddish speaking, Jewish community who were already there.

With Ezra's tailoring skills he could earn a living and taught his three sons everything they needed to know to measure, cut, stitch, and create whatever the customer wanted. Adam, David's father was the eldest. These were portable skills that would travel with the man who had them. If the sons needed to move on they could take their trade with them. Everyone needed clothes.

Things went well for the family and when Ezra's sons were old enough to contribute to the business, they set up a shop and developed a reputation for superior quality men's suits and ladies' formal dresses. The City of Liverpool was thriving through its shipping trade and this growth was creating a wealthier class who could afford and wanted to buy fine clothes. It was already a receptive, cosmopolitan city.

Adam moved into manufacturing. Imports of cotton, silk and other textile commodities flowed through the docks from India, China and other Asian countries. The Saffer's' were able to access this quality produce and the wholesale business grew. They sold across England and to The Netherlands and France. David's Uncle Samuel travelled to New York on a mission to find new customers. He found plenty of new buyers, as well as a wife. He stayed and created a new import and distribution company on 7th Avenue in Manhattan which then bought much of its cloth from the family business in Liverpool.

Arthur realised life could be precarious for ordinary people when there was conflict and turmoil, especially if they were seen as different to the local community. Like the itinerant Irish navvys who came and went and were avoided. He'd only ever known stability with his own family who for several generations had lived in and around Loughborough. He felt he had nothing of much interest to share with David during these conversations.

But David wanted to hear about the Walton's, their different family life, Arthur senior's desire to keep them out of the 'fluff' mills, their political discussions and ability to disagree with each other without having a punch-up, as David and Ben frequently did. And about being encouraged to think freely and develop personal opinions to be respected.

Politics was never discussed in the Saffer home. His father, Adam, was involved with the Liberal Party and Town Council. The family's business history in tailoring and cloth was what drove Adam Saffer's politics and why he was close to Sir Maurice Levy. A great believer in education and opportunity, Adam made sure his firm provided apprenticeships for young men working on the machines and maintenance. And for young women in sales, accounts, clerical work and product design. Their innovative designers were always recognised by their names appearing in a fancy script on the label.

There were regular surges in Anti-Semitism in Russia and Eastern Europe with many Jews fleeing the worst areas. Some had sought refuge in safer countries, including England. They arrived in family groups and settled in traditional immigration entry points such as the East End of London, Liverpool, and parts of South Wales. In some places it caused a rise in local tension and violence. The response of the British Government was to try to prevent more refugees from coming by introducing an Act of Parliament in 1905, which Sir Maurice fought against.

David didn't know how wealthy his family was, but they really were extraordinarily rich in comparison to the Walton's. For many years Sir Maurice, who headed Hart and Levy, another wholesale cloth and tailoring business similar to the Saffer's, and Adam Saffer had been competitors and great friends. They were also quiet philanthropists who diverted a significant part of the profits of their respective businesses into charitable causes. Much of this went to support new arrivals from Eastern Europe and also to provide funds to feed striking workers in Britain.

The motivation for the first of these causes was obvious, but to those who knew little about their family backgrounds, the second appeared to be totally incompatible with their positions as wealthy businessmen. If known to the wider public and political allies in the Liberal Party, the donations to support the families of the striking Rhondda miners in 1910 would be held up as examples of political hypocrisy of the worst kind. Big business and worker's pay and welfare should be a source of irreconcilable class conflict in the view of many. Sir Maurice and Adam Saffer should sit on one side of this issue, the strikers on the other. But striker's families were going hungry and the instincts of both men, driven by the poverty and social deprivation that they knew could quickly overwhelm anyone, drove their financial support. The hunger and plight of new Jewish immigrants and striking Welsh miners wasn't really so different.

Adam made this point to his sons on a regular basis.

4. No. 17 Clarence Street, Loughborough.
Arthur's home.

When the shop closed Arthur could take a short-cut through the rear service courtyard and narrow lanes to avoid the Market Place. But as he stepped out, he could hear the excited calls of the evening newspaper sellers:

"Austria at war with Serbia",

"Germany to be next",

"Latest war news" and other howls to get the attention of anyone in hearing distance.

'Grubby' Joe had the pitch nearest the shop. So called for his unkempt appearance and tobacco-stained fingers. Whilst all the paper sellers were referred to as "boys", Joe was probably in his 30's, but looked closer to 50. He liked a drink, resulting in his permanent good humour, a jolly drunk. As a recognised fixture in the centre of town, people knew this was the only way he could earn money, and the non-temperance lot took pity on his situation and bought papers from him.

Arthur paid his halfpenny to have the already folded paper thrust into his hand. Opening it up, the headline read, "Germany sends Ultimatum to Russia." Apart from recognising the country names, the sentence meant little.

On getting home he used the rear alley and gate straight into the backyard, pushed his head into the kitchen to let his mum know he was back and caught a whiff of freshly baked cake. Another recipe from *"Mrs. Wheatley's Famous Range Baked Cakes."* His last year's Christmas present to his mum who had a passion for baking.

He washed in the yard and changed out of his work clothes. Tea would soon be ready. Mutton stew with carrots, onions and rosemary, boiled potatoes, and runner beans; a winter meal in the middle of summer. It was Thursday; it was predictable, as it would be in every other house in Clarence Street. The menu would be different from house to house, but these working families generally ate on fixed list of meals set by the day, all year round, summer and winter. And something sweet afterwards, even if it was just a piece of cake.

As Betty dished out the stew on the scullery table, Arthur was off.

"Germany sends Ultimatum to Russia dad. What does that mean?"

After a pause, his dad replied.

"And how was your day son?"

Arthur recognised the rebuke.

"Sorry dad. We got the stock-take finished and the rest of the time flies by working with David. He's not from working stock like us. He tells me about his family, and they know lots of important people and have plenty of money. We laugh a lot, and it's very ordinary. Dippy said he'd teach us how to make some basic ointments next week."

He paused briefly.

"So what about this ultimatum then dad?"

Whilst his dad was slicing chunks of bread from the round cob loaf on the table Arthur could almost hear his brain working. After forking a small potato, stirring it around in the stew gravy, lifting it to his mouth, chewing and swallowing, Arthur senior put his fork down.

"An ultimatum is an order to do, or not do something, which if ignored will have consequences. We know the countries across Europe have been creating alliances for them to either influence or provide protection for others. What we have now is two blocks of friends standing opposite each other. It's team building, a bit like when you were at school and picking pullers for your tug-of-war team. The bigger lads usually get the first slots and then the smaller lads follow on."

On finishing this sentence, he cut a piece of meat and ate it before continuing.

"When that Austrian Prince was shot a few weeks ago, the man who did it was from Serbia. The Austrians "tug-of-war" side includes the Germans and Turks. We're on the other, with the French and Russians. They're all the big lads. Serbia is one of the smaller ones, and you remember that on Tuesday the papers said that the Austro-Hungarian Empire had declared war on Serbia to punish them for killing their Prince. But the Serbians are big pals with the Russians who've said they'll protect them if any of their team starts getting pushed around. Austria blames Serbia for the killing as it was a Serb that did it. As this has happened each team member is being sucked into the fight. Have you got all that?"

"I think so."

This time it was a couple of runner beans that were cut in half to make a more sensible mouthful. They were large, fresh, and vibrantly green.

"But countries can't just go to war. They have to get their troops prepared, get them to the places they might be needed. It takes time, especially with really big countries like Russia. Both Russia and Germany have been planning and building vast new railway networks in order to do this. Germany's is ready, Russia isn't. Now, as they've started getting their army ready, the Germans have said if Russia doesn't stop, they'll be at war. This is what The Echo is reporting today. The order is to stop mobilizing; the consequence of not doing so is war."

He stopped talking, knowing there would be more questions, he focused his attention on the still warm plate of food in front of him.

There were a few moments of silence as all three ate more of the stew, dipped bread into the thick gravy and digested the world's geo-political situation in their modest, terraced working-class house.

"So, if Britain are one of the big lads, does it mean that we will definitely be involved?" asked Arthur.

"And if these countries are so far away, why do we have to pitch in?" he continued.

At these questions, his Mum answered.

"Come on Arthur, you know the British Empire is a big part of the world, and we rule many countries and people in faraway places. We've had many wars in India and Africa. Being far away doesn't mean we aren't bothered by what other countries are doing."

His dad added.

"We have our Empire; we'll always be a big player. For a long time, other European countries have been building their own which has led to conflicts between them and us at times. A few years ago, Italy claimed Libya in North Africa, which at the time was being ruled by the Turks. Their Empire, the Ottoman, is old but unstable. The Germans and French were rowing about Morocco, another Ottoman 'province', and Britain sided with France telling the Germans to back-off - twice!"

"There have been wars between countries in Europe to create bigger states or independence for national groups, for example where the people are united by speaking the same language – German, or Italian for example. The problem with this is that in many parts of Eastern Europe, you can't easily wrap a border around all of the people who speak the same language. I did hear that there are a load of German speakers in Russia. Vulgar Germans, I think they're called. Seems a strange name to give them."

Mis-stating the fact without realising it, but it may have been what he thought. He went on.

"All this jostling for land and power and trying to pull the same language speakers together. People who see themselves as being part of the same nation with their leaders following policies to build new, united countries has led to nationalism – a belief in the superiority of your people and country. Another source of conflict that can result in a dislike and disrespect for people in the next country, like falling out with the neighbours on a big scale. Especially if they think there are members of their own nation living and being mistreated over the border."

"Because we're an island, we've had our scraps with the Welsh and Scots, but that was ancient history. We pretty much get on with each other now. But nationalism can cause war as well, especially with the neighbours."

"People do love their countries though and the British can be very self-centered, patriotic and passionate when it comes to our Empire and the threats we see others making toward it."

The three of them continued eating without speaking for a few minutes. They were interrupted by a mewing and turned to the open door to see Mrs. Davy's ginger cat from number 13 strolling in as if it owned the place. A tomcat that was pathetically small and skinny and was sure to have been the runt of the litter. Geno often appeared around this time with his remarkable amber and orange stripes that covered his back, flanks, and head. His mint green eyes with pupils that looked like vertical ellipsis were split by a pure white nose, and whiteness on the bottom of his face, neck, chest, and paws. He was a strikingly handsome cat. Mrs. Davy would not be home yet; he was hungry having been out with Sonny, his brother, and the other street cats for the day. He expected a saucer of milk which Betty duly provided. Community cat lapped the dish placed close to Betty's chair, then rolled onto his back waving it's paws at the apron belt strap teasingly hanging down. Sonny sometimes appeared too, but not today.

Arthur senior interrupted the quiet interlude.

"There's a couple of other things I'm aware of that has caused tension between Britain and Germany. For a long time, we've had a big powerful navy that we needed to support and protect our empire and trading interests. The Germans are now quickly building theirs and that's seen as a threat to British imperial power. And the last thing is that the King, the Kaiser, and the Tsar of Russia are all cousins and I believe there is no love between them, in fact more jealous rivalry. A typical family feud."

Arthur now had a whole bunch of reasons as to why there might be a war. He knew his dad kept himself well informed by speaking to colleagues and friends. As was the case in all of the factories and workshops in the town, few of these men had formal educations beyond learning to read and write. They were avid readers of newspapers and political pamphlets enjoyed intense political discussions at work, in the pub and often out on the streets during these long summer evenings.

5. Alice Baker.
Saturday 1st August 1914.

As suggested by his dad, by Saturday the first team members in the two pan-European Alliances were beginning to make good on their treaty obligations. The dominos were falling. Germany declared war on Russia in response to no action on the ultimatum and in support of Austria-Hungary against Serbia. As the news reached the Loughborough Echo in time for a special afternoon edition, 'Grubby' and the paper boys were hollering the message like a kennel of barking dogs throughout the centre of town.

"War more likely over there",

"Britain and France next in line",

"Echo has it all."

The three girls working the Saturday afternoon shift, Eileen Patch, Frances Simpson, and Alice Baker were getting excited by what they could hear and Mr Martin commented on their lack of attention. Mrs Sheldon "had words" several times for them to calm down. Neither were generally disciplinarian, so to extract any comments on behaviour was unusual. Arthur picked this up through the frequent trips in and out of the shop from the stockroom. It was only him today, David never worked on Saturdays, as agreed by Mr. Martin and Adam Saffer.

Dippy was in the lab making up various concoctions. When he needed something from the stockroom, he would call through to Arthur who found himself being pulled from shop to lab and back again. There was a lot going on so Arthur hadn't had a break. Around three o'clock Mr. Martin, who'd seen all the activity told him to disappear to the staff room for twenty minutes. Alice was also there with a cup of tea and a piece of the fruit cake that she'd brought in to share. Curly, fair hair with alert, blue-green eyes and a jolly, fizzy manner. Always smiling or laughing, popular and clever too – she came top of the class in her last term at school. It was her birthday; she was seventeen today and had been in the same school as Arthur although in the year above in age. They knew each other quite well, with many mutual friends and were relaxed in each other's company.

"Have some cake, Wally. My mum made it for us all here today. She's a good baker."

He'd already poured himself some stewed tea into one of the metal mugs they used in the lab and the stockroom. He knew about good cake from home, and Alice was right, this was good too.

"My brothers are both saying they'll join up when it starts. It's bound to happen now. Everyone says so. What about you?"

"Well, I don't think I can Alice, you have to be eighteen to properly join the army, unless your parents sign you up as a bugler or something. I know your boys are older, so they'll get in. It'll be over too quickly for me to reach enlistment age and to be honest, I'd not even thought about it. Apparently, we have close to a million men in uniform and our pals, the French have got four million. Seems a lot to me, they might not need your brothers and very unlikely to need me."

Alice went on. "But what if they are needed, and others too. I'm worried of what might happen to them." She looked anxious too, leaning forward on the edge of the seat with her hands clasped together. Not her usual positive manner at all.

"It's a bit early to worry Alice. We're not at war yet and they're not in the Army. If they do join up, they might not even be out of training before it's all over."

Trying to lighten the mood he finished with.

"You'll have plenty of time to worry about all that stuff when the bullets start flying."

Finishing her tea, she looked over the top of the cup, and with narrowing eyes and an unamused, tightening mouth said.

"Not helpful Wally. Enjoy your tea and choke on your cake. I need to get back."

At that she stood up, swept both hands down her apron to brush off some crumbs and straighten it and flounced out of the staff room retaining her bitter stare at Arthur. He knew she wasn't really offended by the admittedly flippant comment. They were long-term friends and despite the stare, her eyes told him so.

6. Syphilis ointment.
Monday 3rd August.

Monday's were busy at the chemist. Working people who fell ill over the weekend and couldn't afford to call a doctor would come in. The service girls in the larger town houses were also shopping to get fresh produce from the market. They would come by to pick up orders put in last week, now ready for collection.. There was a lot to be done in the stock room. With David away on Saturday, weekend deliveries were usually left till Monday to be checked off and stored. The boys were well rehearsed and efficient in this. They split the shelving jobs between them and ticked off the items on the delivery lists. Everything was cleared and shelved by midday, in between providing whatever was needed for the shop.

They then got a call from Dippy.

"David, Arthur, come back here!"

David almost bounced on his heels and with his irrepressible energy ran down aisle four in response to the call. Arthur walked steadily down aisle three, knowing that too much speed in the stockroom attracted a rebuke. David knew this too. Sure enough Dippy's first comment was.

"David, I've told you many times, slow down. It's not a greyhound track, you haven't just been released from the starting gate!."

"I'm sorry Mr. Diplock, just keen to help" was David's answer, said with a disarming smile.

"Okay, okay. So I mentioned we'd do some preparations this week to start educating you both on the use of various salves, ointments, and potions. We'll get started later this afternoon as we have an unusual syphilis prescription for Colonel Allard, that pompous ex-Indian Army Officer that we see occasionally. He should have been more careful with his body parts when he was in the Queen's service. Oh, and you two lads are not to mention names to anyone outside of this place. Is that clear?"

They looked at each other with their eyebrows raised in mutually surprised faces.

Diplock was small in stature, pug-faced and bespectacled. Half-rimmed glasses rested permanently on his conveniently upturned nose. His head bowed forward, a result of many years of having to peer over the specs. The very little hair he had sat like two cotton-wool balls on either side of his head. Bushy, unkempt, professorial eyebrows grew without restraint above piggy blue eyes. He was clever, irreverent and had little respect for anyone except Mr. Martin for whom he'd worked with forever. His "Dippy" nickname was a true reflection of his personality. He could be tense, nervous and anxious, especially outside of his comfort zones in the lab and stockroom. He was irritable and his mood could swing dramatically. David had speculated that some of the noxious fumes and use of dangerous chemicals had affected his head.

"I'll dig out the recipe for the ointment and we'll start at about four o'clock. I'll let Mr. Martin know you'll be unavailable for a while, he's aware we'll be doing some training. Right, if you've got time to chatter, get two buckets and get the stockroom and outside alley mopped over."

The boys got the mopping done. It was almost four when Dippy squeaked again from the lab.

"Right chaps, come through and let's get started."

Dippy was sitting in the middle of the work bench, and off he chirped like an excited sparrow.

"Okay, first a history lesson. If you know or don't know what syphilis is, I will tell you anyway. It's a nasty disease that is spread by sexual relations between infected men or women. It can only be transmitted between them by sexual intercourse. Many carriers are prostitutes or sailors travelling from port to port. This is why it is a particular problem for soldiers and sailors travelling the world and no doubt why our 'Colonel Blimp' has it. They pick it up in ports and camps across the Empire and bring it back to England. They should be more careful."

He sounded preachy from a high-pitched point of view.

"In fact, it wasn't known in Europe before Christopher Columbus discovered America in 1492 and his happy but unsuspecting crew brought it back from the infected natives over there. All those Latin sailor and soldier mercenaries then spread it through the cities and towns of Europe. It has four phases: initial infection of the contact area, usually the growth of ugly but painless spots. Then a few weeks later the victim will get some red and brown rashes over the body, especially his palms and soles of his feet, small sore eruptions in the throat and other body parts, maybe some fever and headaches, a bit like a very bad cold, except the rashes. These will all go away after several months, so it seems the disease has gone – but it hasn't. Its lurking in the body before its final flourish. This can come years later and in this last phase we can see damage to multiple organs, movement problems, numbness, fits, blindness and tumors on the bones, open sores the growth of pink fleshy tissue on the skin that are called gummata. It's all very unpleasant and now you know about it make sure you steer clear of getting it."

He stopped talking and his small porcine eyes stared at them one after the other. "I mean it!" He suddenly trilled, jolting the pair of listeners.

"Any questions so far?"

Neither David nor Arthur said anything, they just shook their heads with looks of astonishment. It was the first time they'd heard Dippy speak at length about anything, and he either really knew his stuff, or told a good story.

"It's rare here in Loughborough, but when we see it, we can provide some things to help. On this occasion 'Blimp' is into the last stage. It was probably picked up many years ago when he was a young officer. His doctor confirmed by letter to Mr. Martin that he now has some sores on his body for which our solution will help ease the pain and irritation but won't cure it. We'll be making a mercury based ointment, the recipe of which I have here. I need you to get each of these ingredients before we mix it up. Your familiarity with the stock room and Mr. Martin's bench in the shop will get you most of them. If you can't find them, ask. Let's not waste too much time on this. That's the list of what we need."

Dippy finished with placing a short list of barely decipherable writing on the bench. They read through it, confirmed between them what they thought it said and then Arthur read it aloud to Dippy.

"Mercuric chloride, two ounces. It says for this we'll need some Hydrochloric acid to heat to extract the Chlorine gas and some Mercury to then mix with the gas in a sealed flask. The acids are in aisle one."

They were indeed, but inexplicably on a high shelf that needed the wheeled ladder to get to. This was supposedly to put them out of reach of passing shopgirls as they weren't deemed dangerous enough for the lock-up. Arthur continued.

"Caustic soda granules, two ounces. Boxes of that in aisle three. A finger-nail patch of Gelatine leaf, aisle two. Two ounces of formic acid to heat up to extract the something gas. I can't pronounce the name Mr. Diplock"

"Formaldehyde Arthur. It's a strong smelling gas." Dippy responded.

"Thanks" said Arthur trying to repeat the word a couple of times with only partial success and a smile for effort from David, before moving on.

"Anhydrous lanolin, one ounce. That's the brown greasy gunk in tubs in aisle one, and finally five ounces of Vaseline from aisle two."

Dippy then said, "Right you've got all that. Be careful there's some tricky stuff there. Here's the key Arthur to get the Mercury. We also call it quicksilver – it's in the locked cupboard. It's clearly labelled in a bright blue glass bottle with a rubber bung."

Arthur took the key and the pair of them turned to go back into the stockroom. As they walked back David said.

"You get the acids in aisle one and I'll get the leaf, lanolin and Vaseline from aisle two, and the caustic soda."

As they walked into the room, Arthur placed the key on the counter to the left of the door under one of the wall-mounted cabinets. David scurried with his usual enthusiastic speed to get his ingredients, whilst

Arthur pushed the wheeled ladder along the length of aisle one to climb up to the higher shelf. David, completely ignoring Dippy's advice to be careful was rushing. He got his items and returned to the lab to deliver them as if he were in a competitive race. He then went back into the stockroom, picked up the cupboard key and zoomed down aisle four. Unlocking the cupboard with his right hand he opened the door leaving the key in the lock. He immediately saw the metal label stating 'Hg. Mercury' on a small chain over the blue bottle and plucked it off the shelf placing it on the counter underneath. He closed and locked the door, picked the bottle up, holding it awkwardly between his thumb and little finger. He then walked at pace back down aisle four.

Arthur had collected the acids, had descended the ladder and walked down aisle two to the lab door. He was reaching for the door handle just as David came around the corner, having to abruptly pull up to avoid a clash. The mercury bottle flew out of his gammy left hand, hitting Arthur on the leg as it fell and crashed onto the floor spilling the contents. The bright shiny liquid metal split into a thousand tiny ball-bearings that shot off in every direction across the floor and under the closed door into the lab. It was now obvious why it was called quicksilver.

"Shit" they both exclaimed is horror when they saw the outcome.

Arthur placed the bottles of acid on the counter where the key had been. The lab door was pushed open by Dippy who wore a face of indescribable anger. He then erupted with a series of vile expletives directed at the two of them, but in particular Arthur to whom he'd given the key.

At this point Arthur realised and quickly understood the consequences for David of this disaster, given his prior employment at the mill resulting in the hand disability. It would wreck his chance to get into the family business, under his father's demand to bring a skill or expertise to it. He also knew there were plenty of other jobs and trades in the town he could try out if he needed to.

"I dropped it" he said immediately. "I was trying to carry the acids and the mercury, and it slipped out of my hand."

David stared at Arthur in total disbelief and said, "It was me Mr. Diplock, I took the key and got the bottle."

More swearing squeaked from Dippy as Mr. Martin, having heard the initial crash of glass and Dippy's shouting, appeared with a puzzled face, turning to complete shock as he saw the silver debris of tiny balls skittling on the floor.

"Arthur dropped the mercury flask Mr. Martin, these two were no doubt racing to get the bottle with no regards to the danger of their actions."

It was now Mr. Martin's turn to erupt in a way they'd never seen before, shouting, but no swearing at the pair of them, demanding to know what they were thinking, mucking around with dangerous chemicals. His anger was directed at both boys, but the whole time he was looking at Arthur with a diarrhetic stream of invective on their behaviour. At the end of this angry and uncharacteristic rant he closed with.

"Right, you two will now clear up this mess, collecting all of the spilt mercury with dustpans and getting it into another receptacle. Put on protective gloves and under no circumstances touch it with bare skin or touch any part of your face or skin with the gloves after they've been in contact with the mercury. It is dangerous, which is something that clearly hasn't registered with you yet. When you've finished, put the gloves in the stove to burn and then leave the premises. I'll decide what to do with the pair of you in the morning."

At that, he took Dippy with him, and they went forward to the shop deep in conversation and casting looks back to the lads. As soon as they'd gone David spoke.

"Why the hell did you say you'd dropped it. You've put yourself in the shit when it was me and my problem."

"But if it's your problem David, it's a complete disaster ...... forever. Because, as you've told me, you have a future in the cloth trade. One of us is likely to be sacked over this, if not both. There are loads of things I can do, lots of jobs in the factories and mills across the town. Look, two good hands."

He held them both up wiggling his fingers in demonstration replicating something David said and did in jest on a regular basis.

"I can do those jobs, you can't because of your knackered hand. You need to be here more than I do, and when the war starts, maybe I'll go and put a uniform on. You're smart enough to do good and clever things, but if Mr. Martin thinks it was you, you'll get the chop. That will cause all sort of problems with your dad too."

Arthur then added.

"It's done now, and we have to clear up the debris. No point in trying to undo this. They think it was me and that's how it should be, and no matter what you try to do or say, I don't think their minds are for changing. Now let's get on."

The discussion continued back and forth as they donned gloves and found the metal dustpans at the back of the lab in the mop and broom cleaning cupboard. David was irritated by Arthur's intervention and his believing it was the right thing to do as the consequences for him were manageable. David's future was predictable, provided the bumps in his road were surmountable. The mercury drop might just have been a bump too high. It was this reasoning that was rattling about in Arthur's head. Not with absolute clarity, but enough to be able to justify his actions to himself, and he believed David would ultimately see things the same way.

They hung up their white coats and left through the alley door turning left toward the market square where they could hear the excited calls of the paper boys.

"Belgium invaded", "Germany on the march", "Belgium in flames" "Britain at war by the end of the week" "Crowds and recruiting in Trafalgar Square."

They both bought a paper from Grubby Joe and folded it under their arms before agreeing they just had to face the consequences in the morning. David crossed into Market Square and Arthur turned into Biggin Street to walk north and home.

7. Tynte House, Ashby Road, Loughborough.
The Saffer's home.

Arthur had some time to think. Was the job at Martin's really his future? It was a good job, in a clean, relatively safe environment, if you excluded today's events and the gases, the volatile metals and the acids. He smiled to himself in wry amusement. It was great that his mum had pushed him into it, and it wasn't in one of the many industrial plants in the town where almost all of his mates worked with a constant risk of physical injury. The places his dad didn't want him to work.

From today's newspapers he was told, war by the end of the week. He was tall and strong, and increasingly felt that he would, and should be a part of this for his country. Of course, he had nothing of the depth of understanding as to all the causes of the crisis. He didn't feel personally threatened and didn't hate the Germans, Turks or any other Europeans he didn't know. As he walked toward the old and very grand All Saints Church, a plan began to crystallize, and his demeanor changed. His physical frame appeared to grow in stature, his pace became more confident, and his eyes peered far ahead. He now knew what to do.

He was startled and his thoughts interrupted by a familiar female voice that came out of thin air.

"Wally, you're out of the shop early today, and looking very strident.

It was well before five o'clock; the earliest the stockroom boys would get out.

It was Alice coming from his right along Sparrow Hill, walking purposefully and carrying a covered wicker basket crooked in her right arm and held to her front. She wore a pale salmon-pink lace dress, with a darker pink sash around the waist. The sash matched a ribbon tied around the wide-brimmed straw hat perched on her head, topping her fair tresses hanging down and framing her pretty smiling face. Seeing Alice brightened Arthur's mood immensely. She hadn't been at the shop today and knew nothing about 'the mercury drop'. He wasn't about to tell her either.

Immediately ignoring the implied question, Arthur answered with.

"Oh, hello Alice, where are you off to?"

She nodded to the large building.

"The Church are collecting tins and food for the poor; my mums sent me over with some. We have a new radical priest with some strange ideas on changing the words in hymns, but we stick with it. We're here every Sunday, it's just what we Baker's do…… "

She trailed off, and then.

"So why are you off early then?"

29

"Well, we'd finished everything we needed to do, and Mr. Martin let us go."

He knew he sounded evasive. Alice knew it too but didn't press the question. There was clearly something going on.

Arthur changed the subject. "You'll have heard the war news then. There'll be a lot of change now Alice."

And then asked, "How do you think I'd look in uniform?"

She wanted to ignore this but couldn't.

"You're too young Arthur, you told me yourself. I've got to drop these things off before five o'clock, so I can't stay talking and wasting my time with you. Much as I'd like to, she added with her warm smile. It's been nice to see you. I'll see you again tomorrow, I have an afternoon shift."

With this she bounced off on her heels, crossing Church Gate through a convenient break in the light motor traffic and occasional horse-drawn carriage. There were crows squawking in the tall, leafy canopy that stretched across the road from the ash trees on both sides. They seemed to have read Arthur's thoughts and were laughing at Alice's final comment. He wouldn't be going into Martins, not tomorrow, not ever.

*

David left Arthur at the top of the square and walked south. He sometimes jumped on a motor bus that ran the twelve miles to Ashby-de-le-Zouch and passed his home, but today he'd walk the twenty minutes back to Tynte House. He needed thinking time too. There'd been no need for Arthur to take responsibility for his mistake. He knew he'd been stupid by rushing from an urge to compensate for the hand disability. This was his problem that he had to contend with every day, yet for almost everything he did and everyone he worked with and met, it was never an issue. He usually volunteered the reason for the missing fingers knowing people would be curious. After an initial explanation by him it was never mentioned, unless he did, and was using the finger absence as a joke prop.

As he walked, he started to accept Arthur's reasoning for jumping in, despite his initial dismay. He was now annoyed with himself that he thought Arthur's reaction had been because he'd felt sorry for him, which was clearly not the case. David realised their talks had made an impression and it was true, his path was mapped out with familial constraint and lack of choice, assuming no bumps. Arthur was able in more ways than just physical. He had the ability to choose what path to take, what working trade he might apply himself to and to map his own future.

He was now walking past St Mary's church which distracted him and drew his eyes every time he went past. It looked like a classic mini-Greek temple prompting the same mildly amusing thought every time. 'What were the Greeks doing building temples in the middle of England?' This was then forced out by something more serious, what would he tell his father? It was entirely possible that he might already know. Mr. Martin could well have telephoned Adam and given him the details. So, it had to be the absolute truth with an explanation as to why Arthur had put his hand up to take responsibility.

David turned left into the tree-lined drive and could immediately see the cream-coloured canopy roof of the Crossley motor car their driver used to ferry Adam about. He couldn't see Shellard the driver anywhere, which meant he was probably having some tea in the cloakroom with Mrs. Golson. The car meant his dad was already home. There would be no stewing on events, he would need to tell him straight away. Fortunately, Adam had always been approachable and easy to talk to despite a facade of sternness and discipline.

He reached the house where the front door had been left open to let air circulate through and walked up the porch steps. On the right as he entered, the study door was closed, he rapped lightly with a little trepidation.

"Come" the voice from inside said loudly. Adam was sitting at the desk with his reading glasses on which he peered over.

"Oh, hello David, I wasn't expecting it to be you. I thought it would be Mrs. Golson with some tea. You're home early."

Rather formally, David spoke. "Hello Father, Wally and I were sent home a little earlier as there has been an incident in the stockroom. I need to tell you about what happened unless Mr. Martin has already called you."

Adam removed his glasses and looked serious. "No, I've had no conversation with Mr. Martin."

This was of some relief to David as he was now able to explain what had really happened instead of having to unpick an already incorrect story. He went through the whole incident, including much of the chat between him and Wally as they were clearing up. Mr. Martin had sent them home so he could consider what he might do with the boys. His dad's eyebrows lifted sharply when David talked about the acid, the rushing, and the dropped mercury. He nodded and watched his son closely as he spoke without any need to interrupt for clarification. With the story finished, Adam left a silence as if to give the impression he was thinking about it. But he wasn't. He'd recognised why Arthur had done what he'd done and the obvious friendship that had evolved between the two boys.

"Well, young David, this is a bit of a mess, isn't it?"
A rhetorical question: he wasn't expecting an answer.

"I think we need to let Mr. Martin decide what to do. As you know, we've known each other for many years, and I know him to be a fair man. My guess is that he will already have seen through this. And the lesson for you is more haste, less speed. This is a direct consequence of you rushing everywhere. But I do think I'd like to meet your friend, I believe his proper name is Arthur, and have a chat with him about this. Do you think he'd be okay to come here to see us this evening?"

David remembered his dad's dislike of nicknames and was surprised by this concluding comment.

"I don't know dad; I can only ask him."

"Right then, do you know where he lives?"

"I know he lives in one of the terraced houses on Clarence Street, the road opposite Paget's, but I don't know what number."

"Okay. So, I suggest you get Shellard and ask him to drive you there. find Arthur and tell him that I would very much like to meet him and talk to him. Assure him that I know what has happened and I think I understand his actions."

Adam was measured and conciliatory. Much to David's relief, there was no irritation or annoyance.

*

David left the study and walked along the corridor turning left into the kitchen. He could hear Mrs. Golson and Shellard talking in the rear room. He knocked on the door and apologized for interrupting them. The staff were treated with respect and politeness. David explained to Shellard what was needed in terms of the use of the car, but with no other details as to why Arthur was to be invited to Tynte House. Mrs. Golson listened, was intrigued but said nothing.

Shellard knew Paget's Hosiery factory and they would find Clarence Street from there. They drove back into Loughborough retracing the steps walked by David. Back up Ashby Road into the Market Place, out of the top onto Church Gate and then onto Nottingham Road to Paget's. Shellard spotted the Clarence Street road-sign immediately opposite the factory gate and turned left into the street lined on both sides with identical looking two-up, two-down industrial workers cottages. The distinguishing feature for each one was a brightly painted different coloured front door, reflecting individuality and pride for each home.

There were two women talking on the roadside path, one carrying a small baby, and a bunch of small children running around the street, some of the boys kicking a football. They looked a bit grubby and snotty, but most kids of that age do. The women looked at the car as Shellard stopped. There weren't many private cars on these roads and even fewer that actually stopped in Clarence Street. David stepped onto the footpath and crossed over to where the ladies were.

Very politely he said.

"Excuse me, I wonder if you can help me. I'm looking for the Walton's house, in particular Wally, sorry Arthur Walton."

The women chuckled and one replied.

"Wally to most of us too young sir, but yes his name is Arthur. Number 17, with the bright red door, further down on the left. Go past the gap in the houses you can see, that's Duke Street and then a couple doors from there. You'll see the door number."

"Thank you, I appreciate your help."

David crossed the street back to the car where some of the bolder children had started gathering and gawping. Shellard had engaged in conversation with a couple of them through the car window.

"It's down here a bit, I'll walk, and you can follow on with your new friends when you're ready."

Shellard smiled at the comment.

David reached the red door, number 17 in brass figures on the vertical centre panel and a small brass knocker at waist height on a horizontal panel. Not the only red door in the street, but this was a very noticeable, bright, post-box red. He rapped the knocker twice and waited a few moments until the door was opened by Mrs. Walton with a look of surprise.

"Hello, I'm David Saffer, I work with Wally, sorry Arthur, in the stockroom at Martins. Is he about please Mrs. Walton?"

"Hello David. Yes, Arthur has mentioned you to us. I think he's in the back yard. I've just got home myself, so I've not seen him. Wait there a moment, I'll get him."

She turned and walked down the hall through the scullery to find Arthur sitting on a wooden chair in the yard reading the looming war news in the Echo.

He looked up as his mum came out of the door. Before he could speak his mum said.

"Arthur. David, your friend from Martin's is at the door asking for you. I hope everything is ok?"

It was a question needing an answer, but not yet, and without responding to it, Arthur said, "I'd better see what he wants then."

He stood up and walked to the front door. Betty stopped in the scullery not wanting to interfere but kept a keen ear to the conversation. Unfortunately, the boys spoke in quiet tones, not whispering, but not quite loud enough to pick up what was being said.

David blurted out the speech he'd rehearsed in his head.

"Wally, I've told my dad exactly what's happened and about you taking the blame. I had to, as you know Mr. Martin is a friend of his and he would have found out soon enough. He said Martin needs to deal with this as he sees fit. He also says he understands why you've done this and would like to meet you and talk about it. My dad can appear a bit intimidating in his black suit business attire, but he's a bit soft with me and Ben. He knows you and I have to deal with this and the consequences. He just wants to meet you."

As he finished, and without noticing due to his concentration, Shellard with his very official looking chauffeur cap and the Crossley car slowly appeared outside number 17, with a small crowd of young kids excitedly running after it.

Arthur was surprised by David's speech and then completely distracted by the arrival of the car immediately outside of his house. Peering over David's shoulder at the car he asked.

"Is that what you came in David?"

David turned around.

"Yes it is. If you're good to come back with me in it, I'm sure Shellard will bring you back here afterward."

Arthur had travelled on motor buses, but had never been in a private car, so this would be new. Without further consideration as to why David had come he replied.

"I'll just get my jacket."

He walked back to the yard to collect his jacket and ever-present flat cap worn by all working men in the area. As he came back through the scullery he said.

"David has come to take me for a ride in his family's car. I won't be too long mum."

"Okay. We're having ham and salad for dinner, so I'll plate some up if you're late."

*

Shellard loved to talk about the car and as this was Arthur's first time in a family owned vehicle he was full of questions. They'd just finished as they turned off Ashby Road into the drive and sped up through the hornbeam avenue. They stepped out, walked to the porch and up the steps to the open front door. David saw the study door was open so his dad would be elsewhere. He showed Arthur in and told him to wait there while he went to find Adam. Mrs. Golson told him his parents had taken a walk into the garden and would probably be checking the poplar trees where some of the tightly packed upturned branches needed lopping. She said she'd take some tea through to Mr. Walton.

It had been a whirlwind afternoon for Arthur, and he was now taking in the plush plum coloured room, the comfortable looking leather settee and bay window chairs, the sea-scape pictures, and the huge desk. Suddenly and unexpectedly a voice.

"I've brought you a pot of tea Mr. Walton and some apple cake. There's an extra cup for Mr. Saffer. Help yourself as he may be a few more minutes."

Mrs. Golson placed the silver tray with matching teapot and white china cups on the end of the desk. Arthur thanked her as she left the room. He was a bit surprised at the courtesy being shown, nothing he'd experienced before. This didn't happen in the streets where he and his mates lived. He spent a few minutes admiring the pictures on the wall and then poured himself some tea. With cup in hand, he turned toward the fireplace and caught sight of the curious metal object on wheels on the white marble mantelpiece. It was quiet with no risk of being seen, so he placed his cup and saucer on the mantel next to it and picked up the object.

In the warm summer weather, the metal felt contrastingly cool and comfortable in his hands as he turned it over. To Arthur it looked like a vertical tobacco box to be opened from the front, but this wouldn't make sense. Concluding it was some kind of ornamental trinket, he held it up to have a closer look. There was a crude picture scratched on the metal, obviously meant to be uniformed, perhaps a soldier with a peaked cap. Opening the tiny door, hinged at the top and bottom with a wire twist, he saw scratched lettering on the inside. Almost completely illegible, he could just make out the last four: an R or a P, an O, definitely an R and finishing with a clear T. He closed the hinged door, with its very imperfect fit. In the atmosphere of the smart room, the thing was oddly out of place, knocked up by an amateur. Perhaps Mr. Saffer had made it himself as a young man and kept it as a personal treasure.

A sudden noise from the front doorstep and Mr. Saffer appeared at the study door not giving him time to replace the metal 'thing'.

"Hello Arthur, I see you've found our treasure. I appreciate it's not hidden very well! We call it the 'Report Box'."

Adam had a friendly, welcoming smile.

Arthur struggled slightly to get it back into its place. Looking a little embarrassed he replied.

"Sorry Mr. Saffer. It looked so odd I wondered what it was."

"No, no harm done. It's robust enough in its own way."

Adam spent some time telling what little he knew of the box. Of his dad, Ezra leaving Lithuania and having to look after it. This was now his job. One day it would be Ben or David's to care for, until it was collected, as he firmly believed it would be. Once he'd finished the story he said.

"Arthur take a seat in the window here and tell me about what happened today. David's already told me some details. I just want to understand."

They moved to the alcove at the front of the room and sat opposite each other in the Chesterfields looking across the laid out chess board. Arthur recounted the events of the afternoon with Adam listening attentively without commenting until he'd finished.

"Thank you Arthur and lastly, why did you take the blame for this."

"Well, I know from David that he's at the chemist as part of his education. He'll be able him to come and work in the clothing business. For me it's my first real job, but there are lots of other things I can do. David doesn't have the same choices as I do. I didn't do it because I feel sorry for him, but because I can get work elsewhere, he can't."

Adam smiled paternalistically and wiggled his left hand, emulating David's regular action.

"I'm naturally grateful Arthur. You didn't have to do this, but I respect what you've done. I can't intervene in any way with Mr. Martin, and we'll have to let him reach his decision on what to do tomorrow. After that if we need to get you something to do at Saffer's of Loughborough, I'm sure we'll be able to. Thank you for coming up to see me and I hope you enjoyed the car ride."

*

For the drive back home, David sat Arthur in the front of the Crossley. As they trundled through the tree lined drive to the gate Shellard started talking about the car again and wouldn't stop. Most of which was technical, with some numbers on horsepower and engine size that went over Arthur's head. He also mentioned that when he was at the factory collecting it, there were some Army Officers there from the Royal Flying Corps looking at the cars.

"I thought they flew, but no they need cars as well. I guess they're needed to collect the pilots when they crash land in those flimsy looking flying machines", he added as they arrived back at number 17.

As Arthur entered the door his mum called from the front room where she was now sitting with her evening knitting. It was about six-thirty.

"We've eaten Arthur. I've put some on a plate for you on the table."

"Thanks mum." He replied walking straight through without stopping to speak. He knew his dad would be in the yard with his evening pipe at this time and he didn't really feel he wanted a conversation with either of them.

The plate was on the table covered with a small linen cloth and next to them a salt dish and a glass bottle of 'Heinz Salad Cream' that had just appeared in the grocers shops. A real creamy vinegary treat to tip on top of the normally bland lettuce, tomato, and cucumber. There was some tea in a pot from which he poured himself a cup and sat down.

After a few minutes, Betty came in.

"What was all that about then Arthur? Did you know David was coming round? You should have told me. I would have offered him some cake."

"No, I didn't mum. He was out doing an errand for his dad, and he knew I'd never been in a motor car, so he came by to give me a ride."

Of course, it wasn't a lie, but not the whole truth either. Betty knew it too. She didn't want to press him though.

"Well, I guess you two talk about a lot of things at work, so it was nice of him to do that."

Whilst he ate he read the evening paper. There was a big picture of crowds in London tossing their hats into the air looking patriotic, and smaller, similar pictures from Paris, Berlin, and Vienna.

When he went to bed that evening he wrote a short letter to his mum and dad, which he put in an envelope and would leave on the scullery table in the morning. He took the smaller of the two canvas bags from under the bed and packed a couple of shirts, vests and underpants, some socks, and a spare pair of trousers. The bag was then shoved back under the bed. He would put his work gear on in the morning and leave as early as he naturally woke up. Tap's knocker-up service wouldn't be required on the 4th of August 1914.

8. Departure.
Tuesday 4ᵗʰ August 1914.

Inevitably, he slept badly. Normally he would be able to get several hours of decent sleep before Fred got in from his late shift to create a waking disturbance. The brothers were used to the unsatisfactory arrangements and accepted them because they knew nothing different. It was common in the working-class households where siblings were crowded into the bedspace available. However, tonight he was still very awake when Fred came in.

The warm August night didn't help, but it was the busy thoughts crowding his head that caused the wakefulness. Confusion around the constant talk in the newspapers, the shop and just about everyone he met over the threat and now certainty of war with Germany. Was it a national patriotic war or would it be a revolutionary class war?

More confusion around the disastrous mercury drop incident at work that would lead to either him or both him and David losing their jobs at Martin's. The unexpected thrill of his first ride in a private motor car, being treated like a gentleman by Mrs. Golson at Tynte House. The pictures, and strange item, and his surprisingly open discussion with Mr. Saffer. Added to this mix of thoughts, feelings and emotions was a clear picture in his head of Alice and her final words to him when they met, "I'll see you again tomorrow, I have a morning shift."

He tried to clear his head and recite some of the Latin names for potions in the stockroom to exclude the intrusive clarity of the day's events. Nothing worked. So, when Fred came in his eyes, hidden in the dark of the night were wide open and alert. His brother could tell he was awake.

"Something wrong?" Fred asked.

"No, nothing."

"Don't lie to me Arthur, I may look dull, but I'm really not that stupid."

Despite the four-year age difference, which seemed a lot in their young lives, the brothers were able to share confidences. Arthur got Fred to agree to this and briefly explained that as a result of the stockroom mercury accident he was quite sure he would be getting the sack from Martin's. That he'd taken responsibility for it and why, and he'd be leaving in the morning to travel to London to enlist in the army. He'd seen the pictures of enthusiasm and recruitment in the Echo and for him this was his way to escape, to be part of a great adventure. There was no argument as to what the war was all about, it was now something Arthur would be doing, despite his age. He'd written a letter to explain this to their parents which he would leave in the scullery in the morning. He'd be leaving as early as possible so as to miss them.

Fred listened and understood that his brother had made up his mind and there was no point in trying to persuade him otherwise. They spoke for some time until physical tiredness overwhelmed Fred and eventually Arthur succumbed as a blanket of mental fatigue lay over him providing fitful rest.

The early morning light woke him up shortly before five. He got up and dressed as quietly as possible. He pulled the packed bag from under the bed, turned to go out of the door when he caught sight of Fred stretching out his right arm with his hand open and summoning.

"Arthur, come here." whispered Fred from his now satisfied, spread-out position filling the bed.

He turned and took Fred's hand in his. They both gripped each other and looked one another in the eye.

"Be careful. Write and tell us where you are."

"I will Fred. I'll be fine."

They smiled warmly at each other, and Arthur left the room and the house via the scullery door, dropping the letter to his parents on the family dining table. He thought he heard some movement upstairs, as he went out into the yard to collect his razor and shaving brush, the final things to place in the bag.

*

At that time of the morning there were very few people about, except Tap, who gave him a wave and a puzzled look from the other side of Clarence Street as they passed each other. He then saw no one on the few minutes' walk from home to the railway station. He bought a third-class ticket to London; being told by the uniformed and grandly walrus-mustachioed ticket clerk he would arrive at St Pancras Station.

"As long as it's in London".

"And you won't be wanting a return ticket young sir?"

"I'm not sure when I'll be back" Arthur replied.

The clerk looked directly and questioningly into Arthur's eyes and paused as if he was expecting something more. Nothing came.

"Okay, that'll be nine and six. Next train on platform four over the footbridge. You'll see the teashop has just opened and you'll be able to get a bun and cuppa to take onto the train if you like. There's also a dining car on the train. Third-class is at the rear."

Arthur handed over some coins from the small leather, pocket-sized money pouch he kept, thanked the clerk and took the ticket. He had several half sovereigns and other coins worth about four pounds that he'd saved up over time from his twelve shillings a week pay.

Crossing the bridge he heard the trains piercing, steam powered approach whistle and looking along the line he could see the dense clouds of white smoke puffing into the warm early morning air. The round black coloured, smoke box door with a big brass headlight set above it was just coming into view. With the chimney immediately behind the headlight, the rest of the train was obscured from sight by the smoke.

He'd have time to get a tea and walked toward the open window that served the platform customers from the teashop. In doing so he recognised through the window Mrs. Higgins from Number 3, Clarence Street, who ran the shop. He quickly turned away and briskly walked along the platform to get closer to the rear of the train where the third-class carriages would be. He really didn't want an early morning conversation to explain his presence and getting a train to London.

He found an empty compartment. The train built up speed and rhythm. Arthur leaned into the corner. He removed and folded his cap to provide a small makeshift pillow which he then propped his head on against the rear cushioned headrest. Within a few minutes he was beginning to doze with the repetitive rocking motion sending him into deeper sleep. He was barely conscious of a couple of stops where no-one entered the compartment. At Kettering a middle-aged couple with a young boy entered from the corridor.

He stood up for politeness when the lady entered. She apologized for disturbing him and asked if the empty seats were occupied. On hearing they weren't, the three of them sat on the seats at the other end of the compartment. The lad was their grandson who they were taking to London for a special summer visit and a show, The Pirates of Penzance. They exchanged small talk on the weather and a little on the likely war. No one entered their compartment at the further stations; Wellingborough, Bedford, Luton, and St Albans. He took in the window views of the rolling county countryside, the villages they sped through with church spires in Northamptonshire and the church towers in Hertfordshire. He'd never taken so much interest in the shape of a church belltower, wondering how many of them contained bells from Taylors of Loughborough.

The small towns and villages started to disappear with fewer fields until they reached the nicely named town of Cricklewood, and then few green areas to see. The young lad moved to the seat opposite Arthur to peer out at the great growing metropolis. The fields had been replaced with buildings of all sorts. From stretches of embanked track he could see out over a different urban landscape of densely packed worker's houses and some smart streets of large, semi-detached and detached homes, some of which were quite grand. Occasional rows of shops and factories with tall, round chimneys. London looked big, sprawling and a little grim.

9. Martin's, Loughborough.
4th August 1914.

The previous day's incident brought Mr. Martin to the shop earlier than his usual ten o'clock. He hadn't been absolutely convinced by Arthur's explanation, but Arthur had been the one to admit responsibility. Martin was also well aware of David's tendency to race about the place, and this had caused numerous collisions of no consequence in the past. He'd warn them about their behaviour and dock Arthur's wages for the breakage. By doing this he was certain the real culprit would pay, they'd sort it out between them. But Arthur hadn't arrived, and this was puzzling as one thing Martin knew from the short time he'd had Arthur at the shop was that he was punctual and diligent.

David was in. He was also concerned about Arthur's absence. He'd been directed to register an order of medicines delivered from Boots in Nottingham. It would take a while with only one on the job, so he focused on this.

When Mrs. Walton entered the shop, the bell above the door rang. Mr. Martin looked up as did the others; the bell drew people's attention. He was holding a small bottle of medicine and in deep conversation with a concerned looking young mother clutching a coughing baby.

"Hello Mrs. Walton. Please come around the back here where we can talk."

He led her behind the retail counter and the wooden drawer rack to his space at the rear of the shop.

"I'm sorry Mr. Martin, Arthur won't be in today. He wrote me a letter about what had happened yesterday and thought he would be sacked as a result. So he's taken a train to London where he's going to try to enlist in the army."

Betty was in tears. "He may be rejected if they realise he's too young, but as you know, he looks older than his age, so we don't really expect him back."

Mr. Martin was temporarily speechless. He wasn't expecting this.

"Mrs. Walton, I'm most grateful to you for coming in to let me know. I'm very surprised. It's been a difficult thing for me to deal with. The two boys work well together, a little exuberant at times, but that's youth for you. I'm not sure which one was actually responsible, they both claimed they did it. I had decided not to sack either of them but give them a warning."

He paused and his eyes drifted as he took a short time to think through Arthur's actions.

"I think Arthur has been rash in his decision but also very brave. We'll probably see many more young men going off to the forces soon."

"Thank you Mr. Martin." Although his comment didn't make Betty feel any better.

David, having no idea of Arthur's intentions was incredulous. He'd got his head around his motivation for taking responsibility, but to take it to this crazy length was beguiling. Martin explained that he wasn't sure who to believe, but the incident would now be laid to rest, despite its seriousness. David would need to slow his pace when on the premises and make sure no further disasters occurred.

*

Alice breezed into the staff room shortly before one to start her afternoon shift. She was humming to herself an unidentifiable, but bright tune. Jane was on a short lunch break, sitting with a cup of tea reading an old copy of 'The Ladies Home Journal' from the numerous magazines lying about.

"Hi Alice, how are you?"

"I'm well, thank you Jane. As you can tell, Mrs. Sheldon has now got me on afternoon shifts having a done a stretch of mornings. It's funny how she likes to swap things about."

"She likes to keep us on our toes, but I don't mind. I'm on the ten to three, middle of the day hours right now." After a short pause she added. "So you won't have heard about Arthur then?"

Alice was hanging up her light jacket in the small cupboard to be replaced by her white shop-coat. Looking back over her shoulder.

"No, I haven't. I saw him on his way home near the Church in the afternoon; it was a bit earlier than usual, which I thought was odd. What's he done then?"

Jane had already left before the previous day's accident, so the tale was second hand as she told it to Alice who's eyes were growing wider. Jane finished with.

"And he's only gone and disappeared to London early this morning to join the army."

On hearing this Alice slowly sat down, her bright, airy demeanor imploding and her posture crumpling. She then promptly burst into tears and through the deep sobs, heaving shoulders and wringing hands said,

"I knew there was something wrong............. He didn't tell me.............. Why's he done that?.................... He's too young........................ He told me...................... sitting right here, that he was too young................. oh Jane, he's so stupid."

Jane was taken aback by Alice's sudden emotional response and tried to comfort Alice, who she now realised had something for Arthur. It had never been obvious. After a few minutes she went to get Mrs. Sheldon who spent a while calming Alice down. Throughout her time in the chemists that day, Alice felt on the verge of welling up whenever she wasn't busy with customers. Several times she had to go to the back of the shop.

10. Enlistment, Trafalgar Square, London
4th August 1914

The war in Europe lasted longer than anyone could have possibly imagined. Millions of ordinary people, especially young men across Europe and elsewhere in many other countries, lost their lives. Fathers, brothers, sons and boyfriends volunteered in the first two years and in Britain, from 1916, were conscripted. An industrial war of incomprehensible destruction, death and injury. A large number of those who survived to return to civilian life were scarred and damaged; if not visibly then mentally. They'd seen friends and foe blown up in the carnage of artillery barrages, gassed, mown down by machine guns and burnt alive by flame throwers. The men that returned were not the same men that went.

Arthur enlisted roughly twelve hours before the war was declared on the 4th of August 1914, a couple of months before Kitchener's appeal for volunteers with his pointing finger. From St. Pancras station he made his way on foot to the jingoistic festival atmosphere in Trafalgar Square to add one more body to the queue of men of all classes wanting to enlist on the steps of St Martin in the Fields. He joined the Royal Artillery by raising his hand in response to an ornately uniformed, mounted Horse Artillery officer asking who could ride a horse, despite only ever having sat on one once.

On that day the squad of artillery recruits were marched from behind St Martins to the Honourable Artillery Company's (HAC) headquarters on City Road next to Finsbury Square. They had medicals and those successful were marched the following day through the wealthy streets of the financial district, the impoverished Jewish area of Whitechapel and through the docks to the northern pier of the Woolwich ferry. In the new squad were two other men who were to become his closest army friends, Eric Amos and Frank Abraham. They were both initially reserved, impenetrable characters, but over time, various incidents, adversity and ultimately merely surviving the war they became very close.

*

Arthur's first recollection of Frank was on the march to Woolwich. Out of the HAC gate they turned right and retraced their steps back down City Road past the bowling club in Finsbury Square where at this time of the morning there was no one to be seen. There were very few people about, but then not many were active in the financial markets in the City of London before ten o'clock. Just past Moorgate Station they turned left onto London Wall and had the rising sun shining straight into their faces.

The 'marching' rhythm was quickly established with only the occasional,

"Lep…….. Lep………. Lep, Right, Lep," from the escorting sergeant and bombardier to help them along.

The buildings were grand compared to Loughborough. Many with at least six floors. Most had their names on brass plates and were more subtle than the hotels, cafes, and shops Arthur had seen coming along The Strand the previous day. There were many stockbrokers, banks, and insurance companies. They continued walking east into Aldgate and then Whitechapel High Street where the pavements on both sides of the wide thoroughfare were packed with large, wheeled country wagons, each one carrying stacks of bundled straw. This was the hay market that took fodder brought in by carts trundling in from the Essex countryside and wharfs in the docks. Each wagon was a massive haystack. There were already buyers who'd come from stables all over London to get food for their horses, or to buy hay to sell on in the areas they came from. Horses were still a vital component of the London economy, and this was the main source of food and stabling hay.

As the squad turned right onto Commercial Road it was all very different. The buildings were smaller in height, mostly now only three or four storeys high with a growing number of the kinds of shops to be seen on most town high streets. Many had unrecognizable lettering alongside the English version of the business name hanging above the 'Kosher Butchers and Poulterers'. The workers here were busy hanging a vast array of dead birds and butchered meat on hooks that were then raised to cover the front of the store. Two small boys appeared at speed from inside carrying chunks of meat on their shoulders which they promptly flipped onto a counter at the front to be neatly arranged by a slightly older butchers boy of no more than twelve years. The two carriers quickly disappeared to get the next slabs.

There were 'Bagel Bakeries", a term, alongside 'kosher' that was unfamiliar to Arthur. He also saw the word Yiddish in several places and recalled a dig made at one of the men as they were waiting for the medicals the day before. Many shops were now starting to open, shutters being pulled up and folded back, awnings pulled down over the pavements.

The people here were different too. The few men walking about wore similar knee length black jackets, had significant bushy beards from very dark to fluffy white in colour depending on age. They wore Homburg hats and were not speaking English as they called to each other in greeting. Arthur was seeing the huge contrast between the rich financial district they had now left to the run-down immigrant East-End.

There were small children in the street, many of whom were bare foot and in ragged clothes. They looked at the marching men from skinny faces with big, curious, and universally dark eyes. Compared to what Arthur had seen in London so far, this was clearly a poor area in complete contrast to the wealthy streets they'd marched along the day before. Some of the bolder kids were skipping about in front of the squad when a voice was heard shouting in an unfamiliar tongue.

"Hey, ir kinder, geyn aoys fun di veg oder mir geyn iber ir."[1]

On hearing what was said, the response from the seven or eight kids was immediate as it was amusing. They were shocked to hear their own language coming from the troop of recruits. They squealed with surprised laughter and scurried as a group away from the front of the marching men where they then stood on the pavement. They were laughing, pointing, jumping up and down, clapping and cheering as only excited kids can do. It was warming to see.

From the rear came a shout from Sergeant Thomas.

"Thank you Abraham, most helpful!"

And then from Bombardier Hay walking to the squad's right in the road.

"Eyes front number one squad. Lep…….. Lep………. Lep, Right, Lep."

They marched on to their destination on the Thames.

*

Frank was a quiet thoughtful man who appeared to have a self-imposed protective moat around him. In the early days of training at Woolwich the shield was always up; he never talked about himself in those first weeks of intense basic training. Reserved and circumspect, he would observe the intimate banter of the others without contributing. It wasn't that he was unfriendly, but constantly uneasy, almost anxious. He was also fit and competent all round and from the NCO instructors perspective he blended in with the crowd; a good place to be so as not to draw attention. He provided help and support to the other recruits without being asked. If he saw someone without the skill trying to sew on a button when he knew drill boots needed bulling, he would volunteer for one or the other, and do a decent job on whatever it was. His advice on tailoring and practical skills were used widely across the squad. Whenever asked about his home and family he simply told people they'd come from Eastern Europe a long time ago. No further elaboration was ever offered by Frank, another brick in the castle wall.

*

The slow development of Arthur's friendship with Eric Amos started in training and was cemented during the years in France. For all the soldiers at the front, letters from home were extremely important. Arthur did well

---

[1] Yiddish. "Hey, you children, get out of the way, or we'll walk over you."

as it seemed not only his mum was a good writer, but he also got intermittent mail from friends and regular letters from Alice. Some of the gunners were known not to get any mail at all.

Eric Amos, an itinerant Scottish labourer was one of these. Known as 'Aims' Amos he was quiet, self-sufficient, and insular. He'd been very difficult to get to know. Over time this hard man with piercing blue eyes, a fair complexion and a long square face had revealed more about himself to other men, including Arthur and Frank Abraham. He only vaguely recalled his early childhood in the Glasgow slums as one of hunger and begging. One day, he thinks he was about seven years old at the time, he returned to the tenement block and found his bedridden mum dead in her bed and his two younger sisters on the filthy wooden floor crying.

The perpetual drunkard of a dad had gone and they had been left in the squaller of a room not fit for animals. The following morning some men arrived to remove the body and three kids who were handed over to the Glasgow Parochial Board to be separated and homed in different orphanages. He never knew what happened to his sisters and never saw them again. His new home, The Oak Tree Children's Home had been an early Victorian lunatic asylum. Intimidating arched oak entrance doors in a large portico between red-bricked gothic spires. It was now a boys home for about 300 orphans and miscreants who the authorities deemed to be the same thing.

Education was cursory, a few morning lessons on reading and arithmetic. Afternoons were spent working in the extensive grounds surrounded by a ten foot wall, tending the fruit and vegetable plots, and looking after the animals reared to supposedly provide food for the kids. They saw little of it, but the staff were all rotund and florid faced. A couple of gardeners who were no part of the supervisory team were the only ones to engage in a kindly way with the young lads. The place was mainly controlled by older boys who were responsible for their own small gang who would be marshalled to "classrooms" of 50 at a time or to work where directed by the skeleton staff. It was a tough cruel regime with physical abuse meted out constantly, and this was in spite of the occasional visit by inspectors, known as "The Cruelty Men", whose job it was to check that no abuse was taking place.

Amos became suspicious and self-centred in this environment, but somehow retained a sense of humanity that would surface when another boy was in real trouble and needed a friend. He managed to run away, really an escape, with another lad when he was about 12, not really being sure of his own age. They managed to get some casual day-rate work for some pennies on a construction site before he moved on from town to town, never wanting to get returned to Oak Tree.

This drifting life on the edge of society, moving further south all the time, never knowing where he might find work or get his next meal, continued until he found himself in the middle of London in August 1914 and enlisted. He knew he could easily manage an institution like the army and the chance of three meals a day drove him to sign up. Unlike Arthur, he'd never sat on a horse in his poverty riddled, marginal existence but the elevated officer in Trafalgar Square looked to be managing okay. Amos thought he could do that too and so it proved to be the case.

His quiet, unassuming demeanour also meant that Amos went unnoticed most of the time. Only when he spoke in his deep voice and almost impenetrable Glasgow accent would he draw attention. Arthur had an ear for the voice, it sounded just like a friend from home's dad, Jock Wallace. So there were occasional needs to translate, which they both found amusing and created an odd linguistic bond.

There was something else about 'Aims' Amos that steadily permeated the men through training, his constant small acts of uncalled for kindness. He would take boots to clean when their owners were struggling to organise themselves in training. Press kit in the same way. Carry webbing like a pack animal when on physical training for unfit, stumbling colleagues. Before he ate himself, he'd collect food for those on guard duty on the gun position to make sure they received it as hot as could be delivered. Amos was often the first to respond without request when a gun or limber got bogged in the mud and needed grunt and groan shoulder effort.

In the absence of anyone else offering, he agreed to remove with a pair of pliers, a rotten tooth causing excruciating pain for his gun commander lance bombardier Taylor who just wanted rid of the agony. Amos gripped, tugged, and wiggled, released the offending molar and plenty of blood, but once the trauma had gone he'd relieved Taylor of the pain. For Taylor it was a supreme act of kindness as he was unlikely to get to one of the few frontline dentists anytime soon. Apparently Amos had done this before on a building site.

*

As Amos was known never to receive a letter, those that did would share their own and read them to him. He wasn't a good reader himself and not all letters of course, mainly family and friends, and certainly not those from sweethearts.

Arthur's mum Betty wrote at least weekly, sometimes more. Her letters were, understandably repetitive and full of local news and gossip. These were shared with 'Aims' Amos and worked like a weekly magazine serial story to the point where if a regular character wasn't mentioned for a couple of weeks, Aims and Arthur would discuss what they might be up to.

She wrote about her small world in and around Clarence Street, the local shops and Loughborough market that she went to every Friday. There was always a paragraph on Arthur senior and Wilfred who had written short notes a couple of times each; no doubt bullied by mum into sending something. She mentioned the same people on a regular basis, moaning about some, praising others, and too often relaying sad news of death and serious injury of young men from the town that was reported in the Echo. Some of the men he knew, many he didn't. Betty was well aware that Arthur was not in the Infantry, so would not be going 'over the top'. He was less vulnerable in that respect, and his risks were different. There was also a regular snippet on Geno and Sonny, Mrs. Davey's ginger cats. Usually a story describing their comedy double act. Amos was always grateful for hearing these letters as they described a home and family he never knew and reminded him of good things from the country for which he was fighting for but had little experience.

Arthur senior died during the war, his chest eventually squeezing the life out of him. Alice and Arthur became sweethearts writing when they could. Alice continued to work at Martin's on Saturdays. When the men went off to war she became an accounts clerk at the Hart and Levy textile factory where the whole of production became uniforms and military kit for the war effort.

His good friend from the chemist stockroom, David Saffer landed a job as the secretary and man-Friday for the local Member of Parliament, Sir Maurice Levy, a business and family friend of Adam Saffer, David's dad,

Arthur managed to survive despite being blown up and hospitalised for some weeks after the First Battle of Scarpe near Arras in April 1917. Both Eric and Frank did too. The mental defences they both started with enabling them to get through relatively unscathed.

Part 2.

1. Demobilisation. Grantham, England.
Friday 21st March 1919.

Bombardier Frank 'Abs' Abraham, Gunner Eric 'Aims' Amos and Lance Bombardier Arthur 'Wally' or sometimes 'Cosher' Walton were sitting in a large training room with about forty other men waiting to be called to the two desks to have their final discharge papers stamped. They would then be released into a 'Land fit for Heroes' they already knew would be no such thing. It was Friday 21st March 1919. They wore ill-fitting civilian discharge suits having handed in all their uniform items to the Harrowby Camp Dispersal Unit stores, manned by a grey haired Quartermaster Sergeant. He waddled and wheezed as he called the items being handed in whilst his civilian storemen ticked a list on a clipboard. He might have seen action in Egypt in 1880, if ever. Much of this uniform kit would be re-cycled into a civilian clothing market where need not fashion dictated what some people could afford to wear.

They were some of the last of the 1914 volunteers to be discharged from 63 Brigade, Royal Field Artillery before the unit number was put into cold storage. There were a few others in the NCO hierarchy, of the battery there too. Men who were the 'Trafalgar Square Veterans', as they'd called themselves.

In the Grantham room a man called Abbey had been processed and was now leaving with a broad smile. Abraham was called next to the same desk. They thought it was to be alphabetical. Frank said as he stood up.

"The pubs will be shut by the time they get to you Wally. Me and Aims will be tight before you get done."

Blessed with surnames beginning with 'A', they were used to getting the right kind of priority treatment as Frank described it. At that moment the Sgt. at the other desk called 'Young'. They now realised it was the double-ended process, one from the start and one from the end of the alphabet to try to create some fairness. Unusual in an organisation like the army. Almost certainly an initiative from the processing Sergeants. The next call was 'Worboys', so they knew Arthur would be dealt with soon. The beers seemed suddenly closer.

The truth was they had no plans to get drunk. They had places to get to. Frank would be on a London and North Eastern Rail company train heading south to Kings Cross in London to get home to his family. He knew what this meant today and he wasn't looking forward to it. He'd be home before last light on a Friday where his extended family would be gathered to welcome him back and to celebrate the Sabbath. Aunts, uncles, cousins, people he couldn't place in the family tree if it were drawn on paper for him. Some neighbours, possibly the Rabbi and others important to his parents. The local butcher, Mr. Koppelman, ('Always good to keep in with the butcher', Frank's dad would say).

It wasn't seeing all these relations and other people that didn't appeal. He could deal with it by externalising the whole thing. It was a duty that had to be borne. He'd had plenty of those over the last four and a half years. It was the religiosity expected of him that would rankle. Like many men who'd gone to the war with some semblance of a belief in a God, he'd lost that belief. Trying to reconcile a higher being with the horrors he'd seen had become impossible. These thoughts were deeply personal to Frank, he never shared them with others, not even Arthur. He was sometimes seen writing in a notebook. When asked his response: 'just personal stuff'.

*

Arthur was taking Eric Amos to his home in Clarence Street. A train to Nottingham from Grantham and one change to Loughborough. A trip that would take them about three hours. There were two reasons for this. Eric had nowhere else to go. He'd never said as much to anyone, certainly not to Arthur. But amongst the cohort of long-servers, they knew that Eric, whilst surviving the war, might not survive the peace. At no time had Eric ever asked anything of anyone. However, without any expectations of payback, he was always there. On the 'A' sub gun he never stopped delivering whatever was expected of him. He dug a latrine twice as fast as anyone else, claiming those dirty bastards might shit where he could tread in it otherwise.

Frank frequently said it was really Eric that saved Broncy in the collapsing cottage, and he deserved the military medal bravery award. If this ever came up, Eric would usually mutter something along the lines of 'complete and utter bollocks.' Then he'd walk away.

So Eric was to meet his mum and Wilfred who already 'knew him' through Arthur's letters. Betty had often said to bring Eric to meet her after the war.

The second reason was that Arthur and Frank had a germ of an idea of a plan which they'd mentioned to Eric. When they did so, he said little in reply. He nodded at the time and a few days later said he'd thought about it and if they thought it was a good idea he was up for it. Effectively putting the complete onus of the decision on the other two.

Arthur was still only 21 years old. He'd been in the army for four years and almost seven months and at this moment in time he could think of nothing else but military service. He was deeply in love with Alice and he knew this was reciprocated. But he couldn't see in his immediate future being married and settled in Loughborough. A quarter of his young life had now been in uniform fighting in the war. Whenever he thought about a future he became confused. He had no idea what kind of work he'd find or whether he would get any at all. This army life was all about comradeship, stability, teamwork, service to country and community. He didn't feel ready to leave the experience he'd had for an alternative he couldn't conceive. For very different reasons he was as fearful of the uncertainty as Eric.

It wasn't long before Arthur was processed and issued with his 'Class Z Reserve' discharge papers. Arthur had to ask the Lincolnshire Regiment Sergeant the question.

"Class Z Sarge? It makes it sound like we're at the bottom of the system. What does this mean?

The Sergeant peered over his half-moon reading glasses.

"You joined for the duration of the war, did you not Lance Bombardier Walton?"

"I did Sarge."

"Well some of our politicians are not yet sure whether the Germans might start it all again."

He picked up a slip of paper with a short, typed paragraph printed on it.

"For our more curious Reservists ……… that'll be men like you Bomb., we give them this. It's what Mr Churchill said in Parliament a few weeks ago when asked what 'Class Z' meant. We think it's the most appropriate explanation and it saves me the bother of having to explain to questions from men like you Lance Bombardier Walton."

It was said in an expressionless monotone manner, in the same way he'd said it thousands of times before to the curious of the 70,000+ men and 2,000+ officers who'd passed through the demobilisation process. He passed the slip across the table for Arthur to read:

On the 3rd March 1919

Mr. Walter Perkins, Conservative MP for New Forest and Christchurch asked the Secretary of State for War "what are the duties and obligations of men placed on demobilisation in 'Class Z' Reserve, and, particularly, will they be required if necessary to intervene in labour troubles or other civil disturbances?"
Mr. Winston Churchill answered.

"The only immediate obligation on men passed to Class Z Army Reserve is that they have to notify change of address to their record offices. This in any case is necessary in order that they may receive their medals in due course. Soldiers in Class Z will be liable, at any

time before the end of the War, to be recalled to the Colours in case of urgent military necessity only."

The Sergeant then said.

"It basically means if the Germans kick off again you'll be called back, but you won't be expected to shoot at strikers or rioters in Britain."

He stamped Arthur's release slip and then added.

"Unless its Fenians............but then only in Ireland. Right that's you then, off you go. Enjoy the rest of your life Mr. Walton!"

*

The three comrades now free from uniforms but apparently not from their obligations left the gates of the demobilisation centre onto Harrowby Lane and turned left toward the market town of Grantham. They each had an army haversack carrying some additional issued clothes and personal hygiene accessories. More transport lorries were arriving with men to be discharged after an overnight stay and a number of lectures on what they might now expect as civilians. They crossed the bridge over the river Witham following the Manthorpe Road which ran into Watergate. They were headed toward Grantham railway station. It was approaching lunchtime and they'd agreed to discuss their idea over a farewell beer. They stopped at the Black Dog pub where they ordered two pints of Soames bitter and a pint of mild for Frank.

Up until now, on the half hour walk their chat had been light-hearted and reminiscing. At a table under one of the old black painted beams Frank opened their main agenda item.

"So we know there continues to be a need for soldiers in the regular army and we heard on the ship from Calais of the soldiers in Russia right now. The rumour was they will be looking for more men for that campaign. We've talked about continuing to serve. From what I've read and heard, it's very unlikely the Germans will resume the fighting, the peace talks have been going on since late January. So with nothing else happening the only option is to re-enlist in the regulars. What do you two think?"

Eric answered first.

"Well as you know, I'm not sure what being out of the army will mean for me. I'm not even sure where to start. It's good of Arthur to be taking me home to meet his family. But what happens from there on, I don't know."

Then Arthur.

"You'll be made welcome in Clarence Street Eric. I'm sure there'll be a fine cake for us when we get there later. I know my mum is happy that I'm bringing you to meet her. Loughborough has got plenty of industry, textile factories, iron works and rail yards, so finding work should be okay. For me though, I don't know it's the immediate future I want either."

The discussion went on for about half an hour, wrestling and vocalising their own thoughts, concerns, anxieties and motivations that by now had been done many times before. They finished their drinks decided not to have more. It was time to go.

They agreed to get back to some kind of peace to see how that felt and what it might be like. Frank's parents had recently had a new phone installed so they could speak at times if Arthur was able to access a public telephone.

2. Churchill's call for volunteers.
April 1919.

It hadn't worked out so well for Arthur and Eric when they returned to Clarence Street. The first few days were okay and sure enough when they arrived there was a fantastic fruit cake waiting for them. Betty was like a mother hen insisting on taking care of every aspect of the two returning soldier's welfare. It was great to be eating home cooked food and to be looked after. But this did not deal with the two men's restlessness.

Wilfred was now married with a one year old son he'd called William Arthur. He called him Billy the Kid and told his brother he wanted to call him Arthur William. His wife wouldn't allow it, saying if his brother never made it home from the war, every time he called his son's name he would be upset. Wilfred argued that wouldn't be true, and that every time he called his son's name, it would remind him of all the good things about his brother Arthur. The good news was that Wilfred and his wife Emily were living at her parent's house a few streets away. Eric could occupy the boy's bedroom at the front of the house and Arthur would be sleeping in the main living room.

Alice quickly realised that the man she loved had returned in a different state of mind to the man she'd seen at David Saffer's house in London, as recently as six months earlier when he was on leave. It was nothing explicit or overt. Several times he tried to explain to her the feelings of immense relief and satisfaction he felt at being back. As well as the guilt at the dead friends lost. Like Frank, he was also faithless, he could be angry at religions and believers in a God that could allow this to happen to all the families who'd lost brothers, fathers, sons and daughters too. Alice 'believed' in a routine, 'Church every Sunday way' and whilst they never argued the point because she wisely just listened to him, it was an area of tension. But whether he didn't have the vocabulary or ability to express his feelings effectively, she didn't really understand. How could she?

Patience, humour and empathy helped enormously. Alice had these attributes in abundance. She recognised the good deed Arthur was dong for his friend Eric who was clearly a lost soul. Initially, quiet, reserved and aloof, Eric and Alice developed their own relationship to the extent they had a few private jokes at Arthur's expense. As Eric warmed a little, Alice arranged for a few of her girlfriends to join them to walk out in the evenings as the light stayed longer and the cold temperatures of early spring started to go. It seemed that Marjorie, Madge, a strong willed lass with a bundle of brown hair and who liked to tease anyone who seemed strong enough to deal with it, and Eric got on well. Madge's humour was ruddy, factory floor, industrial. Perfect to throw at this Scot with his unfamiliar accent and protected, distant persona. On occasion with Madge and Eric walking some yards behind them, all Arthur and Alice could hear was bursts of deep laughter and high pitched giggles. It felt normal and warming in the moment.

*

Arthur received the telegram early on the morning of the 9th April from Frank. Being from Frank, it was short, sharp and to the point, reading.

"Arthur, call me on Whitechapel 284."

After Betty had boiled a couple of eggs and made some toast for their breakfast, the pair walked down to the Infirmary where there were some phone booths installed for the public. They were rarely used as so few houses had telephones. Arthur put threepence into the slot and asked the operator for the number on the telegram. The other end rang several times and was answered by an old man's voice with a very thick European accent. The voice switched to what the untrained ear would think was German. Arthur had heard enough occasional Yiddish from Frank to recognise the language. Within a few seconds Frank's familiar east London cockney sounding voice came onto the phone. He knew it would be Arthur.

"Who's ringing this number, scaring the old-folks?"

Arthur laughed of course. Frank then came straight to the point.

"Have you seen the news, Churchill's call for volunteers to go to Russia? The government put an announcement out yesterday morning. The Times newspaper reported today that over 60 men had already responded. They're looking to recruit two Battalions of experienced men including some gunners......... that'll be us Arthur. Because we've been demobilised, we'll technically be 'civilian volunteers'. It has nothing to do with being Z reserves, but if you need an excuse at home, you might use that one. What do you think?"

No flannel or opportunity to digest what had just been said. Frank being frank. Sometimes he even quipped, 'now let me be frank with you'. Or 'frankly speaking'. Arthur paused for a few moments, then said.

"I'll have to speak to the Scot."

"Of course you will, but you know he'll do what we decide. A little detail then. Enlistment is for one year, the aim is to protect the withdrawal of our existing troops and we'd only be used in defensive operations, not to attack the Bolsheviks."

"I'm not so sure now Frank. Eric's met a young lady and they seem to be quite sweet on each other."

There was silence on the line.

"Frank.......... Frank.......... Are you there?............ Frank."

"What do you mean he's met a young lady. What are you doing introducing him to young ladies? I've never seen him show any interest in women."

"Me neither. It was Alice who thought it might be a good idea, and it seems to have been so. I'll speak with him and let you know."

"You do that Wally and call me back in twenty minutes."

The phone abruptly went dead and the operator said.

"Thank you caller, would you like me to reconnect."

"No, no thanks we're done for now."

Arthur took Eric to a cafe on Baxter St. that he knew and used frequently to get cakes, pies and sandwiches when he'd worked at the chemists. The proprietor was a large bundle of jowls and jiggles who clearly enjoyed her own fare. She stared at Arthur as if she recognised but couldn't place him, while a young waitress took their order. He explained what Frank had said. They ordered tea, which arrived in a white porcelain teapot and were presented with quite delicate matching tea cups. Another short conversation covering ground they'd covered many times recently, but more useful to Arthur to help him clarify his own thoughts. After a few minutes they'd volunteer. Arthur decided to string Frank along for a bit, it was almost thirty minutes later when he called back to agree they were up for a new adventure.

*

Arthur and Eric got the train back to London few days later. Before doing so there were some difficult conversations with his mum, Betty, and even more so with Alice. He had genuinely looked into employment options, but nothing had any appeal whatsoever. Both women tried to explain that why should work have any appeal. A job was to earn money to live a life, get married, start a family. It all sounded wonderfully domestic and he was sure it would be ...... but not for him yet. He countered to Alice that she enjoyed her work in the office as an accounts clerk at the Hart and Levy factory, to which she acknowledged she did. She then added that many women's jobs had already been transferred back to men, although she'd been told she would be kept in her role. The fact that Sir Maurice always acknowledged her when he visited had something to do with it. She knew that too.

Arthur tried unsuccessfully to obscure his need to retrieve his comradeship and decision to get back to the army with his 'Class Z Reserve' discharge slip. In a fit of pique Alice concluded his immaturity meant he wanted to be with his pals rather than her. This hurt Arthur but was probably true. Immaturity or some kind of invisibly close ties created during the war, he didn't know. Eric resolutely refused to talk about it, prompted by hints from Arthur it might be best to say nothing. It might cloud the issue. Eric was quite happy to remain silent.

3. North Russian Relief Force (NRRF). HMS 'Czarina'.
13th May 1919

So this is how they found themselves at 7.00am. alongside Frank and the artillery contingent of 40 men; part of almost 750 other 'civilian volunteers' who would be collected from Woolwich, Tilbury docks and then Newcastle. A remarkable group of very experienced and bemedaled war veterans. Added to this number were officers named on the manifest plus many additional officers who'd forgone previous commissioned status to serve as 'other ranks', O.R.'s. Marching as a military disciplined body of men onto the south pontoon of the Woolwich Ferry, where they'd disembarked from the 'Francis Duncan' named ferry almost five years ago. Neither Arthur nor Frank could remember the 19th Century artillery officer it was named after, they just recalled being told by the escorting Sergeant. Eric remembered the name though. He said.

"Not as stupid as I look then?"

To which Arthur replied.

"You couldn't possibly be as dumb as you look Aims, otherwise you wouldn't be able to march in step like the rest of us."

They laughed as they stood about waiting with the other gunner volunteers, smoking and drinking tea or coffee from a horse drawn mobile stall recovered from the war. Frank observed how familiar and reassuring it all felt. Queuing under the lifted awnings, above which there were signs for 'Tobaccos, Cigars, Sardines, Tea, Coffee, Bovril'.

The ship they were waiting to board was the appropriately named HMS Czarita. At 347 yards long and 38.2 yards wide, the twin funnelled steamship had been used as a troop and stores carrier for much of the previous five years. It was taking men from many different infantry regiments to create two Brigades under the command of the highly decorated Brigadier General George William St. George Grogan VC, DSO and bar, and Brigadier General Sadlier-Jackson DSO. Additional support units of artillery, engineers, signals, Machine Gun Corp and Army Service Corps were all present on the Czarita. There were no horses or field guns on the ship, these would be supplied in Russia on arrival – so the nominal officer commanding the artillerymen, acting Major George Sumpter, had been told.

Grogan was 44 years old with a square, chubby looking face. Originally from Devon. A well-liked and respected commander of men. After Sandhurst he was commissioned into the West India Regiment and first saw colonial service in the Sierra Leone Hut Tax War of 1898. The British governor, Colonel Frederic Cardew sought to implement a new tax to fund the colonial administration's expenses based on the size of the hut. Ten shillings annually for a four roomed hut, anything smaller, five shillings. For subsistence farmers this was unsustainable and 24 tribal chiefs petitioned against it. Without the tax being rescinded, several ethnic groups rebelled. Cardew deployed his soldiers to suppress the revolt, including Grogan's unit.

A scorched earth policy was executed, burning farms and crops. Eventually, Bai Bureh, the Temne leader surrendered on 11th November 1898. He was exiled to the Gold Coast and 96 other rebels found guilty of murder were executed. The colonial forces suffered 67 killed and 184 wounded. Local casualties were unknown. For Grogan, as a young officer, he fought and witnessed an asymmetric war of British power over African natives. Very typical of the 19th Century British Empire.

After service with the Egyptian army up to 1907, he returned to build a career with the Worcestershire Regiment. His two DSO awards were for frontline gallantry in the trenches leading his men. His VC citation from an action near Jonchery-sur-Vesle in France in May 1918 defending against a German advance read:

His action during the whole of the battle can only be described as magnificent. The utter disregard for his personal safety, combined with the sound practical ability which he displayed, materially helped to stay the onward thrust of the enemy masses. Throughout the third day of operations, a most critical day, he spent his time under artillery, trench mortar, rifle and machine-gun fire, riding up and down the front line encouraging his troops, reorganising those who had fallen into disorder, leading back into the line those who were beginning to retire, and setting such a wonderful example that he inspired with his enthusiasm not only his own men but also the Allied troops who were alongside. As a result the line held and repeated enemy attacks were repulsed. He had one horse shot under him, but nevertheless continued on foot to encourage his men until another horse was brought. He displayed throughout the highest valour, powers of command and leadership.

Grogan was a soldier's officer. Brave, experienced, effective and he knew his men and how to get the best from them.

Brigadier General Lionel Warren de Vere Sadlier-Jackson was 42, also with DSO and bar. He would be commanding the Brigade of re-enlisted volunteers. As a young officer he'd served in the Boer War as a staff officer, present at several actions including the Relief of Kimberley. He was wounded, recovered and continued to the end of the war being mentioned in dispatches several times and awarded the DSO. He entered The Great War as a Captain in the Army Signal Corps and through rapid promotions was a Brigadier by October 1917 commanding 54th Brigade. Clearly a little eccentric, he became notorious for his unkempt foppish hair and driving around the rear areas in his blue Rolls Royce picking up stragglers.

On the 21st August 1918 at Albert he led his troops to take their objectives and was wounded in the knee by machine gun fire. He collapsed on the battlefield, brought in by his men, he spent the next few months recovering in England. He was awarded a bar to his DSO as a result of his leadership in this action.

So the two commanders of the 8,000 men of the NRRF were brave leaders of men. They had been appointed to their command positions and were pleased to be able to continue their active service; for them this expedition was a part of their military obligation to Britain. The quality and recognised bravery of these units was further enhanced by another eleven VC holders who'd volunteered and were part of the same travelling cohort of the three gunners. There were many officers with Distinguished Service Orders and Military Cross's and other rank soldiers with Distinguished Conduct Medals and Military Medals as Frank held.

From a horrendously long war to another conflict for which these men didn't know what to expect. They were inspired and motivated by many things, some indefinable. Back in 1914 with the rush of volunteers for Kitchener's New Army, patriotism, jingoism, defence of the Empire, risk of German invasion, as well as many personal reasons drove men to volunteer. Now was different. For some the change from army to civilian life was too fracturing leading to instability, unemployment and poverty; the money and guarantee of being fed was an attraction. As was the camaraderie. High expectations of what peace would mean for up to four and a half million demobilised men were quickly shattered, especially for post 1916 conscripts who felt entitled to a payback from the country for the service demanded from them; and for the disabled, their sacrifice.

The Force was assembled and sold to the volunteers on the premise of a rescue mission of the thousands of Royal Marines and other soldiers already in the port of Murmansk and its hinterland. Rescuing fellow soldiers was one of the reasons thought to have attracted so many VC holders. Retrieving and supporting fellow soldiers provided legitimacy and cohesion to the mission. The British soldiers at every level needed to know they had a specific purpose, giving them focus, cohesion and also underpinning confidence. Certainty and stability within a clearly understood hierarchy created psychological comfort for some.

Motivation for some officers might have been political. They would have known enough about the Bolsheviks and the impact of revolution in Russia to understand that if it spread to Britain the transformation of a privileged class structure, from which many benefitted, would be total. Finally amongst the many motivational pulls, there may have been a few war-mongers wanting to continue killing. Murderous psychopaths would rarely find the discipline and rigour of a military existence satisfactory, so this number might have been none, or very few.[2]

HMS Czarita was ready to leave by high tide on the 13th of May at midday. Released from the ferry jetty it whistled loudly, slowly pulling into the centre of the Thames, here known as Woolwich Reach, to steam imperiously toward the open sea. At Tilbury half an hour later they were joined by HMS Stephen. A days sailing in the North Sea to another smaller embarkation at Newcastle and then several days across the North Sea to track the Swedish coast into the Barents Sea before heading 'East-South-East' to Murmansk and then to the White Sea port of Archangel.

Very few of the volunteers on board the Czarita had experienced any more sea than the short crossings from Britain and France. Some had been at Gallipoli and Salonika so knew the Mediterranean, a body of water that could be rough, but being non-tidal was nothing like the North Atlantic. For most sailors of the Royal Navy the rolling waves meant, maybe 24 hours of sea-sickness. They knew it would go once they got their legs. For the soldiers it was the worst sensation they'd ever experienced. Over the first day it afflicted almost everyone, although some only briefly. Many felt they just wanted to die, and one poor soul from the Welsh Guards who was known to be suffering badly went missing, recorded as lost at sea, presumed to have thrown himself overboard. After two days Arthur and Eric felt okay, Frank took another day. They then started to enjoy the voyage.

The three men were now part of a force that had a clear and well defined mission: to ensure the safe withdrawal of the units already committed as part of the greater war they'd just fought. This is what they'd signed up for, but at the international political level it was a little different. They had given up their stripes and reverted to the rank of gunner on volunteering. Many others in the other units, including some senior NCO's and 'Gentlemen Officers' had done the same

---

[2] "The North Russian Relief Force. A Study of Military Motivation in the aftermath of the First World War."
Carol Boylan, PhD Thesis, 2016. (See acknowledgements).

4. Russia's war and revolution.

Russia had been one of the most significant British and French allies in Europe from August 1914. The war on the eastern front covered massive areas of land, requiring the commitment of millions of Germans, Austro-Hungarians and Turks, many of whom would otherwise have been deployed in France, Belgium, Italy and the Middle East. As well as soldiers and officers, huge quantities of resources and materials were needed. German occupation of land in the east meant the requisitioning of local food produce, raw materials and production capability to be converted to support the fighting soldiers.

The country was a vast empire of 170 million people from many ethnic groups, less than half ethnic Russian. The demographic diversity of nationalities and its land mass meant that control from the centre by the Romanov family of Tsars was in many places, fragile. The attempted imposition of a common Russian language and the Orthodox Church increased tensions across this diverse population. A backward agricultural economy with mainly subsistence farmers lived a medieval rural existence.

The political and government infrastructure was corrupt at all levels. Before the war the ruling Russians were conscious of the growing tensions in Europe, the increasing imperial aggressiveness of Germany, the vulnerability of the adjacent Ottoman and Austro-Hungarian Empires. They'd been making attempts to grow their industries and in particular to create rail transport links to their western borders. This was not due to be completed until 1917.

When the war started in 1914 there was some loyal support for the government during the mobilisation of troops. There's nothing like an international conflict to galvanise the patriotism and the population. Initial campaigns went well with the occupation of Poland where the Russian army were able to harness local food resources to sustain the men. Very quickly the Germans and Austrians responded with the Russians suffering a devastating defeat at Tannenberg in August 1914. The Russians withdrew to their borders. They did manage to beat back German attacks at Masuria which resulted in a lull in the fighting. This didn't stop millions of refugees heading east putting additional pressures on an already collapsing supply system. War on Europe's eastern front ground on in a more mobile way than in France without any decisive outcome that couldn't be managed by throwing more men into the frontline.

Britain and France quickly recognised the strategic importance of Russia's war in ensuring the Axis powers had to keep the front stocked with men and equipment. They knew that keeping Russia fighting was key to winning. Despite having potential access to huge numbers of men through conscription, there were many exemptions, including the usual medical, physical, religion and randomly through a lottery process. If a man was the family wage earner he gained exemption, leading to over 2 million marriages in the peasantry in August 1914. They also had to be trained, fed and transported to the front which, in a vast undeveloped country created huge challenges.

In 1915, without success being delivered on the battlefield, Tsar Nicholas II dismissed his Commander-in-Chief and took overall command. Things got worse through the next two years as the Germans stretched the front further north into the Baltic States creating more offensive pressure. To the south the Russians made some progress against the Austro-Hungarians but this stopped when the supply lines were elongated and failed to maintain momentum.

By 1917 the cohesion of the Russian army and society was fragmenting. Displaced civilians and peasants had fled east to the cities looking for work, food and shelter of which there was little available. The level of hunger and privation was obvious and increasingly unequal. The aristocracy and profiting industrialists had all they needed, the workers and peasants next to nothing. In March 1917 the women of Petrograd, the Russian Capital, protested over the rising price and shortage of bread. Coal for bakeries was short and flour was being withheld by 'capitalist speculators'.

The army was called out to deal with the crowds, but these men were now conscripts with no wish to fight foreign enemies, even less to kill fellow Russians. The soldiers and factory workers elected a soviet (council), the political socialist intelligentsia inveigled their way into leading the uprising and negotiated the end of saluting, the military death penalty and the election of officers in the army. Into this societal fragmentation came Lenin, a long standing socialist intellectual who combined charisma with leadership, oratory and organisational skills.

Over the next six months, attempts by more moderate politicians to steady the country and assemble a stable government failed. The army's ability to attack the enemy diminished, morale collapsed and many soldiers tried to make their way home. By November, the only political organisation with any coherence were the Bolsheviks who assumed power by occupying the Winter Palace in Petrograd, in an action that was almost bloodless. The soldiers in the building refused to resist and members of the Provisional Government, the administration trying to rule were arrested. At the front the army was collapsing, refusing to fight and according to Lenin "voting with their feet".

Lenin and the Bolshevik leaders quickly arranged an armistice to preserve and focus on their own revolution. On the 3rd March 1918 Russia withdrew from the war by signing a Treaty at Brest-Litovsk (B-L), a Polish town then occupied by the Germans. Russia ceded vast tracts of Imperial Russian land in Eastern Europe to the Axis powers. The treaty enabled forty German Divisions to be transferred from east to west giving them numerical superiority for the first time, at least until the Americans arrived in greater numbers over the spring and summer of 1918. Ludendorff's final flourish Spring Offensive was enabled by the B-L Treaty.

Most European politicians were completely focused on the war on their doorstep. But for the belligerent Winston Churchill, the War Secretary in Lloyd George's government, who's international horizons were wider, the situation in Russia needed a response. An initial desire to protect British military assets that had been delivered into the northern ports of Murmansk and Archangel developed further. Firstly when the Czech Legion[3] were considered under threat from the Bolsheviks, and secondly the unwillingness to continue fighting the Germans. Lord Curzon at the Foreign Office had additional concerns on Russian threats to the British Empire in India and other Far Eastern dependencies. So troops were also landed in Caucasia in the south and Vladivostok in the far east to work with the Japanese and Czech's to secure the Trans-Siberian railway and contain the Bolsheviks to the west of Russia.

Beneath the geo-political motives there was also widespread political fear and hostility toward the type of socialist ideology espoused by the Bolsheviks. The international implication of Marxist calls of "Workers of the World Unite", could lead to the overthrow of many governments. So not just the British, Japanese and French but the Americans, Canadians and Italians also sent troops to fight the Bolsheviks and contain the worker's revolution. The Czech's had their own force there too. Smaller contingents from bordering nations such as Finland, Poland, Estonia and Greece were also active.

After B-L, Russia descended into a civil war with multiple unaligned military forces known generally as the "White Russians" fighting the Bolsheviks across the vast open spaces of the country. Russian opposition to the south came under the leadership of General Anton Ivanovich Denikin, an Imperial Army professional and veteran of the disastrous Russo-Japanese war of 1905. Nikolai Nikolayevich Yudenich, a Muscovite with a similar history to Denikin led the White Russian forces out of the Baltic states. The most powerful Admiral Alexander Vasilyevich Kolchak. Born in Petrograd of Romanian parents; his father had been a marine

---

[3] 70,000 plus PoW's captured by the Russians who were formed into a force to fight against the Axis powers. They were Bohemians, Moravians and Slovaks; ethnic groups wanting independence from the Austro-Hungarian Empire. They'd taken control of the Trans-Siberian Railway and were potentially stranded there.

artillery general at the Siege of Sevastopol in the Crimean War. From 1918 to 1920 Kolchak was recognised internationally as Russia's head of state based in Omsk, Southern Siberia, also a stop on the strategically important Trans-Siberian railway.

Other forces under the white anti-revolutionary flag were motivated by nationalism including ethnic groups of Georgians in the Caucasus, the Don Cossacks from Ukraine and the Ural Cossacks from the Kazakh region to the north of the Caspian Sea. In many cases these men fought their Cossack compatriots within the Bolshevik army who had sided with the revolutionaries.

5. The Trial.
Norwegian Sea, May 1919

Feeling more comfortable after the bouts of sea-sickness on the first few days the army men collectively failed to understand how the sailors of the Royal Navy could tolerate these floating death-traps for more than a few hours. To the three gunners, losing sight of land seemed completely stupid. They discussed at length the incomprehensibility of ever volunteering for such a hair-brained idea, and as with August 1914, this was little to do with the global geo-political situation. They had time to spare and despite this they were never able to establish which of the three of them was to blame. As these close friends bantered and joked between themselves, many of their artillery colleagues billeted in the same bunkroom became familiar with the arguments each one tried to make….. unsuccessfully.

Support was garnered and then lost by each man. It became a running theme of amusement to a wider group and the light-heartedness was good for general morale. In this claustrophobic environment of a new group of unfamiliar men forced to live together in very close proximity for the two weeks at sea, the ability of the three friends to keep the mood light became important.

About eight days into the trip, on witnessing the banter one of the Leading Seamen, Henry Holt known to all as 'Harry', suggested to the artillery section Sergeant, Bradmond Raybury, an ex-RSM with an extraordinarily calm and commanding countenance, that a mock trial was needed to allocate responsibility for the 'crime' of press ganging two of the three of Arthur, Eric and Frank. Harry Holt had become a popular sailor amongst the soldiers on board. Now, the same age as Arthur at 21, he'd been on many of the supply convoys to Murmansk and Archangel, including the ferrying of the Royal Marines in 1918. Outgoing, with a positive manner that found the best in everything. Even when the soldiers were at their worst with sickness in the force five weather they met in the North Sea, he regaled them with tales of what a force eight felt like. As if it were something to look forward to.

Harry Holt came from Wandsworth, just south of the Thames in London. Living with his family on Warple Road , close to Wandsworth Town Station on the 'East Putney and Wimbledon New Railway Line, 1889'. This was an area of industry that had grown up on the wet tidal flood-lands at the confluence of the River Wandle and the Thames. Within a few minutes' walk from their terraced house there was a tram depot, gas and chemical works, various wharves and warehouses on the river, Osier's Fireworks factory where his father worked, the Southwark and Vauxhall water works, The Union Brewery, Thorley's Food works and The Ram Brewery.

Harry claimed his love of the sea came from all the time he spent on the Thames tidal beaches that he gained access to from steps by the lock for the Wandle Canal Dock. As a young child he'd join his dad and other local people 'mud-larking' in the river, looking for washed up and lost treasure that surfaced in the daily tidal movements. They would scour the mud and filth for anything of value which could then be sold. He found a Roman silver coin once but was deeply disappointed when the local sweet shop refused to accept it. His mum persuaded him to give it to the town museum where it sits with a card marked 'Henry Holt's Roman coin found in the River Thames, 3rd June 1908'. His dad always joked the best find he'd made was a gold ring worth five pounds. After removing the hand attached to it, Mrs Holt now wore it on her wedding finger. He found this hilarious every time. Unsurprisingly, she pretended she didn't and responded with a faux verbal telling off.

The mock trial would need a Judge independent of those on trial. He volunteered his services for this, claiming he was well versed in the procedures from reading about Captain Thomas Anstis *"Mock Court of Judicature to try one another for Pyracy"* as he and his crew waited for pardons from George II near Cuba in 1722.

"It's a Mock Court Holt. How can there be procedures?" asked Sgt. Raybury.

"Of course the procedures aren't documented, I make them up as we go along."

Holt replied with a conspiratorial wink.

A jury of eight men would be needed and these were selected from some of the infantry volunteers. Each defendant could have an advocate or represent themselves. The trial would be held in the ship's canteen. Harry had to work some of his persuasive magic on Frank who never liked to be the centre of attention. However, he agreed that it would provide a morale boosting distraction for the men on their mess sitting, limited to 120 of them which was the capacity of the dining room. Over the war years Frank had become more artful in his aloofness. He was now very different with his close mates and had been so with some of the others in 'A' Battery. His promotions and Military Medal helped him and he could now appear more friendly and interactive socially, but it was an act that he'd developed to wall in the real Frank. Arthur and Eric knew this. They also knew that when he turned on the act, it was very convincing. Frank decided to throw himself into the spirit of the charade and represent himself.

Word spread about the Czarita of the mock trial and it genuinely seemed to lift the spirit of both crew and soldiers. A young Captain approached Sgt. Raybury with an offer to get involved. Jack Mitchell came from Alresford, educated at Winchester School as a day pupil and had served with the Hampshire Regiment during the war in Divisional Headquarter staff roles. He'd qualified as a Barrister in 1914 but immediately responded to Kitchener's pointing finger appeal. Jack had a first class degree in history and a first class brain which the army sensibly and unusually used where it was best suited, dealing with the administrative complexities of just getting things done. His legal skills had also been applied in numerous Court Martials for desertion and cowardice. Not one case he'd been involved in led to the execution of the accused soldier. He'd maintained a record of protecting men from a military firing squad in a process that he considered barely legal itself.

A thorn in the side of some of the military hierarchy, his reputation amongst fellow lawyers and the legal profession grew. At the end of the war he just wanted to get back to the courts with attractive offers from various chambers in London. However, the army, Winston Churchill at the War Office and the Judge Advocate General under which military law fell, had other plans. They needed to get a lawyer into the North Russia theatre to deal with a number of mutinous actions conducted by British soldiers of the Royal Marine detachments already there. There was no one better qualified than Jack Mitchell – because his planning skills and knowledge of logistics would also help the extraction of men and kit back to Britain. A bonus for the Exchequer.

Mitchell also enjoyed humour and laughed easily despite the weight and seriousness of the law. Whilst not having come across Mock Trials before, he thought, perhaps it was a Navy thing, he knew this would be good for the men. Sgt. Raybury suggested Capt. Jack Mitchell as Arthur's advocate, which he was happy to accept.

Eric on the other hand had decided that his advocate would be an ebullient, supremely self-confident Glaswegian ex-Sergeant Major from the Highland Light Infantry. William (Billy) McIntyre, (Military Medal and Bar), had been with the 2nd Battalion when the war started, a corporal at that time, seeing his first action at the Battle of Aisne in September 1914 where he sustained a minor flesh wound on his shoulder. He'd grown to believe he was invisible to the enemy by surviving the war with no further injury at Ypres and Loos in 1915, The Somme the summer of 1916, Arras and Cambrai in 1917 and the advance on the Hindenburg Line in 1918. And these were just the significant actions.

He'd seen many comrades die and get injured and appeared to veer to the edge of insanity if he ever stopped to reflect, so he tried not to, except when he drank. He'd re-enlisted for Russia after realising that peace in Glasgow meant unemployment and hunger. Other men avoided McIntyre when he managed to get hold of a bottle of spirit on the ship. He was known to completely abstain from drink when in action, always refusing his rum ration. A man of real contrasts, he was self-educated, reading whenever and whatever he could and liked to boast that he'd read the complete works of Dickens. McIntyre had also organised his battalion's entertainment shows when out of the line. In that context he liked to see himself as a Scottish Fred Karno, the English music hall impresario.

The other ranks canteen was organised for the trial. Along one of the long sides a small platform had been created at the very front for the Judges Bench with a green baize cloth draped over it, hammer and gavel borrowed from the Officers Mess. The room had been laid out with as many chairs as could be fitted with the central seats of the front row having small cards with 'Reserved' written on them. A number of the Relief Force officers and the ship's Captain, Angus Buchan, a white bearded veteran of northern supply convoys, had expressed an interest in coming to see the proceedings. They needed entertaining as much as any of the men. To the right of the bench were two more desks at 90 degrees, with three seats for Frank, Eric and McIntyre on one, two for Arthur and Captain Jack Mitchell on the other. To the left, two rows of four seats for the jury who's been picked from a lucky dip of men who'd put their names in a hat the day before.

Arthur and Capt. Mitchell had met several times to prepare a defence, with much laughter creating preposterous and absurd reasons as to why Arthur had been led, firstly by Frank and then Eric to be marching up the boarding planks of the Czarita.

The advocates were allowed an opening statement, there would then be a set of the same questions posed by the 'Judge', leading seaman Harry Holt to the 'defendants' which he might vary and add to as he saw fit, and finally a closing statement. The principle aim of all involved was to elevate what had been the kind of matey interpersonal banter between the three men, that had already become popular amongst the artillery volunteers, to a common level. The friends were comfortable enough with each other to know that nothing said would be taken as genuine hostility. They'd shared plenty of harsh words in times of real stress to know what all this was about.

*

By 7pm. the room was full of the loud noise of talking and laughing. Sgt. Raybury took the hammer and banged on the gavel three times to get the attention of the public gallery. He projected his voice across the room in the finest parade ground style.

"Gentlemen of the North Russian Relief Force, ship's crew of the Steam Ship Czarita, sirs at the front here and the mice and cockroaches of the kitchen that might be listening."

There was an uncomfortably embarrassed look amongst the officers and a small cheer from behind them. The truth was no matter what measures were taken, there was always vermin of sorts being transported on ships and everyone knew it. Raybury continued.

"We meet tonight to establish who is to blame for these three men, Gunners Abraham, Amos or Walton, for them being on this ship bound for the sunny climes of north Russia. I'm told that when we get there the winter will be over and the ice in the ports will have melted."

An audience cheer, that evolved into a groan.

Raybury introduced each defendant and their advocate. As he did so each man stood and took a small bow. All were uniformed and wore their respective service cap.

"The court will be presided over by leading seaman Harry Holt who claims to have knowledge of these things."

As he finished this sentence he waved his hand toward the far end of the room where, from the kitchen door behind the serving counter Holt emerged wearing a judicial looking black cape and in the absence of a wig, what looked like a white tea-towel draped over his head. A loud cheer went up as the men recognised their popular colleague. It was indeed a tea-towel that he'd grabbed in a last minute flash of inspiration as he'd exited the kitchen. Holt made his way to the bench, took his seat, explained to the room what would happen and then called on Frank to make his opening defensive statement.

Frank stood and spoke about meeting the other two on the day they enlisted in August 1914, recounted a number of humorous tales from training and the war. Claimed he was always an outsider and never sought or needed the friendship of the other two, that they were malignant influences and that despite Amos's apparent quiet, unassuming manner, he was an accomplished hypnotist who could control the will and actions of others when he chose to do so. Wally Walton on the other hand was a positive, personable man who lulled his fellow men into trouble with good humour and affability wherever he went. Frank spoke for about ten minute and drew laughs from the public gallery and from his friends for his delivery and the ridiculousness of his fabrications.

Holt than asked Frank questions from his prepared list and a few others that he made up at the time. Frank's acting of the role of an easily influenced follower might have been convincing had Holt not pointed out that he was the only one who'd chosen to represent himself.

On completion, Holt banged the gavel called for order in the court as chatter erupted amongst the audience and the jury and called for McIntyre to speak on Eric's behalf. Billy McIntyre's pitch started as if it were a lesson in Scottish history. He talked about the uniqueness of the hardy ancient Scottish tribes of Picts, Celts and Caledonians who resisted the Roman conquerors of the rest of Britain; and then the Gaels and Picts who united in the 9th century to resist the Viking invasions. It was clear he knew the history of his country which took him ten minutes to reach the Act of Union in 1707 where the English took over. At this point Holt banged the gavel.

"We appreciate your monologue on the fascinating history of Scotland, but I'm not sure how this relates to the case in hand. I'd just like to remind you Private McIntyre that you've reached the time limit for opening statements."

"Another minute or so, Your Honour and I'll have made my point."

He continued, ignoring Holt's comment by referring to the intellectual enlightenment in the 1700's, Watt's steam engines, McAdam's roads, Mackintosh's macs, Smith's invisible hand.

"Gifts the Scots have given to the world. But since then our nation has been ruled from London. We are the victims of English colonialism, our men used by imperialists to build the British Empire. It is my point that my friend here, Gunner Eric Amos, a quiet man, with much to be quiet about, has been influenced and led into this mission by two silver-tongued tools of English imperialism and suppression who sit there before you."

He finished waving his right arm with a dramatic flourish toward Arthur and Frank and sat down next to Eric who's shoulders were bouncing up and down in laughter. After a moment to let the cheering and clapping die down, notably from a clutch of Coldstream Guardsmen, Holt was heard to say.

"I have no particular wish to influence the jury here, but I've never heard such complete and utter twaddle."

He then questioned McIntyre.

"Just to be clear private McIntyre, you did volunteer for this force yourself?"

"I did Your Honour."

"Without being lashed by a silver-tongued Englishman?"

"That's true Your Honour."

"And do you understand the meaning of the word irony?"

"I do Your Honour."

McIntyre had a big grin on his face as Holt went through his list of questions. Eric, in Eric's way, answered most with either a yes or no. The men in the room knew his reticent nature and were enjoying the interaction of Holt trying to engage with more dialogue. When asked what role he'd had in Frank's award of the Military Medal, his answer stretched to.

"I helped remove some bricks."

Holt asked. "Would you like elaborate?"

Eric paused and appeared to be giving it some thought. He allowed the tension in the room to build for about thirty seconds and then replied with perfect comic timing.

"Nooo."

The room burst into laughter. Holt moved his head from side to side in a show of despair, the long sides of the white tea-towel flapping on his shoulders making the scene even more ridiculous. Banging the gavel he shouted for order in the room before calling Captain Mitchell for his statement. Mitchell stood to give his opening remarks.

"Thank you Your Honour. My client, Gunner Arthur Wal...."

Before he could finish his first sentence Holt was hammering the gavel on the block.

"Order! Order! Captain Mitchell, you referred to the defendant, Gunner Walton as your client, is he paying you?"

"Err....... No Your Honour. Professional habit I guess."

"Professional habit? You're not in the Old Bailey now Captain Mitchell. He's a defendant. It's a Mock Court abuse of protocol, you'll need to be sanctioned."

Jack Mitchell was smiling at the nonsense being played out. Leading Seaman Holt was enjoying his moment of power in the limelight. The audience were enjoying the spectacle. Arthur was chuckling with his elbows on the table and head resting on his fists. Mitchell spoke.

"My apologies Your Honour, I wasn't aware there was a protocol."

"I hope you're not opening a debate on this Captain Mitchell. Sanctioned, yes sanctioned. I think The Queen of Hearts in Alice had it almost right."

Holt paused, banged the gavel and shouted.

"Off with his.......... hat!"

The room erupted in a big cheer. The officers at the front were laughing and clapping at the ritual humiliation of a fellow officer, all in the good cause of humour. Mitchell removed his peaked cap, revealing his neatly cut fair hair. He placed it on the desk and tried to continue his opening remarks. His defence was to emphasise Arthur's youth when he enlisted, technically before the war started in 1914. In a style that was comically theatrical with repetitive over-emphasised alliteration he told the story of the 'calamitous, chemical, catastrophe, the elemental emergency, the mercury misadventure', which led him to flee from an ogre of an employer. He landed in the same recruitment cohort as Abraham and Amos who have been leading him astray ever since.

Holt asked his questions of Arthur, challenging him on his promotion to Lance Bombardier when Amos apparently refused. Picking up on Frank's charge that Eric was an accomplished hypnotist, he claimed he must have been in a trance like state. The raised eyebrows and rolled-eye look on Holt's face told the room what he thought of this.

He then addressed the jury and asked if they had any questions for the defendants or advocates. A Scot from the Cameron Highlanders asked Billy McIntyre if he could explain what happened at the Battle of Culloden. McIntyre was on his feet and into his second sentence before the gavel came down on that one. A Yorkshireman from the Duke of Wellington's Regiment sporting a VC ribbon asked if Frank could detail the rates of fire for artillery field guns and then added 'and why do the rounds drop short on our own heads?'. This got a cheer from all the infantrymen before order was restored.

There was then a break in the proceedings while the jury considered their verdict. The ship's Captain Buchan had arranged for some beer and rum to be made available for the event. Tea and coffee for the abstemious, of which there were few. After fifteen minutes Holt returned to the bench, banged the gavel and the men returned to their seats with a great deal of chatter and noise. It quietened down when Holt asked the elected member of the jury to act as spokesman. It was the Cameron Highlander by the name of McLeish who stood. Holt asked.

"Have the jury reached a decision?"

"We have Your Honour, sort of."

"What do you mean, sort of."

"Well I'm afraid we're not unanimous, which I understand is what is expected."

The Scot looked amongst his fellow jury members.

"We are split between ourselves over the three gunners."

Holt raised both his arms in a fake presentation of despair.

"So I will write on this paper my verdict as to who is responsible for bringing the other two along with him and pass it to you. Add it to the jury's decision and let's get a result."

Holt passed the slip to McLeish who read the name without expression.

"So now tell me who is the guilty party."

McLeish responded. "Well we now have three votes for Amos."

Men started laughing again in anticipation of what they could now expect.

"Three for Walton.........."

And before he could finish calling the perfectly, three-way hung jury verdict the room had already responded with applause and cheering. The mock trial pantomime had failed to pin the blame on any one of the three friends. It was the right verdict for the evening enabling the continuation of the banter and the wider interest on something that would never be decided. When the partisan cheering for whoever they supported died down, the white bearded, Santa-Claus lookalike, Captain Buchan stood to address the room. He thanked Sgt. Raybury and Leading Seaman Holt for organising 'the great show trial' as he described it, and also Capt. Mitchell and ex-Sergeant Major McIntyre for their participation. Then the three gunners for being

"such tremendous, good sports by allowing themselves to be exposed to the Mock Court and sharing some of their personal stories. Without unusual evenings like this the passage to north Russia would be insufferable for us all."

He hoped all had enjoyed the spirit as well as the content of the trial despite it being inconclusive. The appreciative clapping and verbal response in the room told him everyone had. Arthur, Frank and Eric returned to their bunk room with the rest of the gunners who were proud of their colleagues for agreeing to participate.

The gunners were satisfied they had been able to bring some humour and improve morale amongst the volunteers and navy crewmen who attended, and even the officers. A few more tots of rum from an acquired bottle finished the evening off. Arthur lay swinging in the hammock reflecting on events. A typical military 'something' created out of nothing. He dozed off thinking that one thing his army life had told him was to volunteer for nothing unless you were certain of the outcome, and how the hell he ended up on the Czarita.

6. Archangel[4] Docks.
June 1919.

Archangel. Biblical Chief Angel. Michael, Gabriel, or Raphael? Or the angel Jophiel, also known in Judaism as Dina with her flaming sword? Ariel, Azrael and Chamuel, who make vaguer appearances in canonical writings. All of these embodiments of spiritual 'leaders' of angels created an idea of some kind of idyll. The reality was more like naming the incredibly productive yet disgustingly smelly, industrial fishing port of Grimsby, 'Paradise'. The port of Archangel would never be a tourist attraction.

It was 05.20 am. Arthur had woken early and had sensed from the noise and vibration of the ship's engines they were being piloted by a local tug into the final port of their destination. They'd called into Murmansk a few days ago on the 3rd June to drop off supplies and pick up more men and then sailed south-east as part of a fourteen ship convoy along the Kola peninsula to turn south into the White Sea. Much of the sea was still covered by winter ice with ice-breakers leading the British convoy of ships sailing in parallel.

The ice was late breaking up this year, the winter had been long and harsh. A channel had been created enabling access to the Dvina river delta and the protected port of Archangel. The tug needed to negotiate the multiple branches of the river through the islands, water channels and ice hazard. The early hour meant that only the merest hint of dawn was breaking. There had been blanket grey skies yesterday, likely the same today. Difficult to tell right now as all Arthur could see were the few electric lights from the windows of the harbour's official buildings and the burning braziers lit by the piece-work dockers already waiting in anticipation of the arrival of more foreign ships. Numerous lights flickered in the hinterland behind the dock area where the city spread away into a distance.

The NRRF volunteers had orders to be ready to disembark by 8.00am. That probably meant midday in the commonly used 'rush, run, wait' army method for getting soldiers from A to B. Arthur stood for fifteen minutes or so on deck, watching the pilot tug towing the larger steam ship onto the dockside. Other men came and went off to get tea or an early breakfast from the ship's canteen. He stayed, enthralled by thoughts of now being two weeks away from Britain in this new world. It seemed to get lighter, the small harbour city revealing the contradiction from its name. Wooden,

---

[4] As it was known to the British. Archangelsk locally then and today.

dark, dirty, dishevelled and very far from the angelic implication. It looked grim. It was grim.

Cold too. When up on deck he'd worn an issued great coat and the 'Sarah Nicol's' Saffer balaclava he'd retained from the supply sent to the Battery during the war. He was already glad he'd done so. He knew Frank still had his but Eric had either lost or swapped this very useful and warming hat for a more attractive but now discarded souvenir. Today there wasn't much wind, had there been so he would've gone below after a few minutes. Well below freezing, the coldness felt brittle and penetrating. A great deal of winter snow still lay on the roofs of the dockyard warehouses where there was no heat to melt it. Some huts had no snow indicating warmth inside. Arthur was pleased to think they would only be in northern Russia for the summer months when they'd been told the climate was similar to Britain despite being so much further north.

In true army style, the men were ready to disembark by the allotted time, only to wait until their time slot was reached. It was 10.45am. for the gunners on the disembarkation schedule. Descending the gang-plank to the dockside wearing webbing underneath great coats and carrying their large haversack's, the unfamiliar sounds of Russian voices filled the air. The burning braziers were now isolated from the men who'd lit them for warmth. They were engaged with unloading the Czarita hold.

Two small cranes were lifting boxed supplies loaded onto wooden pallets, long ropes threaded under the wood and tied above to create a sling. In the hold the British sailors were loading smaller bundles into large net slings that swung wildly when lifted. The cranes seemed to be dancing in unison, one releasing its pallet on the dock, while the other picking up a net sling from the hold. The latticed lifting boom of each crossing at the midway point of the traverse from hold to dockside.

The gunners deposited their haversacks into a waiting military truck that, much to their great surprise, had an American flag painted on the driver's door. They hadn't been made aware that the Yanks were also involved in the operation. No driver was to be seen, but the British Sgt. Major directing dockside affairs was insistent it was reserved for the artillery section. Major Sumpter, inappropriately named the 'Battery Commander' of enough soldiers to man and supply no more than three guns accepted the Sgt. Major's direction. He was rushing to an officers briefing on the local situation so had no time to argue. Sgt. Raybury paraded the gunners and told them they'd be marching to a transit camp, leaving at 2pm. They were issued with meal tickets to be used at an American YMCA canteen set up in one of the buildings by the front gates of the dockyard.

On the dockside the heavily bearded stevedores who Arthur had seen waiting by the fires had removed their top-coats revealing a thick brown protective work apron. Like a string of ants carting twigs and leaves to a nest, they ferried bags and boxes on ancient looking sack barrows from the deposited cargo pallets and slings to the log built warehouse behind. The sound of the metal rimmed wooden wheels rattling over the cobbled dockside dominated the air. A wheel had come off one of the barrows. A young looking docker, whose sparse red beard contained no grey and contrasted with the other men's predominately greying black and brown growths was arguing emotionally with a uniformed official holding a clip-board. He was perhaps below the age of military conscription or revolutionary usefulness, as the others were over.

Eric, with his pre-war knowledge of subsistence life said to the others.

"It's piece-work. If he can't work, he won't get paid. It'll be his responsibility to bring the tools for the job, in this case a barrow that's in working order. He looks young, it's a very old barrow he's inherited or bought from an old man. He'll now have to get it fixed at his own expense. So losing at least a day's pay and the cost of repair is a double blow for him."

There were some other barrows propped up against the warehouse behind the foreman that red-beard was gesticulating to with his open palm waving at them. The foreman with his palm facing the ground, his arm and his head moving from side-to-side was responding with a repeated 'nyet' mixed in with a host of angry, sounding harsh words. The docker held his hands together as if in prayer, clearly pleading with the foreman. Eric again.

"I think red-beard wants to use one of the other barrows. They'll belong to other men so the foreman won't let him. I've seen similar things many times on building sites."

The row continued for a few more minutes until red-beard threw up his arms with a string of angry abuse that the foreman ignored. The young docker then lifted the damaged barrow onto his right shoulder and clutching the wooden wheel in his left hand stormed off along the quayside, talking to himself through his immature, straggly growth. They watched him walk in front of the next wooden structure, this one a much smaller, gaudily painted, two floored, multi-windowed house with four doors painted purple, red, blue and yellow. It was completely incongruous in the docks. As he walked past there appeared, at some of the windows and doors, numerous women in similar white shawls and headscarves covering coloured patchwork dresses. They started calling to red-beard, each one trying to attract him in by waving.

"It's clearly a brothel." Said Frank with a moralistic undertone.

As the gunners watched, a man in uniform emerged from the blue door. His peaked cap was louchely pushed back on his head in a slovenly careless way. He walked toward the truck and seeing Sgt. Raybury shouted.

"Are these your men Sarge?"

"Yes they are, Private?" His upward inflection created the question.

"Pickens Sarge, Jericho Pickens, my pals call me Jez. From Green Bay, Wisconsin. Right there on Lake Michigan. Weather very much like here, cold and then colder. Is the truck loaded?"

"It is Pickens. Are you the driver?"

"Co-driver Sarge. I ride along shotgun to keep an eye on the driver, Kranz his name is. And to look out for locals wanting to steal the contents."

"Where is Kranz?"

Pickens looked about the dockside in an insubordinately theatrical way, that didn't expect to find an answer. Not seeing his mate he shook his head with a tombstone grin missing several alternate front teeth.

"Still in The Ladies House of Pleasure I'd guess Sarge. Still bringing pleasure to the ladies."

His unpleasant, gaping mouth spread more broadly at his own little quip.

Raybury had been around long enough to know that when some soldiers had time to kill they usually found their own vices. Whoring, alcohol and gambling the most ruinous. A positive atheist, he also included any form of religion as a lost cause vice as well. Probably in his early 50's, his dad had been a soldier in India in the 1850's where he'd been caught up in the Mutiny and witnessed the viciousness of both soldiers and the local people. The old man had taken a local wife who he doted on. Very unusually he'd brought her back to Britain, settling in Blackheath on a street called 'Tranquil Vale'; appropriate to help counter the horrors both he and his wife had seen in the barbaric Mutiny fighting.

Brad was the product of this loving relationship that transcended all the interracial marriage difficulties of the time. Being close to Woolwich, the Royal Artillery was always going to be his destination. Still extremely fit when many were discharged for being 'no longer fit for service'. Now a well-travelled soldier of great experience himself, going back as far as Egypt in 1888, The Sudan, the Boer war in South Africa and firing mule-pulled screw guns along the North West frontier in India.

With a weathered, wrinkled face, no hair on his head, a thick grey handle-bar moustache, he had two more distinguishing features. A small part of his skull was missing where he'd been struck by a razor sharp Arab scimitar, the skin being roughly stitched back together by the 37th Battery barber-surgeon at the Battle of Firket fighting the Mahdist army. The scar covered a dent on the top of his skull that had subsequently been decorated by a tattoo of black stitches and a trickle of red blood. Raybury was drunk in Cairo and his mates thought it funny at the time. After this first tattoo which told its own story, he felt compelled to get inked wherever he went. With the exception of his visible skin, his face, neck and hands his whole body was covered with pictures and scenes, some of questionable quality, that told the stories of his army career. On occasion this illustrated man claimed his body continued to re-enact the events the art depicted. He'd never married, saying the army was his wife and that she'd put up with him, when a real women never would.

"Okay Pickens. We're marching out at 2pm. You and Kranz need to be here at 1.30 to run ahead of us."

"All-righty Sarge, we'll be here."

Pickens then called to the gunners with a thumb indicating the brothel.

"They'll take your meal tickets if you have no coins boys."

He clearly knew the process for new troop ships arriving.

Before dismissing the parade, Raybury said just loud enough for his men to hear.

"If I catch any of you lot coming out of 'The Ladies House of Pleasure', you'll be on a charge and disease alert. Don't do it."

Most of the men did the sensible thing and drifted off to the YMCA. Passing the brothel, the women emerged again calling to the British soldiers. Arthur could see they was nothing attractive about them. Like his view of the city from the Czarita coming in, they looked past their best, mucky and now with aggressive sounding unrecognisable words streaming from mainly toothless mouths. The few not shouting gripped small white clay pipes in the corner with their lips in a lop-sided face contortion making them look even uglier.

*

Called the 'Log Cabin', because that's what it was, the YMCA canteen run by the American voluntary organisation was clean, warm and a haven from what the men had already seen of the cold, wet and gloomy quayside. They'd been in Russia only a few hours and were still inside the dock complex. What did they expect? War, revolution and now foreign occupation forces were not factors to attract tourists, and they were not tourists. The canteen's four long rows of tables, each could seat about 40 men, already had a crowd of British and Australians from their ship occupying two of them. Smaller groups on the other tables were speaking in French and with American accents, some of whom turned out to be Canadians.

There was also a bunch of Czech's, part of a large contingent up to 70,000 ex-Prisoners of War. Once part of the Austro-Hungarian army, they were released by the Russians to fight against the Central Powers in their cause for independence. These men were in a heated discussion amongst themselves, babbling in their Slavic tongue. The room was loud, raucous with laughter and chat, and dense with cigarette, pipe and cigar smoke from some of the Yanks.

Joining Arthur and friends going to the YMCA were two other men they'd become friendly with on ship. Henry Budge and Michael ('Taffy') Davis (Military Medal). Similar to Arthur and Frank, both ex-Bombardiers who'd volunteered as gunners.

Taffy Davis was a short, excitable, barrel of a Welshman from Maesteg, a coal mining town in South Wales. He was a true believer in God, the Christian faith and an afterlife, attending with his family the Bethel Baptist Chapel in the centre of town. Every Sunday for the family service, Saturday morning and Wednesday after school for 'Sunday School'; he couldn't work out why it was never on a Sunday. When younger he didn't really understand the faith teachings. The joy came from a local giant of the Maesteg Rugby Club, a Mr. Moyle, who gave all the boys the opportunity after every session to run about the Queen Street playing fields next door throwing an oval shaped ball to team mates and trying to tackle the other side when they had it. Grappling in the mud was more fun than kicking a round-shaped ball. His size, shape and love for the rugby scrum, and then as a miner blessed him with an un-Christian like, local nickname, 'Pit-prop'.

Deeply religious himself, he carried his faith lightly and personally. He rarely shared it with others. He'd been down the pits before the war where he'd developed skills installing props and pillars in the coal seams. The war enabled him to escape a job he hated in an environment he increasingly feared. He was in Kitchener's New Army as soon as the appeal went out and managed to hide in the artillery for three years before being transferred into the 19th (Glamorgan Pioneers) Battalion, The Welch Regiment. He was now digging sap mines under enemy trenches, back into the surroundings he loathed. During 1918 he'd been trapped in collapsed sap shafts twice, the second time winning his Military Medal by calmly controlling and digging out three men from the inside using his knowledge of props and where to site them. He'd saved their lives but ruined his head. He wasn't the only one in the gunner's bunk room that would talk and writhe in his sleep until he'd wake up screaming, covered in a cold sweat. He was the only one who'd then take himself up on deck to see the rest of the night out regardless of the weather. He needed an open space to recover.

Henry Budge, Budgie, had been a baker's boy at his uncle's bakery in the market square of the old castle town, Warwick. Until conscripted in

1916, his life was mapped out. He was destined to become a baker and one day inherit his unmarried uncle's shop. Hopefully marry, have kids and they would become bakers too. In contrast to Davis, Budgie loved his job, in particular during the long days of June at 5am when perfectly light cycling to the surrounding villages of Hampton-on-the Hill, Budbrooke, Leek Wootton and Bishop's Tachbrook. When he'd finished his working day at 3pm he'd walk from his home in Crompton Street through the castle grounds down to the River Avon. He'd spend several hours fishing for Chub, Roach, Tench and Perch with Ethelfleda's Mount, the remains of an old Motte and Bailey fort, and the historic Warwick Castle just over his left shoulder.

Leopold Greville, the Sixth Earl of Warwick knew Budgie, although Budgie didn't know who the man was who would occasionally appear and tell tall stories about salmon fishing in Scotland and Norway. It followed that the castle staff knew Budgie, everyone knew Budgie, and because the Earl let him fish, they all turned a blind-eye.

Budgie was also keen on machines. In the winter months in bad weather his bike would be taken apart, maintained and reassembled once a week. His uncle had made him responsible for the upkeep of the Werner and Pfleiderer, belt-driven kneading machine which drove a large piston with a pushing arm on an irregular cam that replicates the arduous physical movement of a person. This was the only kneading machine for miles around. The apprentice baker was immensely proud of the large rattly contraption. In March 1916 he was drafted into the Field Artillery and fell in love with the field guns. To hear him enthuse about their mechanics was like a man describing his wife or sweetheart. He finished the war as a bombardier in a field gun battery with a reputation of conjuring up bread from the most limited ingredients. Budgie Baker ran nicely off the tongue.

*

It was some hours since they'd eaten, they were hungry. At the counter a rotund grey-haired women in a blue apron with "YMCA" in white letters across the top, beneath it in smaller letters, "Portland, Oregon", was controlling the food distribution with a dull metal ladle. She, and a much younger, skinny colleague in the same apron were serving the short queue of soldiers choosing what to eat. As the older women moved her large size gave her a distinct waddle as her weight was thrown from leg to leg to create enough momentum for her body to take a step. When Arthur and the others got close she turned to shout over her shoulder into the kitchen hatch behind her, in the rapid, aggressive sounding Russian language. The cook in the kitchen barked back. She then turned to the young skinny women and said in an American accent with a rhythm.

"Natasha, more ooh-whaa[5] on the way."

"Thanks mom. More hungry men here."

The contrasting scene of the Russian/American, mother/daughter, fat/skinny caught the British troops by surprise. A couple of them looked on with slightly gaping mouths. 'Mom' could see the confusion and waving her ladle in mock confrontation she growled.

"You got a problem boys? You're jaws are on the floor."

She was laughing at them. Natasha was too.

Frank was next to be served.

"No problem from us ma'am, just a little confusing with the English and Russian. We arrived early today so just finding our way around."

"It's a confusing place young man. People here from everywhere. It's a big country. No one in charge."

She paused and ran her eyes along the queue of men.

"Except here……. where I'm in charge!"

She waved her ladle again, making Natasha chuckle heartily.

"We, …. me and my daughter have come from Portland, Oregon, as you can see on our bibs. Volunteered to return to the country of my birth to look after our American boys. Born in Pete's, down the road there. Saint Petersburg to some, Petrograd to others. I come back here and get a hotch-potch of strange people from all over the world with open mouths like you boys on vacation from that there Engerland."

She had a big jolly smile on her florid face enjoying the interaction. At the end of her sentence she used the ladle to point at each of the five British soldiers like a fairy-tale ogress. The cook bellowed from the kitchen. Mom blasted back in Russian and turned to the kitchen hatch to lift a large black cauldron which she placed in front of Natasha.

"Right, enough chat boys. What'll it be."

Using the ladle as a pointer, she said.

"Murmansk cod, cabbage and potato, that one's fish and berry pie, cabbage and potato and ooh-whaa……. with potato………… but no cabbage."

She said 'ooh-whaa' in expectation of the men knowing what it was.

Arthur was standing directly across the counter from the fair haired Nordic looking Natasha. He braved the question.

"What's ooh-whaa?"

She flashed her piercing sky-blue eyes back at him and loud enough for all the men to hear replied.

"Local fish soup. Fish, potatoes, onions, carrots, celery, some herbs and black peppercorns."

---

[5] Ukha, pronounced 'ooh-whaa'. Traditional Russian fish soup.

She then beamed an attractive smile. Peering at the soup cauldron Arthur asked.

"And what's that staring at us?"

"Ah yes, fish heads. You don't have to eat them......... if you don't want to. They're in there for flavour. The soup tastes good, very hearty, you should try it, you'll be seeing a lot of it while you're in Russia."

Arthur accepted her persuasive sales patter and opted for the soup, a clear broth packed with pink and white chunks and the vegetables described. He would discard the fish heads. Budgie was next in line and being interested in food generally, fish in particular, he also engaged with Natasha.

"What kind of fish is in the soup?"

The jolly smile disappeared from the girl's face in order to reply. It was the kind of banter that she and her mum had grown to enjoy. Looking with faux disdain at Budgie.

"The same fish that's in the fish pie."

"And what's that?"

"Fishy sea fish caught this morning, fresh as you like. You're welcome to ask Vasily our cook what it is, but he only speaks Russian. I can tell you that the Murmansk cod is cod-fish. If you want to check out the fish heads and recognise any friends, you might be able to work it out yourself."

Her charming, embracing smile promptly returned when she finished. Budgie opted for the pie with its oven browned layer of mash on top, which she doled out generously with more potatoes and well-boiled white cabbage. He'd check the fish heads in Arthur's soup. The food was hot, tasty and generous. Fish was to dominate their diet for some months to come, but never as pleasantly served as at the Archangel docks YMCA.

7. Dyer's Battalion, Archangel.
June 1919.

Some of the section of gunners retained their old war ranks to ensure there was a semblance of hierarchy which is needed in any military organisation, just to make things work. They were assembling on the quayside at the requisite time of 1.30pm. Sgt. Raybury was not there which was fortunate for the two men who sheepishly appeared from an alley to the side of the brothel. These two ex-Sgts themselves, Riley and Caldwell got away with it here as neither Raybury nor Captain Sumpter saw them. Kranz and Pickens were nonchalantly leaning against their truck full of the gunners kit, Sumpter's was in there too.

Raybury arrived with another man in a U.S. uniform, and then Sumpter. The gunners were told they would be marching to an American camp six or so miles away along the North Dvina River, it would take a couple of hours. It didn't really matter where it was, the men were going where they were directed and thought they trusted Raybury's map reading skills to get them there. They needn't have worried, the 'dough-boy' was to be the guide through the town and out the other side to the camp. Their kit would be taken ahead of them.

Before they set off, Sumpter briefed them. The next two weeks would be spent familiarising themselves with the guns likely to be available to the White Russian, anti-Bolshevik units that they were now to help train. Not the relief expedition planned for quite yet then. The guns would be the French 75mm light gun, the British 18 pounder brought in with the Canadians and possibly the Russian 122mm light field howitzer with its lumpy 52 pound shells. Canadian artillery units were already present in the region with British guns. They would be attached to support the Canadians for periods when they weren't training the Nationalist units.

Carrying their Lee Enfield rifles in marching order the artillerymen were led by Raybury and the American, Sgt. Brodsky, past the Ladies House of Pleasure with associated waves and calls from the working women. Past the YMCA Log Cabin and out of the dock gates in a north easterly direction for a few hundred yards, then turning south east to cross the Kuznechevsky Bridge over one of the many deltaic branches of the partially ice-bound North Dvina River splitting into tendrils before disgorging into the White Sea.

Through the low level, log buildings, none more than three floors high, they marched in an easy way whilst being ignored by the local people going about their business. It was several degrees above freezing with melt-water running from the deep piles of winter snow cleared from the roads. It accumulates from October and usually disappears by June. The road was broken and muddy in parts, other places fairly solid underfoot. It wasn't raining, sleeting or snowing, a good thing. The thick threatening grey and white pillowy clouds occasionally breaking to reveal a patch of blue.

The only vehicles on the road were military. They looked familiar, the same transport trucks used in France. There was a tram network in the central areas of the city that had been kept operating by the Americans since the local workers went on strike during the winter and then abandoned their jobs. The assumption was that many had joined the Bolsheviks further south, or volunteered for the White forces in the area where they had a better chance of getting fed. The foreign governments were bringing vast quantities of food into the region from the sea to supply their own men and had been doing so since early 1918. The local economy was now dominated by the needs of the Allied armies and the expanded population of many bourgeois refugees fleeing from the Bolsheviks. The traditional food supply chain from the hinterland had broken down with the revolutionary forces controlling areas of territory, rivers, roads and rail networks. In the countryside peasant farmers concentrated on subsistence which in this region meant hunting, fishing and hardy pigs.

With the section of men all being highly experienced veterans, the march was relaxed. It was a means to get from the quayside to the camp, not a parade ground demonstration of soldierly discipline in front of a bunch of brass-hats. The route took them south east where to their right was the vast river. Hundreds of yards wide at this point, it collected water from a huge river basin with innumerable tributaries stretching hundreds of miles into the heart of this enormous country and the Ural Mountains. The river ice was melting and for several months it would be navigable for as far inland as the city of Kotlas.

The Allied forces and the Bolsheviks were making good use of the unfrozen water to ferry men and supplies from Archangel as far down the river as tactically possible. The flotilla of naval ships were working the supply routes. This included HMS Sword Dance, subsequently sunk by the Bolsheviks in June 1919, and river gunboats HMS Hyderabad, Cicala, Humber, Monitor, Borodino and other boats acquired from the Russian navy and re-purposed with new Allied guns fitted. There were also long river barges laden with timber. The supply of the primary source of building materials and fuel for the region had not been disrupted by the war and revolution.

To their left a dense boreal forest of trees including spruce, Scots and Siberian pines. Up to 100 foot high, the trees blocked out much light at the ground level leaving a barren, plant-less forest floor. Below the canopy level, where the green needled branches captured the light and thrived, the branches were bare and broken. From the road the men could only see thirty or forty yards into the forest before the tree density stopped the view. There were some small settlements set back from the track along the route, women dressed in black, scraping in vegetable plots, pigs being fed scraps by small children, smoke trailing out chimneys. It looked like, and was a poor, brutal existence.

*

The purpose of the NRRF as sold to the British people and the re-enlisted volunteers of Sadlier-Jackson's Brigade was to ensure the safe and efficient repatriation of men and supplies sent there after the Bolshevik revolution in October 1917. But as with many military interventions by Britain throughout the 19th Century, once the soldiers were in theatre, local circumstances and domestic political objectives changed.

Locally in Archangel, Brigadier General Ironside, the theatre commander held a birthday parade in honour of the King on the 1st of June at which the now well trained Slavo-British Legion, known as Dyer's Battalion, were recognised and presented with their Colours. There had been a need to beef-up the White Russian, nationalist forces due to the withdrawal of the French and most of the Americans. The Royal Marines had been expressing their disaffection with still being in Russia long after the Armistice in Europe. Letters had been sent to their commanders threatening to commandeer a train to return to Murmansk. They were increasingly unwilling to risk their lives in what they had concluded was a pointless mission. The Italian's were also on the verge of mutiny. So the three hundred Russians trained by Dyer were expected to become the core of a new force.

Lieutenant Royce Dyer was a Canadian war veteran from Quebec. He'd worked as a butcher before the war, enlisting as a soldier in 1914. He spent much time in the Ypres salient, on one occasion being gassed and found in a ditch two days later. In 1916 he was wounded at The Somme. After recovering in Britain he was sent to Archangel as a Sergeant where he won a Distinguished Conduct Medal on attacking the village of Onega:

"He set a fine example to his men ..... and from a very exposed position successfully engaged an enemy machine gun at close range with his Lewis gun. He showed marked courage in taking up new positions with his gun under heavy machine gun and cross rifle fire."

This action drew Ironside's attention who commissioned him with a task to recruit and train criminals released from local prisons as volunteers to fight with intervention Allies. With other British, Canadian and Australian officers, this well trained unit of ex-prisoners became known as Dyer's Battalion, so called due to the respect he gained in the recruitment and training process. Some of these men, effectively political prisoners themselves, were known Bolshevik sympathisers. So at the recruitment stage Dyer filtered out the real political activists which he called 'the bads', keeping the 'less bads' and 'probably harmless'. Those that remained were given political lectures to persuade them of the anti-Bolshevik cause. As time would tell, with only limited success. The initial military and political training went well. Ironside optimistically messaged London that he had the foundation of a new Slavo-British Legion.

The Russians in Dyer's force seemed to respect and commit to this energetic Canadian officer. Unfortunately he was not to see them in action, contracting broncho-pneumonia in December 1918 and dying on the 30th. The ex-prisoner soldiers were saddened by Dyer's death and carried a portrait of him when on parade in the manner of an Orthodox religious icon. Without his leadership and stringent selection criteria the process of recruitment was relaxed. In order to get more men a hundred Bolshevik deserters were enlisted. These men, who'd already proven to be unreliable, were added to boost the headcount. It was to prove fateful.

Bolstered by the arrival of Grogan and Sadlier-Jackson's Brigades of the NRRF and the apparent success of creating a locally raised and well-trained unit of hardened, although politically suspect local criminals, General Ironside's new aggressive confidence was revealed in an article published in the first edition of the *"Gazette of the Archangel Expeditionary Force"* (GAF). It was created by *'The Times'* journalist, Andrew Soutar for the benefit of the British Forces feeling a long way from home and bereft of any news beyond their own unit's gossip and rumour. It reported the details of a discussion Ironside had with a representative of the White North Russian Provisional Government. The broad plan was to use the summer months to advance east along the North Dvina River to the city of Kotlas and link up with the Siberian Command under Admiral Kolchak, the internationally recognised head of state. This strategy would enable the Siberian Army to move its headquarters west to Archangel from Vladivostok, making the unlimited flow of food, weapons, munitions and other supplies made by the allies Supreme War Council in Paris easier to fulfil. Conditions had to be met for the promise to stand.

Ironside's public disclosures printed in the GAF were giving away plans that Churchill had been developing but hadn't disclosed to the War Cabinet. He was now bounced into it. Exchanges between the Prime Minister Lloyd George, busy at the Peace Conference in Paris, the Army General Staff and Churchill resulted in the sanctioning of Ironside's offensive plan. Convenient for Churchill that he could hide behind the local initiative. But few were fooled by the man who knew the strategic importance of rivers from his days as a young cavalry officer in Egypt, and the successful use of the Nile to re-conquer the Sudan with General

Kitchener. All detailed in his book *"The River War"*, written in 1899 about his time in the Queen's Own Hussars where he participated in the Battle of Omdurman in 1882. This knowledge, combined with his ideological opposition to Bolshevism only ever meant the intervention in northern Russia would be expansive.

*

For several weeks Capt. Sumpter's troop of artillery trainers were billeted in a large log camp built for the Russian army, more recently occupied by the Americans and French Foreign Legionnaires. Their time was spent training a cohort of a hundred of the unsavoury volunteers of Dyer's battalion on British 18 pounder guns. The ex-prisoners were quick and willing learners but not what anyone might call friendly. The dynamics of these men felt odd to the gunners. Few of them spoke any English. Those that did, a limited vocabulary which they used to try to translate when possible. As a result, much of the work was by demonstration and execution. This worked as there was ammunition allocated for the training and so much open forest space to the north-east without any known human occupation, that the guns could just point in that direction and fire. Similar to firing into the Thames Estuary at Shoeburyness.

Every military organisation of Dyer's Battalion replicated that of the Allied forces. The men appointed to the NCO ranks had been selected during the earlier training and in general seemed to inspire the confidence of their fellow soldiers. It was usually a man who had some English vocabulary wearing the bombardier's stripes. These men were already familiar with what was required of them as infantry soldiers, and were now being converted to the joy of gunnery. The trainers worked in pairs, Arthur and Frank; Eric had been teamed up with Taffy Davis. The Russians were taught in crew teams of six, exactly the same as the British men had been through in those distant Woolwich days. One evening in the camp's log-cabin canteen over a supper of venison stew and a grain similar to pearl barley, Arthur raised an observation directed at Frank.

"Have you noticed when the Ruski's take fag breaks they tend to be listening mainly to that little fellow."

Knowing exactly who he was talking about and deciding to feign ignorance, Frank answered.

"Which one Wally, there's a couple of them on our crew, plus they all mix up with the other crews."

Picking up on Frank's deliberate awkwardness, Arthur got his own back.

"You know, the one with the beard."

The men at the table in earshot of the exchange all made looks of disbelief at Arthur. It was Taffy who said what they were all thinking.

"They've all got bloody beards you idiot."

"Of course they have Taffy but old dumb-arse here knows who I'm talking about."

Frank was smiling benignly, enjoying the moment.

"What about him Wally?"

"It seems strange to me that he is able to capture the attention of the other men. I mean he doesn't stand out in any way. He's as competent on the gun firing drills as the others, but no more than that. Okay, I admit, he picks up things quite quickly, usually before the drill has been translated by the corporal. He listens to us carefully. If I didn't think we're already using all the English speakers, I'd guess that he knew what we were talking about without the translation."

While he was talking he rolled a cigarette with some course black tobacco given to him by one of the Russians. It was strong and bitter on the throat. The local men liked it and shunned the mainly US tobacco that was available to the foreign soldiers. He lit the fag and said.

"Having said that, this little guy is not everyone's pal. Yesterday when the gun drill session finished and they broke for tea, he was surrounded by four others including the one missing his right ear, as he went to the canteen. They were trying to walk him to the back of the cabin, he didn't look very happy. I followed and got there as 'one-ear' had titch by the throat up against the cabin wall. It was looking ugly. I shouted at them and the gang quickly walked off in the other direction. The little man was roughed up but okay. I think he let his guard drop as he caught his breath, saying 'Thank you, thank you,' a couple of times and then 'Spasibo, spasibo'. Whoever these other lot were they had no time for titch."

On the table with them was a lad from London, Corporal Alex Vinokurov, known as Vinny, a Royal Fusilier of the London Regiment. He was born in Smolensk and arrived as a five year old with his family in 1904. His father, a University Lecturer had been involved in the growing intellectual anarchist/socialist movement in Russia. Their lives were perceived to be at risk from the Tsarist police, the Okhrana and his parents fled to save themselves and the family, him and two older brothers. They'd settled in an enclave of Russian intellectual émigré's living on Lorenco Road in Tottenham, a northern suburb of the growing city. A cheap place to live and away from the poorer immigrants fleeing anti-Semitic persecution who settled around Whitechapel – where Frank's family were. Vinny was well educated by his parents in an environment of constant intellectual debate about the people, politics and future of Russia.

Vinny spoke English with only a mere hint of an accent and had been used by Dyer and the other training officers as one of the main translators, a function he was now performing with the gunners. He'd kept his distance from the Russian men believing that none of them could be trusted. After Arthur had spoken Vinny said.

"You need to understand a little more about these men. Two things in particular. Firstly, they are a mixture of criminal criminals, in prison for things like theft, possibly murder and waiting to hang; violent crimes – beating other gang members up, stealing pigs and the like. You'll be able to recognise this group from the tattoos they have on their necks and hands. Missing fingers, or maybe ears."

The gunners tried not to glance at the highly tattooed Sgt. Raybury.

"Some will be covered in them, the members of gangs get tattooed in prison as a status symbol. And then there are the others in prison because local bureaucrats, politicians or the police thought they were a threat to the Tsar and the ruling establishment. Socialists, anti-royalists, democrats, anarchists. Clever, thinking people who want a different government, one for the people, run by the people. Political prisoners really. Both criminal and political groups are considered dangerous in different ways. Your little man Wally, Privakov his name is, comes from this second group. He'll be a Bolshevik sympathiser, a 'politico' as we call them. We didn't take them at first, but orders from the brass meant we had to. They wanted to get the number of Russians recruited to the White cause higher."

Frank then spoke.

"So your saying we're training men who have more in common with the enemy than with the Whites we're supposed to be supporting?"

"That's exactly what I'm saying Frank. Both groups volunteered for one reason only, to get out of prison. All around us this country is falling apart. They were not being fed properly and treated brutally by the guards. When society collapses the prisons are the last place anyone cares about. So when Captain Dyer went to look for volunteers, he got plenty of both sorts. Winter in a Russian prison is not appealing in the best of times. Getting out and fed by an occupying army suited them just fine."

Frank again.

"So that's firstly and there's something else as well."

"There is. Even though the criminal criminals are hard men, they come from a background of religious piety, respect for their parents and ancestors and before the revolution, unwavering devotion to the Tsar, believing he was chosen and anointed by God to rule the vastness of Russia. The war and revolution has changed that a little. They still need to be led and have someone to look up to, but no longer the old Romanov regime. This is where Privakov comes in. He is a good talker and tells them that the Bolos will win in the end. They are fighting for the people of Russia. Us, the Americans and the rest of the foreigners will come and go. The men here need to make sure they are on the right side. His persuasiveness is giving them hope and a vision to believe in. Even murderers need to believe they have a future, now they've escaped the rope. Privakov tells them it's red not white."

When he'd finished there was a contemplative pause before Budgie spoke.

"So do you think he understands English then Vinny."

"Probably. I know he can speak French; I heard him cadging a cigarette from a Legionnaire a while back, and it was a proper conversation. So he's not quite what he seems. Wally's right that he attracts and holds an audience. But outside of us seeing that, he keeps a low profile and gets on with what's required."

The discussion continued and Vinny added additional insight into some of the Russian national characteristics. In particular how this new armed and trained body may not be the allies that the generals and politicians in London think they are.

8. Topsa and Troitsa.
June 1919.

General Ironside was now putting his plan to link with Admiral Kolchak into action. The initial incursion to reach Kotlas on the North Dvina river deep into Russia started on the 19th June. Arthur, Frank and Eric were part of a section of six gunners that included Budgie and Taffy Davis, travelling upstream on the gunboat HMS Cockchafer. With two 6 inch naval guns and a thinned out crew of 40 men against a full complement of 53, there was a need for additional men to operate one of the guns. Sgt. Brad Raybury commanded the field gunners on Cockchafer. The previous day the Royal Navy men had shown them the drills, but with their combined experience the gunners could fire just about any field or naval gun. From the boat they were to support the land attack on two villages. On successful completion, Raybury's artillery section would be landed to join the rest of Sadlier-Jackson's Brigade continuing upstream.

The objective of this mission was to secure the villages that had been fortified by the Bolsheviks, to then be used as a base for further incursions along the river. The Cockchafer had some narrow channels to negotiate to reach its overnight position on the 18th June from which it would deploy its guns in support of the land attack. The first group of villages centred on Topsa, was to be taken by two Battalions of the 3rd North Russian Rifles under a Colonel Voulichavitch, who were to use the forest cover to move above the village and then attack in a south-westerly direction pinning the Bolshevik defenders against the inescapable barrier of the river.

The second village, Troitsa, a little further upstream would be approached by a wider flanking march north of the Russian Rifles by two companies of the 2nd Hampshire's under the command of their heroic but volatile Commanding Officer, Lt. Col. John Sherwood Kelly VC. A South African with a distinguished military record going back to the Matabele Revolt in 1896. Awarded the DSO for action in Gallipoli and the VC at Cambrai in 1917. Gassed and wounded several times, he was a brave, inspirational, controversial and sometimes reckless leader of men.

*

The gunners were below deck on the Cockchafer sitting in the mess drinking sweet tea. Corporal Alex Vinokurov was with them. His language translation skills had become important in the training process of Dyer's Battalion and were now needed in the field with Russians being put into action ahead of the NRRF brigades. He'd be dropped off with the gunners. Eric spoke.

"Well I can't remember ever being so comfortable travelling into battle. All those bloody midges coming out at night to suck your blood. I wouldn't have though it could get hot here with all that ice and snow we saw on arrival. In these forests where the boys are marching now, it'll be really nasty."

The riverside tracks were marshy and difficult. The infantry and land artillery bringing the guns in with second-rate horses had suffered the daytime June heat and humidity. Lack of sleep on the route to get to the villages, 180 miles south-east of Archangel also wore the men down. During the long day the gunners stood on deck to see the vastness of the country they were moving into. Miles of nothing but riverbank with the dense pine forest right up to the edges and an occasional break to bring a small settlement or an individual cabin into view. Where any people were seen, they were women and old men who stared out from the land at the boat passing by. A wave by one of the soldiers drew no response from the adults. On two occasions at the settlements a few children ran along the bank waving and shouting. Vinny commented.

"Too young to know who we are and what this means. Their parents can't be seen by anyone to show any recognition to us. It would be thought they are taking the side of the foreign invaders. The Bolos would respond accordingly."

To ram this point home, another clearing emerged a mile or so further on. A collection of what remained of a group of cabins came into view. A wooden jetty stretched a few yards out from the bank. Blackened, smouldering wood with smoke trails still rising from the burnt homes. No people could be seen apart from three adult bodies hanging from two trees. One was a partly naked women. Vinny again.

"We've all seen the carnage opposing armies bring to each other. But that's different to the hatred and atrocities that a people can inflict when at war with themselves. Life is cheap here. Death from the seasonal cold, disease, childbirth, feuding neighbours, wild animals, it's all common here. This village was probably fired by the Bolsheviks. But it could have been caused by neighbours with a score to settle over land or the sale and non-payment for a pig or milking cow."

The river gunboat continued its journey upstream for the rest of the day and as the light eventually began to fade late into the evening it pulled up to a holding position that had been identified on an earlier reconnaissance. About 6 miles short of the target villages, the boat remained here until 2am. The men slept, played cards and exchanged stories. When they started moving again the gunners assembled in the canteen waiting for the action for which they were needed.

As they sat around they were listening to the London raised Russian, who they weren't really quite sure what to make of. He told an unexpected tale. Referring to the burnt settlement and the hanging bodies he started by saying a childhood memory taught him how little some people valued the lives of others.

"My family moved out of Russia when I was a kid and we sailed across seas and took trains overland into a vast dirty city where we understood nothing of what people were saying. Maybe my dad knew some of the language, I don't know. It was London. Smoky and dirty, hunger and filth everywhere in the poor areas. I spoke no English when we arrived. As I remember, we lived with other families for a while. Around Whitechapel where your family is Frank. Dad was always clustered with other men in the evenings wherever we lived. For the first year we moved every two or three months. I started learning some English with other kids on the street but there was no schooling. They were all Russian, Latvian or Polish. Many were Jews fleeing the pogroms, but not all. We eventually stopped moving with a home in a place that felt like the countryside. A short walk took us to marshes and reservoirs. Tottenham it was, some called it Little Russia. It felt like a community. Russia without the bitter winter cold and nasty summer midges."

Frank listened attentively and said nothing. Vinny took a long puff on the grey clay pipe he'd taken to smoke on his arrival in the country of his birth. He then paused staring at the ceiling before continuing. The boat engine was chugging in the background.

"My dad got a job at a factory nearby. I think they made rubber tyres and other stuff. It meant he could earn money during the day and every evening he'd have meetings with his mates plotting and scheming and drinking vodka. One morning I was playing football on the street and one of the other boys I'd got friendly with said he had to take his dad's lunch pail to the factory, did I want to go with him? We dropped it off, passing it through the gate and were walking away when we saw a car pull up and a working lad get out. They were opening the gate and two men appeared trying to grab the lad's leather bag. We then heard shots and started running away. The two men who'd grabbed the bag were running up the same road and some other people were trying to stop them. It was close to Tottenham Police station. Two coppers without hats appeared chasing the thieves who I was told after, had tried to steal the wages for the week."

The men were listening silently intrigued by the story.

"One of the policemen shot at the thieves. The car from the factory gate had now joined the chase along with some men on bicycles. As the car approached the thieves started shooting back at it. We tried to turn away but my friend …….. Ralph his name was, suddenly screamed and fell over backwards clutching his chest. There was blood on the front of his brown coat and his cap had fallen off. It was a cold day in January and I remember shivering and being held back as some people put him in a bicycle tow-cart to take him to hospital. Afterwards I was told he died before they got there. The man who shot the pistol was only about thirty yards away and he knew he'd shot Ralph. I could see him smile when the boy screamed and fell over."

One of the Naval officers appeared at the door telling them they needed to be at their firing stations in 15 minutes. Vinny finished his story.

"I was taken home and I remember when I got there I was sick in the hall, cold and sweaty, and couldn't stop shaking. The papers the following day reported the two men had stolen a bag of money. From where we saw them they ran across to the marshes and the reservoirs. They shot a policemen too. Hijacked a tram and then a horse-drawn milk float which they crashed. I think they stole another cart before being cornered when one of the men tried to kill himself but failed. The other one broke into a cottage where the police followed him from hearing the screams of the women who lived there. The thief had locked the door. The police broke in and found he'd shot himself in the head. He died when they pulled him outside. The incident was in all the papers the following day. Twenty three people were hurt. My friend Ralph and a copper both died."

Vinny paused again.

"My mum kept all the newspapers which she made me read years later. It turned out the two men were radicals, like my dad. One of them was from Latvia. I was never sure whether dad knew them. I think he did because he was very odd for some days after and my mum wouldn't speak to him. The funeral was huge and I was allowed in one of the carriages with mum and Ralph's family. My dad didn't even go. They reckoned hundreds of thousands of people lined the streets. Ralph and the copper were buried near each other in Abney Park Cemetery. It taught me that desperate men don't care who gets in their way and will kill them if they have to. They just don't care. Ralph was a good boy .... and my pal. Shot dead in a London street."

He then went quiet, puffing his pipe and staring at the table. Arthur wasn't sure whether to believe the tale until Frank broke the silence.

"I remember it being in the papers, and with so many Russians, Poles and Latvians in the East End, it was all anyone talked about for weeks afterwards."

*

The Cockchafer's engines had slowed to a throbbing hum as they negotiated the last mile. The naval gunnery sergeant gave them a final briefing, including no cigarettes to be smoked on deck, and they moved to their allocated gun. A naval crew manned the other. Vinny came up to watch the action. There was dense cloud cover threatening rain, no sign of a moon. The Indian inky blackness of the night was disturbing for the field gunners as they wondered how the helmsman steered the large boat. They had seen several grounded boats on the shifting sand bars of the low flowing summer Dvina river.

As their boat was quietly creeping along to try to maintain an element of surprise, a torch flashed a signal from the north bank. This was the White Russians forming up point; the main Topsa village another four hundred yards to the east. At 3.35 am. the two six inch guns on the river boat opened fire with a salvo that lasted twelve minutes. Arthur and the field artillery gunners managed to get 15 rounds away, the experienced naval gunners, 24. A precisely timed four minute gap was followed by another seven minutes when their contribution finished and the Russian Rifles would attack on the ground.

When they started firing it was several minutes before Bolshevik rifle, and then machine gun fire was returned from the bank. The enemy were clearly taken by surprise. Pings and ricochets could be heard between the heavier booms of the naval guns. Toward the end of the first fire mission, some light artillery guns opened up, firing out from the village. It was known the Bolsheviks had some in the area. No rounds hit the Cockchafer, all of them going over the top of the boat into the far bank, a few splashed in the river. Only Vinny was conscious of the shells going overhead. In the dark of night the Russian gunners couldn't get the range of the mid-stream target. At 3.58am. the Cockchafer's guns stopped and it withdrew downstream until reaching a mooring at Kurgomen, where the White Russians and Kelly's Hampshire's had set off from. The boat would remain here until first light when Arthur and the other army men would be dropped off.

Starting at 6.30am., with little sleep, they were set down on a small jetty and immediately made their way along the well-trodden track with all the signs of a battalion of soldiers having passed down it the night before. Deeply rutted transport and horse drawn, field-gun tracks had churned up the route. The early morning persistent drizzle adding to the slithering discomfort. The six gunners plus Vinny had been issued with light-weight US army capes, oiled to keep out the wet, with deep collars that could be turned up against wind and rain likely to trickle down the back of the neck. Unusually good and practical kit.

In command of a small unit of highly experienced soldiers, Sgt Brad Raybury had adopted an affiliative style of leadership. The men knew what was expected of them and would cooperate as a team to deliver results. There was no doubt they had to, as another huge issue loomed over the presence of all the British soldiers on this mission. They were already 200 miles from Archangel and there was no chance of any kind of reinforcements if things went wrong. It was all very well Winston Churchill in the cosy War Department offices in Whitehall looking at the route of a river and thinking it a highway across Russia. It was quite another to throw a few hundred men into the isolated depths of the country, in the middle of summer with the flowing water level dropping daily and getting worse. It would soon become impossible for the navy boats to navigate any further upstream.

It took over an hour to march along the boggy, churned up track to reach Topsa and rejoin the White Russians they'd been training. Their initial attack was being seen as a great success with the last few Bolsheviks being cleared out of buildings on the eastern side to which they'd withdrawn. All resistance had ceased by 8.20am. There were 150 enemy dead and 450 prisoners, of which 100 were wounded. However, close to a hundred Whites had been killed or wounded and seven of the British 'advisors'. An insignificant number in the context of the slaughter on the Western Front, a real shock to the small number of British men present here. When they arrived the gunners were buoyed by the success of their contribution from the Cockchafer. This was tempered significantly by the deaths of colleagues and the high number of deaths amongst the Whites. By the time the news of this small victory reached the London press, it was reported by *The Times* under a banner of *"General Ironside's confidence justified – Russians' brilliant operation"*.

In complete contrast to the success at Topsa, Colonel Kelly led his two Companies of Hampshire men into a confused affair. According to General Ironside "they failed to take any part in the fight'. According to Kelly there were numerous good reasons not to engage. Having reached their forming up position and holding it for two and a half hours, Kelly withdrew the Hampshire's back into the woods. The position was insecure and ammunition supply had failed to arrive. The difficult night march through marshy forest; the tail of his column not reaching him until midnight; not knowing the progress at Topsa through local communication failure; exhaustion of soldiers and officers with a couple of hours rest over two hot, humid days with little food; stiff and alert Bolshevik resistance; the risk of being surrounded by an enemy well prepared and motivated; concern over the fate of wounded, were all additional disadvantages at Troitsa. Kelly was a man who could be impulsive, but his concerns here were primarily the tactically untenable position his unit had been placed in. It transpired that the Bolsheviks had been alerted to the planned attacks on both villages, had reinforced Troitsa and set up strong defences. On the ground, Kelly had read the situation and concluded it was a trap into which he wouldn't commit his men.

Despite the disagreements between Ironside and Kelly as to what actually happened, the strategic plan of trying to reach Kotlas continued.

The politicians in London were being fed limited reports by Ironside, not recognising the increasing difficulties of river navigation, the remoteness of the units now deep into Russia and the exaggerated, but in reality very flimsy commitment of the trained White Russians from Dyer's battalion.

9. Dyer's Battalion Mutiny.
7th July 1919.

Arthur, Frank, Eric, Budgie and Taffy, under the command of Sgt. Raybury were attached to the four gun battery of the Slavo-British Legion which included men from Dyer's Battalion. Their role was to act as advisors and continue to train a unit of about fifty men. Vinny, their interpreter had been absorbed back into the HQ establishment of Sadlier-Jackson's Brigade. They would now have to rely on their very limited Russian language skills and the English of the Russians.

The British and Russians assembled after a partial withdrawal from Troitsa with no expectation of attack from the Bolsheviks in the forests on the north bank of the Dvina River. Arthur's section and the Russian gunners had been billeted in some deserted forest logging cabins near the village of Gorodok, half a mile from the main infantry units. Equipped with wooden cot beds, stoves and plenty of logs to burn for cooking, they were comfortable and surprisingly cool in the shade of the tall pine trees. There were about twenty poor quality, commandeered horses, enough to move the four guns and ammunition limbers, but not all the fifty or so men.

The gun battery of 18 pounders left by the Canadians before their withdrawal was under the command of a Captain Ilyavich who spoke little English, but limited French and they scraped by. Despite other reported mutinies by White Russian soldiers, the British gunners felt alert but comfortable with the Dyer's men until very early on the morning of the 7th July. They were disturbed by a noisy commotion heard in the clearing outside the log cabins. It was just beginning to get lighter from a dusky gloom at around 2.30am., when the gunners were disturbed by the sound of Ilyavich shouting and numerous others joining in. Then some shots creating immediate concern in the British hut. Frank was the first to the door when a bullet hit the frame splintering wood into the cabin. He slammed the door shut.

"Shit, we're being shot at."

Raybury was surreptitiously peering out of the window. He was his usual calm self.

"I'm not sure we are Frank. I think they were shooting at the two men who were running our way. There are bodies lying in the dirt now. It doesn't look good though."

More shouting. Irritated words in Russian which was an angry language at the best of times. Looking out of the window whilst standing well back in the dark room so that they couldn't be seen easily, the British men watched a number of the Russians gesticulating and bellowing at each other in the early dawn half-light. Some more shots. No more bodies fell. These were fired into the air as a means to temper the situation. A man could be seen without a weapon repeatedly pushing both hands face down in a 'calm-down' gesture. A group gathered around him and he disappeared amongst the visual shield of the crowd.

Raybury spoke in his controlled, untroubled manner.

"We need to wait to let them get the shooting out of their system before we find out what's going on. In the meantime, Taffy, get that pan on the stove and we'll have some of that lovely black tea....... Unless anyone has seen a milking cow locally?"

Arthur replied with a groan.

"No chance of that. The last cow I saw was in that steak pie we had on the ship coming over. I'm not even sure it was real cow. Probably horse meat for us and steak for the navy."

They watched the men of Dyer's Battalion, the men they had trained over the last few weeks to become operationally effective artillerymen as they shouted and argued with each other. A couple of riders arrived and one left after more talk. There was some pointing toward the cabin they were in. No one approached them. The two bodies were dragged away. Eric said he thought one of them was Captain Ilyavich. The other may have been his orderly.

Things had calmed down until shortly after 7 am. three men walked toward the cabin. Arthur was on 'window duty' watching as the others were sitting about a wooden table cleaning rifles or packing away kit in their small packs. Whatever was going on, they had to be ready to move quickly.

"Brad, we have a delegation."

Arthur opened the door as the Sgt. and the other men stepped outside carrying their weapons. The Russians appeared unarmed although the group in the yard were watching carefully with their rifles poised. Immediately recognisable, flanked by taller, older looking men with thick, greying beards was the diminutive Privakov. He hadn't been part of the gun battery; he must have been one of the riders appearing earlier. Taking a pair of round, metal framed spectacles from his tunic breast pocket, he read from a prepared script. Initially only looking at Raybury, the little man spoke in heavily accented but understandable English. He now looked less soldier, more university academic.

"Sergeant, and comrades. Patriots of Russia will no longer fight our brothers and sisters and the Bolshevik cause for the working people of our great country. This morning there have been some deaths including two men here. Traitors to the revolution. Others are British and Russians from the officer class and their servants. This is unfortunate but inevitable. We do not want you in our country and your continued presence is unwelcome."

It didn't sound good at all.

"Most of 'C' company and some of 'B' company of what was known as Dyer's Battalion, as well as our men here will be joining the revolutionary cause. We'll be taking the guns with us to add to our armoury They are needed further east. You are now our prisoners; hostages if you like. Your countrymen have now stopped more patriotic men joining us."

Glancing up and adding menacingly.

"At least for the moment."

As he looked up scanning the British soldiers in front of him he caught Arthur's eye. He paused. There was a very slight nod of the head in recognition.

"We will be moving away from here in half an hour. We do not expect you to resist in any way. It would be guaranteed death to do so and I know you are not stupid men."

He looked again at Arthur.

"But you will need to surrender your weapons. I will appoint someone to arrange this. They may be returned to you at a later time, when our soldier's soviet decides your fate. My Bolshevik comrades have no special anger toward workers and soldiers of other countries. Men like yourselves used as puppets and exploited by capitalist industrialists and politicians. But we do have some leaders amongst us who are ruthless hot-heads and difficult to contain."

He paused and looked straight at Raybury.

"I can't tell you any more at this point Sergeant Englishman. Half an hour, be ready to leave. I will have your rifles collected."

He then bowed his head a little toward Raybury and gave another small nod to Arthur. He abruptly turned and walked away to the apparent bemusement of his two minders who jumped to follow. Privakov was then shouting orders at other soldiers, two of whom ran to the cabin to collect the British rifles. Oddly, they didn't take the ammunition, of which each man would have had over a hundred rounds in their webbing pouches.

As they made their final preparations to leave the log cabin they heard four more rifle shots.

*

The mutiny and defection to the reds of about 150 men from Dyer's battalion resulted in the immediate deaths and severe mutilation of three British and four Russian officers, as well as a number of their orderlies. Two other British officers died of their wounds, one of whom, Captain Barr had been shot numerous times before swimming out to the river monitor, HMS Humber to alert the crew. Barr died of his wounds after being awarded the Military Cross for his actions. The incident was an embarrassment for General Ironside who'd put his faith in the Slavo-British Legion. He claimed it was the action of a very few determined men in one company only, who led the mutiny.

Ironside's view was reported by *The Times* journalist, Andrew Souter, a few days later, contrasting what he really knew. His copy was probably deemed to be politically expedient at the time, both in Northern Russia and Westminster. Souter wrote some years later that some junior officers, including Captain Barr had expressed to him concern over the commitment of the men in Dyer's Battalion. Concerns which the junior officers had not passed up the command chain, which ultimately had cost Barr his life.

Ironside's response was to disarm the remaining soldiers of the battalion and use them as a labour unit. His belief that local Russians could be trained and would commit to the anti-Bolshevik cause was destroyed. To emphasis his need to regain control and deter further mutineers he messaged London that he planned to execute up to twenty alleged instigators. The War Office replied immediately that no more than the British casualties should be considered for the death penalty. The final outcome was twenty five were charged with mutiny, eighteen condemned to death, seven commuted and eleven shot.

Back in London, Churchill was incensed and in a letter to the Chief of General Staff wrote:

"The names of these Russians should be carefully recorded and never lost sight of. They are guilty of the blackest treachery conceivable..... When it is possible for us to demand their exemplary punishment, we must not fail to do so."[6]

The international legal position was decidedly dodgy. The 'mutineers' deaths caused resentment amongst the local population and the five hundred newly recruited men to the Slavo-British Legion forced to witness the botched execution. Carried out by 'loyal' Russians of Dyer's Battalion who probably 'aimed-off' with the five rounds they had. Only four of the eleven were killed outright. The witnesses, including sailors and other sightseers then watched as British officers used their revolvers to kill the seven survivors, one shouting, 'Long live the Bolsheviks' as his final words.

The deaths of the British Officers and men alarmed and demoralised all the members of the NREF and other intervention forces in Russia. They'd lost faith in the White Russians who they'd trained but whose cause they now realised was unpopular across the country. At Onega, another White Sea port 120 miles south west of Archangel, a Russian Regimental

---

[6] Churchill's Crusade, Clifford Kinvig. P202

commander and most of his officers were shot, their positions being handed over to the Bolsheviks. The deserting soldiers burnt their uniforms and returned to their homes. Disaffection was spreading, the ability to contain the dissent and internal resistance within the White Russian forces diminishing and a growing belief in the futility of the British mission increasing.

10. Bolshevik Captivity.
July – September 1919.

As prisoners of Privakov and his band of mutinous Bolsheviks, the politics between Ironside and senior officers in theatre, and Churchill and the War Office back in London were now irrelevant to the six British men. It was now about survival in a currently hot, inhospitable, heavily forested, thinly populated country. Even without these challenges, which applied to the Russian men too, there was the difficulty of managing their captors. None had experienced captivity in the hands of the Central Powers during the war. Had they done so, they speculated between them, it would have been nothing like this.

An expression used by Privakov sprang into Raybury's mind the morning of the mutiny, 'but we do have some leaders amongst us who are ruthless hot-heads and difficult to contain.' He recalled it as they marched away from the log cabins into the depths of the forest. There were four dead bodies. Clearly shot in the temple, stripped of their British issued uniforms and boots and macabrely sitting up against four consecutive trees to watch the guns depart. The Russian and British men could take this as a message. Despite the facial destruction caused by the pistol, Arthur noticed the last one had an ear missing.

For the first week or so the routine was the same. As it got lighter from the semi-darkness at around half past two in the morning, a few minutes later each day, the bivouacked soldiers would be stirring. They slept in clearings on the forest floor where centuries of undisturbed fallen pine needles had created a soft bed of malleable comfort. A fresh, pleasant smell of the trees filled the air as the men awoke and the chill of the night was driven away by the rising sun sending beams below the canopy. The forest waking up to remember it was supposed to be the hot sweaty season. For sleeping, Arthur and the British crew wrapped themselves in their oiled capes as the heat of the day and the cold of the night created a heavy due. Raybury had each man, himself included, doing a one hour guard duty through the short 5 hours of semi-darkness. On a rotation basis it meant that one man got to rest without disturbance one night in six. They needed some alert eyes, not because they felt threatened generally but the risk of irrational behaviour by their captors was high. Privakov had said as much.

In the first hour of the day each section in the camp would light fires, boil water for tea and ablutions. The water from the close proximity of the Dvina River meant there was always a good supply for washing clothes and the body and for cooking or boiling. The men were encouraged to fill their personal water bottles from the small tributary streams that ran down through the forest. It was going to be cleaner as no one could tell what detritus might have been dumped into the river upstream. To start with the British section shaved most days. They'd then sort out tea and something to eat from rations provided by a giant, jolly Finn in the role of Quartermaster. Apparently a real criminal, not a politico. He was reputed to have used a butchers chopper to remove the hands of a debtor.

Several inches taller than Arthur, with almost white-blonde hair and an easy laughing manner, the Finn made sure their rations were no different to that of the Russians. Dense, black rye bread and meat of some kind, frequently supplemented with a variety of mushrooms and edible fungus. During the course of the day the Finn would send two of his men into the forest on horses to hunt and forage. Depending on what was already in store, they would know what to look for. If meat were needed they would reappear hours later and miles further along the column route with a couple of deer or wild boar being dragged by their horses. On one occasion, a brown bear arrived, so big they'd had to bisect it at the waist to share the load. A few days later a fully grown she-wolf. The Finn was ecstatic. He marinaded the meat in a salt, vinegar, rosemary and a nettle mix and that evening offered small fire grilled pieces alongside the venison stew. Apples and pears, hazelnuts, walnuts, berries or fungus would be collected in hessian sacks strung like saddle bags. Every day they came back with something and everything was shared equally between Bolsheviks and British.

By 4am. they would be on the march. Due to the shortage of horses, the battery's four guns and ammunition limbers were pulled by four horses only, not the usual six. Under the control of the Finn, three other wagons contained some tentage, food and water, shovels, axes, double-ended wood saws and other kit. There was a two carriage, rolling field kitchen and stove acquired from the Americans. An ingenious late western front invention that could be fired up on the move with stews and soups cooked ready to consume when setting up camp at the end of the day. This one had a small brass manufacturer's plate on it that proudly read: "The Taylor Rolling Kitchen. Eclipse Stove Co., Mansfield, Ohio. Mobile food for Military men." It had travelled a long way.

The transport arrangements changed the day the camels arrived. The foragers were late back and instead of food they were each towing four, double humped Bactrian camels. It was a foraging day and they'd come across a settlement where they traded the food they'd collected and a bonus deer they'd shot, plus some rifle ammunition for the camels. Not only could they tow the wagons to release the horses, but they would also produce milk for the bitter black tea brewed constantly. In the unlikely event food became really short, the animals could be butchered. With the camels switched to the Finn and his store wagons, the horses were released back to the guns.

Six horses meant better progress. Good news because wherever they were headed was far from where they started. With the exception of two planned half hour stops at 10am. and 4pm. they kept moving all day at a steady pace for the men on foot. If this timing went to plan they would be covering roughly 4 miles an hour. Sixty miles over the fifteen hours of daylight. Ludicrously ambitious. The reality was that on a very good day they achieved less than half of this. Exhausting for men on foot, with problems or barriers on the route creating unplanned stops, each of which had to be overcome.

*

In the order of march the six British men were to the rear of the four guns which led the column. A few days after setting off, the lead gun slithered off the track where it fell away sharply down to the river. They were moving upstream on the north western bank toward Ironside's, Churchill's and the White Russian's original offensive objective, the city of Kotlas. The inexperienced Bolshevik gunners had no idea how to recover the gun. Without invitation, Raybury led his men forward ignoring the protests from a nominal, ineffective guard. Reaching the wayward gun they met a growing group shouting, waving, pointing and shrugging. The horses were still attached to the towing harnesses; one was injured, baying and nodding aggressively in fear. It was a chaotic scene of incompetence with none of the Russians knowing what to do.

Arthur, Frank and Eric had been here hundreds of times and under Raybury's general direction and the application of their 'bogged-in many times' knowledge, they set to work. Taffy and Budgie unhitched the horses and led them away; all were fine, just anxious at the depth of the drop they could see to their right. The currently useless Bolshevik captors were instructed to collect logs and fallen branches to fill and pack the ground under the wheel, uselessly spinning in the air. This bolster would provide some balance when they tried to move the gun. A thick eight foot branch was used as a lever with three men and Eric hanging on it to lift the wheel higher to jam more packing beneath. Once done, a combination of pulling the harness towing tackle and pushing from the rear where they could get access started moving the gun back onto the track. The operation took a couple of hours, with one last heave and push getting the ordnance square onto firmer ground. When completed the Bolsheviks gave a cheer, enthusiastically patting the backs of their 'prisoners'.

Privakov was absent and witnessed none of this. His apparent deputy, a strong, red-bearded man with a grizzled, scarred, moonscape of a face; more brawn than brain, stood and watched. At the final recovery point he

107

turned away without expression. The horses were re-hitched and the column fell back into marching order. Most day's march terminated around 7pm depending on an appropriate place to pull up. The Finn would have a hot meal on the go so the men could eat on arrival and rest immediately. On this particular day, Privakov returned to the camp shortly before last light which was around 9.35pm.

The British men were sitting around their own fire having eaten well from the venison stew with potatoes, swede and some kind of ceps that were giving an 'other worldly' aura. Relaxing and disorienting at the same time. Whatever had been foraged for the pot that day was a little different. As the darkness came in, Privakov appeared with his bulky minder who was clutching two bottles of vodka.

"Can we join you Sarge Englishman?"

It was clear that Raybury's name was difficult for him to pronounce, so he didn't bother. They sat down on the soft pine earth close to the fire. Then referring to his man he said.

"Klechov here told me of your men recovering a gun today. We, well most of us, know you did this for the respect of the artillery ordnance, not the Bolshevik cause."

He smiled at himself. As an unexpected touch of irony, it worked.

"We, I mean those of us you have trained and know, always have supported the Bolsheviks. We know your passion here is the artillery. You, like us, are working men of England. We are ordinary working people of Russia, Poland, Estonia and of course Finland."

As he said this he raised the vodka bottles as if to show what the Finn could provide.

"Your men and we Bolsheviks are brothers and comrades under the yolk of the historic aristocracy. Kings, Kaisers, Tsars; their dandy's and empire builders; the bankers and owners of capital. We, the ordinary working people, the proletariat, want no more of it. I'm sure the working men of England will reach the same view. You are industrialised, you lead the world in manufacturing and trade. Your imperialist expansion and that of Germany, France, Italy, and others mirror the monopoly economic power predictions of Marx. Our leader, Lenin wrote in his pamphlet, *'Imperialism, The Highest Form of Capitalism'*, about the world of the 20th Century being dominated by a small number of countries with monopoly market powers over resources, trade and finance capital. As the highest form of capitalism, Marx's analysis of history through dialectic materialism dictates the inevitable collapse of the capitalist economic system. What you see here in Russia today are the first revolutionary stages of a changing world order. Workers of all countries unite!"[7]

Privakov stopped speaking and looked around the fire at the six pairs of British eyes staring at him in puzzled silence. He started laughing quite heartily. It was the first time any of them had seen him being anything less than completely serious. In a slightly embarrassed tone he said.

"I'm sorry my English friends. I really didn't come here to give you a political lecture."

He continued chuckling to himself as he uncorked one of the bottles. Even the grizzly bear sitting next to him was smiling. Not that he understood what was being said. Taking a swig as a courtesy to show it wasn't poison, he passed the bottle to Raybury who did the same. He then shook his head.

"Whoaa, that's strong stuff!"

More laughter around the fire. Privakov answered.

"It is, it is! He tells me its real vodka, Finnish vodka. We Russians drink piss-water and why do we bother?"

Raybury passed it to Frank on his right who in his eminently sensible way took the smallest sip possible. Privakov again.

"I came over to thank you and your men for your help today. I heard you defied instructions to get to the problem. I got a little carried away in my rant. I've been at a meeting of political commissars attached to different Bolshevik army units. We have to preach the word of revolution to the soldiers. In some cases, as with the men here, we also command the units. In many cases, especially with the Cossack and the Siberian units, we don't. Those men can be wild and have a different, self-interested, more insular and local view of the world. Our commissars have a difficult time with them."

The bottle had gone around and Klechov passed it to Privakov who placed it inside the crook of his crossed legs.

"I also wanted to explain to you and your men that we don't see you as our enemies. You're here by accident of your rulers and now under our temporary care if you like. Good instructors, we learnt a lot. Obviously not how to get guns back on the road though."

He smiled again and set the bottle off on another round. Looking and pointing at Arthur he said.

"The man you call Volly saved me from what would have been a nasty beating or possibly death in the training camp. I'm grateful to him."

He smiled and nodded at Arthur in a warm genuine way, and then his expression changed and he quietly added, linking the camp incident.

"You may have seen those men as we left the hutted camp. They were no good. Common criminals and not required for the revolution."

---

[7] Imperialism, The Highest Form of Capitalism' Lenin. First published 1917.

He paused to let this comment settle.

"I will now do everything I can to enable you to get back to your country. It won't be back through Archangelsk though. Do you have any questions of me?"

Frank jumped straight in.

"How come you speak English and why didn't the officers know?"

"Well they probably did know. They knew I was in prison for political crimes, but it made sense for me not to volunteer my voice to the friends of the White's, as you call them. I studied in Berlin and Paris and then taught for a while in London. I lived on Bloomsbury Square, near the museum of Britain. It's a wet, smelly, crowded city, London. Not like the beautiful wide streets and parks of Paris, or the cultured cafes of Berlin. But you have a good attitude to free thinking and I did learn English there. It was a good place to meet other like-minded socialists. I did some work with Kautsky and Engels."

These were not names apparently familiar to most of the gunners and he didn't elaborate. Frank knew of them both as socialist thinkers. The bottle arrived back empty and he uncorked the second sending it on its way.

"I should tell you a little of what we're doing. We need to get these guns south to the City of Vyatka[8] and into the hands of our comrades there. They will be taken further east by train where the rogue imperialist Admiral Kolchak has his forces, mainly Siberian and Asiatic men, and where we have a need for artillery."

Raybury then asked a question.

"If we're not getting out through Archangel, why not and then from where?"

"There are two main reasons for that. One, an accident of being located with the gun battery at the time of our departure from your British force. We couldn't leave you behind. Some of my men wanted to kill you. I wouldn't have it. So you had to come with us. That was the argument we were having at the camp. I now see you as part of our unit until we deliver the guns, and you will be treated as such. After recovering the gun today, the rest of the men recognise that too, and their suspicions of you have mainly gone. However, I do not trust them all and you shouldn't either."

Taffy commented under his breathe.

"I don't bloody well trust any of you."

In his thick Welsh accent the Russian didn't catch the words, so he ignored Taffy and carried on.

---

[8] From 1934, named Kirov after Sergei Mironovich Kirov a Soviet politician and Bolshevik assassinated in 1934.

"Although I do understand you will not see it that way, that you are English soldiers and you will want to get home. But I'm sure you'll agree, this is the best option for now."

Privakov paused as if he was thinking. The darkness having closed in and the only light coming from the numerous wood fires dotting the forest edges either side of the track and casting giant flickering shadows amongst the trees. Raybury gave a verbal nudge.

"And the second reason?"

"Yes the second reason. We have a long way to go across forested country. About 750 versts[9], 500 or so of your miles, almost due south. It might take us thirty to forty days; it could be as many as sixty. This is difficult country to cover, even on the tracks, as you have already seen. We'll be into September by then, maybe October if it rains a lot. Rivers and seas in the north will be starting to freeze. If your fellow soldiers and other foreign compatriots haven't left Archangel by then, and we understand from our spies there is already talk in London of a general withdrawal. In fact its why you came here in the first place unless I'm mistaken? To help recover your men and equipment?"

None of the artillerymen commented.

"Perhaps you were misled, perhaps not. But the point is from where we'll be there may be better ways to leave Russia. East by train from Vyatka which will connect with the main east-west rail line, the Trans-Siberian railway. Or south west to the Caucasus, the Black Sea to negotiate with the unpredictable Cossacks. Neither will be easy, nor safe and much will depend on the situation on the ground and the local commanders. I can't guarantee anything right now, particularly your safety, but I can arrange for papers for you after we have completed our delivery. To explain your presence, contribution and hopefully provide safe passage. These might help you get through Bolshevik lines when the time comes."

As Privakov finished speaking the second vodka bottle now empty, completed its second circuit. He stood to leave, as did his gorilla.

"Remember you are not our enemies. We are the same working people, from different countries. You will be treated as comrades by me and my men here for our time together. I now wish you a restful night."

Once he'd gone, the six men sat for some time around their own fire adding a number of logs cut by two of the Finn's men, experts with a two man tree saw and both handy with an axe. Fires around the camp were starting to fade. The Russians about them started their regular evening singing that closed out wild forest noises that were heard in the quiet of the night. Low humming songs that drifted from one fire to another as a new

---

[9] A Russian measurement of distance, about two thirds of a mile, 1.1km.

verse was picked up by the next group. Soothing and comforting, like lullabies. Whilst listening to this they discussed their situation. Budgie referred to it as a 'predicament', to which Raybury responded.

"I prefer 'a little difficulty' Budgie. Predicament sounds a bit terminal. We currently don't seem to be at any risk from Privakov and his party. With his plans we're going to be attached to them for a couple of months according to his timings. So, unless anyone has any better ideas, I reckon we need to bide our time, get on with whatever they need us to do and deliver the guns to their next destination."

The gunners agreed they had little option here. 'Predicament', 'situation', 'dilemma'. It didn't matter what they called it, they were stuck with the remnants of Dyer's artillery battery until something significant changed and that wouldn't happen deep in the Russian forest. They agreed the only course open to them was cooperation. The following morning as the unit was preparing to start that days march, Klechov appeared with the Finn's two foragers, each of them carrying two rifles. Their return was a good sign of the trust Privakov now had in the British men. Their individual identity papers which had been taken on the day of the mutiny were not returned.

*

Arthur and his five colleagues reconciled themselves to the fact their immediate future was best served by contributing to the Bolshevik cause. Not in an ideological sense, more the best staying alive strategy on offer. Even so Privakov had started to enjoy practicing his English whilst trying to convince the men of the inevitability of the proletarian victory over the capitalist classes. As he began to realise that collectively they would not be swayed he started trying to pick them off individually.

Learning that Taffy had been a coal miner, a key industrial worker, and eventually getting an ear for the accent, the Commissar targeted him in particular. This suited the others, because as long as the Welshman was getting an earful from the revolutionary, they weren't. Davis was phlegmatic about getting the attention. It was only ever at the end of the day when they were sitting around the fire, and Taffy did his best to use it to his advantage in efforts to learn the Russian language. He amused himself with the thought that one day he might be able to preach revolution in the Welsh valleys...... in Russian.

Privakov's attempts to engage with Eric were met with a blank refusal by the Scot. In terms of communication, Eric had, to a large extent, retreated within himself, focussing only on what was needed from the British men and then adding more with a small group of three Russians he'd help train. Arthur and Frank knew that for Eric familiarity of those around him drew out his best. The ex-convicts in Dyer's battalion knew little about soldiering. Eric did what he could in many small ways from demonstrating his button sewing skills to building a one man shelter with forest debris and whatever else was available. He didn't talk much, he showed them by demonstration, he made no attempt to speak Russian other than 'da' and 'nyet'. The hardened criminals respected the surly Scot without ever understanding his impenetrable Glaswegian accent.

Frank had become Raybury's right hand man. His constant detachment was still there, but Raybury had worked out that keeping some distance was Frank's way. Along with Arthur and Eric, Frank was bringing the influence and contribution of half the team. The other two were happy to defer to his wisdom. They'd now been together as soldiers and friends through so much that little needed discussion between them; total trust existed in the decisions of the other men.

Privakov was wary of Frank. One evening he mentioned the name Abraham to Raybury and repeated several times, "Yevrey?". Raybury just shrugged his ignorance. The fact was that he didn't know what 'Yevrey' meant but could guess. He didn't even know if Frank was Jewish, so the question was as unanswerable, as it appeared irrelevant. A week or so later Privakov had worked out the English word was "Jewish" and he asked Frank directly. On confirmation he said that many of the best socialist thinkers were Jewish including Karl Marx, the founding father. He'd been in prison with another man called Abramovich which is how he'd made the connection. He said after the revolution the Bolsheviks welcomed many Jews into their ranks and they opposed anti-Semitism where they could. Frank maintained a polite attitude toward Privakov, but his distance from his faith was now so great due to the war years that he rightly assumed this was another angle Privakov was using to persuade the Workers of the World to unite.

Of the British men, it was Budgie who'd settled into the temporary captivity, as promised by Privakov, in the best way. For two reasons. Firstly, their route to Kotlas continued down the North Dvina river which had an abundance of fish just waiting to be plucked out. Budgie had ingratiated himself with the giant Finn they called Arvo and persuaded him to let him go fishing as part of the foraging efforts. The Finn spoke some English he'd learnt from crewmen on fishing boats working in the Gulf of Bothnia. So one morning when the camp packed up and set off, Budgie was lent a horse and sent fishing with a wooden rod he'd made, and twine with instructions to rejoin the column in the afternoon. On the first day he returned with a couple of fine salmon and half a dozen trout, a great treat for the fish loving natives from around the White Sea. This became his morning duty and a task he relished.

The second reason was also food related. They'd passed through a logging settlement where they'd picked up a sack of white wheat flour, a rare find, which the Finn had little idea how to use; his bread making efforts in the mobile oven were confined to heavy black rye bread. Budgie used his baking skills to create something much lighter using a little of Arvo's precious yeast, salt, a little fat, water and plenty of kneading. It may not have sold in the Warwick market square, but the forest Bolsheviks thought it a gift from their new revolutionary comrades. Budgie was also making positive efforts to learn Russian and Finnish. So whilst the others picked up useful words and expressions on and around the movement of the guns and the care and exercise of the horses, his exposure to the men around the quartermaster created more opportunity to trade words. Some of them were trying to learn English too. It filled their time, strengthened comradeship and they all laughed at mispronunciations.

At the end of the marching day, after the men had been fed, Privakov would take a tour of the open fires around which groups of the Bolsheviks would congregate. Wet, newly washed kit might be strung up drying in front of the fires and they would be talking, possibly drinking Vodka of which there seemed to be a regular supply through the Finn. He would approach the British fire and always make a line for Arthur holding out a cigarette made with the course black Russian tobacco. Privakov was never seen offering a cigarette to another man. It became a routine. The Russian would remain standing and would hold up a light for Arthur, forcing him to stand. As he took the fag and put it into his mouth to be lit, Privakov would say the same thing every time.

"Volly, a token of my thanks to you. They were dangerous men in that training camp who wanted me dead. They probably would have killed me had you not appeared. No longer a problem."

He would then add.

"We are not at war with you English but we don't want you fighting in our country."

After these opening lines the conversation would move on to the days move, incidents they might have overcome, the food they'd eaten, fish from Budgie's catch or forest animal meat, or reliving the funny moments that soldiers need to capture in order to stay sane, even if they are notional enemies. He rarely bothered Arthur with the socialist politics. In these conversations Privakov spoke quietly, as a friend, not a proselytising revolutionary. It seemed to be his release where he climbed out of the costume and became the bloke in the pub. They laughed and came to enjoy each other's company. There was an emerging trust and respect between them.

The British men had stopped shaving, grew their beards and started to look like their revolutionary comrades. Frank quietly expressed his personal opinion that he'd always thought Arthur and Eric looked more like convicts. To him, their grizzly, hirsute faces confirmed as much.

11. Cossacks.
September 1919.

The artillery column crossed the North Dvina River from the north side at the small village of Dyabrino crossing to Krasnoborsk. In some years during the summer months it was fordable at this point using sand bars that appeared mid-stream and a large island that created two channels. Not this year. They waited for two days until a pair of flat-bottomed wooden ferry barges arrived one morning. It meant rest for the men, horses and camels; swimming and washing in the river and fishing lessons from Budgie. The crossing was downstream from Kotlas which Privakov had decided to avoid and skirt on the opposite western bank. It was unclear from the messengers Privakov was seeing whether the town was in the hands of the Bolsheviks or the White Russians. The communication channels were provided by riders being sent out from Privakov's artillery unit and other Bolshevik units thinly spread across the countryside.

The journey continued for several weeks, recrossing the river to head south east near Bobrovnikovo. This time the river was fordable. Now into early September the temperatures were dropping sharply at night and wet weather was slowing progress along all the forest tracks and navigable routes. The many small settlements they passed through were untouched by the tumult of the recent war in Europe, the revolution and the civil war being fought in parts of their homeland.

These people had a simple, subsistence existence. 'Loggers and piggers', Arvo called them. The countryside slowly started to change with patches of cleared and agriculturally cultivated land imposing itself between the trees. Proper fields. The people were now 'diggers and piggers', which Arvo found very funny in his ability to find humour everywhere. The Russian army principle of feeding from the land was now supplemented by what they could trade and sometimes just commandeer from the villages.

Arvo's laughter stopped when the first burnt village appeared. A few dozen, still smouldering cabins spread around an open central area like a village green. The track bisected the settlement and the column was led right through without stopping. It was an atrocious scene that the eyes could not avoid. A dozen or so men had been hung from trees and were swinging gently in a light breeze, in sharp contrast to the violence of their deaths. In the centre a pile of bodies were covered in flies with scavenging dogs peering suspiciously at the men and horses passing through. It was clear these bodies were women and children who'd been shot. There were two young women, semi-naked some yards from the others. The British men had seen many terrible things during the war, but the total destruction and murder of a village and its population was not one of them. There was no talking, just shock. A couple of miles further on, another hamlet raised by fire and terror. Fewer bodies, but still hanging men.

In the middle of September the sun set at around 6pm. so they would start to find an appropriate camp area from around four o'clock. It had been bright, clear weather so a night in the open was easier than finding billets in a village somewhere. Privakov thought they were still a week away from Vyatka and the completion of their mission to deliver the guns. Arthur had been riding the lead horse of the lead gun on this particular day, a role he knew well but meant he was one of the first to see the horrors. The horsemanship of all the British men had been noted by the Bolsheviks. The daily duties were now spread between the men regardless of nationality. He was removing the horse harnesses when Privakov appeared on his horse with Klechov alongside.

"Volly, I'll be going ahead to find out what's happened in those villages. I think I know. It may be Cossacks, but we'll see. When you meet up with Sergeant Englishman, tell your comrades that tonight you must have your fire at the far side of the clearing. I don't want them to appear and meet with you when I'm not here. Keep your Bolshevik comrades between you and the track. The Cossacks are unpredictable and cannot be trusted."

His comments were made with a voice of concern.

He rode off, continuing along the route the guns would follow the next day, a Sunday. There was a clearing to one side of the track stretching a couple of hundred yards into which the unit spread. The night was quiet. Sentries were posted on the track at either end of the camp to check anyone passing through. Outside of a few locals, no-one of any consequence did.

Privakov re-appeared during the early morning preparations to move. Sunrise at ten minutes past five. He pulled together his Bolshevik NCO's and Raybury to brief them. Speaking Russian to his own men to start with, they were then dismissed and he spoke to Raybury who noticed his tired face, irritated demeanour and the real giveaway, bloodshot eyes. Privakov was not a big man and could take a drink, but an evening with the hard drinking, hard living Cossacks would be a challenge for anyone.

"There's a regiment calling themselves Cossacks eight versts further on at Murashi, about 500 men and others. We have to pass through their lines. I have met with their commander, a major elected by his men who goes by the name of Pavel Krasnov. Quite young, maybe thirty, the son of Pyotr Krasnov, a real Cossack general who has already led his men, the Don Host[10] against the Bolsheviks in the Ukraine and Poland. He may still be

---

[10] Host – Cossack Army Unit.

doing so. His son Pavel claims to support us, but the truth is they are only interested in themselves. They are war-lords; land pirates if you like, most of them support our enemies."

He stopped to take a tin mug of sweet black tea passed to him by Klechov. Privakov claimed the camel milk made him sick.

"These villages were destroyed by his men. He claimed they'd been hiding grain and other food and in the past they had fed men supporting our enemies. He was told this by peasants living in Murashi. I spoke to some of them. There'd been local conflict between their neighbours and the people killed. Yevrey people. Jewish. It's not unusual Sergeant Englishman for neighbours to turn on each other in times of conflict, and when bands of armed men with no loyalty to anyone roam the country. Especially here in Russia now, where there is no law. Local agitators do it to favour themselves, to divert the aggression to someone else, to acquire the land and animal stock from those killed. And there is always a hatred of others who are different. We oppose this kind of murder. We'll execute offenders and disband their units. But as you'll understand, there is nothing we can do here with these men who call themselves Cossacks. They are supposed to be honourable people, respect other men. If what the villagers say is true, they are not real Cossacks."

"You say we have to go through their lines. Is that dangerous for us?" Asked Raybury.

"Do you mean 'us' as in our artillery column? Or 'us' as in you Englishmen?"

Privakov never saw Taffy and Eric Amos as anything other than English.

"We British."

Privakov thought for a moment.

"Ah....... Well....... I think we will try to keep you and your men low key. We don't need to draw attention to you. These men have few friends, nor enemies. Their loyalties flow depending on where they benefit at the time. You pose no threat to them as part of my unit. So we plan to spread your men about the column, as we have been doing, and just march on. The tracks are getting better and we should make fifteen versts today..... provided there are no hold ups."

He concluded cautiously. This was the first time Raybury had seen the small man anything but supremely confident, something he didn't share with his section. However, he did tell them that Privakov had referred to the men ahead of them in disparaging terms implying they weren't real Cossacks.

*

It was approaching 9am. on a cool mid-September morning, with large white cotton-wool clouds floating across a clear blue-sky background. At the head of the column was Privakov and a couple of his NCO's – men with no military experience prior to their training after being released from prison. Both as thuggish looking as Klechov who today was tailing the procession of guns, men and the Finn's camel drawn covered wagons and mobile kitchen. The British men had been 'demoted' to marching as crewmen, except Budgie who'd increasingly become part of Arvo's QM team and rode on one of the store wagons.

The column meandered through the forest which had narrowed to the edges of the track. A short distance ahead in the trees they saw a small group of men at a checkpoint. A horse rode away from them. Privakov exchanged a few words and the guns were let through. They wheeled along the track at a steady walking pace to keep as concentrated in length as they could. Turning a corner and exiting a stretch of dense trees they came to the Cossack camp. It straddled both sides of the track with no apparent order and stretched down a shallow incline for perhaps half a mile. A chaotically arranged series of round tents of various sizes each flying a coloured flag; blue, orange, red, brown and others for the visible distance. Some flags further along had a cross in the centre, the first ones a crescent with a star. Horses and ponies of many sizes and colours were tethered in ground-pegged rows close to the larger tents. Loose chickens and geese strutted around pecking the thin grass and dirt. The camp had an established feel.

There were numerous big fires with triangular frames above them holding black iron cauldron's being tended by women dressed in long brightly coloured red, orange and yellow dresses, their heads covered in equally colourful, patterned shawls and scarves. For the British men and probably the White Sea convicts, the big surprise was the children of all ages running between the tents, the horses, the fires, the rows of wooden frames with clothes laid over some to dry. Other frames had hares and odd looking, large black and blue feathered birds hanging, some smaller brown ones too. On seeing the birds Eric and Arthur had the following exchange.

"Capercaillie…….. Horse of the woods."

"What's that Eric? I see loads of horses."

"Not those horses……… The birds. Capercaillie. You get them in the Scottish Highlands. I've not eaten that for a while. Shall we get one?"

"I don't think so 'Aims'. Privakov was clear about getting through this lot and not engaging with them."

"Yes, but it tastes good, a real treat."

"Not one of your best ideas. That's out of the very few you've ever had."

Eric nodded at Arthur's response. The pair of them were smiling at each other. The short dialogue broke the tension they were feeling being in this strange place.

The Cossack men had been inside the first group of tents and they started emerging as the guns moved along the track. Most had white shirts and billowing green or blue pantaloons; those that wore hats, white, brown and black bear-skins, some with a thick fur ring surrounding the lower part of the head covering, some taller and others shorter in height. There were impressive beards on a few, even more impressive drooping moustaches on most. The men, women and children who were coming to stare at the guns rather than the soldiers moving them, looked Turkic and Asiatic. These were nomadic people from the south of the Russian Empire, Uzbeks, Turks, Georgians, Kazakhs. Expert horsemen from the steppes and around the Caspian Sea. The smallest children from these tents were standing close to their mothers watching from a distance, those a little older running close to the track on either side shouting at the Bolsheviks, mainly in dialects they didn't understand. It was clear these people were not from one place, not an ethnically homogenous group as might have been expected.

Further along the track, across a shallow ford were tents with crosses; perhaps twenty large ones and many smaller. Here there were no kids running about. There were numerous congregations, men women and children, kneeling in front of black robed priests with round pill-box hats widening a little from the bottom to its flat top. The hats had a black veil draped down the neck. The worshippers were chanting in response to the priests words and the swinging of a smoking incense burner. The pleasant smell of this could be picked up by the marching soldiers and little attention was being paid as they made their devotions to the Russian Orthodox church. Many Russians were deeply religious, as reflected here. Having a diverse unit of Muslims and Christians within his band of brigands was clearly a leadership success for Pavel Krasnov, and further evidence that these were calling themselves Cossacks for convenience.

They'd reached the edge of the camp as the prayer services were ending. The kids ran toward the guns to join the others shouting at the soldiers, some of whom had spoken with them. A few hundred yards ahead another checkpoint was manned but there was no barrier to stop the column. Privakov was approaching the checkpoint as three horsemen galloped toward it from the right of the track, coming from the largest marquee looking like a low-level circus 'big-top'. Privakov pulled up and as he spoke more horsemen arrived at the checkpoint. The discussion got heated and lasted about ten minutes before the little man and his minders rode back to the big-top. The column of gunners lit cigarettes and pipes and waited. A short while later one of the minders returned. The guns and Arvo's QM wagons ahead of the marching British men pulled off the track. It was clear the stop was going to be for some time.

Budgie walked back from the wagon he was driving to explain to the British what he thought he knew as the Finn had explained to him. It was nothing sinister. The day was September 21st, the day the Orthodox Russian church celebrate the feast day of Saint Jonah,

"Swallowed by a whale," Budgie said.

As he mentioned this, Taffy spoke.

"I remember from my Bible Classes, one of the best stories in the Holy Book 'And the Lord appointed a great fish to swallow up Jonah. And he was in the belly of the fish three days and three nights. The sea stopped raging, God intervened and the fish vomited Jonah onto the beach where he lived happily ever after……. Or something like that."

Budgie replied with an unconvincing smile.

"Yes, something like that Taff. Arvo mentioned it was something to do with fish. I thought he was suggesting it was all in honour of me. Apparently not, but Jonah is also a prophet in their Holy Book."

Nodding in the direction of the crescent flags.

"So today they can all celebrate. The Cossack leader wants Privakov to stop for a few hours to join his people in their celebrations. We've got some salmon and trout for them; they've slaughtered some sheep that they'll share with us."

Taffy again. "Mutton eh? Well I'm stopping, I don't know about you lot."

Raybury was listening with a frown. Frank looking toward the guns ahead of them added.

"I don't think we'll have much choice lads. They're unhitching the guns."

Just beyond the checkpoint the ground to the left of the track opened up enough to park the guns, the wagons and line up the horses and camels. Budgie had returned to the wagon he was driving, unhitched the camel and was busy getting the mobile kitchen into action. Privakov returned after meeting Krasnov, he looked furious. Shortly after he approached Raybury and Frank.

"I'm not sure what Krasnov is playing at. We'd agreed last night that he would not interfere with our progress and let us through. His Bolshevik Commissar was with him then, a weak looking man who surprisingly spoke up for us getting on with our business. This morning the Commissar has been called away 'on urgent business', apparently in Vyatka, where we're headed. He'll be away for several days. If what I'm told is true."

He kicked a small rock away from the ground in frustration.

"We've been stopped at his invitation to enjoy some Cossack hospitality. It would be insulting and difficult to refuse. He wanted us to remain here overnight. I said no. We compromised and we'll leave at 3 this afternoon. He's been told we have some foreigners with us. I think one of my men told the kids running about which was passed back to him. He wants to meet you later. I have no reason to believe there is anything sinister in this, other than genuine curiosity. Many Russians never meet anyone other than their family and countryfolk. However, we should be cautious."

*

Over the next few hours the camp atmosphere became celebratory, like an old style town fair, village fete or county show. All the adults and teenagers were involved in some preparatory activity. The women, constantly shouting at the smaller children, were tending the cauldrons and scrubbing the mud off potatoes, turnips and chopping other green vegetables. They would occasionally break out into liturgical chants and then more uplifting tunes that sounded like work songs. The young and toddlers clutching the hands of their slightly older siblings came over to look at the big guns, things they'd never seen before. Privakov gave the nod to allow the lawless kids to climb. It was easier than his men trying to stop them.

There was a narrow strip about 300 yards long and 40 wide between the tents on one side of the track and the treeline being roped off by some teenagers. Alongside this strip some open sided square marquee's were being erected. Four large open log fires that had been burning fiercely as the column passed by earlier were now large piles of hot red and white ashes. The spits over two of them each had half a carefully butchered cow, split down the middle. The other two fires each had four sheep on the spits being turned slowly by extremely bored looking youths, the fat dropping and hissing on the ashes below. A number of smaller fires had a row of the game birds roasting. All over the place there were small groups of men practicing acrobatic high kicks and back flips. Contrasting, familiar and strange looking instruments, were being blown, beaten, strummed and plucked. The camp had the sense of the medieval about it.

After handing their personal weapons in to Arvo for safe keeping, the Bolsheviks and gunners were given freedom to roam within the camp. Privakov gave three strict instructions: to be back at the gun-lines by 2.30; they were not to engage in any conversation with women or girls and were not to drink alcohol. The third probably the easiest to comply with as the Cossack camp rule was no drinking before the sun went down, and even then only the Christians drank alcohol. As they walked about, and despite the seeming chaotic nature of the camp, everyone was busy with a task of some kind. As agreed with Krasnov three rifle shots would signal the time the soldiers needed to return.

Privakov spent the morning in the main camp tent which housed the Cossack leader and his close lieutenants. They discussed the broader geographic area, identifying, with the aid of maps, who controlled Vyatka, the Trans-Siberian railway to the east of the city, what was happening further south in the Caucasus and whether the White's under Admiral Kolchak with his Siberian army had secured Kotlas, from where Privakov knew the intervention allies in the north were supposed to be headed.

At midday, Klechov and his fellow minders were sent out to collect the British section to meet the Cossack leader. Budgie, in his improving but still broken Russian tried, without success, to extract from the goons something on what this would entail. They were met at the entrance of the round 'circus top' by Privakov who walked with Raybury and the others toward a screened off section. Men were milling about the rest of the tent, some with large, long and skinny hunting dogs tethered to hand-held leashes. It smelt a mixture of incense and tobacco smoke. In one area a number of wooden chests were being guarded by four men with standard Russian issue M1891 Mosin-Nagent rifles. A manual bolt actioned, 7.62mm cartridge loaded from a 5 round magazine. Archaic compared to the British Lee Enfield's, but these were the common local weapon, although rarely seen with the eighteen inch bayonet attached as they were here.

A flap was pushed aside by a giant Cossack, also with a bayoneted rifle, and they walked into Krasnov's inner sanctum. He sat at a desk flanked by two other men, the three of them peering at one of several maps laid out. He really did look young with fluffy facial hair pretending to be a moustache on an intelligent looking face and alert blue-green eyes that flashed at the men entering his private office. To the amazement of everyone, he spoke in heavily accented but fairly fluent English.

"Welcome, my friends to our humble Host of Cossacks. I understand from your commander here, Grigorey, that you have become accidentally mixed up in our countries political affairs. Through no fault of your own, I understand. I heard there were foreigners amongst his men. I was hoping either French or English. As a child I had governesses from both countries and haven't practiced for many years. Had you been Italian, I would have had no interest in you."

He chuckled to himself. His lieutenants left and a steward appeared with a silver tray of glasses containing sweet black tea.

"First we can talk for a short while. Afterwards you can eat and enjoy some entertainment and then you can go on your way. There'll be music, dancing, singing and horses. You'll like what our boys can do on horses.

Before that you must tell me about England which one day I hope to visit......... And what you think of our great country."

Krasnov asked the questions The next thirty or so minutes were spent with the men talking about home, the British Army, the war, why they came to Russia, did they think the Allied forces would stay, would more foreigners arrive and various other topics. It was clear that he was trying to gauge which way the winds might blow. As the six British men had been out of touch with their own commanders for over two months and had no idea, whatever they said was speculative and extremely vague. Raybury did his best to make this clear. The Cossack leader was surprisingly erudite and articulate. When he failed to find the English word he and Privakov would come up with something that worked.

Frank noticed there was little said about the revolution and the current political tumult engulfing Russia. He thought this might be because it mattered little to Krasnov and his followers who was nominally running the country. The band of men he led would do whatever they liked, wherever they liked anyway. They were not peasants, soldiers or students. Nor the industrial proletariat, so they didn't fit into the perceived menu of revolutionary groups. They were a wandering, muddled tribe of opportunists without ideology or affiliation. Ruthless and dangerous, as had already been seen in the villages, yet today he was personable, even charming. He finished the audience by hoping they'd enjoy the festival in honour of Jonah, a holy man for our Christian church and our Muslim Brothers.

They left to hear unfamiliar music coming from the roped off field to which they now headed. They found the Bolshevik gunners congregated close to one of the large fires at one end of the field. Nearby were trestle tables covered with colourful patchwork cloths, trays of vegetables and meat was being cut from the carcass of the spit-roast cow and sheep. At one of the 'A' frames the spit had been lifted and spun away from the embers to enable access for the two carvers. They used bayonets, which must have been razor sharp as the cooked flesh was being easily sliced onto trays being held by several boys. Once full they would take the meat to the tables and return with another empty tray. At the tables, women in their colourful dresses and shawls were serving the food. Arvo had wheeled his mobile kitchen up. He and his small crew including Budgie were pulling metal pots of fish stew from the ovens to contribute to the feast food. Budgie had collected more plates from Arvo's stores. Today it felt like their army issue mess tins would be out of place.

The musicians were moving to the centre of the field and as they did so only one man played what looked like a large penny whistle. Combining high and low flowing notes in a series of short and repeated blasts that replicated a calling forest bird.[11] Eerie as it was compelling. Two large kettle drums were set down twenty foot apart, and between them were arrayed a dozen musicians. Some wooden pipes with antler horns attached to the end which produced a high pitched reedy sound[12]. Two men had small metal horse-shoe frames with a flexible piece for twanging, which they held to their mouths. Using their mouth shape and breath they could create boings and metallic hums.[13] A small barrel shaped drum with a tuft of horse hair at one end which was jerked by the player[14] to give a haunting tone. There were some large stringed instruments looking like lutes, and then out they came, two of them. Not obvious at first, but Eric Amos saw them being blown into with a pipe.

"Bloody hell! Bagpipes. I've come all this way for a Cossack Party and they have the nerve to play me the bagpipes."

Initially Arthur and Frank didn't get what he was talking about until they saw the balloons expanding under the left arms of an old looking man and a younger one next to him. They blew into an upright wooden tube on one side, the balloon got bigger. The player held a tube on the other side facing the ground and started running his fingers up and down. The unmistakable, painful to English ears, background skirl of the pipes was heard.[15] The others were as shocked as Eric.

"Can you play them Aims?" Asked Arthur.

Eric glanced across at him, pausing before he spoke.

"Oak Tree Children's Home. That dreadful place. There was a man who worked there in the gardens, Macky we called him. He told us what to do, when to plant and pick stuff. He was one of only two who ever tried to teach us anything interesting. He taught a few of us how to play the pipes, some the penny whistle. One tune only, The Black Bear. He said it was an old marching song. The other's tried to stop him but he had none of it, he just ignored them."

Frank added. "You've never told us you played the pipes."

"You never asked. Anyway, one tune only, hardly playing the pipes."

People were now sitting around eating as two troops of Cossack men entered the field from opposite ends. From one end dressed in loose white shirts and billowing green trousers, the other red shirts and blue trousers. They marched in to stand either side of the musicians. Krasnov was stood straight in front of the band on an upturned wooden box so he could see and be seen. He spoke for a few minutes to his people, whatever he said

---

[11] The instrument, a Floyara.
[12] Zhaliyka.
[13] Drymba. (Jew's Harp).
[14] Buhay
[15] Duda

sounded uplifting. He then turned towards Privakov and said a few words in Russian getting a polite clap from the Bolsheviks. Spotting the British men stood in a group he added.

"And welcome to my new English friends who have come so far to enjoy our Cossack hospitality."

"English, my arse." Muttered Taffy, whilst the others also gave Krasnov a subdued clap.

They'd actually felt accepted by this strange band of nomadic 'land-pirates' for the short time they'd been there. Krasnov called out to the band and they struck up. Thundering drums, bagpipes, whistles, wooden horns and strumming strings now combined into a rhythm that stirred the dance troops. Each group moved in rows dipping, bouncing, kicking and squatting, interspersed with claps and cheers. They spread along the long edge of the field, breaking up with individuals taking small solo dances as their comrades clapped and shouted along with the crowd. The two troops closed back to the centre, standing opposite each other in a row as a single dancer stepped out to perform his speciality moves, then followed by another man from the other troop. It was competitive, exhilarating and the gunners had seen nothing like it.

As all eyes were focussed on the show in front of them, Frank had stepped away to have a quiet word with Raybury. The two of them then spoke to Privakov, who strode with a smile on his face along the back of the onlookers to Krasnov.

The athletic Cossack dancers finished. The band played for a short while as in the open field behind them markers were being placed for the next event. When they finished, the giant tent-flap attendant could be seen, if anyone had been paying attention, walking out to speak to the old piper. The fluttering forest bird whistle shrilled as the kettle drummers picked up they're drums and walked away with the rest of the musicians, except the old piper. He walked the other way toward Privakov's men only observed by Frank who put his arm up to attract attention. There were puzzled faces in the watching crowd, not sure what was happening. Most of the Bolsheviks were talking amongst themselves, as were the British section standing around Raybury.

Watching the piper get closer, Frank announced.

"Right Amos, show us what you can do."

Eric hadn't been paying attention, with his back to where the band had been. He hadn't seen the piper who was now diligently wiping the mouthpiece with a not very clean looking rag.

"Step forward my Scottish friend and play us The Black Bear."

Eric realised he'd been set up.

"You are joking, I've not blown into a bag like that since I was a kid. I'm not starting again now."

Arthur and the others were laughing. Frank again.

"Of course you are Eric. Look around, all these people are now expecting something. We can't just leave them waiting. Come on, grab the pipes."

At this moment Krasnov appeared with Privakov, but they stood well back, just watching with amusement. Eric was shaking his head in an exasperated way, realising that doing nothing would be even more humiliating. He tried an excuse.

"It'll be different, more or fewer finger holes, not the same sound."

Frank took the pipes from the old man who nodded graciously and grinned broadly showing a toothless mouth.

"How many finger holes should there be Eric?"

"Eight."

Looking at the instrument carefully, Frank confirmed.

"Lucky you, eight there are! We're all set then!"

With a sinking feeling of resigned despair and being caught in a gag by someone he thought a friend, Eric reluctantly took the pipes.

"You bastard Abraham, I'll get you back for this."

They were now surrounded by Bolsheviks and Cossacks. Eric used his tunic sleeve to wipe the mouthpiece again. A strap to hold the pipes in place went over his head onto his right shoulder with the pillow shaped bag under his left arm. In his head he didn't believe this was going to work. Success would be to get any noise at all. Holding the chanter, the tone pipe, four fingers from each hand confirmed there were eight holes. He blew to inflate the bag a couple of times and settled it under his left harm with which he could maintain some pressure on it. Needing several long puffs; it was bigger than the highland pipe bags he'd learnt on. It was a long time ago, but he did know how to play that one tune.

He got the drone going. It was strained, there was some whistling and looks of amazement on the faces of many standing around, especially the Cossacks. He tried to play a few notes to warm up and steadily worked out a balance of air and arm pressure. Playing these felt different to the Scottish bagpipes which were more complex. After a few minutes of tuneless droning he tried stringing some notes together. The Black Bear had a jogging tempo believed to be played in the Jacobite Rebellion on the march home. These pipes had a different pitch and the first few bars sounded tuneless and screechingly awful.

Eric persisted and slowly got his fingers remembering the pattern. Stopping for a minute he started again. The tune came through and with more confidence he repeated it and it got better. The crowd had started to clap to the bouncing rhythm. As a final flurry he started a short march up and down with people clearing the way in front of him. Pipe music meant movement; he couldn't play standing still. There were plenty of wrong notes, but not enough to make it too painful and for the tune to be lost. After several minutes and three repeats he thought he'd done enough. He stopped fingering and let the drone subside. The people about him cheered and clapped. They'd never seen a man come into their community and play their pipes. Even Krasnov and Privakov looked as if they'd enjoyed the performance, not gentle on the ear, but they expected even worse. Unstrapping the pipes from his right shoulder Eric passed them back to the old toothless man who bowed his head and then beamed a grin or grimace, Eric couldn't tell which.

*

With the pipe interlude complete, the Cossack horsemanship was on show. Three pairs of horses entered the field being controlled by a single man standing with a foot on each horse. After circling the field several times they performed numerous acrobatic feats, laying alongside the saddle, somehow managing to manipulate themselves under the belly of the trotting horse and getting up on the other side, lying off the back attached to the saddle by the ankles. All impressive circus-act feats. Not stuff that Arthur would be trying anytime soon.

He was a good horseman and could see the great skills needed to control the horses like this. Next out were two riders carrying a flag pole between them and a third man initially standing astride the horses. As they trotted around the field, the standing man climbed onto the shoulders of the two riders using the flag pole to steady himself. The finale here were six ponies entering the field with young riders, none looking over the age of ten, one tiny lad probably half that age. They performed individual acrobatic tricks to demonstrate their skills. With their agility and light-weight, they could stand, spin, hook their foot in the stirrup to lean at near horizontal angles, all to the clapping and cheering of their families and friends.

Arthur reflected on his first time on a horse, Alma in Taylor's foundry yard arranged by his now dead school friend, Sam Wallace. Despite all the death and destruction he'd witnessed in the five years since then, grief for the loss of his good friend, being a strange, creeping, black emotion, unexpectedly intruded. Deep in the heart of Russia, he suddenly felt an overwhelming physical and emotional distance from his home, his family and of course Alice. He was still only 21 years of age and managed to suppress this puzzling sense by looking over to his two friends, Eric and Frank, Aims and Abs, who'd become as close as brothers. As he did so they were looking back at him whilst ominously in conversation with Privakov and Krasnov.

At the far end of the field two groups of horses were assembling. The coloured uniforms of the dance troops could be identified as being worn by the riders, clearly a team from each of the twin communities in the camp. Running into the field were men on foot some hammering into the ground small wooden posts with an iron hoop hanging on a nail, others were carrying man size poles which were erected. These also had hooks with hoops hanging on them high up at head height. When the props had been placed in the field the men doing so collected more hoops and stood close to a post or pole until each one had a marker. It was becoming obvious to the British men that this was to be the Cossack equivalent of tent pegging, something Arthur's mates knew of his high level of competence. He smelt a rat and was right in his suspicion.

Horses started trotting down the field as if being shown by their riders where the posts and poles were. And then a riderless mount was being led by a man on another horse along the far side of the field where many spectators now stood getting a better view far away from the tented area. Taking in the full circumference and being led by a white shirted, green trousered rider with an unusual white hat taller than many of the others. Most were watching the team members but Arthur only saw the approaching horse with an empty saddle. He became vaguely conscious of a presence close to his right shoulder as the rider stopped to their front in the roped off field. The rider towing the horse shouted something in Russian, which the instantly recognisable voice of Privakov quietly translated from over his shoulder.

"Volly, Captain Abdulin commanding the Muslim men says he has been told that one of their guests is handy at 'obruch'. Hoops in English. Your two friends tell me it is you."

Without looking at him, Arthur replied.

"I think someone told you well before the Captain here was informed."

Arthur was now staring at Frank and Eric standing some yards away smiling in anticipation. The Cossack rider spoke again.

"He said that in honour of their guests travelling from another country to attend today's celebrations he wishes to invite our hoops expert to join his team in the competition."

Turning to face Privakov, Arthur said.

"And now I think your captain is taking the piss as well."

Privakov was nodding a little, smiling too.

"Well perhaps Volly, perhaps. But we and you are their guests, and I know they would be genuinely pleased at your participation. You saw how they enjoyed the piper."

Arthur knew he had no choice, but equally it wouldn't be an onerous chore. He was competent, but today, perhaps not quite so confident for lack of any practice. He gave his two friends a sarcastic grin and wagged his index finger as if to say, 'I'll get you back'. Stepping forward he ducked under the rope. Captain Abdulin was nodding as he passed the reins of the lively grey horse to Arthur. They rode back to the entrance end of the field and purely through hand signals the Cossack indicated to Arthur to follow him along the course of the targets.

In this Cossack format of tent-pegging there were eight in all, three man height poles and five low-level posts. A metal hoop on a hook had to be whipped off with the sword as the horse rode by and if successful could then be discarded onto the ground where a young lad – there were already a number of them around the course - would recover the hoop and return it to the post or pole in time for the next ride The men would ride out on the right of their strip, circle left and return, four targets out and four back.

After being shown the course, he and other men rode up and back a number of times to get familiar with the challenge. Speed, pacing between targets, dexterity, good eyes and horsemanship were all equally important to compete. A loud hand bell was rung by a grey bearded man who was waving the riders from the course. Things were about to start. Arthur left the field to join the other four men in his team, all now dismounted and collected together chatting excitedly to each other. Darker in the face and all several inches shorter than Arthur, they represented the Muslim Cossacks in the camp. They'd watched Arthur as he'd ridden his mount and had already been impressed with the movement and control he had over a horse he'd never sat on before. He joined the group and listened. By now, time had provided all of the British men with a fractured understanding of some Russian, but these men were speaking a different language.

The group were approached by a young women with a dark complexion and large black eyes glancing modestly at Arthur. In a red shawl and multi-coloured patch-work festival dress, she was poised and beautiful. Over her arm was a white cotton blouse, the same as that of the other men. They pulled Arthur in, it was friendly and all were laughing, including their guest. Indicating at him to remove his tunic and shirt, he did so, revealing the slim muscled torso of a young man honed by constant and arduous exercise, the sight of which made the young women giggle and pretend to hide her face with her hand. They weren't expecting him to change his trousers. He put on the loose fitting blouse and was passed a black papakha[16] to match the others his team wore. A close fit on his head, but it would do. Although he couldn't see himself, he now looked the part, at least from the waist up.

By holding up his right hand and splaying his five fingers the team leader indicated to Arthur that he would be number four. Good enough for them to recover the race with their last, presumably best rider if Arthur proved to be a dud. They all mounted, were each handed a gently curved shashka[17] and the first horse for both teams approached the field entrance where Captain Abdulin stood with a rifle. Arthur then noticed a tall pole next to Abdulin to which one of the fat black and alive, 'horse of the woods' birds was being tied upside down, shrieking and flapping. He had no idea what this was about. Above the squawking, Abdulin called to the men trying to settle their now excited mounts. Then appearing to count down, which some standing about him joined in, he raised his rifle and fired into the air.

Arthur's team were on the near side closest to the tents where the Bolshevik men were. The first horse on his team reared up at the rifle whilst the other shot off. The crowd instantly yelled and cheered for their man. A lot of brightly coloured scarves waved in the air, the kettle drums from the band started banging out a repetitive thud, thud, thud, thud rhythm. This was slowly picked up by the crowd which each beat being matched by a 'hey, hey, hey, hey'. It was noisy and exhilarating.

The slow start for his team resulted in the first rider losing about twenty yards on the opposition. The winning team would be determined by the number of hoops successfully collected which was always very close in number. It couldn't be determined by observation during the course of the race with so much movement and noise going on. In the event of these being the same, the first team to cross the line with their last horse won. When a hoop was successfully hooked a cheer went up in the section of the crowd closest to the feat. The second horse had been able to make up ten yards which was subsequently lost by the third, they still had some space to make up as Arthur's race was about to start. He held his sword up to be struck by rider three as he'd seen was the relay handover signal.

He set off, the other team in front, with the beating kettle drum thudding, the 'hey, hey' resounding from the crowd and a general cacophony of noise filling the air. The Bolsheviks and his friends had been scouring riders to spot Arthur and now recognised the bigger man compared to the others. A loud cheer went up from that quarter of the

---

[16] Papakha – the Cossack woollen hat which could be in black, white or shades of grey and brown. The name has Turkic origin.

[17] Shashka. Single edged, single handed sword, with a gentle curve to allow cutting and thrusting.

field. The first hoop was a low post. He leant down from the side of the grey and missed it. The was an audible 'ooooh' from the crowd. The next was on a pole and he missed that too, with a similar reaction. He got the next low hoop to a widespread cheer and was only just able to discard it from his sword before lining up for another low one. Success and another loud cheer especially from the Bolsheviks who he was now closest to, having to wheel around for the return stretch. He was making up time as well, spotting that the other rider was now only about ten yards ahead. With two out of four hoops, he didn't know how that rated.

Spurring his horse on he missed the next high hoop, sacrificing accuracy for speed. Slowing his pace only slightly he secured the low six and high seven and was still making up ground. These successes generated widespread cheers from everyone whose attention was focussed on the foreigner who rode and 'obruched' like a Cossack. Undercover in one of the tents, Krasnov and Privakov were both enjoying the spectacle with pleasure and pride respectively. The former from the sense of unity and joy his diverse band of Cossacks were getting and sharing from Jonah's feast day. The latter from seeing his English friend who he still felt indebted to, displaying his skills and being cheered by these hard, nomadic people of Russia.

Thirty yards to the last low hoop which he was lining up perfectly for having got his eye in. He whipped it off and felt it rattling down his shashka until he flicked it away. Now completely focussed on the forty yard stretch to the finishing line, he made up another five yards on the opposition finally crossing at the same time, striking his last team-mates sword and setting him off. Five hoops in the bag and the lost distance made up, Arthur heard universal cheers from all around. The last two set off and were matching each other on the first stretch until the other team rider took too long a turn at the top end. For the home stretch Arthur's man raced along missing two hoops and securing the other two. As he crossed the line ahead he closed in to the post with the squawking bird and cut the tether releasing it to flap in the dirt with its legs still tied.

Four men who'd been on the course returned with their tallies of hoops which were passed to Captain Abdulin. He rode off to report the result to Krasnov in the main tent. The riders had all dismounted and were all slapping each other on the back and lightly punching others on the shoulder. Several, from both teams put their arms about his shoulders in a respectful brotherly, but uncomfortable fashion. Demonstrative displays of tactile affection were not the British soldiers way. They were provided with cold tea and a fruit juice of some kind by some women, including the attractive, black-eyed girl who'd provided the shirt. Arthur thought she wanted it back and started unbuttoning it. She waved her hands and pushed them toward him in the air indicating he could keep it, clapping her hands to acknowledge his efforts and passed him his army issued shirt and tunic. He went to remove the papakha and she shook her head at that too.

The two teams remounted and rode back to the centre of the field to hear the race result called out by Krasnov. The red shirts had secured 21 hoops, the white shirts 22. A quick bit of mental arithmetic told Arthur that most men picked up four or five, so his tally was more than respectable. His winning team leader was handed the fat bird cut down from the pole. No longer wriggling, it's neck had been wrung. The team captain handed it straight to Arthur accompanied by a slap on the shoulder and various words that sounded friendly enough. After the token prize had been awarded the horses were ridden away and Arthur made his way back to the Bolsheviks. Men women and children behind the rope were clapping and cheering him carrying the capercaillie carcass by the feet. It was clear these people were from both religious groups. He was being lauded in appreciation for winning and taking part.

The British men were all together and Arthur swung the bird at Eric as he reached them.

"There you go Jock. There's your bloody 'horse of the woods'. Something I've just risked my life for, without intending to. I hope you choke on a bone."

Eric nodded.

"You've done a great good job Wally. You're everybody's hero….. for the moment. Just enjoy the attention. I did for my few minutes. Now it's your turn."

Budgie added.

"The bird looks a good one. I'll get Arvo to roast it for us later."

*

The men needed to return to the guns to prepare to move out. The Cossack families were dispersing from the field and tents. Some of the younger kids and teenagers came over to watch the Bolsheviks re-hitch the guns and move their troop back onto the track. All set to leave by five minutes to three, they were standing about as Privakov re-appeared accompanied by Krasnov and some grey-beards; the more senior of his men. He spoke to the column in Russian for a few minutes before switching to English.

"Our friends from England."

Taffy winced; Eric didn't care.

"Today you have been our unexpected guests. My people have enjoyed having you amongst us. Thank you for your participation in the music and obruch. Tent pegging, I think you call it."

As he said this he nodded at Eric and Arthur before he continued.

"These are difficult times for all of us. We Cossacks, our Bolshevik allies and you men who find yourselves here by accident of your military calling and the decisions of your politicians in England. We hope you will be able to get back to your homes one day. I know you have seen some terrible sights on the road here. A result of enemies acting against our interests."

He stopped speaking briefly and pulled a folded note from his jacket pocket, which he then said.

"This is a telegram from Lenin sent to and distributed by the Penza Soviet to me and other leaders last year in Nizhny Novgorod. I will read from parts of it.

Comrades! The kulak[18] uprising in your five districts must be crushed without pity. You must make examples of these people.

Hang publicly so people can see, at least 100 kulaks, rich bastards and known bloodsuckers.

Publish their names.

Seize all their grain.

Single out the hostages as I previously instructed.

Do all this so that for versts around people will see it all, understand it, tremble, and tell themselves that we are killing the bloodthirsty kulaks and that we will continue to do so...

As you can see, we are being instructed by our leaders to root out and kill enemies of our revolutionary movement. Those people were kulaks. Do not think badly of us because of this. I know, as soldiers, you would do the same thing for what you believed in and for your cause."

Raybury muttered.

"Indiscriminate murder and rape of women and children, I don't think so. Even Privakov wouldn't be so barbaric."

Krasnov continued.

"Your commander here thinks highly of you and the contribution you have made to his mission, now almost finished. I have agreed to add my name to the papers he will provide to send you on your next journey. Thank you my friends and good luck."

With that he turned about and rode off with his small entourage trailing behind. Privakov passed by the British men.

"He's trying to excuse himself from the village massacres. It won't work. My men have learnt enough to know what happened. They weren't kulaks, they were poor peasants. His brutality will go into my reports for the Vyatka District Soviet Command."

---

[18] Kulaks – richer landowner peasants.

The column pulled out with some of the men waving them off, the women waving their colourful scarves and the kids running up and down excitedly shouting, just like the kids in Whitechapel back in 1914. Arthur was back on the lead horse on the front gun. A small group of young women were the last ones along the track. The beautiful black-eyed girl only watched Arthur with her beaming face. He could barely take his own eyes away to carry on. He still wore his Cossack hat.

That evening they had roast capercaillie, foraged mushrooms and Cosssack supplied cabbage traded for some high-smelling venison. Arvo provided a bottle of spirit he'd also procured from the Cossacks. He called it medova; a sweet vodka produced by adding honey.

12. Freedom from 'Custody'.
Early October 1919.

Several days later the guns were delivered to a Bolshevik camp at a town called Murygino on the flood plain of the Vyatka River. The settlement was on some high ground to the north of a large, curved bend looking across marshy wetlands with meandering curves and ox-bow lakes. Located about six miles north west of the city of Vyatka the quickest route into the city was by boat. The Bolshevik gunners had been billeted away from a small army camp occupied by the main Red military force and Soviet administrators. They'd been placed in an abandoned country house set in a couple of acres of formal gardens surrounded by a ten foot wall.

They discovered it was the country estate and summer house of a rich merchant family called Klobukova. The name was engraved on a stone set in the entrance porch. Built on the eastern bank of the River Medyanka flowing in from the north, a tributary of the Vyatka. There was a small inlet and jetty onto the Medyanka from the estate garden.. The grand house had been stripped of anything that could be easily removed, and much that needed tools, carts and organisation. Room doors, chandeliers, lead water pipes, stair bannisters, wooden wall panelling, skirting boards and even some floor boards had been ripped up.

Privakov had been absent for several days whilst his men and the British rested and amused themselves in their country house accommodation. It was good to have a roof and solid walls about them as the weather was now becoming autumnal. It had been raining steadily for a couple of weeks, starting the evening of St. Jonah's feast day. Arvo and his foragers, of which Budgie was now deemed to be a key man, were busy finding, trading and sourcing food from the local camp of revolutionary soldiers nearby and traders from Murygino. They'd been eating well because they were organised, had guns and therefore very persuasive powers when needed.

However, it was now evident that food supply amongst the general population of peasants was a problem. Every day outside of the gates of their mansion a group of women and children collected and pleaded with anyone entering or leaving for food or money. They were country folk, kulaks or subsistence farmers who'd been evicted from their land, either by Bolshevik soldiers or one of the lawless, unanswerable bands of men like Krasnov's.

Budgie was particularly affected by this as he was in and out of the gates more than the others on his fishing trips. Not being able to ignore the pitiable state of some of these people he would leave in the morning with some food to give them, usually last night's leftovers. Every afternoon he would return and leave them the two largest fish in his catch, out of the eight to ten he caught. Arvo noticed this process resulting in them having a shouting match, both descending into curses in Finnish and English and a few mutually understood in Russian. The following morning Budgie failed to assist the Finn in his usual routine. Arvo, looking unusually miserable approached the British men as they were drinking camel milked tea, sitting on wooden boxes in front of a huge open fireplace with a crackling log fire. Speaking in English.

"Budgie, we shouldn't have fought. You were right. I was wrong. We now do this properly. The revolution is to improve the life of the workers and peasants in Russia. Not to see the people starving when the soldiers eat well. We need to share our rations with these people. We are better able to obtain food, so each day in the afternoon we have a soup kitchen. Agreed?"

With his solemn face he looked directly at Budgie, who retained a blank look as he listened.

His face broke and he smiled.

"Agreed".

Arvo's manner changed completely.

"Yes, yes, agreed, agreed. That's it Budgie, that's it. We're a team again. A team. Partners. We drink to that. I get some vodka."

He quickly turned as if to go back to the kitchen stores. Budgie called after him.

"No Arvo, no! We don't drink to that."

"What, we don't drink to that?"

"No we don't. We don't have to drink to everything. How about we sort some bread and cheese for the people now, and then soup later on."

"Good idea Budgie, good idea, we do that now."

The pair of them walked out of the big formal room empty of furniture. Arvo had his giant arm around the shoulder of the smaller Warwickshire man. They were now babbling together in Russian having reformed their partnership. Over the next few days the front gates were opened twice a day to feed the hungry, dispossessed families.

*

It was the 6th October when Privakov returned in the early afternoon, a Monday. His reappearance was by a small motor launch that landed at the Medyanka river inlet jetty. The boat looked like a family pleasure craft for leisure trips with a seating area at the back partly covered in a blue canvas awning. It might even have belonged to the house or another close by. Witnessed by Budgie who was trying to teach Eric some fishing skills at the time, they watched Klechov at the wheel over-shooting the landing spot ..... twice. Privakov, standing in the boat was getting visibly angry until Budgie called for a rope tethered to the prow and pulled it in. As he stepped onto the jetty Privakov cryptically said, with some irritation to Budgie as he strode past.

"Don't let him steer, he's useless." And raced on.

There were numerous items he immediately needed to deal with amongst his own men. An administration office had been set up in what was once a library. Some desks and chairs were obtained as well as a pair of Remington type-writers that produced Cyrillic script and a roller printing machine. The disciplinary list included one man getting extremely drunk and assaulting a young local women. He was found comatose close to the incident by other soldiers in Murygino and returned to the grand house. Within an hour of Privakov's return this man who'd originally been in jail for murdering a women, had been shot. The politico's ruthlessness was back for all to see. An example needed to be made and discipline maintained.

Early afternoon Klechov had been sent out to find the British men. Arthur and Frank were deep into chess games they were playing with two Russians. Neither looked like winning so the interruption was convenient. They assembled with the others, except Budgie who was out with Arvo procuring rations. In his library office two clerks tapped on the typewriters copying out a selection of hand-written notes strewn on the desk.

"Sergeant Englishman, Volly, and my other friends. Our time together is nearly over. I have instructions to transfer the command of my unit to the Kazan Soviet and they will be taken further south. I will return to Moscow and from there, who knows."

He shrugged his shoulders, now not knowing his immediate future. Opening a silver cigarette case they'd not seen before he took out one for himself and as he always did, proffered the case to Arthur who took one. Privakov flicked the box shut and with second thoughts reopened it and passed it to Raybury, pushing his hand pointing at the others.

"Have a cigarette gentlemen."

He lit his and passed the match box to Arthur who then passed it on. They all had matches so Eric placed the box back on the desk behind which the Commissar was standing with his back to them all. He was peering out of the window looking down into the kitchen garden where the shot soldier was still tied to a wooden chair that had been re-erected after falling over from the impact of bullets on the body. He would leave it there as an example to the others. Abruptly turning to face the five men in his office he said.

"The situation is difficult. I am under pressure from the Soviet to hand my prisoners over to them. It is something we cannot resist, they have over two thousand men available in the area. Tomorrow my men transfer to them. As you know they are ex-prisoners. Some may be motivated to fight for the revolution, many will try to return home. You English men are a problem."

It wasn't sounding very encouraging. The gunners were glancing at each other with concerned looks. Privakov was back to contemplating the dead man. Looking out of the widow he then said.

"To be more precise, you men are my problem."

He paused before further elaboration.

"I promised you that I will do my best to secure safe passage for you to get home to England. I intend to keep that pledge."

He now sat back at the desk.

"It starts to get light at around six in the morning. We will be rising at five thirty and moving out at fifteen past six. No breakfast, Arvo will issue some dry rations tonight. I'll be marching with them on foot, now the horses are gone, to the military camp in Murygino to fulfil my orders to transfer the soldiers. But not you. It's the Political Commissars in Vyatka who now want your company. Not being military men they like to start the day later."

He rolled his eyes disdainfully.

"So they have requested I leave you here with a guard. They will send men to collect you later in the morning, but not before eleven. You will notice there are a few hours between us leaving and those lazy bastards arriving. I don't know what their plans are for you,"

Raybury spoke.

"Commissar Privakov, I don't think I quite understand what you're telling us here?"

The question was acknowledged with a nod but left unanswered.

"This afternoon I will prepare some official looking papers that verify who you are with our stamps. Unfortunately your English identity papers are now in the possession of the Vyatka Soviet. Our set will inform Bolshevik officials that you have been released to return home..... if you have a need to use them. I've said before, Vyatka is an important station on the Trans-Siberian railway and trains are moving both west to Moscow and east to ..... well ...... somewhere further east."

A small smile appeared at his inability to provide an eastern city destination.

"I wouldn't recommend heading to Moscow. There are many soldiers in Vyatka from many parts of Russia, in different uniforms and other costumes. Its chaotic right now."

He stood up and started walking toward the door to show them out.

"Okay gentlemen I know you will have many questions that I am presently not able to answer. I have much to do now to prepare for handover tomorrow…….. and your documents of course. So please excuse me."

*

They filed out feeling puzzled by this meeting. They'd been sleeping in two garret rooms on the third floor in the roof space of the house to which they returned. Trying to work out what the Russian was intimating in his explanation of what would be happening the following day. Frank applied his logical brain.

"Let's start with what we do know. One, Privakov's Bolsheviks, this lot, are coming under the command of someone else tomorrow. We don't know who they are, but we're not part of that transfer. We are now political prisoners and are due to be handed over, well, collected by the political administration in Vyatka."

At this moment Budgie came into the room. Raybury briefed him on what had happened before handing back to Frank who started his points again. He then got to the second.

"Two, he confirmed he would provide us with Bolshevik papers. Ours are with the Commissars and we won't get them back. Three, he then was careful to mention precise times and I think this was for a reason. Remember, he restated his commitment to try to help, and he has shown trust in us over the last few months. So these timings were indicating something, perhaps the opportunity to move out ourselves. And finally, four if you like, he mentioned the railway was operating despite all the chaos. "

The other men had listened to Frank's breakdown and were thinking this through when Raybury spoke.

"Thanks Frank. I suppose we can add to that his comment on not to travel west. It seems there may be an opportunity to escape, if that's what we're calling it, depending on what guard arrangements are put in place. With the horses gone with the guns, we'll be on foot too."

Budgie interrupted. "There's a boat."

"A boat? What do you mean?" Asked Raybury.

"You know, something that floats on water. Sometimes small with oars, sometimes big with giant engines. Or even with sails, often on the sea, that kind of thing." Budgie enjoyed his creative answer.

Frank then added with a comment they used often.

"Don't be a bird Budgie. What are you talking about?"

Eric answered the question.

"He's right, there is a boat down on the jetty. Privakov came back on it earlier."

Eric went on to explain the mess Klechov made of landing his only passenger. A lengthy discussion took place about, the size of the launch, whether it would carry the six of them plus their kit, which now only consisted of personal webbing and a small pack with barely a change of uniform. They had their rifles and some rounds of ammunition which had never been removed. Budgie then recalled the odd comment referring to Klechov that Privakov made as he angrily left the jetty, 'Don't let him steer, he's useless.' Perhaps there was something in this too.

They agreed that the four who hadn't seen the launch would take a walk in pairs to view the boat during the afternoon. Budgie said as a teenager he'd spent time driving small motor boats on the river Avon at Warwick Castle ferrying aristocratic guests downstream to Stratford-upon-Avon to visit Shakespeare's birthplace. This one looked similar; he was convinced he'd get it moving.

The big house became an ants nest of activity over the next few hours especially with Arvo's three men which included Budgie. They had adopted a militarily disciplined approach to looking after the food and kit stores which had been instilled in them by the Englishman. So naturally he was involved in counting and packing up the items they had officially been issued way back as part of Dyer's battalion, and unofficially acquired over the last few months. The rest of the Bolsheviks only had their personal kit to take care of. Many of them had swapped issued items with the Cossacks to the extent they hardly looked like a coherent unit. Privakov, with no military background had no hard view on the dress of his men. Uniformity meant little. On the other hand, Raybury had been clear that the British had to maintain their issued uniform as best they could until items became completely unserviceable. For them it created an identifiable cohesive and united unit.

Dinner that evening was a fish stew made with bream, roach, tench and an ugly whiskered catfish; all of which had been hauled out of the Vyatka river by Budgie and others. Eric had contributed the 'beardy beasty' as he called it. Arvo thought it was right that the last meal the British men should have with the White Sea Bolsheviks was as traditional as possible. He did a good job, fish heads included. The Bolsheviks knew the following day the men who'd been vital in assisting them getting the guns to their destination would be taking a different path. The atmosphere was comradely.

Privakov had banned alcohol for his men due to the early start. However he appeared at the garret rooms occupied by the Royal Artillery gunners with a bottle of the honeyed medova vodka sourced from the Cossacks. He issued each man with a set of three small sheets of printed 'papers' written in Cyrillic script which had an array of official looking revolutionary stamps dotted over them and his dated signature at the bottom of each one. The name of each man had been written by hand on the top of each page. Privakov explained that these sheets detailed their identity, their neutrality in relation to the revolutionary cause and that the Bolshevik administration sanctioned their safe passage through controlled territory to enable them to return to England by whatever transport was available.

He sat with them to share the medova and talked about the military conflict taking place all over Russia. He was a political man, an administrator, an organiser, an academic he called himself. Commanding soldiers in war, he couldn't do and now he had to move on himself. He thanked them for their efforts, saying he hoped they felt they'd been treated fairly, with respect and wished them good luck in their onward journey. Strangely, there was no mention of arrangements for Raybury's section for the following day and when a question was raised by Frank, he replied with.

"Abramovich, tomorrow will come and time will pass. I hope you all get home one day."

It told them nothing.

As he was leaving he handed Arthur a small, black, leather bound booklet, saying this was a token of respect to the British men, but he felt Arthur should have it in gratitude for saving his life in the training camp. Privakov, surprisingly, seemed genuinely emotional. Arthur looked at the booklet, saw it was small, typed pages of the unrecognisable script and tucked it into an inside tunic pocket.

There was no real need for the gunners to be ready for anything at reveille for the departing Russians. Based on what they'd been told, they would be under guard until collected by agents of the local Soviet political Commissars. Disregarding this, they were all up and ready for something as early as the Russians. They were professional soldiers; this is what they did. Watching them form up and 'march' off in an undisciplined ragged way from the third floor windows, they caught sight of Budgie talking with Arvo sitting on one of the store wagons, camel reins in hand. The Finn moved them off in the light drizzly rain and the two men, now firm friends, waved their goodbyes. And with that the Bolsheviks were gone.

*

The gunners were busy gathering and packing their loose kit together when Budgie reappeared. He was carrying a hessian sack of extra rations given to him by Arvo. Hard black bread, cans of pickled herring, some apples and carrots. He emptied the sack on the floor and distributed the contents.

"You probably saw they've gone."

"Of course we did Budge, we saw it all from up here." Raybury replied.

"They've all gone. There's no one left. No guards, not a soul."

The others stopped what they were doing. Taffy Davis spoke.

"All of them...... all gone."

"I came back through the big entrance hall, checked the main rooms, passed Privakov's office. No one. Arvo said there was no guard left that he could make out."

Now Raybury. "We need to be cautious. We'll move downstairs to the main door. If a guard of some kind is here, that's where they would logically be."

They hitched on their webbing and small packs, now carrying only essentials, picked up their rifles and descended the stripped wooden floorboards of the double sweeping staircase. They checked the rooms on each floor which had been occupied by the Russians. In some the stench was appalling where they'd been used as latrines. With the lead plumbing pipes missing, some hadn't bothered to use the pits that had been dug outside. The ground floor was checked out too. No-one.

Raybury wanted the basement cleared as well and asked Taffy and Arthur to do so. The door was in the kitchen at the back of the house. It was only a two room storage area and wine cellar, already cleared of all stock before they got there. It was very dark looking down the steep steps, a glimmer of light came in from a coal chute at the far end missing it's wooden lid. Arthur went ahead, Taffy stopped at the top of the steps, speaking in a torrent.

"You're on your own Wally, I can't come down. It's a hole in the ground, too dark. It'll set me off. I can't do it. Confined, dark space underground. You know I can't come down. With all that forest living, I thought I'd be over it by now. But no."

He was breathing deeply, almost panting, trying to contain himself.

"I know Taff....... I know. You stay there. We just need to know there's no one about before we work out what to do. One minute and I'll be done."

It took a minute for his eyes to adjust. Without moving very far from the bottom of the steps he peered into the darkness, it was clear no-one was there.

"Job done Taff. We're all good."

"Thanks mate."

"Those steps wouldn't have stood both our weight anyway."

They laughed it off returning to the others. Strong men, hardened to the horrors of war and death carrying permanent anxieties, memories, emotions and mental anguish with the potential to debilitate at any time. They could only deal with it when it hit them and hope support was there when it did.

Joining Raybury and Frank at the front door, Eric and Budgie were out checking the front gate and were also to pass by the jetty to see if the motor launch was still there. To the shock of the four in the house they could see three men walking back from the river inlet. Frank was first to recognise the third man – Klechov, Privakov's minder.

Eric, spoke as they approached.

"We found him in the launch, sheltering from this cold drizzle. Budgie's had a conversation with him."

"Yeah. He tells me he's been left by Privakov and I've no reason to doubt him. Mainly because of what he said next. We can use the boat to take us down the Medyanka and upstream on the Vyatka into the city. Apparently he and Privakov have already identified a drop off point on a bend on the river, due west of the main station which is about two versts away from the landing spot. The boat trip and walk will take around an hour and a half. I now understand his comment about not letting Klechov steer. Privakov had already worked out our escape route."

Klechov just looked on dumbly with his red Viking beard twitching as he looked from man to man. Just beneath this profusion of hair there was a noticeable toothless grin and now, unexpectedly cheerful eyes.

Budgie continued.

"There's more. Once we've been dropped off, Klechov will bring the boat back to the Bolshevik camp in Murygino, pick Privakov up and carry on downstream to Kazan. It'll take them a couple of days to get there by river. So the boat is also his transport away from here, which is how he managed to keep it. By the time the politicos realise we're not here later on this morning; we should be on a train east, if we can get one, and he'll be on the boat heading west."

It was now a few minutes passed seven. Time was key to this working and already being prepared to move they immediately made their way to the jetty. The blue awning had been clipped from the windscreen to the sides so that it now sealed the seating area at the back of the boat from the persistent light rain. It also shielded those inside from the view of eyes on the river banks; important as they passed the Murygino Bolshevik camp. The Russian rivers were major transportation routes and were carefully monitored by every ruling authority way back from Genghis Khan's Mongol Empire to the new Soviets of today. A useful source of taxes for moving goods and militarily, for moving soldiers.

Boarding the boat as it rocked on the water, they squeezed onto the wooden bench seats as Budgie took the helm. Perhaps comfortable for a family of five or six, not so for seven soldiers laden with equipment, in addition to some floor space taken up with some wooden crates belonging to Privakov.

There were few boats on the river at that early hour. In another month it will be frozen solid through to April forcing movement by any distance onto the rail network or horse-drawn sledges, some even used on the river ice. Being protected by the awning from the vertical rain and the horizontal river water splashing from the prow was a bonus, keeping them dry. One at a time the men donned the U.S. issued oilskin capes they'd already had great service from as the rain continued. The river traversed Vyatka city on the north and created a complete barrier to the east. Despite motoring against the current, the launch made good progress with a powerful engine. The river skirted a wooded area, behind which a rock quarry could be seen and a higher level loading jetty protruded from the south bank fully occupied by several substantial river barges. Just beyond this, a low-level unoccupied pier was indicated by Klechov as the drop off point.

Before each man stepped off the launch Klechov gripped and shook their hand vigorously, his ugly well-worn face peeled into an unforgettably grim smile. Saying a few words to Budgie as the last man off the boat, he indicated with his arm the direction of the train station as told to him by Privakov. He then took over the controls and sped into the mid-river stream nearly colliding with a depth marker-buoy.

Frank spoke. "I don't hold out much hope for Privakov right now. I think his future is more precarious than ours judging by Captain Redbeard there. What was he saying Budgie?"

"He said he thought I was a natural sailor and had never experienced such fine river navigation as that he'd just seen. He added that he was sorry to see such an eminent hero of the of the Bolshevik revolution leaving."

Frank stared at Budgie for several seconds. "Cobblers he did."

"Well maybe not. He said, 'walk that way.' We'll hit the railway line and follow it to the station. He also asked if there was enough fuel in the boat, which I thought there was."

"Mundane then. No useful information."

"No, afraid not."

13. Vyatka railway station.
7th October 1919.

They followed a track to the south of the quarry which led them into an area of single storey, wooden, dwelling huts on the edge of the city. Each one surrounded by a similar sized cultivated plot. Little sign of people, except two old crones talking over a wooden fence, eyeing them suspiciously. Stray town dogs initially barked and then ignored them. The huts grew in size until they became two floors and were made of stone and red bricks. In the distance they could see five black onion domes atop round towers and close to those, something resembling a minaret tower. Passing through a wealthier area, the houses became quite substantial; large, detached town mini-mansions, now all abandoned by their occupiers. The reason became clear at a 'T' junction at the end of the road.

Ominously, another makeshift gallows with half a dozen hanging bodies, two of them women, ran along the path on the side of the street. The few people they saw were either miserable looking tradesmen with their heads down pushing hand-carts laden with tools or taking almost empty horse drawn carts of farm produce to market. They knew the food supply system had become dysfunctional because the queues for the soup supply had increased rapidly over the few days they'd had it operating.

It was about ten minutes to nine when they heard the chugging and whistle of a determined steam engine and spotted the white/grey smoke rising into the falling rain. More people were appearing on the streets, including several groups of armed men walking purposefully, no doubt to perform some important revolutionary duty. The only recognition was a general friendly wave, as they did the same. The gunners noted these other armed men paid little attention to them. They reached the rail track on a bend curving away in both directions. More smoke indicated the station was to the left; crowds had gathered in front of the station building.

It looked chaotic from a distance, becoming more so as they closed in. There were umbrella's held above the heads of some, an indication that these prospective travellers were not of the lowest classes. The noise rose in volume, of men and women shouting, babies crying, hawkers calling out with things to sell. Barefoot, wet, bedraggled children clutched items of fruit or vegetable in each hand offering them for sale. They pushed between five or six loosely formed queues trailing out from a marquee enclosing officials and desks, acting as a barrier to the station entrance. The mass looked respectable, but wet, tired and flustered, as if they'd been trying to get somewhere for some time. With winter looming and temperatures already dropping, most wore winter coats and fur hats. Wherever they were going, the uncertainty of the future told them warm clothes would be needed. Only the smallest children in the queues were not carrying or standing close to a suitcase, canvass bag or trussed up bundle of some description. These people were trying to get away from Vyatka. Refugees with the means to use the rail network if they could in an attempt to escape the political and military conflict sweeping back and forth across their country.

There were numerous armed men strolling about nonchalantly making their presence known. Some of these congregated to the left of the main crowd in front of a smaller tent separated from the larger marquee. The station building, a recently built, classical Palladian style symmetrical design of three floors was about 200 yards long. It was split in the middle by a large portico entrance, topped with a pediment roof covering a forty foot high, arched porch entrance in front of a matching square panelled window. Most striking was the paint work. The building was all smooth white plaster with the exception of the window recesses stretching along the two wings on the first and second floors. These were a light, pastel blue, as was the inside rim of the entrance arch and the painted frieze with a repeated white plaster moulds under the pediment roof. Frank had to comment.

"Ignore the decorative paint, but this looks like the training academy building at Woolwich. A bit shorter in length, and prettier with the baby blue contrasting paintwork."

Raybury responded. "Thanks Frank, really observant of you to notice that right now, but it's not going to help us get into the station and onto a train."

Frank smiled back, "Yes, but it is a lovely looking building Brad."

Raybury tutted and shook his head. It was then that Taffy indicated another wooden frame of strung up bodies to the left of the building, partially concealed by some trees.

The rain was easing, their hooded capes had kept them dry and they could now drop their hoods and put their soft peaked khaki trench caps back on. At the Sergeant's instruction the cap badges and any other identifying insignia had been removed from their tunics. These items could draw unwanted attention in an environment where blending in and anonymity was best. It was already clear from the walk from the river to the station there were different groups of armed militia to the extent that no one could tell who represented what organisation, administrative department or from what part of the country. It was a confusion of multiple languages and dialects coming from the irregularly uniformed soldiers and the marginally more consistently uniformed Russians. Nobody had a general authority, except perhaps the men controlling accessibility to the railway. Acting confidently and with a purpose was key to negotiating such muddle.

Budgie volunteered to practice his Russian and make enquiries at the small tent where the armed groups stood. They'd agreed the best story they had was the truth as to what had actually happened to them. As the only evidence that might confirm anything were the papers written in a script that none of them could read, they couldn't risk what they said being inconsistent with what the papers said.

Frank went with him for support, not that he was likely to add anything. The others sat on a retaining wall of a civic garden near to a dozen or so Asiatic looking men dressed mainly in furs. They exchanged cigarettes and tried to engage, with little success. No-one seemed surprised by this either. Russia was a vast country of many peoples and languages. Incomprehension in these circumstances was common and right now, to the British, advantageous.

Fifteen minutes later the advance party returned with news. Budgie explained.

"The Russians are very proud of their east-west railway, as I've just had the Station Master explain to me at length."

Raybury interrupted. "Spare us the monologue Budge. What's to be done?"

"So I take it you don't want to hear about the great feats of Russian ingenuity and engineering then?"

"No. Get on with it!"

"Okay, okay. The trains are still running in both directions. The city is currently under the loose control of the Bolsheviks, but every day there is violence and shoot-outs between armed groups. It's unclear to the railway men here who is red and white. They insist their job is to keep the trains moving until forced to do otherwise."

He paused and lit a cigarette.

"The small tent at the end here are dealing with political and civic officials as well as Bolsheviks and Russian Army military units supporting them. Most of these people in the three rows near to us here want to go east to Perm, Omsk and perhaps even as far as Vladivostok, the Pacific sea port we need to get to. There are foreigners there apparently, our man said, Japanese and Americans, maybe British too. These places are still under the control of Kolchak and the Whites or foreigners, it changes all the time. He doesn't care as long as the trains are running. Others, in the queues further down are trying to get trains west to Moscow. He said all of them going in either direction were the rich or connected."

Frank said. "Explain what you told me the railman said on seeing your papers."

"Okay. He read them with a sceptical face and kept looking at the pair of us and over here to you lot. He then said the papers were to guarantee each of us safe passage. That we were British nationals, soldiers of the working class and no threat to the Bolshevik cause. Our presence in Russia is at the order of our government over which we had no choice. He then said he might be able to get us on the next train east."

Raybury spoke. "Well that sounds promising."

"There is a 'but' though. There is a Bolshevik Commissar in the station building who will need to stamp the papers. He thinks he can arrange that. And the train itself will be under the control and protection of men from what he called the Slavic Legion. I think these must be the Czechs we heard about in Archangel. They will need to accept us on the train too. A group of armed men might be seen as a threat to them."

Now Frank. "The train is due in at five past ten and due to leave at twenty past. It's now twenty minutes to ten. We need to get through this process to have a chance of boarding."

The six British men approached the 'Officials' tent where armed men stood about in different forms of irregular dress. Budgie did the talking as he and Frank presented their papers for stamping to the Station Master and a minion. He was now sitting behind an ornate dining table which may have been looted from a local town house. Taffy and Raybury next and lastly Eric and Arthur who'd chosen to place his Cossack papakha on his head. One of the armed men, a small, skinny, nervous looking specimen, who appeared to be the most senior barked at Budgie whilst pointing at Arthur whose papers were being perused at the time.

"What's he going on about Budge?" said Arthur avoiding eye contact with the Russian.

"He wants to know if you killed a Cossack to steal his hat?"

"Tell him I won it."

Which Budgie did. The Russian burst out laughing, as did his colleagues close by. The railwaymen at the desk focussed on the documents and finally stamped them.

"If your Russian words stretch to it, tell him I won it wrestling one of their champions, and if he'd like to fight me for it, he's welcome to try."

As Budgie spoke Arthur's gaze rose from the desk-checkers to look straight at the Russian's face and he drew himself up to his full six foot. Arthur wasn't an aggressive man but he knew that the situation they were in required confidence and bravado to get through. The weedy Russian stopped laughing looking back at Arthur. His eyes narrowed a little and a telltale nervous, head-shake tic became apparent as his gun-toting courage drained away.

The Station Master stood up, spoke with Budgie and they all followed him beyond the tent barrier into the station building. The odd, quasi-military uniform he wore was too small, looking stretched over his broad shoulders and several inches too high above his ankles, it had been made for another man, shorter and slimmer. Contrastingly his comically Ruritanian, gold braided, black peaked cap was too big for his head. He told Budgie that the bourgeois managers of the station had been 'moved-on'. He nodded with a chilling grin to the gallows at the side of the station with more hanging bodies, four of them this time, all stripped of their clothes in a final humiliation. He, as a lowly ticket-office clerk had inherited the role and the uniform of the Station Master.

In the more confined space, the noise from people already passed through to get a train was much louder. They crowded in, taking shelter from the rain, umbrella's furled, faces cautiously optimistic. The gunners were led to a side office guarded by another soldier in a conventional Russian army uniform wearing an ushanka hat[19]. The room had a blazing fire in a large grate, a double pedestal desk with a green leather top, a filing tray lay on both sides, one empty, one with a six inch pile of files. The Commissar was leaning back on a matching green leather, Chesterfield style office chair. Incongruous in its ostentation, the chair didn't belong here. His black ankle boots were up on the table poking out from the legs of a black suit. A clerk sat at another desk in the corner typing furiously to record the dictation from his boss who stopped speaking when he saw others were following the new Station Master into the room.

The Commissar's role was to control travel and the movement of people of interest. He looked very much like the civilian administrator he was. A widow's peak forehead of thick, black hair brushed back over his head sat above small piggy eyes squinting over half-moon pince-nez spectacles. Above these were neat greying eyebrows stretching back to his temples. A wide brush moustache underlined a regular nose. His mouth looked pinched with a small tuft at the centre of his bottom lip, hairless either side and a neatly trimmed, pointed goatee beard poked out of his long chin, grey hair flecks visible above his lip and chin. In the stifling warmth of the office, he wore a suit jacket, white shirt and tightly knotted tie. He might have been a funeral director in a previous life.

He removed his feet from the desk and stood up with a puzzled, concerned looking face. He and the Station Master spoke quickly, Budgie was struggling to take it all in, but he managed to get the gist. The Commissar was told who the men were and how they came to be in Vyatka, with papers stamped signed and dated by a Military Commissar

---

[19] Ushanka - A fur hat with ear-flaps. Ushi means ears.

Privakov. Budgie had mentioned that Privakov was now on his way west to Kazan and Moscow. This detail was passed on resulting in raised eyebrows. The Commissar thought Privakov must be a very important man. The conversation continued. Budgie said nothing. He didn't want to alert this gatekeeper that he understood at least some of the exchange. The presence of six armed men in his office was intimidating and persuasive. The dialogue quickly moved to getting them on the next train east. For these local bureaucrats, the quicker this potential problem was moved somewhere else the better. The Russians both agreed and the process of stamping, dating and initialling each man's papers was completed.

To ensure the six men definitely became someone else's problem, the Station Master led them through the crowded concourse. On the wide, already busy platform numerous hawkers were trying to sell small items of food and one enterprising man had a tea urn propped on a rickety hand cart. Arthur and Eric watched a number of people buy some tea for which they produced their own cups, glasses and other receptacles. They had some kopeks[20] acquired over the last few months from paid allowances when in the training camp and Budgie trading on behalf of Arvo and selling some of the fish he caught. Arthur presented his tin mug to be filled with an ominous looking black tea. It was stewed and bitter, but warm and not water. Frank's appreciation of the station architecture was growing as he admired the covered footbridge to take passengers over the lines to a central platform and a third on the far side. This strip of eighteen windows were surrounded by bright turquoise painted panels. The central platform island had a few passengers waiting for the Moscow bound train.

A few minutes after ten a whistle pierced the air and drew attention. A grey plume of coal-smoke could be seen on the steam engine slowing along a vast bend from the opposite direction to which the gunners approached from the river. Decelerating along the track, the carriage windows had watchful, concerned looking faces peering out. Men, women and small children; old and young. A Russian soldier was standing in the cab with the driver and fireman; there were others on the small platform linking the engine to the water tender and between each passenger carriage. Nervous faces on the platform watched diligently to try to identify where they might be able to board. But even if they saw space that carriage would crawl past them to stop further along in front of another lucky family.

As soon as the train came trundling in, the Station Master led the men to the far end of the platform. Every indication was the compartments were already full. There would be scant chance of boarding this train. At the rear of the penultimate carriage another two soldiers in a different, dark

---

[20] Kopek – Russian coin.

grey uniform, and then the compartment looked empty. It was explained to Budgie this section was kept for 'official' passengers travelling from the Bolshevik sector into the non-Bolshevik sector. He'd paused and had to think before he referred to it in this way, as if any other expression might be deemed treasonable or disloyal. These guards were men of the Czech Legion who controlled the line further east beyond Yekaterinburg. From Vyatka to there, territorial control was still disputed. However a general agreement, not followed by some of the rogue revolutionary units, had been reached to manage travellers in order to keep the line running. The Station Master would have to negotiate with the Czech Transport Officer to get them on the train and into the official compartment. He stepped onto the plate and disappeared into the carriage.

An imperial moustachioed face with thick beard appeared at one of the carriage windows. The Station Master, at his shoulder, hands were being raised in gesticulation as unheard words were exchanged. Several minutes later the pair emerged, the Czech soldier spoke in halting, careful English, searching for the right words as he spoke.

"My name is Sedlak, Officer of the Legion. I'm in command of this train as far as Omsk. If we can get that far, maybe further. We have problems on the line. Raiders who wish to kill and steal, Cossacks who don't know or care whose side they fight for and uncooperative Bolsheviks acting independently of their Soviets."

He then exchanged a few words with the Station Master.

Arthur didn't think this man looked like an officer, he looked particularly unmilitary with his whiskers and unkempt, wavy shoulder length fair hair tied in a pony tail at the back. On his right arm of the grey tunic with several undone buttons, was a single, thick, faded yellow inverted chevron on a dark green patch with a red border. He knew that a star or pip and crowns denoted officers in most army's up to the rank of Major. It was unlikely even a junior officer would have this lowly command. Perhaps he meant non-commissioned officer. Sedlak continued pointing at the railwayman and looking directly at Raybury.

"I think you are in charge. Nikitin here tells me you need to go east on this train. Your papers are in order and have been stamped for travel by a Military Commissar, a more important man than these petty bureaucrats here. We have foreign passengers already. I think some English, Polish and French. You can board here and occupy box C in the military carriage at the rear. I will have my men remove their things to make space when we move. We are a little spread and can spare a box."

Raybury thanked the Czech as his men started boarding the train, Frank leading the way. At this section on the platform it was ordered and controlled. Everywhere else there was a disorderly racket from passengers trying to board; women screeching, men shouting angrily, children howling and the Russian soldiers on each boarding plate attempting to keep control and order. All civilian signs of desperation to leave the Bolshevik controlled areas.

The carriage had a corridor along one side with the six compartments, boxes Sedlak had called them, accessible through a door opening into the corridor. They passed F, E and D to reach C. On each side there were three comfortable bench seats covered in a deep blue, well-worn material and above these two sleeping racks. It smelt heavily of tobacco ingrained into the soft seat covers. It was an old first class carriage, now reserved for the Czech Legion soldiers. The Russian soldiers currently occupied a similar one at the other end. Arthur, Frank, Eric and Taffy started moving various items of kit onto the seats nearest the door.

Looking out of the window Frank could see that Raybury and Budgie hadn't boarded the train. They were arguing, which was difficult to understand. All six men were highly experienced, had worked very effectively as a team, respected and liked each other. Brad Raybury as section commander had never had to 'command' as such. He managed by expectation and each of them operated accordingly. Budgie's affability and mood was always relaxed and cooperative. What Frank was seeing seemed heated and disagreeable.

Incredibly most of the people on the platform had been able to board the train, squeezing into whatever space was available. In an understanding of the needs of fellow refugees, passengers already on board were making space. Even so there were several family groups that were now being instructed by the soldier guards to move back onto the broad platform. There were railwaymen, including Nikitin shouting to indicate imminent departure and blowing into pea whistles. Raybury and Budgie could still be seen rowing until the pair of them stretched out their hands which they shook vigorously. Budgie passed the sergeant a small leather pouch and Raybury got on the train. The other man walked along to the compartment window, the top of which could be opened for ventilation. Frank called out.

"What's going on Budge?"

"I'm staying here. I'm not coming back."

The others caught the conversation. Eric shouted above the train whistle.

"Don't be an ass. There's nothing here."

"There's nothing for me in blighty. So no point in trying to get back there."

The train started moving.

"Brad will explain. I've got things to do here. Being a baker at home has no appeal, so I'm staying."

Budgie threw up a sharp salute to the men on the train.

"Good luck fellas."

He now waved his saluting arm in the air as the train moved off and he disappeared out of sight, left behind to his own devices in the middle of Russia on the Vyatka station platform.

*

The Sergeant opened the compartment door, stepped in and slammed it shut.

"I couldn't get him to change his mind. The stupid idiot. He told me the other day he had nothing to go back for, was enjoying the adventure and was thinking about staying. He'd got himself a role working with Arvo and thought he could get away with being from somewhere in Russia with his language."

Taffy interrupted. "Well you have to admit Brad, it was a lot better than any of ours."

"Shut up Taff! Not helpful right now."

Raybury sat down and took out a packet of Russian cigarettes, which were passed around.

Now Arthur. "So what's he planning?"

"He said he'll make his way back to the Bolshevik camp at Murygino and link up with them. The Finn suspected that many of the men in that bunch of criminal 'volunteers' would desert as soon as they got somewhere out of the forest. But Arvo said he would stay with the Bolshevik fighters no matter what. It was him that suggested Budgie might play a part and the thought stuck with him."

Frank said. "Well he's taking a big risk just trying to get back to them. But what we know about Budgie is he's resourceful. If he reckons he can do it he probably will."

Holding up the leather purse Raybury said.

"He told me a few days ago he thought he might stay. Not for the revolutionary politics, but for the action now, and no better alternatives he can think of elsewhere. I said he was talking rubbish."

Raybury took a long, thoughtful drag on the smoke.

"He gave me this. It's some money he'd made on selling the fish he caught and the trading he and Arvo did. We might need it and he can make some more if he needs to. There's a letter in there for his parents when we get back. How the hell I account for this to the army, I don't know"

Frank offered. "I'd suggest 'missing in action' Brad. It seems the best description to me."

"Thanks Frank. Missing in action it is then."

14.   Czech Mates – The Trans-Siberian Railway.
October 1919

The ethnic complexity and imperial politics of Eastern Europe in the late 19th and early 20th century's had resulted in numerous local and broader wars and had been the catalyst for the recent global conflagration. Destabilising factors included the decline of the Ottoman Empire, increasing nationalist movements demanding independence within the multiple states controlled by the Austro-Hungarian Empire, the Balkan wars of 1912-13 leading to the almost complete removal of Ottoman control in Europe and the broader pan-European alliance network of the major powers. These led to changing allegiances and control over the panoply of ethnic groups scattered across South East Europe and Western Asia.

Further complication was added by the incredible patchwork of ethnic settlement across the region. German speakers could be found as far east as Saratov on the Volga, as well as in the Ukraine, Poland, Hungary and Rumania. Czechs, Slovaks, Slovene's, Bosnians, Serbs and Croats and large Jewish populations were dotted about in an interwoven patchwork with other ethnic groups across the region.

Within the Austro-Hungarian Empire, Czech and Slovak nationalists under the leadership of Tomas Masaryk pushed for their own nation state after the outbreak of the war. They formed the Czechoslovak Legion to fight on the side of the Allied Powers against their current rulers in the hope of getting support for independence. The Legion grew to over 100,000 men fighting in Russia, France, Italy and Serbia. These units were strengthened by other deserters from the Austro-Hungarian armies and released prisoners of war held in Russia. The majority were Czechs, with 7% of the force in Russia being Slovaks.

After the revolution, with the collapse of the Russian army and before the Brest-Litovsk peace treaty with Germany and allies, the Legion were given permission by the Bolsheviks to travel east to Vladivostok for embarkation to France. Most of Russia's European ports were still blockaded by Germany and the Axis Powers preventing shorter routes to the west. To force their peace terms onto the Russians the Germans launched Operation Faustschlag (Fist Strike) on the 18th February 1918. The Legion fought successfully with the Russians at the Battle of Bakhmach in the Ukraine, the Germans trying to prevent their evacuation east. However, continued distrust existed between the Bolsheviks and the Czech negotiators led by Masaryk, who ordered the Legion to remain neutral in the Russian civil war.

Attempts by the Bolsheviks to disarm the Legion's soldiers failed resulting in sporadic fighting along the length of the Trans-Siberian Railway as the Czechs stretched out on their move east. In July 1918 Vladivostok was under Legion control and declared an Allied protectorate. They controlled much of the railway but morale was falling for lack of Allied support and increasing Bolshevik military strength and organisation. Despite control of towns and cities along the line in central Russia and Siberia and the track itself being unclear, trains continued to run, sometimes to a loose timetable, mostly not. From Vyatka there were many refugees travelling east as well as trains completely commandeered by Bolshevik units for as far as they had some territorial control.

*

The gunners boarded the Czech train on the 7th October 1919. Over the next two weeks the soldiers fell into a routine of cautious cooperation. The Bolsheviks, about a dozen of them, occupied a carriage at the front, the Czechs and now British at the rear. They would patrol the whole length in pairs to ensure calm was maintained amongst the passengers and to show an armed presence. The reality was the people on board were refugees fleeing whatever it was that frightened them so much to force them to leave their homes. Everything they knew and owned was left behind as they headed into an unstable, unpredictable future. The passengers were mainly families, sometimes three generations with a mother, grandparents and young children.

Men of fighting age were absent, either conscripted into the White Russian army, press-ganged into the growing Bolshevik forces or hiding. In this environment serious trouble was unlikely on the train; disagreements were generally over space and sometimes food and water in the crowded, second and third class carriages without compartments. People had had to bring their own food with them or they could buy provisions from the platform and trackside hawkers that appeared at every official and unofficial stop along the way.

The mainly single line track from Vyatka to Omsk to connect with the main track of the Trans-Siberian railway was over 1,100 miles long. Plans to upgrade the line creating several east-west branches incorporating the other important cities of Nizhny Novgorod, Yaroslavi, Kazan, Perm and Yekaterinberg had been postponed in 1914 leaving a series of impressive stations along the route serving an inadequate track system. Passing loops and sidings enabled the locomotives to pull over allowing priority trains heading west to continue without delay. These stops were numerous; a train of civilian refugees was low on the list of transport importance. The loop stops were useful for taking on more coal and water and attracted the sellers of food items and drinking water.

As they left Vyatka, Sedlak spoke with his peer in the Bolshevik guards, a man called Bulavin, to explain the situation with the new armed men who'd boarded. The Russian rarely left his carriage, was drunk most of the time and had been in a stupor during the stop. He had no interest as the British men would be continuing with Sedlak once they reached the limit of Bolshevik control, therefore it was his problem to deal with. The Czech asked Raybury for his men to support the Czech military guard on the train. This made sense given the depth of professional experience the gunners had, that they were armed and that their interests were aligned in getting the train outside of the zone predominantly controlled by the Bolsheviks.

Marek Sedlak was in his mid-thirties, originally from Prague, the capital of the Austro-Hungarian province of Czechia. The British thought they understood a little of the Czech Legion and their desire for independence, but to confuse matters, and in truth to amuse himself, Sedlak only ever referred to himself and his men as Bohemians. Frank tried to get some clarity and was told through a smiling whiskered face and kindly, blue, twinkling eyes that the newly declared Czechoslovakian state included many Slovaks, Silesians, Moravians, Hungarians and an awful lot of Germans. Bohemians were the smart, cultured, artistic people from the beating heart of Europe that somehow had to build a country from this collection of 'others'. This was said in such a way as to be clear to Frank that Sedlak was toying with him.

From a professional family of Lawyers and Doctors, at a young age Sedlak discovered he could draw and paint quite well and decided he would be an artist. This was rejected as nonsense by his parents, the choice being the law or medicine. He was enrolled at the prestigious Imperial-Royal Real Gymnasium where he tolerated the strict academic regime and continued to draw. At the age of 16 he left home and travelled to Munich, surviving by drawing and selling caricatures of tourists. His feet took him further west to Zurich and then Paris where he spent several years before crossing to London. Always drawing pictures and when really hungry he would get kitchen porter's jobs where he was paid a few coins and what he could eat. Brussels, Amsterdam and Berlin were covered on the route back and after many years and now in his late twenties he got back to Prague in July 1914. At this point in his story he'd shrug his shoulders and say that his 'timing could have been better.' He'd missed his national service in the Austro-Hungarian army, was immediately conscripted and by Christmas 1914 he was on the front as a stretcher bearer. 'So it was medicine after all', he quipped.

After several near-death misses, he was taken prisoner and ended up in a camp with many other Bohemians who the Russians knew were against the Axis powers. The Czech Legion had been created by many with similar stories. Sedlak was not a soldier. He was very likeable and understanding of the people he now felt responsible for. He was committed in his own mind to doing everything he could to get his train and it's passengers to safety. Raybury and the British men quickly realised they had an ally in Sedlak who they needed to support in his unwanted role.

*

There were two elements to the military presence on the train. The first was to be seen by the passengers in a policing role to maintain civility. Whilst patrolling the carriages in pairs, there would be constant attempts to engage with the British men from more forthright and vocal travellers. But the lack of Russian language skills prevented much dialogue. Frank and Eric had discovered a medical doctor who appeared to be in his 70's. This man had some English. He'd seen the gunners and heard them talking to each other.

One afternoon he stood from the wooden bench seat he was sharing with two young children and an elderly lady who turned out to be his sister-in-law. She had a black scarf tightly wrapped around her head which also covered much of her face. The two children, both girls were similarly scarved, theirs were red and yellow. They were sat by the carriage window when the doctor sidled up to Frank and spoke quietly as his eyes darted fearfully from one end of the carriage to the other.

"Doctor sir, I'm a doctor...... was a doctor. My name is Kazimir Malevich. I understand you men are English. You are escorting this train."

"We just happen to on this train travelling in the same direction. You speak English?"

"Small English. A bit."

"There are many different languages here. Sounding similar but different. You're the first English speaker."

"It's true, different talking from the lands of Poland, Ukraine and there are Volga German's. Tartar and Turkic tongues too from the south and the Caucasus. There are others who speak English, you just don't know them yet. My family are originally from Poland, but we lived in Kursk. I moved there to help look after the workers at my brother's sugar factories when they fell ill. He died many years ago, but I stayed to help bring up his nine children. He named his eldest son after me, so I was obliged, but of course I love them dearly. This is my brother's wife, a daughter and her youngest girls."

He explained that he and many others on the train were petrified at being identified by the Bolsheviks as professionals, members of the bourgeoisie, middle class and therefore enemies of the people and the revolution. At the moment the soldiers were focussed on winning the war against the Tsarist aristocrats, Nationalist Whites and foreign interventionists. It meant there were opportunities for people to flee if they had the means to do so. Paradoxically, this made them identifiable potential targets anyway.

Frank realised this man was well informed and had put his trust in the British soldiers. Close by there was another small family group watching carefully and whispering to each other in barely audible tones of what could have been German. An elderly lady, her head also scarf-covered with loose strands of grey hair curling out of the sides and clear blue Nordic eyes. With here were two younger women who looked to be in their late twenties and a boy of about six or seven tightly clutching a canvas satchel.

The doctor continued to speak. "I need to tell you that some of the children have spots, including my two grand-daughters here."

"Spots?"

Frank looked over to the two girls and the small red spots could be seen on their faces. One of them was scratching her cheek and her mother took her hand to place it back into her lap. She gave Frank a nervous look.

Eric added. "Sure enough, they've got spots."

"Thank Aims, I can see that now I'm looking." And then to the doctor.

"What is it, do you know?"

"Ospa, vetryanaya ospa. Spots, I don't know English for."

"Measles?"

"Not measles. Ospa, ospa, spots."

Frank and Eric looked at each puzzled. Then a soft, cultured and unmistakably English women's voice piped up.

"Chicken pox, its chicken pox."

The two gunners turned to stare at the women, their mouths slightly open with the shock of the familiar female tongue. She had an engaging smile on her face having enjoyed the linguistic ambush. Her blue-green eyes showed relief at speaking to the British soldiers, at making herself known as a fellow national.

"Close your mouths chaps, you look like fairground goldfish."

The mouths clamped shut.

"The children have chicken pox. Our boy here has it too and there are several more in this carriage. It will likely spread amongst the children; most adults will have had it when young themselves. I expect you both will have had it. In this environment, there's not much you can do to stop it spreading. I think the doctor will agree."

"The lady is right. You call it chicken pox. Its common here with children and less serious for them, as you know."

Neither man did know, but they nodded in their ignorance of the medical science. Eric spoke.

"So what do you suggest doc? If it can't be stopped and it's not so serious to threaten life, should we do anything?"

"You may be able to reduce the infection rate by placing those with it in the same carriage. This would mean a major effort at one of the stops. Unloading the train of all passengers. This will be resisted by many. Then searching for the infected; people will think this is sinister too and try to avoid close inspection. Who would do it? I would be reluctant myself, as I've already said, doctors are vulnerable to Bolshevik ideology. And finally the other soldiers from both ends of the train may not cooperate."

Frank and Eric listened carefully to Dr. Malevich as he went through his list of options to act or do nothing. When he finished Frank said he'd be reporting the conversation back to Sergeant Raybury and the Czechs in order to decide.

"With the very limited resources we have, the best thing we can do is make sure that anyone infected has access to water. Spots, sorry, pox can affect the throat and mouth. Swallowing is difficult, water important."

The doctor's words were passed back to Raybury and Sedlak, including an appeal not to be approached, which might draw attention. They decided to inform the Bolsheviks that the British soldiers had recognised the virus and what it meant. It would be unpleasant and uncomfortable for the children and possibly adults who contracted it. At the next official or unofficial stop to take on water, the Czechs would collect a central supply of drinking water in addition to that obtained by the individual passengers. They would organise the distribution of this to chicken pox patients. They agreed creating a quarantine carriage would achieve little and cause significant disruption. Sedlak also thought moving the doctor and his family to a compartment in the Czech carriage would protect him; his medical knowledge might be useful in the future.

*

The dialogue with Malevich revealed the presence of the Englishwomen and her incredible story was told to Arthur and Taffy on their next train patrol. Her name was Amelia Redron and she came from a sleepy rural village of Iden in East Sussex. With pride she boasted it was listed in the Domesday Book and close to the ancient Cinque port of Rye. Little had happened in Iden since the Norman 1086 censor catalogued the *'one villager and 7 cottagers with ploughlands and meadows with an annual value to the Landlord, Robert, Count of Eu of 1 pound and 10 shillings'.*

Amelia then got weepy as she described her village wistfully and poetically as a place almost lost in antiquity, approached by sunken, hedge-lined lanes, hiding ploughed fields and apple orchards. Old village churches and oast-houses dotted the landscape. Just a few miles from the old port of Rye, Romney Marsh and the sea, you could taste salt in the air and the marsh sheep mutton. An idyllic place to grow up, living in the Victorian gothic vicarage of Iden Park. The youngest of six children, the only girl, of the vicar, the third son of a Baronet. Her brothers all went to Cambridge, three had been killed in the war, officers in the Grenadier Guards. She had been educated at home by her parents and their many academic friends, and of course the boys when they were about.

As a child Amelia had become intrigued by the name of a nearby village, 'Rye Foreign'. Learning it was so-called because the area remained in the control of a French Abbey in Normandy by a careless English Henry; she couldn't recall which one. She thought to go there she had to speak Franch. By the age of seven she was fluent, the intellectual family regularly speaking the language at home to encourage her. Learning Latin as a matter of course, Italian was a breeze. German and Flemish needed a Governess, the inspirational Fraulein Haas from Aachen who lived with the family for four years. She picked up some Romani and Cockney rhyming slang from the apple pickers who turned up annually in late September. The stairs were 'apples', feet were 'plates', 'whistles' were suits, five pound notes were 'ladies'. [21]

She told the soldiers that in 1912, shortly after her 21st birthday she left home for Paris, employed as a Governess herself by Baron Edouard de Rothschild to his three year old son Guy. Guy's older brother, also called Edouard had died of appendicitis the year before, the tragedy leaving a sense of sadness in the family. The parents paid little attention to Guy and his younger sisters leaving Amelia free to educate the young boy "in the English style", as her role specified, admitting with an easy laugh she had no idea what this was.

When the war started and with Paris threatened, the family retreated to their vineyards in Bordeaux. Amelia's linguistic ambition was now Russian. Her apparent skills and dedication to Guy had been noted by a visitor to the family home, the Countess Marguerite von Toll, a German noblewomen and wife of the Russian Ambassador to Paris, Count Alexander Izvolsky. The Count was the instigator of the Anglo-Russian Convention of 1907 leading to the Triple Entente with France, the diplomatic basis for the war alliance. The Countess's Russian was poor and

---

[21] Apples and pears – stairs. Plates of meat – feet. Whistle and flute – suit.
Lady Godiva's -fivers

teased Amelia gently in Baltic German that no Englishwomen could master the language. Rising to the challenge, the Ambassador's connections found her a role in Moscow with a family called Rappoport.

Three generations of the family lived in an elegant, but not ostentatious town house in the centre of Moscow. Originally from rural Lithuania, the grandfather, Julius had become a highly skilled jeweller. Initially based in Petrograd he moved his workshop to become one of Carl Faberge's 'work master's'; independent workshops producing jewellery, works of art, ornaments and silver for the famous House of Faberge. They would produce commissioned works and create their own designs sold under the Faberge label, as well as their own.

Amelia was now travelling with the Jeweller's elderly wife, daughter and grandson, Isak who she'd been employed to teach English, French and German. Julius had been taken away by the Bolsheviks in December 1917 and they thought he was dead. Many people with links to the Tsar and aristocracy had been arrested and summarily shot. Isak's father, Mikhail was in London where attempts to arrange safe passage for his family through the chaos of Europe had failed. Their only option was now by train to the east.

With her happy demeanour, smiling face and dusty blonde locks, Amelia had the remarkably confident manner of a very smart women who was used to succeeding in everything and getting her way. With her numerous European languages, there were few barriers to communication or misunderstanding when she engaged in conversation. She explained that using her Englishness and bluff in an argument to be allowed on the train; she'd made up quotes from a supposed Lenin proclamation that announced the neutrality of British and French citizens. Her documents were British, those of the Rappoport family with her were faked French papers acquired in Moscow. The matriarch was Irena, her daughter Simona.

As she finished the tale she went on to say some of the Bolshevik guards were becoming increasingly threatening to the passengers, sometimes drunk and searching bags for money and other items. In particular this was happening at night when the carriage door guards changed rota. In her direct forthright way she asked for, and expected additional protection from the British soldiers explaining it was their duty to protect British citizens. Or better still they could move closer to the rear of the train where the Czech and British soldiers were.

The conditions of the train deteriorated as it haltingly made its way over the 530 miles from Vyatka to Yekaterinberg. Each of the third class carriages had only one toilet, a bucket shaped bowl set in a flat steel frame which became the seat. A manual lever opened a flap to drop the contents onto the track, the rushing air below creating a difference in pressure to extract the waste. That was the theory anyway. They were only supposed to be used when the train was moving, not always possible with multiple stops. Men took to urinating from the open connecting platforms between the carriages and when water was available, some more practical women made efforts to keep the facilities clean.

With little to do on the train, an inability to sleep properly when sat cramped together on the hard wooden benches, the stress of the Bolshevik soldiers acting unpredictably and exerting their power on the vulnerable civilians and the stress of uncertainty for the future, many of the passengers were irritable. An insignificant incident could trigger disagreements that had potential for, but rarely did erupt into violence. In most carriages wise heads of older men and women would intervene to keep the peace thereby containing the volatility. The three nationalities of soldiers might be called on to arbitrate in disputes. The Bolsheviks would respond with threats. The others acted to restore calm where they could, pointing out that the train was only moving and taking passengers at the good grace of the controlling authorities, which at this point were the Bolsheviks.

15.   Comrade Krupskaya.
22nd October 1919.

The train had been travelling for two weeks with numerous stops in siding loops to take on water and coal for the engine. In that time they'd covered about 400 miles with another 100 or so to reach Yekaterinberg. They'd been held overnight in a small town called Shalya and the following day, the 22nd of October, they trundled slowly to a settlement called Sarga Capra a few miles further on, pulling into sidings. There was no station here, only a signalman's box directing the traffic. Once the train had stopped, the signalman appeared to let the driver know he had telegraph instructions to hold all east bound trains until further notice. The news quickly spread causing a barely repressed panic amongst the civilian passengers.

There was nothing that could be done by the Czech soldiers or the train crew. Sedlak approached Bulavin, the Bolshevik commander with a request to investigate, who having run out of vodka, and needing more, did so. Taking the signalman back to his box-tower, he emerged an hour later with news that they would be held here for at least 24 hours to allow some troop trains and a 'Political Transport' through. It was unclear what the latter meant. Despite the small size of this very rural village, locals had already appeared with items of mainly fresh food, fruit, vegetables, eggs and river fish, being offered for sale up to the carriage windows. With knowledge of the minimum delay period, Bulavin and Sedlak agreed the passengers could leave the train.

Initially many were reluctant to do so. Sgt. Raybury indicated to Amelia and Dr. Malevich this was the opportunity to move compartments to which Sedlak had agreed. They led the way off the train and others followed onto the scrubby ground surrounding the loop, the coal chute and water tower used to replenish fuel for the engine. Most of the village was to the west of the track. To the east, trees encroached, beyond which could be see the small River Sarga. The temperature in the middle of the day was a few degrees above freezing and would be plunging at night. For the journey so far no-one, apart from the soldiers had been able to walk any more than a few feet from where they had space on the train. Just being able to walk about was a relief, the bodily movement providing some warmth under the winter coats these people had had the forethought to pack.

The military experience of the five British men now took precedence. They stood together watching more passengers stepping down from the carriages when Frank spoke to no-one in particular.

"This is already chaotic and will only get worse. We need some organisation."

Raybury thought out-loud.

"You're right Frank, this could be a mess if we don't sort it."

Sedlak was walking towards the group with two of his men. He'd reached the same conclusion, but his lack of organisational skills left him without a place to start. Raybury sent him to get Bulavin who he knew would be equally clue-less. With the other gunners he planned a number of actions he then shared with the Czech and Russian commanders.

1. When close to the train, passengers would need to remain on ground adjacent to the carriage they were travelling in. Unless directed otherwise.

2. They could exercise away from the from the train between the track and the river.

3. Passenger working groups would be organised to collect firewood, needed to generate heat for warmth or to cook if they had the means to do so.

4. Hygiene was becoming a problem. So, soldiers would dig latrines a short way into the trees. One for men, another women and children, this one shielded by cut down fir tree branches for some privacy. Although external toilet facilities might be distasteful for many of these bourgeois women, the train toilets would be closed.

5. A group of passengers would be selected to go right through the train washing out all the toilets using water collected from the river. Those chosen to do this were the troublemakers that all the soldiers knew. Hopefully it would encourage them to be more cooperative in future.

6. Clean water would be accessed to replenish drinking supplies. The village was likely to have a number of wells.

With the three commanders in agreement the British dealt with the latrines believing the risk to passenger and soldier health was high if this were neglected. The Bolsheviks the wood collection, the Czechs the water and also took responsibility for a light-handed supervision of passengers around the train. Some simple things that would make a difference for the short period they'd be there.

The night was extremely cold, the fires burnt strongly providing warmth and comfort close to them. Most passengers returned to their wooden benches and train floor to get some sleep as the flames died down in the late evening. It had been unusually dry for this time of year and the rain still kept away. In the evening, where people had obtained some fresh food and means to cook, it had become communal, with crackling flames burning unseasoned wood. There had even been singing of traditional songs and an old man produced a battered violin that he played sad, lamenting tunes on.

*

Around 8.15am., shortly after the sun rose on the eastern horizon a train full of Bolshevik soldiers travelling toward the sun passed along the track. Seeing the giant locomotive engine with its oversized hopper-shaped chimney followed by twelve packed carriages created a silence amongst the refugees. Another went through 20 minutes later. These first trains sped away and disappeared into the dense woodland enclosing the track a few hundred yards beyond the siding loop joining the main route.

Concerned tension rose as the passengers speculated on what they were seeing. It got worse when a third troop train drew to a halt just beyond the loop exit point. After ten minutes or so the soldiers started alighting to form up in squads along the trackside under the shouts of NCO's and Officers. The sky had clouded over, leaving a blanket of grey and a light drizzle dampened faces. Another engine could be heard in the distance, the reducing chugging sound indicating it was slowing down. It eventually stopped on the track, parallel to the refugee train on the loop, a gap of 200 yards between the two.

This last was nothing like the first three. Only four carriages long, it was gaudily decorated in caricatures, men in uniforms, idyllic scenes of fat-faced, rosy-cheeked children and peasants dancing and scything flush fields of corn. There were wooden carts being towed laden with root vegetables of impossibly bright colours and gangs of workers striding purposefully toward factory gates and mine-shaft lifting towers. These were pictures of the post revolution society the Bolsheviks were planning and promising for the people of the Russian Empire. This train was designed to carry the message across the mountains, steppes and frozen wastes to these people.

Arthur and Taffy Davis were standing with Dr. Malevich when the train stopped. Painted on the side of one carriage in Cyrillic script were words the Doctor translated without being prompted.

"The bourgeois owners of the theatres poisoned the spirits and minds of the people. Now the theatre belongs to the people."

Malevich started chuckling as he read another message.

"Working people of Soviet Russia, brush your teeth daily, learn to read and write and take precautions against French pox."

Taffy spoke.

"They have a way with words these Bollys! I guess it's not chicken pox they're referring to here. So Doc, do you think they've stopped to put on a show for us and the trainload of ruthless soldiers down the track there?"

Malevich looked at the Welshman with piercing serious eyes not understanding the attempt at lightening the situation. Arthur saw that men and possibly women, it was difficult to tell with their winter coats and hats, were stepping down from the painted train, most of them carrying a brass instrument.

"Well it looks like their planning some sort of entertainment."

The Doctor shook his head.

"It's unlikely to be a benign theatre production. No such thing exists in Russia now, even less likely at a remote forest siding in the middle of the country."

Arthur responded.

"Come on Taff, let's see if Brad knows anything."

Raybury had spoken with Sedlak and Bulavin. The Russian agreed to approach the painted train, as he did so the band started playing some stirring martial marching music. The Bolshevik soldiers began marching back to the scrubland between the main track and loop where the two stationery trains now were. One of the painted wagons, a cattle truck, had the doors slid open by non-uniformed men in black tunics, Party officials. They started unloading bundles of pamphlets tied together with string. The soldiers were brought to a halt to parade in front of the open cattle wagon. At the parted door opening a trestle table was erected and draped in a red cloth with a yellow hammer and sickle facing the soldiers.

It was a senior political Commissar from Moscow that Bulavin spoke to who explained the train was part of a Soviet information initiative delivering the revolutionary message to the people of Russia. The soldiers were compelled to listen to the speech as were the passengers of Bulavin's train. On hearing these people were refugees, the Commissar would consult as to whether they would be allowed to continue their journey east. He was then told that trains were moving in both directions with the approval of the local Soviets through which the Trans-Siberian railway and its feeder lines, including this one from Vyatka and Perm. Regardless of that decision the civilians would also need to assemble behind the Bolshevik soldiers. Even Bulavin recognised the difficulties trying to stop his transport would create, not least with British men on board. Without mentioning this, Bulavin used the painted message to make a point. Nodding toward the 'teeth brushing' lines he said.

"This train carries pox."

At which the Commissar became very attentive.

"Pox?"

"Yes, pox."

"What kind of pox?"

"Do I look like a medical doctor?"

The Commissar eyed him suspiciously. He was an urban left wing intellectual from Petrograd with close connections to the Bolshevik leadership. He was struggling to comprehend a conversation about pox on a train in the middle of the forest miles from his view of civilisation and socialist revolution.

He became abrupt and disdainful.

"Whatever pox it is, those people will listen to Comrade Krupskaya. You will organise them to attend Mr...... train-man. They will assemble twenty paces behind the soldiers. Far enough to keep your pox away. All of them, men, women and children. The old and infirm too, all of them. And after we've gone, you take your diseased people east as far as you can get. We don't want them in Soviet Russia. Twenty minutes the speech starts. Go and do it."

"Of course."

Bulavin returned to convey the message to Sedlak, Raybury and the others. They would need to listen to the Comrade, whoever he was, and then be on their way. The soldiers dispersed to round up the passengers. A line was marked in the dirt behind which they had to stand and wait. The brass band played and stopped, a group of two men and three women sang some revolutionary songs, some light rain feathered the faces of the waiting audience. The Commissar appeared on the makeshift stage platform looking out from the cattle wagon door at the expectant faces of the soldiers and refugees. He started speaking, projecting his voice out to the people. Arthur and the others stood behind the civilians, amongst the Czech soldiers, not wanting to draw attention to their presence. Having no idea of what was being said, they observed the parade of Bolshevik soldiers in front of them, responding with unenthusiastic cheers and claps at the appropriate times.

This sermon seemed to be ending after about 15 minutes. He was the warm up act. There was some movement in the dark depths of the wagon as some figures shuffled about and he made an introduction, lifting his right arm to welcome Comrade Krupskaya forward to the covered table. The soldiers clapped and cheered. There was a rustle of polite clapping amongst the refugees. Playing an involuntary part to the event, their middle class courtesy trumping their distaste at the proceedings. Unexpectedly, a tall women stepped forward, the Bolshevik soldiers enthusiasm increased, the British men were baffled.

"What's this all about Frank?" Arthur asked.

"Who knows? Whoever this woman is, the crowd appear to know and like her. Well maybe not 'like'. She's obviously someone though." He added with fake sincerity, "let's see what she's got to say, shall we?"

"You're expecting her to speak English then?"

Frank shrugged and smiled. She launched into her speech, starting slowly, with a well-pitched voice that carried across the assembled crowd.

Dressed in a light-grey coat, her head was uncovered revealing a chubby, round, serious face with fair to greying hair and concentrating, slightly bulging eyes. Much to Arthur's disappointment, but not surprise, it wasn't in English. So they listened to her speak with obvious conviction, emotion and wildly gesticulating arms, not having a clue as to what she was saying. This went on for about half an hour whilst the audience stamped their feet to keep the blood moving. Fortunately the drizzle eased off. The speech finished with enthusiastic cheering from the corralled soldiers.

On finishing Krupskaya moved back into the dark and could then be seen with the Commissar stepping from an end door onto a connecting link and into one of the painted carriages. The small group of aides around the table quickly cleared it away and the cattle wagon door slid shut. The regiment of soldiers were marched back to their train and the band struck up some more stirring military marching music. It was all a bit puzzling to the British and many of the Czechs who walked back discussing the events with their heads shaking. When loaded, the military train pulled away followed by the brightly painted 'Soviet Information Initiative' transport carrying the formidable Comrade Krupskaya, whoever she was.

The refugees re-assembled close to their carriages with a hum of intense conversation. The British men headed toward their compartment at the end of the train where the Czechs were heating water for tea over an open fire. This was mainly for the passengers with whom they increasingly felt a communal spirit. Dr. Malevich's family group and Amelia's were also close by having been allocated their own compartment 'box' in the Czech carriage. Recognised as useful for the Doctor's medical skills, Amelia's languages and for added protection of a British citizen. Sgt. Raybury was talking to Amelia and they both strode toward the other gunners.

"Sergeant Raybury tells me there's a bit of confusion over what we've just seen."

The men nodded and agreed. Amelia explained.

"Comrade Krupskaya, Nadezhda Krupskaya?......... The name is unknown to you? .... Mrs Lenin? That's who you've just seen preaching the revolution. Wife of the leader of the Bolsheviks and the revolution. Now you can see why the soldiers listened attentively and it made sense for us to do the same."

Frank asked the question they all had.

"What's she doing out here rallying fighters who already seem committed to the cause?"

"She's been part of the revolutionary cause for many years and supports everything the Bolsheviks do. She spoke a little about the need for complete political change in society, but most of it was on transforming the education of the Russian people. She said she works for the People's Commissar for Education. Krupskaya is a powerful women. She's been married to Lenin for over twenty years. What she said was probably not very important for the soldiers. I think she'll take any opportunity to get her message across, and in this country there are many poorly educated children. So I think it's a good thing."

Frank replied. "What, the revolution?"

Amelia tutted with raised eyebrows and a telling-off finger wagging at him.

"Education Frank, education. All children should be able to read and write. That's what Mrs. Lenin is saying, and I believe that too."

Her face then broke into an amiable smile and she theatrically flounced off to rejoin the Rappoports.

Arthur spoke. "I think she likes you Frank."

"Bugger off Wally!"

Wholly uncharacteristic of Frank to swear, and defensively so. Arthur thought the feelings might be mutual.

16. Onwards from Omsk.
November 1919.

The presence of Comrade Krupskaya heading east was evidence of the increasing progress and confidence the Red Army had developed through 1919. By November the Siberian White Russian armies under the command of Admiral Kolchak were in retreat. Shortly after the VIP 'Information' train moved off the signalman was able to allow the refugee train from the siding loop to continue its journey. This had the surprisingly beneficial effect of a clear run over the next hundred or so miles toward Yekaterinburg where they formed a peculiar three train convoy. The military transport, Krupskaya's propaganda carriages and the desperate civilians fleeing east in their slipstream.

For different reasons there were few delays on the next long leg of almost 600 miles to the important city of Omsk which they reached mid-morning on the 7th November. Initially they still followed the Bolshevik soldiers which eventually stopped at Tyumen, as the Czech train did, to refuel with coal and refill the water tank. The Bolshevik soldiers detrained and were replaced by one of the last platoons of Czech soldiers cooperating with the Bolsheviks to protect the working of the line west of Omsk.

The Russian engine driver and fireman disappeared too. They were concerned about their own safety and had been clear they would refuse to continue the journey beyond Tyumen. To get them this far Sedlak had to bribe them with roubles supplied to him by the Legion and he'd now run out. One of the new Czech soldiers had been a train fireman in Vienna before the war and claimed he knew enough to drive the locomotive. He said the firemen's job could be done by anyone who could lift a shovel. What they didn't know was that Krupskaya's Moscow Commissar had communicated ahead that a civilian "plague" train was to be given a clear pathway. The train was identified by its number, IRS850-5761, and as this passed through each signal box or junction the information was forwarded to the next box.

The small contingent of British soldiers on board this particular refugee train were now swept up in the chaos of many thousands fleeing east to escape the advances of the Red Army. When they arrived, the garishly turquoise coloured art-nouveau station at Omsk was crowded with people desperate to get away from the city. It was known that within days it would fall into the hands of the Bolsheviks. On two designated platforms, a more orderly evacuation of White Russian Siberian Army troops, and others was being organised. In the preceding weeks, as the Reds advanced, regiments from the 15th Siberian and 11th Ural Divisions had mutinied and shot officers who refused to transfer loyalty to the Bolsheviks.

*

The train had been at Omsk station for a couple of hours, the refugees trading for provisions where people could. Sedlak and his colleagues were engaged with a Czech Legion quartermaster and were able to acquire extra tinned food and a substantial amount of warm military clothing. The QM explained it was likely to be abandoned and fall into the Reds hands if he couldn't issue it in the next few days. He also pressed Sedlak to take picks and shovels for the onward journey, they'd be needed at some point to dig snow off the track to keep moving. Sergeant Raybury and Sedlak, who remained in command of the train for the Czechs, had discussed the next steps of the journey east.

Brad pulled the gunners into the compartment they occupied to go over the options now they'd crossed from territory nominally claimed to be under Bolshevik control to White Russian territory.

"We've seen there are significant Czech and other military organisations here. Clearly Whites, but a multitude of different uniforms with irregular head-dress. I guess supplied by the allies through Vladivostok. I've seen some Polish, Americans and couldn't be certain, but possibly some of our lot too."

In fact, whilst most had left, there were still numerous British troops and administrators in Omsk. The lack of communication between the gunners and any British military establishment since being caught up in the Dyer's Battalion mutiny, meant they were unaware of the strategic and military situation in Siberia, or anywhere else for that matter. Cigarettes were lit up and blue-grey smoke filled the closed space. The daytime temperature now rarely got above freezing. Small heating stoves were present in some carriages, but so far they'd lacked the paraffin fuel to light them. Raybury went on.

"Somehow we've managed to get through to an allied controlled area. Not to remain so for very long according to Sedlak and his compatriots. As we know ourselves the Reds are on our tails. We do now have a choice. Well, it may be a choice, it may not. That will depend on what we, collectively, think……. Sounds a bit Socialist when put that way, I guess."

"Get on with it Brad."

Eric threw in. He never could tolerate the pre-amble.

"Okay. For you Eric, we stay on this train, with Sedlak and his bunch. They're as keen as we are to get to Vladivostok."

"Or what?" said Eric, now goading Raybury.

"Or we look to join one of the military trains which lowers the risk of the next four thousand miles of hostile tundra, freezing forests and isolated railway track that we need to get across."

Taffy, in exasperation. "Four thousand miles? We're not going back the way we came are we? We must have covered that already. How big is this place?"

"It's big Taffy, very big. But we do know where we're trying to get to."

Arthur then spoke. "You said it may be a choice, or may not?"

Raybury again, pointing out of the window with the thumb of his right hand.

"We've seen what's like out there. The disorderly, hectic scenes. The chaos. It's only going to get worse in the next few days. I've spoken with Sedlak who's pushing at an open door with the Legion storemen to get supplies for this train. The man doesn't think he'll see more Czech soldiers passing through. He wants to empty his cupboards and leave himself. So this might be a better choice for us."

Arthur again. "So the choice is this train or a military train."

Raybury took a deep breathe.

"Maybe not Wally."

There was general puzzlement.

Now Frank. "You're not being clear Brad. Not like you at all."

"Okay Frank. We have Bolshevik issued papers that we can't read and don't know what they say. Nothing else to prove who we are. There are all sorts of people out there with perfectly legitimate papers from both the military and civilian authorities. I suggest, at this point, in this place, in the middle of a breaking down country and society, trying to convince anyone to let us onto a military escape train heading east, taking up precious space ahead of people with the right documents, is going to be difficult."

The men looked at each other. Until now their Privakov issued papers had got them out of Vyatka, approved by a party apparatchik. They were still on 'that' train. Raybury was right, Omsk may not be the best place to test out their validity outside of the Bolshevik regime.

Eric abruptly concluded the meeting.

"Right then. Decision made. Better the devil we know. We stay on this one, where the people need our help. Not another one where we're looking for the help of others."

He stood up, picked up his rifle and left the compartment.

*

With the crowds in the station and filling the platforms, very few refugees got off for fear of not being able to re-board. Much like the passengers of their own train, the platform people were a mix of mainly older men and women, along with mothers and children. It was the families of the middle class, the bourgeois professionals, lawyers, doctors, teachers and businessmen who'd been given a passage through, all to maintain the ideals of keeping the railway open. With the Czechs controlling the line and providing some protection, the Russian railwaymen were also playing their part where they were willing to do so. Here were also the usual platform hawkers trying to sell items of food, cigarettes, various bottles and other containers of water and even vodka was proffered.

The atmosphere felt frantic, desperate and near panic with the railway being seen as the last means of escape from the advancing Red Army. Kolchak's forces and control over them was collapsing. Several hundred miles to the west, Tobolsk, the old capital of Siberia had fallen to the Red Army in late October with the immediate assimilation imposed of the 'Soviet System'. Also known as the Red Terror; a political regime of torture and death to eliminate anyone believed to be against the Bolshevik revolution. This was the brave new world the refugees were fleeing from. This bad news was filtering back to the Allied governments.

Reuters reported. *"The civil government is evacuating Omsk. Admiral Kolchak's army is retreating on the whole front."*

The Times in London. *"Lacking prestige and power, either as a representative government or as a dictatorship, the organisation headed by Admiral Kolchak has proved incapable either of assuring victory in the field, or of the efficient administration of the country."*

To some of the senior allied officers in Siberia; the British, American and Czech, it was no surprise that Kolchak was failing. As far back as December 1918, Major General William Graves, commanding the American forces in the east wrote from Vladivostok in a memo to Washington.

"All information that I am able to obtain leads me to the conclusion that the government headed by Admiral Kolchak cannot last. Representatives of the democratic class all state that the act at Omsk on November 18th has resulted in cementing and bringing together all elements who have been opposed to the old Russian Government.....................

I have also been informed by representatives of the democratic class of people that the same methods are being pursued by Admiral Kolchak that prevailed in the time of the Czar. Russian troops in Siberia are arresting and murdering people and basing their action on the authority of Admiral Kolchak that everyone opposing the government should be punished." [22]

Kolchak had been generously supplied with uniforms, weapons, ammunition, vehicles and other kit by the British and other allies. A year later his brutal method's, no different from the Bolsheviks, had failed on the battlefield, failed to retain the support of military units and had proved no different to the old regime of violent repression. His multiple failures led to the observation by a British Warrant Officer from the Railway Mission in Vladivostok describing a situation where, after a local uprising against Kolchak,

"both government troops (Kolchak's) and insurgents are wearing British clothing and boots and firing British ammunition out of American rifles and Canadian machine guns.........There you have it in a nutshell, the result of Allied help to Russia."

From the Omsk Military Stationmaster, Sedlak had learnt that the train he commanded had acquired the "Plague Train" moniker, and had been prioritised with green signals when possible. He quickly recognised the potential benefit this might have and agreed that he should leave the station later that afternoon of 7th November. At this time of year it started to get dark at around 5pm. Heavy clouds were threatening snow, little had fallen so far in the month that snow was heaviest for Omsk and the central Siberian region. With daytime temperatures now peaking at below freezing, the heavenly signs looked ominous. The train pulled out at 4.30pm. Other heavily armoured troop and civilian trains with fewer military personnel, mainly the Czech Legion for protection, had also departed earlier in the day. There were now hundreds of trains travelling east using both lines of this completed section of the Trans-Siberian track. This volume of traffic should enable it to keep open when the heavy snow fell, as it always did.

With issues of surplus warm military clothing, including forty pairs of winter fur boots, almost a hundred heavy winter coats and ushanka fur hats, drums of paraffin for the stove heaters, plenty of tinned and dried food and water, they were now well stocked for the continued journey east. This train of refugees by luck of being commanded by Sedlak and not being recognised as part of the railway engine establishment was in a far better situation than most. Omsk fell to the Bolsheviks a few days later on the 14th November 1919. Many Siberian soldiers who didn't melt away in the general military collapse, or immediately transfer their allegiance to the Reds, and thousands of civilian's left behind would die from hunger and exposure as they fled east on foot as the impossibly harsh winter descended on what became known as The Great Siberian Ice March.

---

[22] Papers Relating to the Foreign Relations of the United States, 1919, Russia - Office of the Historian

Whilst the passengers on the refugee train were relatively comfortable and protected by the efforts of Sedlak's Czechs and the British, they quickly became aware of the abject misery of many civilians making their way east along the path created by the railway. For the first few days out of Omsk there were hundreds of people struggling to move in the falling snow and freezing temperatures. Lining the sides of the tracks and in a desperate state, it was very obvious that few would survive. Those trying to walk were pleading for help and there was nothing that could be done. The train was already beyond full. As the days went by the refugees on foot became fewer, the collapsed bodies increased as items of clothing could be seen lying on the banks in cuttings where the snow hadn't yet covered them over. The trudgers were replaced by a number of sledges being pulled by weak looking ponies. The carts over-laden with possessions, the starving and ill trying to hold onto the cart as it rocked over the compacted snow doing its best to throw them off. If they did it was certain death.

Arthur and colleagues became aware the risk this might be the fate of everyone on board a week later when they passed some broken down engines and burnt out, abandoned passenger carriages in sidings at a number of small town stations. The Czech platoon who'd joined the train security crew under Sedlak were familiar with the line and where to stop for more coal. The bigger town depots would be depleted quickly, smaller towns were the best chance. They learnt that lack of proper rail engineers; they'd not been paid for months and deserted their jobs, meant no repairs could be done that required relevant expertise. Unless a solution could be created by the crew or soldiers on board, the train would be emptied and the fate of the civilian passengers and soldiers was at the mercy of the elements. For most a cruel, agonizing death in the bitter cold Siberian snow.

Another resource problem for all the engines was water for the boiler. Vital to keep the train's moving, the trackside water towers were either empty or frozen. Sourcing water from trackside 'wells' which were generally holes broken into river or lake ice, was a competitive and dangerous task. So to keep the boiler topped up as best they could, Raybury and Taffy had beaten a flat metal panel they'd broken off the side of another train into an open triangular hopper with upturned sides. The broad end was leant onto the open fire door. Snow was collected in baskets in a human chain whenever there was one of the numerous halts, and tipped onto the plate where it quickly melted The water ran into the narrow end which fed it into empty paraffin cans, then poured into the water tank for the boiler. Taffy had the idea from a piece of cooling machinery used in the mines. This process became a constant duty for the two firemen who themselves were either British or Czech soldiers as part of a well organised rota created by Raybury and Sedlak.

The bitter cold, day and night was relentless for everyone on board. At least the train provided some shelter from the snow and winds that whipped it about creating blinding blizzards and dune like drifts. After a couple of weeks toward the end of November the paraffin for the carriage heaters ran out. People dressed in as many layers as they could to keep warm and the military surplus clothes helped. In most carriages the refugees had rigged something up to cover from the inside the now permanently closed windows. This helped stop small draughts coming in and sealed the view from the daily horrors of the destitute, dying and dead bodies scattered alongside the line. But they were confined to their crowded, dirty carriages and couldn't move about.

The soldiers were active with work needed all the time. On board this was the maintenance of some order by patrolling up and down, guarding the carriages at night, fireman and driving duties as the sole Czech soldier who'd got them away had trained others, providing hot water for drinking from the only heating source now available, the engine fire-box, and trying to deal with minor mechanical problems not related to the locomotive. All day and night they needed to provide lookouts for marauding bands of partisans sympathetic to the Bolsheviks, or just brigands looking for loot. As the temperatures dropped, these duties on the open platforms between carriages were reduced to one hour shifts, any longer might result in frostbite and an inability to move through frozen limbs.

Arthur would keep his brain active through the cold and tiredness by recalling past events and trying to remember every detail. In particular the warmth of the too small bed he'd shared with his brother until he'd left home and the many insults thrown at him as he 'accidentally' woke him up in the morning after Fred's night-shift. All the work and physical movement meant the soldiers were better able to keep the blood flowing to provide some body warmth.

Train breakdowns and track congestion led to slow progress and long halts where those controlling the track gave priority to senior officers and military trains including those of the British Mission in Omsk and their entourage, and a regiment of Poles, the latter allowed through by threats and duress. When several locomotives were stopped and a queue formed, soldiers from trains at the rear, believing they might not move again would move to the front train by running over the roofs of train carriages ahead. Some of these were British, part of the residual Omsk contingent. They'd move in small groups of three or four men. Raybury discovered a platoon of the Middlesex Regiment were several trains back.

A Sergeant Barrett with two men was noticeably shocked to be greeted by Arthur and Eric from the cab platform as they were on melt-water duty. Arthur called out from the engine cab recognising the British badge on a forage cap, the man's uniform covered by a khaki great-coat with a small Union Jack on the shoulder.

"Hello Sarge, where are you off to then?"

Despite the cold, the work was hot, neither gunner was wearing a tunic nor hat.

"Bloody hell. Russian railmen speaking English. I would never have believed it."

For several minutes he shared what he knew of the military and civilian confusion now engulfing the Russian and Allied withdrawal across the thousands of miles from Omsk back to Vladivostok. His small team were the last Middlesex men, the rest of the regiment had left in September. They were armourers, rifle and pistol experts detached to train the White Russians on the British Lee Enfield rifles being issued to them in their hundreds. He added, as fast as they were issued to the Siberian army 'volunteers' and conscripts, they deserted to the Reds, so now aiming our rifles back at us.

When Arthur mentioned they'd arrived in the country through Archangel, Barrett eyed them both suspiciously and shook his head. He had a vague idea that was in the European north of Russia, a long way from where they were now. He then shrugged and told them what he knew of the broader situation. That General Knox, the British Officer commanding the Mission in Omsk was on a train with his staff a little further back and it was thought that Admiral Kolchak in command of the White Russians, with his captured train of imperial gold further ahead, closer to Irkutsk, the next major city. Both the military and civil order was collapsing. As they looked like they were in charge of their own engine he recommended they stick with it for as long as they could to escape east. He wished them luck and was on his way as he turned to add.

"Whatever you do, avoid the British military hierarchy. You're better off with your Czechs, they can act as free agents."

17. Imperial Gold.
December 1919.

Slow progress, numerous stops for higher priority trains, track rebuilding by British, Polish and Czech engineers after incidents of sabotage, refuelling and water production eventually got them 95 miles short of Irkutsk by mid-December. Alongside the tracks were many broken down and burnt out carcasses of the trains that hadn't made it. They passed more than twenty locomotive engines, mostly derailed from the line, always from embanked sections where a carefully timed explosion or deliberately broken rail would send a speeding train down onto its side. There were dozens of wrecked passenger carriages and many more empty freight wagons which was the main target for the bandits and saboteurs.

Despite the almost complete, white snow covering of the miles of featureless countryside with an occasional settlement, the train had just pulled through a dull and grimy looking industrial town called Cheremkhova. They then pulled into a large set of sidings a few miles further south near the village of Grishevo. They were running short of coal and didn't have enough to get them to Irkutsk and beyond. This area was the centre of the of the region's coal-mining industry. Known to the Czechs who'd worked the line over the last year, these sidings were where the open wagons supplying the depots to east and west were loaded with coal. Due to the importance of these sidings, a perimeter defence had been established by a company of Czech Legion soldiers of over a hundred men. It was as safe and secure as any spot on this risk laden journey to freedom.

It was the middle of the day on the 17th December. They came into the multiple track lines with numerous shunters moving engines, loaded and empty coal wagons and a few empty passenger carriages that had been recovered after being abandoned on the line when their locomotives had broken down. To one side were a series of grey, armoured wagons currently without an engine. Flat metal plates were rivetted to the sides like a battleship, the roofs covered with arched plates to provide additional protection from either artillery or attack from the air. There were six of these freight wagons and at both ends an armoured passenger carriage with rifle loopholes where the windows might be. Two machine guns, currently unmanned, sat on the roofs of the guarding soldier's carriages. Another fifty or sixty Czech soldiers surrounded this train.

The outside temperature was -12 degrees, so despite the protection and safety of the sidings very few people got off the train. Sedlak, Raybury and Cermak, the 'Bohemian' Sergeant commander of the new platoon, now reporting to Sedlak, went to organise a coal deposit into the train bunker. Approaching a group of soldiers who looked like they might be in charge, they weren't received well. A White Russian Major and a Czech officer with no visible indication of rank were arguing between them surrounded by nervous looking men. The Czech angrily demanded to know details about Sedlak, why the train had come into these sidings, who was on board, how the British had got there, and a number of other aggressive questions about weapons and intentions. Sedlak retained a easy demeanour, responding to whatever was asked. The Czech officer calmed down. He moved away from the Russian, beckoning Sedlak to join him, as did the other two.

Now introducing himself as Colonel Janecek, he explained he'd taken control of the armoured train on behalf of the Legion and Allies. The Russian officer reported directly to Admiral Kolchak, the train contained the gold reserves of Imperial Russia. Unless they were protected, the Bolsheviks were certain to capture the train. Janecek recognised that Sedlak's refugee train was no threat to this process, but to ensure that was the case it would need to be searched before it could refuel and continue.

This interaction was being carefully watched by Frank and Arthur from the cabin occupied by Amelia, the Rappoports and the Doctor's family. Frank could hear Amelia nervously whispering to the old lady, more a stage whisper to penetrate the hat ear-flap and compensate for a little deafness. To his astonishment and a sense of joy, even linguistic revenge, he caught what was being said. Amelia was speaking a form of Yiddish, not the German he thought from a partly heard snip when they first met a while before. He spoke to her with a smile.

"Zeyn opgehit Amelia, di tingz zenen nisht shtendik vos zey oyskumen."[23]

Amelia looked shocked and now her mouth gaped. Frank then added.

"Close your mouth Amelia, you look like a fairground goldfish."

They both burst out laughing, her quite joyously; him, pleased with himself having created an extrovert moment of humour. Not something his usually detached personality allowed for. After many weeks of deep stress for all of them, Arthur could see a warmth in the exchange not even knowing what had been said. Even the old lady and Isak's mother were chuckling. The boy smiled broadly, not really understanding the interaction, still gripping tightly his canvas satchel.

"What's going on Frank?"

"It seems that this women of a thousand tongues speaks Yiddish too, well a form of it. We'll find out how she achieved this remarkable feat later; I can see Brad's on his way back."

---

[23] "Be careful Amelia, things are not always what they seem."

Which he was, whilst Sedlak and Cermak remained engaged with the Czech Colonel. Once on board, Raybury stood in the first class carriage corridor with his thickening grey beard covered in white crystals where his breathe had frozen. Here he could speak to Eric and Taffy in the soldiers compartment, and Amelia and others with Frank and Arthur in their box. Raybury went through what was said and then concluded with news that Colonel Janecek's men would be searching the civilian passenger's baggage for weapons and the expression he used was 'loot' that he though belonged to the people of Russia. It seemed this Czech officer might be supporting the Red's cause.

"I take this to mean anything his searching soldiers deem to be attractive enough for them to keep. There's nothing we can do about this. We know that almost anything of value will already have been taken by the Bolshevik soldiers, exchanged for food or spent. And of course they have more men and rifles than us, so we are in no position to resist. We have to get on with it in order to get the coal bunker filled and be on our way."

Looking out of the window he could see a group of eight soldiers now with Sedlak returning. Four of them broke off with Cermak heading for the front of the train. Speaking to the gunners Raybury said.

"Sedlak will accompany the searchers. We'll play no part in this."

He turned into the British soldiers compartment next to Amelia's. Eric and Taffy were already there and Arthur followed Raybury. Amelia called to Frank and again spoke in Yiddish, now knowing no-one else could understand. In her confident instructional manner she said.

"Frank, I need you to look after Isak's satchel. We have a Rappoport family item to protect. It's very important to them and they need to make sure it gets to Mikhail in London. Please take it."

She spoke quietly to the small boy and gently removed the bag, passing it to Frank, who naturally asked.

"What's in it?"

"How about we take a look when we know we're safe in Vladivostok. If you and Arthur can take care of it until then. We know we can trust you; Irena and Simona are good with this too."

Frank looked at the old lady who's fur gloved, down-turned hand was waving in the air as if to push the satchel toward him. Simona was nodding and said in accented English, 'please, please, look after it for us'. He took the bag and retired to the gunners compartment as the sound of heavy soldiers steps entered the train corridor. Sedlak was walking ahead of Janecek's men talking to them. They walked passed the British men, staring in at them but respecting they were not there to search allied soldiers. Sedlak told them Dr. Malevich and the next compartment were under the direct protection of the British. The searchers insisted in their orders to search the bags of all civilian passengers, but here they only made cursory looks into the small suitcases and carpetbags and took nothing.

Further along they found and confiscated some jewellery and gold coins they discovered hidden in false sections of baggage. As if there wasn't enough gold in Kolchak's train across the yard. This was more highway robbery by a show of force rather than anything that could be justified as legitimate. Sedlak and Cermak were furious and disgusted by the acts of his supposed countrymen, yet helpless. Afterwards he claimed Janecek and his men were Slovak's, not Bohemians.

It took a couple of hours for Colonel Janecek's two searching Legion sections to meet in the middle to finish the shake-down. Another two hours to get the train coal bunker replenished to maximum capacity, levelled off by men with shovels and then heaped in the middle to ensure it was as full as possible. In darkness they left the Grishevo sidings and the Imperial Gold train behind. Isak's satchel was safe. Irena, through Amelia said it was now in Frank and Arthur's care, as were the Rappoport family.

*

Another week took them through the city of Irkutsk where Sedlak and the gunners agreed they would try to avoid stopping. The potential for the train to be commandeered for military purposes was high; the risk best avoided. Beyond the city the track ran along the southern edge of the vast Lake Baikal, hogging the bank so closely, it sometimes felt there must be no sleepers or ballast beneath them. They were hemmed in between the lake and the vast tracts of the larch and birch forest that surrounded it and covered the land everywhere they could see. In the summer the views across this inland sea would be dramatic. Right now, at the turn of the year it was solid. The white and grey flat ice stretched beyond the horizon; the lake was completely frozen over in the winter months.

Further north the remains of the White Russian Army, now under the command of General Kappel would shortly attempt to cross the lake on foot and sledge to escape the advancing Russians. Up to 30,000 soldiers, their families and possessions and the Imperial Gold made their way across. It was a near impossible challenge, the piercing icy winds blowing off the mountains surrounding the lake bringing the average daytime temperatures to below minus 10.

Looking out of the opposite train window to the lake, the snow and ice covered mountains climbed into the sky, their upper levels disappearing into the clouds. The environment was inhospitable under normal circumstances, in the chaos and disorganisation of war, even worse. However, with their train now east of Lake Baikal, there was increasing distance between them and the Red army, enhanced by a vast natural barrier.

Even so, there was another 1,800 miles to Vladivostok and back onto a single track line of the Chinese Eastern Railway (CER) built by the Russians under a Chinese, Qing dynasty concession to provide a more direct short-cut from the city of Chita to the great eastern sea-port of Vladivostok. Completed in 1902 and managed by the Russians from Harbin, a settlement that grew into a large rail-hub.

18. Buryat Bandits.
January 1920.

They'd negotiated a steady passage along the CER from Chita to Harbin. The Czechs were no longer in control of the line, the White Russians were nominally, but under the close supervision of the Allied military units, mainly a large contingent of Japanese. As an ally of Britain, France and Russia against Germany and the Central Powers, Japan were at first reluctant to get involved in Eastern Russia after the revolution in 1917. When learning the British and Americans were sending ships to Vladivostok in January 1918, they sent their own to land enough marines to occupy the city before the arrival of the others. Troop numbers increased dramatically until by January 1920 there were 70,000 troops and in Vladivostok, Chita and other cities another 50,000 civilians working for large Japanese conglomerate businesses looking to exploit the political disarray and natural resources.

Territorial expansion and annexation was not an obvious motive of the Japanese initially. It became so over time as they supported the local army of Buryat and Chinese men under the command of the Cossack General Grigory Semyonov. The reality was this man was a thug leader of a bandit force, extracting ransom payments from hijacked trains when they could. Protected by the Japanese, he and his men acted as they wished for the length of the CER, targeting the more vulnerable and less well defended trains.

*

On the 6th of January, the Czech refugee train had to stop at Harbin to take on coal and water and to replenish supplies of paraffin and food. Many of the refugees were running out of their own money and already traded what valuables they'd been able to hide from searching Bolsheviks and others along the way. The Czechs had to plead with limited success to the Japanese and a surprisingly large depot run by the Poles.

Now just over 500 miles to go, the train made slow progress out of Harbin for a day when several stowaways came to the attention of one of the Czech train patrols. Three men who turned out to be Italian administrators had detrained from their official transport to enjoy the attractions of Harbin. Only twenty years before it had been a small village until the Russians had selected the location as the base for the development of the CER. Indentured local and imported labourers worked under the direction of Russian engineers. Designed by Swiss and Italian town planners, with buildings showcasing contemporary pre-revolutionary Russian architects, its early style was distinctly European. It quickly became a multi-ethnic, railway boomtown with many Ukrainians, Poles, Georgians and Tatars from south Asian Russia congregating to work. Consulates were established by, amongst others, America, Germany, France and Italy to support their nationals working and trading in a resource and agriculturally rich region.

With its cosmopolitan and fashionable reputation, the three Italians on their way back from the risks and trials of Omsk were attracted by Harbin's reputation for brothels with the most beautiful European and Asian women. They drank, gambled and enjoyed the local 'Houses of Pleasure' until a week later they were stuck and unable to find transport further east. What they did have was money, roubles and Japanese yen to be precise, with which they bribed a now cash-less supervisor to smuggle them into his carriage.

Dr. Malevich confirmed what some of the Czech soldiers had been speculating after the Harbin stop. A fever had been spreading amongst passengers for several days in one of the carriages at the opposite end of the train to the gunner's compartment. First one carriage, where the stowaways were found, and then the next one to it. It was 'sifnoi teiff', the Russian term for typhus. The disease was blamed on the Italians, but the incubation period from infection to obvious symptoms meant they were unlikely to be the cause. The lice could have come from any of the stops since Irkutsk.

In fear of what might happen to them, and not knowing what it was, the family groups had tried to hide their infection from others. Those initially infected were also the ones who'd benefitted from the cash bribe from the Italians. The reality was the increasingly grim and unhygienic conditions and close proximity of the other refugees created a certain inevitability of the disease taking hold at some point. Something the Doctor had feared from the start of the journey. He'd dealt with infected Russian soldiers who'd contracted it on the eastern front. Transmitted by lice, fleas or tics, an inability to keep the body and clothes clean meant once in a confined space, the carriers would reproduce and spread rapidly.

After a severe fever and flu-like symptoms, a rash spread across the body starting from the from the abdomen. The face would keep clear of the rash. So with the intense cold and heavily clothed passengers it was a few days after being alerted to the spreading fever before Malevich was certain. The death of an old man enabled the Doctor to check the body, and this wasn't chicken pox which was still present in some of the smaller children. The body had to be thrown from the train much to the distress of his howling family group, all of whom now had the infection. He was the first of many to succumb.

Again, there was no treatment for the disease that could be applied on the train. Malevich advised the military management of Sedlak, Raybury and Cermak to do their best to isolate the infected carriages and those either side. They would have to stop sending soldiers through the carriages delivering water, meagre centralised managed food and policing. The guards providing security at either end would have to remain outside of the carriages on the connecting footplates that were open to the freezing winter elements.

This sounded fine from a quarantining medical perspective, but almost impractical for the logistics and security of the train. To address this, Raybury proposed that sentry duties be cut to 30 minutes and that the carriage roofs were used by the soldiers to move up and down the train. The driver would need to slow the train down to a crawl to allow for the many switchovers. Further detail was debated, including the strict need to dispose of any dead when the train slowed. Each of the twelve carriages already had an appointed 'senior', mainly men but also three women who were detailed to ensure this heartbreaking task was dealt with expeditiously.

As this was the only option to maintain the train's passage without trying to isolate and off-load all the infected it was agreed to proceed. They knew the typhus would spread but they hoped it would only be less than a week before they reached Vladivostok where the infection could be dealt with more effectively. Once again it was a plague train, but this time more malignant. At this moment, no soldiers were infected, nor any of the Rappoport or Malevich groups, which was immensely lucky for the Doctor who was now high risk.

*

After replenishing the tank of water for the boiler, Arthur and Eric were in the engine cabin. In his broken English and their comical, indecipherable attempts at Czech, Tovec was giving them a lesson on getting the steam engine moving.

"Move this, two handed dial to here, not full-way, more than half-way."

"Three quarters then," added Eric.

"If you say so. Then release brake lever to the left and leave small ejector open."

"Are you following all this Arthur?" Asked Eric.

"Be quiet and learn." Snapped Tovec.

"I'm learning." Said Arthur. The engine was making all the usual hisses and clanking noises heard in a station.

"Good. You be quiet 'Arms', if that's your name Englishman."

Arthur and Eric smiled and now kept quiet.

"Now this lever on the floor, open the cylinder cocks. These levers on the floor on the right, the front and rear dampers, open them. Have you got all that?"

Arthur said, "But we're not moving."

Tovec tutted. "Idiot man. We open regulator to here, just a quarter."

He took the large lever centred above the firebox door and moved it to the required position. The engine eased forward.

"Hope you learn 'Arms', you do it next time."

They were sharing the fireman's duties and apart from when he was in the serious business of giving instructions, which he did most of the time to the two men, the Czech soldier, now engine driver was a warm, well humoured man.

Now the middle of second day out of Harbin the train was moving well. Arthur and Eric were breaking larger coal lumps with a hammer. The fuel would burn more efficiently with a greater surface area and smaller pieces. Arthur was shovelling coal into the engine when the driver moved the shiny brass lever of the regulator to close, thereby reducing the steam flow to the pistons in preparation for braking. There was something about railmen, even though Josef Tovec was still a soldier. The engine drivers always had a rag in their hand to wipe dirt off and polish their levers, knobs and dials. Tovec had his oil-stained rag permanently flipped over his right shoulder.

The train had just reached the peak of a gentle upward slope and peering through the driving goggles Sedlak had obtained for him in Harbin, he could see far enough into the shallow white valley ahead to spot a stationary train. They would have to stop behind it. As the engine slowed on the down slope, the men in the cabin started to hear the rifle shots. The train ahead of them was being attacked by men on horses riding up and down either side of the line.

Groups of nomadic bandits were well known to roam the vast expanses of barren deserts and forests in this lawless border region of Russia and northern China, the last stretch of track between Irkutsk and Vladivostok. Warning stories circulated at stations and refuelling depots alongside tactics for defence. The bandits typically targeted weakness with a limited number of raiders trying to take control of the train. They wanted valuables from the refugee trains they knew would be carrying the relatively well off. If they knew a train carried a valuable or militarily useful cargo, they'd deploy a larger force. Stealing the load from their supposed allies.

The train ahead must have seen them on the slope as it released a series of short whistle blasts to indicate the danger. Tovec repeated this whistle to alert the Czech and British soldiers why they were slowing. A drill had been detailed in the event of an attack where soldiers knew which carriage coupling plates they had to occupy. This was amended with the outbreak of typhus. Now they would take defensive firing positions on the roofs of their designated wagons. In reality a more advantageous position giving the soldiers a smaller target profile and a better view of the attacking horsemen. From their approach this looked like a small force attacking a poorly defended train. They would pull up behind to add their firepower to the defence of the halted train ahead.

It was the clear weather that had brought out the bandits. It hadn't snowed for several days, with vast, clear blue skies covering the endless whiteness on the ground. To the north there loomed some heavy leaden clouds looking as if they held a new snow dump. The train cruised down the slope, slowing as it went, the soldiers carefully making their way along the carriage roofs to take up their allocated firing positions. With the Czechs and British men, theirs was a powerful force coming to the aid of the train under attack.

Some of the bandit horsemen, about six of them, broke from attacking the first train to ride toward the second before it had come to a halt. They knew once it had stopped their advantage of movement would be reduced if its guarding soldiers were of any quality. Skilfully firing as they rode, their first shots hit the engine cabin with resounding metallic pings and penetrating wooden thuds. The train brakes screeched and hissed to a stop. Eric and Arthur could do nothing from inside the engine drivers cabin, so donning their great-coats and ear-flap fur hats, they grabbed their rifles and exited from the side doors at the rear. One on each side, they jumped the five feet to the soft, virgin snow covered ground, sinking and having to recover themselves before the riders returned from their run up the passenger carriages.

Inside the passenger carriages the refugees were cowering on the floor trying to make themselves as small as possible. Panic and fear would be rife. Screams could be heard by the defending soldiers on the roofs. No one could tell if this was just fear or actual wounding, as despite taking cover below the window level, the wooden panelled carriages were of limited defence against the penetrating power of a rifle bullet. The crowded train would guarantee casualties.

Shots were now coming from the carriage roofs toward the raiders and windows were shattering from the armed bandit's fire. In a prone position, in the snow on the ground, there was no way Arthur and Eric could properly see the horsemen, let alone get an accurate shot away.

Arthur managed to kneel up as three more riders peeled off from the first train where defensive fire could also be heard. This gave him a clear view of the men charging towards him. It'd had been a long time since he'd used his rifle against another man. He was breathing heavily with ice particles collecting on his beard, his nostrils burning with the frigidly cold air. He had to calm his panting in order to make a well-aimed shot. Taking a split second to run his rifle slightly ahead of his target, the torso of an Asiatic looking man dressed in Cossack style clothing. He paused his breath, squeezed the trigger at about thirty yards and the man instantly fell from his horse. Arthur immediately felt nauseous, his head dizzy. He shook it vigorously and only just managed to suppress the need to vomit. In this dire situation, his marksmanship had to triumph over his personal anguish and abhorrence of directly killing another man with a rifle. He knew he was a gunner for a reason, the target was always anonymous, somewhere in the distance.

He fired another at the rear of a departing rider firing at his train carriages. This time he hit the horses left hind quarter which led it to collapse to the right throwing the rider into the snow. The horse writhed in the frozen powder trying to regain its footing and fell again with blood now spilling onto the whiteness. The rider had stood and was trying to get to the struggling mount when he was picked off by a shot from above the second carriage. More bandits were starting to ride down the trackside of both trains as if they were now a single unit.

*

On the other side, the snow Eric landed in was deeper, having been blown by the wind into a small drift about ten foot in front of him. Even kneeling gave him no sight of the horsemen, they were hidden by the bank rising to his front. He was useless where he was, contributing nothing to the fire-fight. He crawled forward into the rising mound and was now more elevated. Even so he had to stand to see over the peak where he spotted bandit horses crossing twenty plus yards to his front. Their intention was to suppress rifle fire from the trains where the defending soldiers usually stood or knelt on the connecting platforms between the carriages. They would pick the men off in these positions eventually overpowering the defenders. However, the typhus dictated the deployment of the soldiers on the roofs, making them virtually impossible targets.

Eric took aim at a big man on a small horse. This rider wasn't using stirrups so his legs flapped comically either side. A very skilful horseman, or maybe bereft of adequate kit. Eric's shot also hit the horse, this time in the flank causing it to swerve off, slowing from a strong gallop to a wounded canter. Another easy target for the roof mounted carriage soldiers to target, the rider no longer able to use speed as a defence.

More bandits appeared and were unhorsed or shot directly by the defenders of both trains. Arthur thought he'd hit another horse which he'd seen slow down, but it might have been a shot from elsewhere. This rider was also targeted by the successful roof borne snipers; his mount seen to be wandering aimlessly. There were probably no more than thirty bandits, enough to take over one moderately defended train, but not two with the military strength of the 'plague' train. The final sweep of a dozen or so bandits ran back on Eric's side. Arthur heard a concentrated fusillade of rifle fire striking and ricocheting off the engine metal and woodwork as they continued ahead to run along the same side of the carriages in front. A trail of them could be seen strewn out running up the opposite slope on the far side of the valley.

Eric had waited until he'd seen the withdrawal of the bandits up the slope. He called out in his Scots accent.

"Wally, I've been hit. Plenty of blood. Red as a Rothesay kilt. It's a blighty one for sure."

Arthur reacted immediately.

"I'm coming through the engine cabin Aims. Just stay still."

"Good advice Wally. I've no plans to go anywhere soon. I'll be here when you get here. In fact I can't think of a better place to be."

Arthur lifted himself onto the steps and into the engine cabin. Tovec was at the dials with the fire box open, with the vital job of nurturing the source of power that would eventually get them out of this mess. Without a word, Arthur leapt out of the other side falling into the same deep powdery drift that Eric had earlier. The Scot was lying on his back several yards up the bank, a look of pain through a creased, grimacing mouth. The contrasting redness of the bloodied snow around the top of his right thigh against the unsullied, pure whiteness was startling.

'Shit' was Arthur's first thought. So much blood. We need to stop that. As Sgt Cleverly would say in their training at Woolwich. 'When dealing with a casualty, keep them breathing, stop the bleeding'.

"Let's deal with the blood Aims, then I'll get you to Malevich."

"He'll likely be busy. Tie it up. Pad it up. I'll be sorted. It's a leg wound. I'll be fine."

Arthur knew this was serious. He unbuttoned his great coat, pulled his leather belt off to use as a tourniquet, used his black handled, war issued pen knife with its handy, horse-shoe stone remover tool to pierce a hole in the belt leather and strapped it tightly around Eric's leg. He'd seen this done dozens of times to reduce blood loss on arms and legs. The quickest way to get to the Doctor would now be from the outside of the train. So he took Eric by the collar of his coat and started dragging him back along the train to the soldiers box carriage where Malevich would be able to fix his mate.

It came into his head the last time he'd carried a wounded man off the battlefield. The very young looking Sussex Regiment lad called Charlie, and that it was Aims' song that inspired that feat. Arthur started singing.

"And Charlie, he's my darling,
My darling, my darling ,

Charlie, he's my darling,
The young Chevalier..........................
"Your song Aims, better start singing."
Which he did, not with a great singing voice, but he knew the words to the verses that Arthur didn't.

'Twas on a Monday morning,
Right early in the year,
That Charlie came into our town,
The young Chevalier.

Arthur joined with the chorus and the next verse. He'd heard Eric sing it so often, he knew it well.

And Charlie, he's my darling,
My darling, my darling,
Charlie, he's my darling,
The young Chevalier.

Even though he was badly wounded, Eric started belting the song out.

As he was walking up the street,
The city for to view,
O there he spied a bonnie lass
The window looking through.

And with Arthur.

And Charlie, he's my darling,
My darling, my darling,
Charlie, he's my darling,
The young Chevalier.

*

Frank had been with Taffy on the roof of the British soldiers carriage, his allotted defensive position. He'd dropped down and the pair of them with Raybury and the Doctor had started walking down the train to assess the casualty situation within the refugee carriages and any other soldiers. Sedlak had taken a section of his own men to check that the shot bandits were no longer a threat.

Frank recognised the song carrying across the freezing air and recalled Arthur's action with the Sussex boy. He instinctively knew one of his mates was injured. He was walking on the opposite side of the train and climbed over a link plate between the carriages. In the thick snow he ran with difficulty back to see Arthur and Eric. The Doctor trailed behind.

"We need him inside so I can take a proper look."
Malevich said when he caught up.

Eric wasn't incapable despite the blood flowing, now to a much lesser extent. So with his limping and groaning with pain, and occasional chorus outbursts of the song they got him into a compartment. A stove heater was lit and Malevich cut his trousers above the knee and below the groin to get a good look of the injury at the rear of the thigh. He had to roll Eric onto his side before he partially released Arthur's belt. Doing so resulted in a stronger flow of blood which confirmed for the Doctor that a bullet had severed the femoral artery. He asked Frank to get a bottle of vodka. A large slug was poured into a tin mug for Eric to drink.

Trying to keep things light Eric responded to taking the mug.

"Thanks fellah's, I wasn't expecting a social."

Some vodka was poured onto a cloth to clean out any trouser material embedded in the wound. The patient was lying on his left side, the Doctor could see the torn flesh of his upper thigh where the bullet had gone right through the flesh, missing the bone. He pulled the open flesh together and managed to put in some crude stitching whilst blood still seeped from the wound. Finally a tightened tourniquet bandage around the top of the thigh and he then packed absorbent field dressing pads onto the wound from the central medical box he kept. These were held in place with more bandage strapping. The key thing was to stop the blood flowing. He wasn't to move as this might set things off again. Arthur asked if he'd turned his back on the raiders to get shot in the back of the leg. He got the following response.

"Don't be an ass Wally, when have you known me to turn my back on anything? It was a bullet that bounced back off the engine, I heard the ping before I felt the pain."

It was true of course, Aims had always been there facing whatever was thrown at him from Trafalgar Square on the 4th August 1914 to now.

19. Amelia's genius.

The Czech soldiers linked up with a platoon of Polish men on the preceding train. Sedlak explained the presence of typhus telling them to keep their distance. The young Polish Lieutenant commanding thanked him for the warning. They were protecting mainly European civilian administrators and engineers from Irkutsk, Chita and Harbin. He told Sedlak this section of the line across Chinese territory had been considered low risk, but increasingly General Semyonov's bandits, with the tacit support of the Japanese had been stretching their raids and territorial influence along the whole length of the CER. The Poles believed this attack was the furthest east the raiders would stray, a good run from here might only take half a day to Vladivostok. This gang were opportunists looking for easy pickings.

Two sections of eight men were detailed by the Poles and the Czechs to secure the area, meaning to ensure no bandits were still a threat. The Poles took the northern side of the track, Sedlak's men the south. After a sweep of about 500 yards on either side, the reports totalled eight dead men, three seriously wounded, now confirmed dead and one, unharmed, taken prisoner. A young Buryat boy found next to his dying horse. Probably no more than twelve years old his narrow dark eyes screamed fear. He would be handed over to the authorities in the terminal port. Before then, looked after by Sedlak's men. Four wounded horses had been shot and three fit ones captured. The Polish officer took one that was loaded onto a freight wagon and the others were left with Sedlak. Not knowing what to do with them, he had the saddle and bridle removed and released them.

The Poles had a number of wounded soldiers and one dead. The refugee train two wounded. Alongside Eric, a Czech soldier had a bullet graze his ear. The shock and proximity to his head made him jerk so violently he slid off the roof onto a hard landing and broke his leg. Both train commanders were still auditing their passengers for casualties which might take several hours. Malevich had also reported a growing number of seriously ill passengers. The process of recovery, auditing and treating if possible the wounded and dealing dead typhus patients might also take a few hours.

It would start to get dark from 4pm. Sleepers and logs across the track that caused the Polish train to stop would need to be cleared. They agreed to leave this until the morning and then travel in tandem for the final leg. Quarantine preparations would need to be made for the plague train. They would telegraph ahead at the next manned signal box of which there were many over the last couple of hundred miles of the Chinese Eastern Railway.

Overnight the heavy snow-laden clouds had rolled in and after days of no precipitation, there was a 10 inch dump by morning. And it was still falling. At 7.15 am. it was getting light and ten men were working on moving the track obstacles and shovelling the snow off the immediate area of the line to allow the point train to get effective metal wheel to metal track connection and traction. The work was arduous. After three hours the first digging shift stood down to be replaced by another ten, including some able bodied clerks, engineers and administrators.

Frank and Arthur had been in the first morning snow-clearing shift. They'd returned to the sanctuary of their wagon where Amelia was arranging hot, sweet, black tea for them and other Czech men. They were discussing the snow-track problem. Arthur spoke.

"The Poles tried three time to get their train moving along the line and keep ceasing up. Once moving, the engine weight and wheels should be able to cut through the snow that fell on the track last night. We've seen it work already outside Omsk."

Now Frank, started to speak just as Amelia entered the compartment with two tin mugs.

"It seems to be the slow speed as it hits the drifts ahead. There's not enough momentum for the plough to throw the snow off the track and its getting compressed into hardened packs underneath. This then slows it more until all speed is lost."

"You need to remove the ashpan hopper."

Frank and Arthur turned to stare at Amelia. Frank replied.

"What are you talking about Miss Redron?"

"You need to remove the ashpan hopper. That'll be what's compacting the uncleared snow between the wheels on the track."

Now Arthur. "You're a railway engineer now are you Miss?"

She answered with her big-eyed, English, Amelia smile and faux haughtiness in her most affected cultured accent. They were all on first name terms, but for emphasis.

"Of course not Mr. Walton, but sometimes you have to open your mind to ideas that don't emanate from the most obvious places, like the brains of men. Think about it."

With that she pranced out with, "I've more tea to make, let me know how you get on."

The two men shook their heads, looked at each other and said nothing.

Now on their rest shift, they had three hours before they would be on duty patrolling up and down the outside of the static 'plague' train. Eric had been made as comfortable as possible in the compartment next door which now housed Doctor Malevich and his family. Eric was still bleeding, with his dressings being changed every couple of hours by the doctor's niece. Her two daughters were being taught Eric's song by the man himself in his more lucid moments when the constant vodka supply wore off. At the ages of 8 and 10, they knew no English, or indeed Scottish, they just learnt the words. This kept Eric distracted, but it seemed no matter what the Doctor tried to do to stem the blood flow, it failed and oozed into the dressings.

For half of their rest shift Arthur and Frank would stay with Eric. Raybury and Taffy were doing the same, so there was a constant British presence close by. Amelia appeared at least every half hour to quietly check on Eric as most of the time, the soldiers with him were, understandably, sleeping.

*

Later that day Arthur and Frank were walking back to the front of the Polish Train.

"What do you think Wally?"

"It's a bonkers idea. But look where we are. We're walking next to the train we walked back from six hours ago. It hasn't moved, the sun will go down in three hours, Eric's still bleeding and we've had a dozen typhus deaths with more to come. I don't know where she got the idea from. It looks like nothing else has worked so far."

When they got to the front of the Polish train, Sedlak, Cermak, and Raybury, who'd been brought forward for the consideration of a new idea were deep in discussion with the exhausted, young Polish officer. He was completely committed to his men, his mission, and to get the train to Vladivostok in his role as its commander. There were some senior civilian men on board throwing out ideas yet not volunteering to grab a shovel. Having no authority over them, he could not compel them to dig.

As they reached the engine, Arthur and Frank joined Taffy who'd just finished a shovelling shift. They took several minutes to peer underneath at the ashpan hopper. Its purpose, to collect the burnt debris from the grate under the firebox. This avoided burning ash collecting between the tracks leaving smoking embers in urban areas and fire hazards in rural. Not such a problem in the middle of a frigid, freezing, snow-covered tundra. Sure enough, crushed to its immediate front was a large block of hardened, compact snow. Asking Taffy what he thought, he said it was an inspired idea. He'd seen trains with the ashpans removed in the Welsh valleys in winter, never in summer. He now realised why this was. He looked at Arthur with concern, speaking quietly to him.

"You'll need to go underneath the engine to get at the box Wally. You'll be digging snow out in a very tight space."

He was staring at the engine and the ex-coal miner, decorated for bravery rescuing his men from the tunnels in France gave an obvious involuntary shudder.

"You know I won't be able to help you with this."

"I know Taffs, I know. You're off now. Get back, get some tea and deliver the comfort you've been providing for our sad cargo back there. That's important enough."

Taffy smiled weakly and nodded. He put his shovel over his shoulder. For it was now his shovel that he kept in the corner of their box compartment for his new 'day-job', as he called it.

Arthur and Frank moved toward the train commanders in conference and Frank suggested removing the ashpan. They were not surprised by the same response they'd initially had to Amelia's idea. Arthur added the Welshman's comments. For several minutes the idea was discussed, versus one proposed by a Polish corporal; use explosives to blow a gap through the snow. The latter had other risks, removing the ashpan had few at this time of year, they would try this first.

As his two soldiers had the idea, Raybury said they could lead the execution. They were sent beneath the engine with the right spanner and hammer each to start unbolting the hopper. Lying under the locomotive engine trying to lever the frozen bolts, Arthur's thoughts were this was the best, perhaps the only way to get Eric to effective treatment. Frank was using all his strength on the bolts thinking where the hell did this extraordinary woman come up with such ridiculously plausible ideas. It took two hours lying in the snow with several other men helping in turns to eventually unloosen the bolts, drop the ashpan, clear it of dying embers and haul it out from under the train. Once this task was complete, along with another forty yards of track cleared by shovelers, the point train built up the steam power, opened the regulator and drove at the previously impenetrable snow barrier.............. and burst through. Amelia's crazy plan had worked.

An early night was coming in, the cloud cover blocking out the sun as it set to the west. With the Polish train now moving forward, the refugee train had to follow. The risk of being blocked in again was too high. All of the diggers returned to their respective trains, the young Polish officer almost in tears of gratitude to Frank and Arthur who'd proposed the idea. They embarrassingly accepted the praise, not passing on it had come from a young English governess.

*

Exhausted themselves, they returned to their train. Sedlak's men were chivvying the very few refugees who'd disembarked to get back on board. Taffy needed to be found; they knew where he'd be and Arthur went out to get him. In the two hours Frank and Arthur had been working under the engine, Taffy had been digging in the snow. Thirteen graves for the typhus dead that had been emptied from the train that day, including one four year old girl and her one year old brother. He could not bear to see these families suffer more by not having a Christian burial.

Everyone knew that when the snow melted the bodies would be revealed. It was more likely within a few days wolves, foxes and other wild animals will have exposed the carcass. That didn't matter to Taffy. He'd taken it upon himself to carry the dead body from the side of the train and move about thirty yards out so the family could see him clearly. He then dug a snow grave placed the body inside, stood above and said his prayers on behalf of humanity and the grieving, helpless relatives. He had to give them the dignity of a Christian funeral, knowing how devout the Russian people were.

He had one more to do, a large elderly women who'd been dragged away from the train. Taffy was just finishing digging when he saw Arthur approaching.

"We need to move off Taffs. We need to get back onto the train."

Ignoring what Arthur had said, he answered.

"Give me a hand here Wally. You take the feet where you're less likely to get fleas from her boots."

Arthur did so and between them they slid the deadweight body across the snow into the pit.

"We really need to get back to the wagon Taffy."

"You can go back or wait for me Wally. Either way this needs to be done properly. For those people on the train watching us. For this poor lady to give her the dignity she deserves for her onward journey............. Different to ours Wally, hers is eternal and therefore more important. And important for me and my commitment to my faith. So best let me get on with it."

With the corpse now in the snow grave, a number of prayers were recited, including The Lord's Prayer, that Arthur, even with his complete lack of faith, felt compelled to join in with an Amen. Taffy wasn't to be rushed. He spoke for several minutes with a number of remembered funereal words and prayers concluding with.

"May the road rise up to meet you. May the wind be always at your back. May the sun shine warm upon your face; the rain fall soft upon your fields and until your people meet with you again, may God hold you in the palm of His hand. Amen."

And an "Amen" from Arthur. These were good words, poetic, and sounded meaningful, even to a heathen.

The Welshman then handed Arthur his shovel.

"You can fill it in."

He walked back to the carriage where the women's relatives were calling from the window and an elderly, distressed looking gentleman was standing on the plate linking it to the next wagon. Probably her husband, his hands were clasped together in a kind of imploring, praying motion.

"Spasibo, ser. Da blagoslovit vas bog, ser. Spasibo."[24]

*

Getting back to their carriage, they were given some black bread which they softened in hot tea still being organised by Amelia. With injured Eric in the cabin the gunners shared, Taffy took himself to the end of the carriage and lay down in the corridor. He said it was best he kept out of the way with the infected corpse contact he'd had during the day.

Frank did the first shift to watch Eric who was still bleeding and needed dressings attending to every few hours. He reminded him of the story they both knew so well of rescuing Broncy from under the bricks. Where Frank won his Military Medal and always said it was Eric who deserved it. It was a lively discussion they'd had many times, Frank introduced it knowing it would keep Eric animated for a while.

The train built up some speed and following the Polish lead moved out of the wide shallow valley and over the hills. Soon they were rattling on to the coastal lowlands and the international, terminal port of Vladivostok. Medical aid for Eric, hopefully quarantine and treatment for the typhus carriers, sanctuary for some refugees and the gateway home and asylum for others. For the Czech Legion men, the hope of a boat home. When Arthur came to relieve Frank he found Amelia there as well. Eric was clearly weak but just about awake. Frank spoke.

"Remove the ashpan hopper then. Where the hell did that come from Miss Redron?"

"I read about it Mr Abraham. In a book. You should try reading one sometime........Can you read?......... I can teach you!"

Frank rolled his eyes and shook his head.

"A subscriber to the Railway Gazette eh?"

"Don't be silly Mr. Abraham, do I really look like an oily, callus-handed engineer?"

Arthur was keeping out of this discussion, sitting on the bench seat that his wounded friend was lying on. Eric's head was on a rolled up great coat across Arthurs lap. A small lit paraffin stove providing some heat in

---

[24] "Thank you, sir. God bless you, sir. Thank you."

the dark cabin. Eric was listening to the banter carefully, his eyes moving from Amelia to Frank on the opposite seat, and then to Arthur. He let out a forced whisper.

"I think there's something in this Wally."

"I do too Aims. Give it time and we'll see."

Arthur looked out of the window. In the distance to the east he could see in the darkness of night the light of the Vladivostok city glow. Nothing specific, but he felt they'd made it across the almost 6,000 miles of the disintegrating Russian Empire.

"Nearly there Aims. Not far now."

Amelia again. "I read the book when I was in France. It was called the *'La Bete Humaine'*. The Beast Within. Murderous tale that includes a train stuck in the snow. They remove the ashpan to get the train moving. How was I to know it would work? Nothing else seemed to be, and you had no more ideas."

Amelia smiled triumphantly at Frank who said.

"That was a story Amelia, this is real life."

"I know Frank, I didn't expect you would try it, but I'm glad you did."

Eric whispered again.

"Hold my hand Wally. Get Frank too." Arthur took his right hand.

"Frank, over here."

He moved across and sat on a box on the carriage floor that had contained tinned food. Eric tightly gripped both their hands.

"I won't make it back lads. It's been an amazing journey though. Remember me to you mum Wally, and Alice, and her friend Madge."

"Your friend Madge, Aims. Your friend."

"Of course, my friend Madge."

He tried to smile.

Amelia spoke softly.

"We're almost safe Eric. Stay strong. We'll get you there."

"Thanks Miss. It's a kind thought, thanks."

Looking at Frank he added.

"Be good to the lady Abs, she's very special."

There was an uncomfortable silence for a few seconds as the train sped toward sanctuary and home to Britain. Eric's grip on his mates hands tightened.

"Started as strangers, finished as brothers. Through hell and half-way around the world. An amazing journey I could only have done with you two……….. Thanks lads."

The Scot's grip strengthened again and he closed his eyes. Arthur could only repeat Amelia's words.

"Stay strong Aims. We'll get you there."

Eric lay with his head on Arthur's lap taking shallow breaths. It was only an hour or so to Vladivostok. Frank and Amelia spoke quietly to each other as she explained to him how she'd learnt her version of Yiddish from the old lady and Julias, her husband. They spoke it to each other, a relic from their childhood; his in Lithuania, hers in Poland. Her passion to learn new languages drove her to insist they teach her, as well as the Russian she was there to learn. Frank wanted to ask about the contents of the satchel, but the moment passed as they both fell asleep. The train rattled on.

*

The loud assortment of approaching, reversing, stopping, departing, shunting, manoeuvring and other warning whistles of trains negotiating congested rail junctions in a city station woke Arthur. He was still clutching the now icy cold hand of his dead friend. Eric's eyes were closed, his face now a pale, grey-white, bloodless mask. It was not the look of trauma he'd seen on the many dead bodies over the years in France. No grimace of pain, staring, startled, hollow eyes of shock, gaping mouth, screaming at the world, angry at losing a life not yet lived. Eric looked calmly content in his final moments delivered in his sleep, close to his self-declared brothers.

Frank was still asleep, sitting on the box, his head resting against Eric's side covered in blankets and a coat. Amelia curled up asleep under a similar pile of assorted material. Arthur gave Frank a gentle nudge with his boot causing him to stir.

"He's gone Frank. He never made it through the night."

Arthur was trying to stifle the tears. He tried hard to stop the emotion welling up but just couldn't. His face crumpled with moisture now rolling down his cheeks. Frank's grogginess disappeared immediately he saw Arthur's face. Inside he was in turmoil. Eric, even with his quiet, hard man of the Picts, and Frank with his outwardly, impenetrable, urbane detachment, had been as close as it was possible to be. Arthur was the third leg to this three legged stool. In the moment it was impossible to understand the finality of their relationship. Frank stood up, as did Arthur and uncharacteristically they gave each other a spontaneous bear-hug of comfort. Arthur now openly sobbing into Frank's shoulder. Frank gritting his teeth, tightening his jaw to suppress any hint of the inner despair he really felt.

Amelia was now watching the two soldiers in realisation of what had happened during the night. Her eyes teared quickly. Eric had been the quietest and least accessible of the three men. However, over time she'd seen and learnt how much strength, directness and practicality he brought to what they did. As the Malevich family learnt of Eric's death the two young girls could be heard singing his song.

Part 3.
1. Vladivostok.
11th January 1920

The city was bubbling cauldron of different nationalities with varying interests in the outcome of the Russian civil war. With large diplomatic missions like Britain and America and small office representations like Estonia and Latvia, many countries had a presence. Global imperialist powers like France and Italy, and the more local interests of China, Japan and the White Russians and others eyeing independence from the Russian Empire; the Baltic states already mentioned plus Lithuania and Poland. And of course the Czechs with their substantial, cohesive military forces remained a powerful player along the spine of the Trans-Siberian railway in a competition for power, influence and control.

Tensions between these different armed contingents had erupted in Vladivostok in mid-November 1919 as Arthur and the others were on the train travelling from Omsk. A popular and through the civil war so far, successful Czech Legion General Radola Gajda, had been appointed by Admiral Kolchak to the rank of Major-General, acquiring the nickname the 'Siberian Tiger'. After July 1919 he fell out of favour with Kolchak as the demoralised White Army started withdrawing from the Ural Mountains and disintegrating. Gajda then aligned himself to the Socialist Revolutionary Party, known as the 'Esers'. Pre-revolutionary, agrarian, democratic; they had strong support from the Russian peasantry for their policy to overthrow the Tsar to install a democratic government. In Vladivostok on 17th November 1919 he lead a mutiny against Kolchak's forces.

Bullets were flying in the railway station and marshalling yards located at the north western corner of the protected Golden Horn Bay. From the building they worked, on Mimir Garden, Captain Savory a staff officer at the British Mission noted the confusion in not knowing who was fighting who. He was mainly informed by a young White Russian officer who appeared with a chest wound asking for a doctor. Under the command of a Kolchak loyal, General Rozanov, Gajda's men were finally overwhelmed and beaten into the main station building. The rain was tipping down, the resistance fell and the mutineers, many hundreds of them were rounded up as prisoners. Overnight a hardcore, including Gajda held out. In the morning they were captured and were about to be executed when the senior British officer, Colonel Wickham intervened to stop the slaughter. The Russian officer ordered the machine guns away. He then proceeded to shoot them the next night in the railway station, on stairs leading to a platform with locked doors at the bottom. Lorries took the corpses onto the frozen sea ice where they were dumped through holes. Remarkably, Gajda managed to escape the massacre in the confusion and sailed back to Europe. After telling the detail, Savory's young officer died bravely in his arms without complaint.

This Czech led 'White' Russian mutiny had a serious impact on the local population. Residents of the city were caught up in the response from Rozanov's men. The international missions objected to the shooting and slaughter of innocent civilians. So the following night prisoners were killed by sword and bayonet. Local people now saw the Whites, supported by the international troops as brutal, violent oppressors. Likely no better than the Bolsheviks yet to arrive. Local opinion and favour swung to the Reds and despite their forces still being west of Lake Baikal, the spread of support in the city was far ahead of their physical presence. They were starting to be seen as liberators. Admiral Kolchak transferred his military command to Semyonov on the 4th January. By then his men were out of control, murdering, looting, burning villages and raping wherever they went.

When the gunners arrived on their typhus infected refugee train in early January the local administration was breaking down. Saboteurs and criminal gangs were exploiting the chaos, food and water was in short supply, the city's sanitation system was no longer capable of disposing waste. Effluence was contaminating the streets. The arrival of the typhus borne; plague train had been pre-notified to the rail authorities. With Czech soldiers controlling the train, the Japanese, now the most powerful military presence east of Lake Baikal, cooperated with Czech Legion men who'd remained loyal to the White Russians to manage the train loaded with many ill and dying passengers

It was directed into an engineering shed beyond the main station on the Quay of the Volunteer Fleet. Further along these tracks on the peninsular wrapping around the bay were the dozen or so refugee and troop trains yet to be offloaded of their miserable civilian passengers. These had been arriving for many months and with nowhere for people to be housed before ships were able to take escapees elsewhere, the trains were still crowded with unhappy refugees. Others had been emptied and slowly shipped on. The international missions were closing their own offices and evacuating representatives and any families present.

The Legion had drafted in assistance from a contingent of Canadian Red Cross. The polyglot nature of the city was clear to everyone on arrival, but in this case harnessed effectively to try to prevent the typhus spreading. The Canadians quickly separated those with symptoms and without and processed each group accordingly. Infested clothing was taken and burnt, replacement clothes were issued but much of it inadequate for the time of year and conditions. The refugees were powerless to complain. Their plight continued to be desperate. Both groups were then housed in a vast and freezing tobacco warehouse, but some enterprising younger women amongst them located the railway coal yard and took to stealing fuel for warmth. The Canadians turned a blind eye.

The Czech and British soldiers and those under their 'protection' were dealt with by the Legion. Eight Czech men and Taffy Davis were found to have typhus. Taffy knew that his work burying the infected dead refugees was likely to give him the disease. It was why he kept away from Eric and the others on the last few hours into the city. But these men fell under the Czech medical organisation. Two Czech soldiers died from this group.

Sedlak with the support of Cermak insisted to his compatriots that the British gunners were part of his command and needed to be treated accordingly. Initially refused, Sedlak discovered that a Major who'd been in the same Russian PoW camp in the Ukraine ran the station administration for refugee trains. The Major directed his team to respect Sedlak's demands. At Frank and Arthur's insistence, Eric's body was removed, wrapped in tarpaulin and temporarily kept in a barrack store room. With average daytime temperatures a bit higher than inland Siberia at between -5 and zero, it would be a few days before deterioration had an impact.

As non-infected men, they were quarantined for seven days in a segregated officers room in an Imperial Army barrack block on the western, Amur Bay end of Svetlanskaya Street. Their uniforms were removed, notionally for fumigation. Shirts and underclothes would be burnt, pockets being emptied of personal items beforehand. A complete set of British uniform clothes were reissued. There were plenty available from the large quantity of stores of British kit provided to the Czechs by the British Mission. These had been transported to Vladivostok as part of the greater strategic plans of the Allied Intervention. New boots, great coats and forage caps were also welcome. All now without any regimental, rank or medal ribbon insignia.

The modern barracks they occupied, built by the Tsarist government in 1912 as part of the militarisation of the city had an oil-fired boiler and an extensive, modern, hot-water pipe system. Limitless hot water, communal showers and large tubs with tiled seats within, were luxurious for the Czech and British soldiers who'd only experienced the cold privations of forest and train living for the last five months.

There was a camp barber, a local Chinese man who with the influx of heavily bearded soldiers could see a great opportunity for income. Despite the quarantine, he moved himself into the block bathroom, being available at any time to shave the heavy beards off these new customers. After seeing the results on some other men, the three gunners took advantage. The barber had a few words of English. What he did say many times when cutting and then shaving the very grey, Father Christmas beard from Brad's face was.

"You very old...... Very old man. ..... Too old." And a few minutes later.

"Too old........... Very, very old man for soldier."

When Arthur sat for his turn, he said to the barber, pointing at his chest.

"Very young man........ Very young."

By the time his face appeared from the dense growth and he'd heard his words being repeated back to him dozens of times, he regretted the English lesson he'd given.

The Malevich and Rappoport groups were treated as if they were Czech nationals too. After a few days the Doctor was able to work with the Canadian medics and nurses to provide insights into many of the issues he'd dealt with on the train. Alongside his family, Amelia and the Rappaports were taken to be housed in the luxury of the old German Embassy taken over by the White Russians and Czechs. It was located a little further up the hill on Pushkinskaya Street with incredible views overlooking the Golden Horn Bay, or Zolotoy Bay as it was known locally. The Embassy was being used for a combination of administration and accommodation. Although showing no signs of typhus infection they were notionally isolated for a week before they were permitted to leave the building to try to find a ship to take them elsewhere. During this time the Doctor came and went as he was needed, making the confinement a nonsense.

*

Having been separated from the Rappoports, Frank and Arthur were now in a dilemma with what to do with Isak's satchel. Brad knew about the bag as well, and what was expected. Still unaware of the contents, it had to be returned to the family before they or the gunners left the city. The difficulties in securing a berth for a safe passage were already known. Where people might end up was not. Their lack of legitimate paperwork might make it particularly difficult for the British gunners. One morning after they'd had their usual breakfast of bread and a bitter coffee that was only palatable with plenty of sugar delivered to the isolation room, they had the following conversation. Arthur spoke, trying to organise the challenges of the days ahead.

"In two days our quarantine finishes. We bury Eric the day after. So far we've had no response from the British mission to our messages. That assumes there is anyone left who gives a fig. Sedlak confirmed through his people that most of them are packing up to scarper themselves. There'll be going home through the U.S. or Canada, or south via India and the canal.

We need to find Amelia's lot to return the bag and get ourselves some sea transport out of here."

Now Brad. "That'll be a ship then Wally."

"Well probably. Or anything seaworthy that will get us to a ship. Out there in the harbour Brad there are plenty of these wooden fishing boats. Junks they call them. With the number of people trying to get away from here, I reckon the chance of us getting on a ship are slim. Persuading one of these junks to take us to another place where the clamour for ship space is not so great, might be a better bet."

Brad was nodding and Frank joined in.

"That's a good idea Wally. Has it only taken the five days we've been locked up here to come up with that?"

"Just today Frank. As you've seen, I've been sleeping most of that time. It keeps thoughts of losing Eric away. And probably like you, I feel safe here after the months we've had. So sleep comes easier."

Now Brad spoke.

"It's true. It's been exhausting, but now feels like we're really on the home stretch. So we have things to do. After we've seen to Eric I suggest we split our efforts. I'll try to track down the British Mission to see what they think. Frank can find Amelia. Sedlak's Major should know where they are. And as it was your idea Wally you, can start in the harbour."

After some time discussing the merits of the task allocation, they agreed on the plan. Arthur sometimes wished he kept his best ideas to himself. They also discussed Isak's satchel and thought it was time to check the contents to see what they were dealing with. Frank retrieved the bag from the top of a wardrobe. He placed it on a table where he and Arthur now sat and undid the two leather straps. Inside were sheets of newspaper packed around a blue velvet cloth bag. The contents was carefully removed and placed on the table in the same way it had sat in the satchel. The bag had been made with a double thickness and draw-strings at either end. When these were undone, Frank peered in, then put his hand in to remove the object, which he placed on the table. They were silently staring at it. Nothing was said for several minutes, and then it was, 'Bloody hell,' from Brad, standing behind Frank's shoulder. Followed by more silence. Frank moved the article around so he and Athur could look at it from a different angle.

Sat in front of them was an incredibly exquisite ornament. At its tallest about seven inches. A two-wheeled carriage being drawn by an ornately cast figure in gold of a man in a heavy coat and ushanka hat. His hands grasped the handles reaching forward from the enclosed sedan chair. The matched wheels had a dozen thin spokes inside a perfect circle, all in gold. The rim of the wheel glittered with, what they assumed were small diamonds. Clear, finely cut crystals twinkling the daylight back at them. Each spindle end of the wheel axle had a larger round diamond closing it off. The frame of the boxed-in chair was gold. There was a hinged glass door at the front. The two side panels and door had small windows from the top to halfway, with the back of the box a solid panel. The panels were an unusual green in colour, as smooth as finely polished marble. Inside the carriage also in gold, a military man wearing a uniform and cap. The roof, a square cupola of the same green with more small diamonds running up from the four corners and another lozenge shaped one creating the point.

They stared at it until Frank broke the silence.

"Malachite."

Brad repeated.

"Malachite?"

"Yes, malachite. It's this polished green mineral on the outside. Jewellers use it a lot when they're making fancy pieces. I've seen plenty of trinkets in Hatton Garden windows that had this colouring. I was told it was malachite."

Brad again. "Didn't Amelia say that the old man had been a jeweller?"

Arthur was still apparently mesmerised by the ornament. Frank answered.

"She did. He wasn't an ordinary jeweller though. He ran a workshop that made items for Faberge, the world's most famous supplier to aristocracy and the Russian royal family."

"Right, so this is worth a few bob then? Probably why she entrusted it to you two. Just a thought, do you think it might cover the cost of a first class berth on the next ship out?"

Frank knew he was joking. Well he thought he knew. He then said.

"Right, we know what we have, let's get it back in the bag."

He moved to cover it in the velvet cloth again just as Arthur moved it around one more time.

"Are you okay Wally?"

Arthur snapped out of his trance.

"Yes. Yes I am. I'm good."

To Frank who knew him so well, he didn't seem okay. That afternoon, to fill the time, they played chess between the three of them, Brad having been taught by the other two. He'd picked it up quickly and was now as good as them, all a similar standard. In the six games Arthur played he lost all of them. That never happened. His concentration was elsewhere, but when asked again he replied it was nothing.

2. Star Gazer.
Monday 19th January 1920.

On the day the Czech and British soldier's quarantine finished, Sedlak had arranged for Eric to be buried in a small military cemetery close to one of the sea facing battery emplacements. It was part of the extensive city fortifications the Russians had been building since the late 1890's. Given a boost by their embarrassment of the 1905 war against Japan, they'd yet to be completed. Now, with the revolution, they never would. The cemetery was not too far from the barracks. Sedlak had arranged for a small truck to take the plain wooden coffin, himself and the three gunners. Taffy Davis was still being treated for typhus. The few graves the cemetery contained, marked with wooden crosses were of construction workers and a couple of soldiers who'd died of disease and accidents. The large naval gun emplacements dug into the rock had seen no action, they'd not even housed any ordnance.

Picks and shovels had been provided. The men sat in the back of the American made Ford truck in a solemn mood as it trundled up the roads to the high ground over the city. They stopped at the end of a dirt track, a small host of graves to one side. Arthur and Frank looked about, asked the others to wait for a few minutes and walked further up, about sixty yards, to the top of the hill. They reached the summit and turned to look across Amur Bay to the coast opposite. It was a beautiful view; the clouds were breaking above their heads. On the opposite coast the peninsular island of Peschanyy seemed to be under a single beam of sun, like a theatre spotlight.

Frank spoke. "Eric might see this as one of his beloved Scottish lochs. It's a stunning view."

"It is Frank," and after a pause, "we need to haul him up here and break this frozen ground."

The Czech driver carried the two picks and two shovels. Knowing he'd been detailed to transport a fellow soldier to his resting place, he'd considerately made a small wooden cross the day before. The four soldiers lifted Eric onto their shoulders, as bearers to his final billet. The snow on this high exposed ground was old and hard, but not deep. The wind up here blew it down into the city below. There was a mere breathe of breeze today. They removed their great coats to work. Even the driver wanted to help. It took them an hour to dig the grave. First through a frozen foot of earth and then deep enough before they were satisfied. Their clothes were muddy. It didn't matter, they could clean everything up on return to the modern barracks.

Carefully lowering the coffin on two ropes, they stood, staring into the grave.

"At a time like this we need Taffy." Said Frank.

Arthur replied. "Well he's dealing with his own mortality right now, but you're right he'd know what to say......... As we know, Eric wasn't a religious man. So why don't each of us just say something for ourselves."

"Good idea Wally." It was Sedlak.

"I'll start if you'll let me."

The three gunners nodded while they organised their own thoughts. He then surprised them by starting to sing in his own tongue at a tenor pitch. An occasional flat note amongst the several verses of the serious sounding, anthemic song. The driver could understand the words and he stood rigidly whilst his compatriot continued to the end. On finishing he started talking in Czech for far longer than expected, well over five minutes, with his eyes looking into the grave. He was talking to Eric as if no one else was present. The driver was nodding with a smile every now and then. Sedlak finished the diatribe, closed his eyes, clasped his hands, said a prayer in Czech, then added in English.

"Sleep well my friend. Far from home, but always with us."

Raybury responded.

"Thanks Marek. You can tell us what you said later."

"Maybe Brad, maybe."

Brad then said his piece. He told a short story about how Eric discovered Brad's latent fascination with the moon and stars on a shared guard duty one night at the training camp back in Archangel. It was the first time Eric had pressed Brad for information on anything other than for military necessity. Neither Frank nor Arthur knew about this. Brad said from then on Eric would quietly seek him out on clear nights when time permitted. As they looked into the Ural and then Siberian night sky, Brad taught him the constellations that he knew.

They started with the North Star, Polaris, with its brightness and as a navigation beacon at night. From there Brad said, they identified the Plough, Ursa Minor, Ursa Major, the Twins of Gemini and Orion, the only group that Brad knew the star names. Back in September he'd shared these with Eric too. The Scot decided that Beetlejuice was a great name for a star. Bellatrix was pretty good too, but Beetlejuice was better. Once known to him, on the clear nights they could see the stars, it was Orion's right shoulder that Eric would look to identify first. Ignoring the obvious bright North Star, Polaris. He would nudge Brad to point out Beetlejuice.

"So, my star-gazing friend, whenever I look up to Orion I'll think of you and the idle times we stared at the stars millions of miles away, just wondering what secrets they hold. Eric 'Beetlejuice' Amos, it was a pleasure to know you."

Brad struggled to get his last sentence out. He closed his eyes tightly and a tear rolled down his right cheek. Frank then picked up from him.

"Did you know anything about that Wally?"

"A complete surprise to me. I found him staring at the sky one night but didn't think anything of it. Always a dark horse."

After a short pause. "You go next Frank; I'll take the last leg."

Frank then noted the complete lack of a faith based prayer, in English. He knew Arthur wouldn't add one and without Taffy being there thought Eric deserved a bit of religious insurance, just in case there really was anything in it. A recitation he knew well in Yiddish, he tried to get the English right.

"Respected and praised be God's great name in the world which he created according to his plan. May his greatness be revealed in our lifetime, and the life of our people. To which we say Amen."

Arthur and Brad both repeated the Amen. It seemed the right thing to do.

"Blessed, praised, respected, celebrated, loved and lauded be the name of God, beyond our earthly words. To which we say Amen."

"Amen."

"May there be peace for all our countries. And may the God who creates agreement, bring peace to us all. To which we say Amen."

"Amen."

On finishing his version of the funeral prayer he looked at Arthur and said.

"We have to give him the best chance Wally, even though he wasn't a believer."

Arthur nodded in agreement. Frank went on to say more in another unfamiliar language. It was the Hebrew that his own religious education had embedded in his mind. He came to an obvious finish and Arthur needed to add his words.

"There's no doubt you've been through a lot in your lifetime Aims. Some you shared, most you didn't. You were sometimes difficult, direct and always reliable. It took a long time for me and Frank to get to know you. I'm glad we did. You became a good friend and in my mum's eyes, part of our family. Sharing my letters from home with you helped me in the mud, death and destruction we've seen plenty of. As I am now, she will be very sad to hear you've moved on."

He had to stop for a moment as his voice started to crack up. Unable to speak, he swallowed deeply, screwed his eyes up and wept. Frank put his arm about the younger man's shoulder. The emotion came from the sad moment on the hillside and the sudden intrusion of thought's from home, his mum and Alice. After a few minutes he regained his composure and the words Taffy had spoken over the snow grave of the Russian typhus women came to him. Not recalling them exactly, he paraphrased what he could.

"May the road ahead be clear in front of you. May the wind be gentle on your back. May the sun be warm on your face and the rain fall softly on the ground about you. Maybe you should wear a warm hat too."

Brad and Frank recognised the ad lib that broke the morose mood and both smiled.

"And if there is an afterlife and we're lucky enough to be sent to the same place, may you be safe until we meet with you to revive our friendship. You said it yourself Eric, we started as strangers, finished as brothers. Through hell and half-way around the world. It really has been an amazing journey."

As he tried to get out his last words he was again very emotional.

"We have to leave you now Eric. You have a peaceful bed for eternity".

After a few moments Brad added.

"Good words Wally. You've done him proud",

They filled the grave back in, the driver also helping. It took a lot less time than the digging. The driver then took the wooden cross he'd made; two small, one inch thick planks nailed together and pushed it into the soft earth at the head of the grave. Eric's feet were closest to the steep drop to the shore of Amur Bay. They finished the job and stepped back. Frank then gave each of the men a small pebble from some he'd picked from the soil dug out of the grave.

"We place these on the graves of our friends and family. Some may find it odd that we're doing so on a cross, but no matter. It's the symbolism that counts here. Those of my faith who see these pebbles will know this man had good friends who were here to see him leave for his final journey."

Frank stepped toward the cross and placed his stone close to the upright.

"It's an expression of the permanence of life. Eric's memory continues to live through each one of us."

Arthur placed his pebble on the opposite side of the upright, Sedlak placed his next to Arthur's and the driver, to balance the look put his next to the first one. Brad was rolling his black pebble in his right hand. It looked like a smooth piece of Scarborough jet that a Yorkshire lad he once knew wore with his dog-tags as a lucky charm. It didn't work; he was now under the mud somewhere near Ypres.

In his long military career Brad had stood by the graves of many brave men. The holes sometimes contained a lot more than one, two or a few. Eric had been the first one he'd got to know who'd shared his fascination with the stars. He briefly looked up into the sky with its fluffy white, broken clouds. Then stretching forward he placed his pebble on the far end of the cross, on Eric's right.

"Beetlejuice………… Orion's right shoulder……….. Now on Eric's."

With strained faces Frank and Arthur nodded and smiled. For them both it was a nice end to the journey they'd taken with the taciturn Scot who'd become a beloved friend. From enlistment in Trafalgar Square to a hilltop in far Eastern Russia. An incredible trip, none of them could have imagined.

*

They climbed into the back of the Ford truck and the driver lifted the tail-gate to secure it on each side with a pin in a bracket. The mood was heavy. A few seconds later he reappeared, peering over the tailgate with a sheepish grin. Lifting both arms he held two bottles of 25 year old Glenfarclas, Speyside malt whisky and spoke a few words to Sedlak. The Scotch was not something that Arthur, Frank, Brad and least of all Marek Sedlak were familiar with. They were quite sure Eric wouldn't have been either. Brad commented on the delivery.

"Marek, your driver seems remarkably well prepared for us today."

"Yes, of course. He was told about this detail some days ago. Many of my fellow Bohemians know that Eric died defending civilian refugees from bandits. An honourable death. The soldiers from the train had spread the word. The Captain thought to himself that Josef would be the right man for the job. He comes from a family of undertakers. He knows how these things are supposed to go. The bottles were acquired from the British Mission's Officers Club, not quite legitimately, I understand. Josef said we must now get miserably drunk and tell the good and funny stories about your friend."

He added pensively, "My friend too."

He pulled the cork stopper from the top of one bottle and took a swig. For him a new experience. Almost coughing, his head gave an involuntary jerk as the alcohol seared his mouth and burnt his throat. It was a spirit he'd never taken before, a weird taste combination of apples, pears, honey and a touch nutty. He shook his head again with a small gasp. He passed the Scotch to Arthur who, looking at the bottle in his hand slowly repeated what Sedlak had said.

"Acquired ……….. Not ……. Quite ……… Legitimately…………. Eric would have loved that."

He took a slug and also shook his head.

Brad then asked as the bottle was passed to him.

"So tell us Makek, what was it you said up there?"

Sedlak shuffled on the hard bench seat sitting directly opposite Raybury.

"I just told him he was amongst friends and he'd be remembered."

"That was it? What sounded like a hearty song and five minute to say just that."

Sedlak conceded he needed to explain.

"The song was what I'm sure will become the National Anthem for the new Bohemian state. It's called *Where my home is.'* Perhaps not perfect singing, or the best song, but I thought a good idea up there in the cold."

"It was a good song Marek. We had no other music and I wasn't about to sing 'It's a long way to Tipperary'." Said Frank.

"And I'm glad you didn't." Arthur cut in. "You've an awful singing voice. You can't go about waking the dead with it!"

"What about the speech then?" Brad persisted. Sedlak looked uncomfortable again.

"It was just a legendary tale that my dad would tell me about a heroic soldier who travelled the world. I don't know how he did it, but he had several endings and made it sound different each time. I told the tale and then used the ending where he never returned home but lived on in the mythology of Bohemia. It also seemed right for the time."

The others nodded in agreement and passed the bottles around on the bumpy, jolting ride back down the hill to the barracks. As Josef predicted and directed, they spent the rest of the day finishing the whisky, sharing memories and laughing at those funny times that come back to mind in the intense aftermath of a burial.

*

The barrack room they'd been allocated had four beds, only three occupied, the other available if Taffy recovered. It would have been for a platoon's NCO's. At some ludicrous hour in the early morning, Frank woke up with an aching head and sandpaper mouth to see Arthur sitting at the table. A candle was burning, the electric light being left off to limit disturbing the others. The whisky had already done it for Frank, he needed a piss too. On the table was Isak's satchel, brought down from the top of the wardrobe. The bejewelled, man-drawn, sedan chair carriage was out of the bag. Arthur was staring at it.

"I feel terrible Wally. Why did you make me drink that stuff?"

"Well did you drink the pint of water medicine before you fell out? Of course not. Best thing if you're drunk on spirits. Water before bed. I didn't work in a chemists and learn nothing you know."

Frank shook his delicate head in despair as he went out to the latrines shared by them and the thirty Czech soldiers in the barrack room next door. On his return he sat on the other wooden chair opposite Arthur.

"What is it with this thing Wally. You've seemed a bit obsessed with it since we got it out of the bag. It's not ours you know. We can't keep it."

Arthur knew Frank wasn't being serious. Very obvious and rarely funny. Arthur looked directly at him in the flickering light to the side of the table.

"I don't know Frank. It's a beautiful, ornate, ornament and must be worth a fortune."

"What don't you know? We still can't keep it."

"Yes, yes, it's not that. I feel like I've seen it before, maybe in a picture, a magazine or something, just not like this."

"Well maybe Wally. But tomorrow we've got to start finding a way out of here. Brad's going to the British Mission to see if they can help us, I'm going to find Amelia, the Rappoports and Malevich. I'll take this with me. I think they're in the old German Embassy according to Sedlak's sources. And you drew the short straw, down to the docks for you my lad. You can work out what ships are about and how we might get out of here."

Frank picked up the treasure and placed it back in the velvet covering, and then back in the satchel. "If you think hard enough, it'll come back to you Wally. I'm sure it will."

They both returned to their beds.

3. Hong Kong Bankers.
Tuesday 20th January 1920.

The following morning, the three men left the Czech Barracks shortly before 8.30 am. as the sun was just beginning to rise. It was a bitterly cold, grey, windless day, where the sky seemed to be oppressively pushing down onto the Earth. Greatcoats, hats and gloves were needed. Walking would help warm the body, hands and feet. Sedlak had negotiated a cash payment to the three gunners 'for the military protection duties undertaken on the Czech controlled train from Vyatka to Vladivostok'. They were being paid as if they'd been Czech soldiers during this time. It was partly roubles, partly American dollars and other coins and notes that might have been Chinese or Japanese.

Brad as the notional commander would visit the British Mission located in the abandoned Tsarist administration building at 67 Svetlanskaya Street. Then on to the Canadian Red Cross hospital set up in a disused meat warehouse to check up on Taffy. Frank was to go to the old German embassy on Pushkinskaya Street to return Isak's satchel to Amelia and the family Rappoport. He would try to find out from them what arrangements if any they'd been able to make to leave the city. Arthur to the docks to see what the options might be for boarding a ship in the event that no official help became available.

Frank and Arthur had each written a telegram message they hoped the Mission would be able to convey to Betty and Frank's parents. There'd been no communication home since falling under the control of Privakov and the Dyer Battalion mutineers back in August. Prior to that they'd sent a few letters home and Arthur had written to Alice several times. If there had been any responses, and in the time there definitely would have been, the letters never reached them before taken prisoner. This was an opportunity to say where they were and that they were trying to get home. Brad took these with him.

The segregation of duties made sense, although Arthur wasn't sure what the docks and shipyards on the waterfront would deliver, if anything. Their confinement meant they'd not seen much of the city, so none of them were sure what to expect. They would meet back at the barracks no later than 5pm to share the results. It got dark around 6pm. and they'd been advised not to be out by themselves after sunset. The Red Light area, close to the harbour was known as the 'Bucket of Blood'. Currently recording one murder a night, a dangerous spot for drunk sailors and soldiers of whatever nationality. They'd be carrying their Lee Enfield rifles issued in Archangel and amazingly still in their possession. The weapon demonstrated they were part of an armed force in a city full of men in uniforms, made up of an all-sorts mix of British, Czech, American and Japanese.

After 15 minutes walking east along Svetlanskaya Street, Arthur dropped down some steps to join the Harbour Road over which the main thoroughfare passed. This then swung to his left and stretched out in front of him running the whole length of the waterfront. The road was already full of business. Mainly hand drawn, wooden, rick-shaw carts ferrying fish and seafood produce from the commercial fishing quayside that was much further along the harbour road. A few with military officers sat in them. Wrapped up in thick coats and a military cap of some description needed to keep some warmth in the body.

There were sailors from one of the international naval ships clustered in the first section of the docks that Arthur was approaching. Or they may have been Army officers or Allied administrators returning to their offices after early meetings. Anyone being drawn in one of these rick-shaws early in the morning in the middle of a freezing January needed a good reason to be out. The small, ageless looking Asiatic men with their bowed head and determined shuffling jog all wore an almost uniform thick black tunic and ushanka hats with the ear flaps tied tightly under the chin. Their passengers arms clasped to their front as an additional but pointless protection from the cold.

At this north western corner of the Zolotoy Bay, or Golden Horn Bay to the Europeans, Arthur could see the mile or so expanse of water to the east closing into a cul-de-sac carved into the land like a finger. Looking south-west the exit channel ran toward the barrier of Russia Island and then west to Amur Bay where Eric had his view, and east out to the vastness of the mighty Pacific Ocean......... and home to Britain. It was clear why a trading and militarily strategic city had grown up around this well protected bay.

The ships at this end of the harbour were all drab grey, armed naval gunboats. The American Stars and Stripes could be seen on three, one of which, with the large numerals 117 on the bow had intense activity surrounding it. Cranes were loading items into the hold and a queue of bedraggled looking people clutching bags and some, suitcases were waiting to enter a building. Arthur observed a family group exiting the building and making their way to the gangway to board the ship. The other ships included a Canadian Maple leaf next to a Red Cross on one, two with French Tricolours and half a dozen with the Japanese red spot Rising Sun. Disappointingly, no Union Jacks, so he headed toward what might be the most friendly to a British soldier, the Canadian medical ship.

There were two gang-planks leaning off the ship. From the movement of the few people up and down, one was on, the other off. At the quayside end of the 'on' plank stood two fresh-faced Canadian sailors on sentry duty. Arthur initiated a conversation by asking them how long they'd been in here. Two weeks apparently. Neither men had seen war having been too young to serve. They both came from Vancouver, had volunteered together in 1918 and found themselves on this hospital ship. An officer appeared as they were talking and queried Arthur on what he wanted. He tried to explain, but as soon as he mentioned the need to secure a passage home he was told the ship would be there for at least another month. He should speak to the British military authorities or look elsewhere. He might try the commercial freight ships at the far end of the harbour. Pointing to the busy American boat he said it was departing the following day with a large number of refugees.

He continued his walk along the harbour road until he had to turn away from the bay to walk around a substantial ship-builders yard containing a dry dock several hundred yards long. An unfinished warship was waiting for normality to return. That being the only possibility of it being finished to serve its purpose. There were no workmen and the area was covered in snow through inactivity. Back on the harbour road the next section was full of small fishing junks bobbing at the side of wooden jetty's, their catch off-loaded, the fishermen were repairing nets, lobster pots and other kit. Their hands and fingers must have been immune to the cold. Buckets of odd looking shellfish were being traded on the quayside where the jetty's joined. Along the road to his left were the wharfs and warehouses to salt and process fish for preservation and storage.

Beyond the jetty's there were perhaps a dozen ocean going, steam freight ships, many types of sailing clippers, schooners, pinisi's and larger Chinese junks under sail that traded up and down the Pacific coast as far as Hong Kong, the South China Sea, the Malay peninsula and Indonesia. They were also flagged, some unfamiliar to Arthur, most with the Chinese flag of five coloured vertical stripes, red, yellow, blue, white and black. Each colour representing significant ethnic groups in the Chinese Republic. This flag had been very visible on the last stretch of the train journey through Harbin on the Chinese Eastern Railway. Further down the harbour road there were some more warships and smaller naval launches of the Imperial Russian Navy flying a flag showing a black double-headed eagle with a gold background.

He almost missed it. No flag, so its low-key nature made it almost invisible. A small Union Jack painted on the starboard side bow absurdly next to the boat's name, SS Hamburg. Was it British or German? He was a little confused. A small, ugly, freight steamer with a black hull, a red band at the deck level, a bridge and accommodation section to the rear painted black and grey. There were no sail masts so a boat of this size, a couple of hundred feet long, would hug the coast to within a few of miles. It was tied at both ends to large iron bollards on a heavy duty metal-framed jetty to which a gang-plank was attached. There was no activity around or on the boat but there were two men standing on the forecastle. Dressed for the cold, there were puffs of smoke rising intermittently from the cigarettes or pipes they were smoking.

As Arthur drew closer one of the men saw him and pointed him out to the other. The talking stopped. They watched with curiosity the soldier walking passed the wooden junk to its front with indecipherable lettering. With his rifle slung over his left shoulder he raised his right arm in a wave and called out.

"Hello there. I see the flag. Is this a British boat?"

There was no answer as the two men spoke and Arthur got closer. Then one of them called out.

"Are you British?"

"I am. Bombardier Arthur Walton, Royal Field Artillery."

He thought using his old rank might mean something.

"More recently of the North Russian Relief Force………….. and now here."

There was another conversation on the boat.

"Are you taking the piss?"

"No sir. Why would I do that?"

Now the other one spoke.

"For two reasons. You're in the far east, not North Russia. That's five thousand plus miles away. Perhaps you got lost?"

The two men laughed.

"And secondly, all the British regiments have gone home. I waved the Hampshire's off on HMS Monteagle back in November, the last time we were here."

Arthur realised this wasn't going to be easy. He'd initially felt confident, he was now less so. He didn't think a full explanation would help right now, it would take too long and sound implausible. He tried another tack.

"I come from Loughborough in Leicestershire. Enlisted at St. Martin-in-the-Fields, Trafalgar Square, August 1914, trained at Woolwich and Shoeburyness, then spent four years in France and Flanders. I'm here with three other men. We're looking to make our way back to England."

Another conversation on the forecastle as Arthur stood looking up.

"Okay Bombardier Arthur Walton, Royal Field Artillery ….. and the North Russian Relief Force, come up here and talk to us."

It was a most peculiar sensation that Arthur couldn't recall feeling since the excitement of his first horse ride on Alma in Taylor's yard. Or the morning he'd woken with Alice in David Saffer's mews cottage in London. A feeling of elation, of the world opening up, of a future becoming apparent. Maybe this positive sense released something else too, as at this very moment he remembered where his idea of Isak's carriage came from. A metal frame and battered box on wheels sitting on the mantelpiece in Adam Saffer's study in Tynte House. As quickly as it came, he dismissed the ridiculous thought. There was no connection, the similarity was tenuous at best.

He strode up the gang-plank entering the deck just behind the forecastle with some confidence, the two men waiting at the top.

"Come and tell us your already absurd story young man."

Said the slightly older looking of the two men, both probably in their forty's. Now with a fresh, beardless face, only retaining a ubiquitous army moustache, Arthur also realised he probably did look young.

Introducing themselves as Andrew Armstrong and Ian Taylor, well-spoken bankers and trade financiers from Hong Kong working for the Jardine Matheson trading company. Mr. Taylor explained that the ship was now owned by the Indo-China Steam Navigation Company. The state-of-the-art steamer was indeed German, built around 1910 in, not surprisingly, Hamburg. It had been operating out of the German leased territory surrounding Jiaozhou Bay and its main port of Tsingtao. Not much of this made sense to Arthur, yet it did clear up the German name. In 1914 the territory was occupied by Britain's Japanese allies. The wily German skipper, not wanting his ship in their hands had already sailed south to Hong Kong to concede it to Jardine's. They kept him on and retained the name, SS Hamburg in recognition of his action.

Arthur was led to the bridge tower beneath which were crew accommodation rooms and a small mess room and galley. There was no-one else about. They explained that the crew of six Chinese were all ashore, probably in a gambling house playing Mah-Jong. It was unlikely any of them would return, but there were plenty of other men in the port working the tramp-steamers up and down the coast. The steamer's skipper, a Captain Felix Krull would be with his local mistress. He had one in every major port from Singapore to Sapporo. When they left and the next tramp steamer came in, the mistress would be the next Captain's. It was good steady business for the brothel madam's.

They removed their coats and hats in the warmth of the mess room, heated by coal fired hot-water pipes reflecting the finest German engineering. Although, clearly the senior man, Mr. Armstrong put a kettle on the stove and subsequently made some tea. It was served in china cups, looking clear and greenish in colour, with no milk or sugar offered. It tasted clean and different. Much fresher than the black Russian tea.

Sitting at a screwed down refectory table with bench seats, Arthur on one side opposite the other two, he told his scarcely believable tale. He was listened to with attention, a few questions, raised eyebrows and glances between the bankers. At the end of about forty minutes, numerous cigarettes and two more pots of tea shared between them he finished by saying.

"And that's how the four of us came to be here in Vladivostok. Sgt. Raybury is at the British Mission and checking on Taffy today. So we're looking for a way to return to England. We have no British identification documents, only some unreadable Bolshevik issued papers that have got us this far."

Mr. Armstrong spoke.

"Well I've heard some real fantasies in the world of business Mr. Walton, but nothing that compares to the fairytale you've just told us."

Arthur felt his balloon deflate.

But then Mr. Taylor added.

"I agree, so completely improbable, it has to be true."

They both laughed and Arthur realised he'd got somewhere.

There followed a whole host of specific questions about the journey from the north of Russia to the east. Now in a genuinely interested way as the events described were fascinating. They poked around the detail of being taken prisoner by the Bolsheviks, the celebratory day with the Cossacks, the train across Siberia. Arthur did his best to fill them in.

In return, they told him of the withdrawal of British troops and the failure of the British and other Allied government's Russian intervention to reverse the Bolshevik takeover. The war had changed a lot. Now this revolutionary force appeared unstoppable, not just for the people of Russia, but many believed it would also sweep through Europe and America too. Mr. Armstrong said.

"We're not able to take you and your friends back to Britain Bombardier Walton. What we can do is take you with us when we leave here. We'll be loading a cargo of surplus army uniforms tomorrow; nobody seems to want them here anymore and don't want the Reds to get them. In a couple of days we travel south along the coast to Tsingtao where we'll sell this, pick up a cargo of beer from the old German brewery there, run that to Shanghai where we might buy porcelain or iron cooking pots and so on down to Hong Kong. You get the idea. Our local agents manage the trade, Mr Taylor and I arrange the banking payments and trade finance. Hong Kong is the British Empire's business hub in the far east. There are ships between the port and Britain every week."

Arthur wasn't quite sure about the trading and finance piece. It didn't matter. What these two colonial gentlemen were suggesting was their tramp steamer might be able to get somewhere closer to transport that might get them back to Britain. The four gunners, assuming Taffy was well enough to leave with them, would displace four crewmen which meant they would need to work their passage. There wasn't enough room to carry passengers. The SS Hamburg was scheduled to load and leave by the 23rd January, three days' time. It couldn't be soon enough for Arthur, so long as there was no official military means to repatriate the men.

*

Arthur left the boat and spent a couple of hours walking about the city in the afternoon. Despite the bitter cold, the place was full of armed men and several different types of civilians. There were those looking anxious with permanently cautious faces of concern, often in small family groups. These were walking purposefully to somewhere clutching folders, brief-cases or sheaves of paperwork in their hands. They were probably the lucky ones, transient refugees who'd managed to move off the trains into some other accommodation and were in the process of trying to find a way out.

Another group were local people going about their business. Food was generally in short supply, but product markets were open and it was available at a price. Walking away from the harbour road he'd seen a covered retail fish market with a cacophony of noise emerging. Peering through the ten foot sliding doors he could see local people haggling with the traders over metal pails of fish and seafood. These people were here before the revolution and invasion of their world by foreign armies, they would still be here afterwards.

The final set were small collections of heavily armed men of many ethnic origins. Imposing, threatening, intimidating. Cossacks, Mongolians, Chinese, South Asian and Turkic men were clustered together, frequently spilling out of a café or bar in the streets that ran up the hill from Svetlanskaya Street. Warlords and their gangs that had fallen outside of an organised government or military force. They were exploiting the chaos of a city with no central control and a hinterland where the White Russians were no longer in charge themselves. The Japanese were following their own agenda of territorial acquisition and economic exploitation. They had no interest in maintaining any kind of law outside of their areas of control.

Ignoring the people, Arthur could see all the main buildings on Svetlanskaya Street and those running from it were European in style. They looked similar to those lining the streets he'd seen on the day he enlisted in central London.

*

He got back to the barracks shortly after 4pm. Frank was already there. They agreed to share their day when Brad appeared, which was shortly before 5pm. He'd had trouble locating Taffy but insisted on some sweet tea before he spoke of his search. Sitting at the table they went through the day, Brad first.

"I'll start with Taffy. It only gets worse from there." It sounded ominous.

"He's recovering in the Canadian medical centre. He's almost fit again."

"Well that's good." Said Frank, in a positive way.

"It is Frank. But he doesn't want to come back with us."

In unison Arthur and Frank's jaws dropped.

Frank replied. "Did you say something to upset him?"

Brad gave a false smile at the dig.

"No, no. And it wasn't even the thought of several months on a boat with you two that put him off. Although he did mention the voyage back as part of the problem. I'll come back to that."

Now Arthur. "So what's his problem then?"

"I'll try to explain in the way he did. I guess in a word, motivation. What's driving him. He said he's now at a fork in the road of his own life. One leads back to South Wales with the only option to go down the pits again. Potentially a confined life of pain and mental hell. We know he can't deal with that. He said the other road has revealed itself to him more recently. He's always been a man of quiet faith. We saw how committed he was to be providing a Christian closure for the refugees on the train. Well there are a group of American missionaries helping at the Canadian hospital who are heading into China. They're not evangelistic preachers. They're practical men and women who want to build churches and spread the faith through their good work and example. Taffy will join them. It will be a few months before they go, in the spring when the temperature rises a bit."

Brad stood up and stared out of the window.

"So he can't face a future in the mines and he sees a positive, meaningful existence with the missionaries. And his last negative point was being cooped up on a boat of some kind for three months. It was difficult enough for him on the trip from England to Archangel, having to sleep on deck to quell his nightmares. He won't do that again."

Arthur spoke. "I think we all probably understand why he's doing this. His reasons are very personal and compelling. I guess similar reasons as to why we all volunteered for Russia. We couldn't see how Britain could give us a future after the war. It was pretty grim in Loughborough and in London too Frank?"

"That's true. Grim is a good word for it, although I heard its worse up north. Maybe it won't be much better when we get back. I think things look a bit different for me now though."

Nothing was added but this seemed to be an allusion to the clear relationship that had flowered between him and Amelia.

Brad again. "So moving on. I found what was left of the British Mission. A small administrative cadre of officers and some jumped up, self-important civilians. I eventually managed to get through them for an interview with a Captain Savory. He'd been in Iraq with a regiment of Sikhs; had an MC ribbon on his tunic. Most of whatever they had there was now in packing boxes spread around the offices."

He paused to light a cigarette. Frank and Arthur listened without interrupting.

"Captain Savory heard what I had to say, himself saying very little. Circumspect would be the right word. Suspicious and cautious are others. He asked me for any identification papers. I explained these had been taken from us by our Bolshevik captors who'd provided us with some papers to get through the chaos of Vyatka and central Russia. I showed these to him and he said he couldn't read the Cyrillic script. They might be a shopping list for all he could tell. He then told me the main body of British troops the Mission had to account for, had been dealt with. The regiments and additional detachments had been sent home over the last six months from Vladivostok. He was sure the same was true in Murmansk and Archangel. They'd been warned to be vigilant with regard to potential revolutionaries infiltrating the repatriation of soldiers and selected refugees the Mission was now helping."

Arthur asked. "He's not being very helpful then?"

"You could say that. He did concede that some officers and men were captured by the Bolsheviks and held in Krasnoyarsk. We passed through it a few weeks ago and several thousand miles back. It was the place we stopped for water and saw that pack of dogs going at those abandoned carcasses. The uniformed ones that looked like they'd been lined up and executed."

The men were quiet for a moment as the memory returned. Unpleasant to recall, amongst a long list of such events.

"Those British prisoners, or hostages perhaps, are now part of high level political discussions between Churchill, the British government and the Reds. We are not those men."

"Did you give him the telegrams?" Said Arthur

"I did. He said he couldn't possibly send personal communications through official military channels. He actually said, 'as you can see we are extremely busy here packing away vital documents to return to Britain, we're not a post office service Mr. Raybury. Sgt. Raybury, I had to correct him."

"So is that how it was left?" Asked Frank.

"Not quite. He said he would make an official enquiry to the War Office to try to verify what I'd told him. This would take several days and I should return in a week's time."

Frank again. "It sounds like no help from our military or government officials at this end then. Maybe the War Office will come up trumps. Hey Wally, don't you know someone there who could pull some strings for us?"

"Possibly Frank, if you can find a way for me to get a personal message to him?"

"Good point ….. well made."

Not yet ready to deliver his more positive news, Arthur said.

"So we've lost Taffy to the church and the British army seems to have disowned us. How did you're visit go Frank?"

"Yes, a little better. Not for us but certainly good news for the Rappoport's and Dr. Malevich's family. They'd managed to get away from the general train quarantine through the Doctors ability to contribute to the management of the typhus contagion. Very fortunate by all accounts as there have been numerous additional deaths amongst our passengers. The Doc. was insistent they were all part of the same group and had to be kept together."

Brad questioned. "And that was in the old German embassy building?"

"That's right Brad. Fairly comfortable it seems to be too, compared to the refugee trains in the station and for those in the old meat warehouse where the Canadians have their medical facilities. There's also a number of senior White Russian generals and their families at the embassy. Not surprisingly, Amelia has busied herself finding out who these people are and came across a General Zourabov and his wife. They'd once lived in Petrograd and then Moscow. They were familiar with Julias Rappaport's ornate designs of silver and how respected the Faberge work-masters were. As soon as they heard his wife Irena, Simona and Isak were here, through Amelia of course, they introduced them to some American military administrators. The outcome was messages sent back and forth to Mikhail in London and some exiled aristocratic friends in New York to organise a passage home. The New Yorker's are paying for them to travel to California on an American warship. They'll get a train to New York on the east coast and then sail back to England. The Doctor's family will go to Canada. They'll be leaving tomorrow at 1pm. The ship's in the harbour getting loaded."

Arthur spoke. "Yes I saw plenty of activity around one of the ships. It must be that one."

"I returned Isak's satchel. To say Irena and Simona were full of thanks and joy would be an understatement."

Now Arthur.

"It came to me where I think I'd seen it before Frank. At my friend David Saffer's house. It was in his dad's study. Just a piece of crude metalwork done by a young lad I'd imagine. It's nothing to do with Isak's treasure. A piece of junk really."

Frank replied. "Well that obsession's out of your head now then. So we can see them off tomorrow as I don't expect we've much else going on. How did the docks go Wally?"

"Well I think we may have something to get us out of here as the British army don't want to help."

Arthur went on to describe his meeting with the two English men on the tramp trading steamer heading south along the coast to Hong Kong with stops on the way. From this busy colonial trading port getting transport back to Britain would be much easier. Better news for Brad and Frank with smiles and relief all round. They could see the start of the last leg of their journey home.

4. "Promise you will Frank."
21st January 1920

Frank left the barracks straight after breakfast. The Czechs had employed a Chinese cook to run their mess kitchen. Along with his son, the pair of them had worked in laundries and kitchens on British Naval ships. He could speak a few words of English and always tried to engage with the British men. He insisted they call him Mr. Chan, which they did as a banter-exchanging friendly relationship developed between them. As part of this he would feign insult from something one of them might have said, he'd then grab a large butcher's bone chopper and wave it about muttering in Chinese to his son until the offending miscreant had apologised enough. One day it could be Arthur, the next Frank or Ray.

Over the ten or so days a genuine warmth and respect had emerged between them. With limited resources and supplies, mainly fish and shellfish, pork meat, occasionally fleshless, bony chickens, ducks and 'other birds', he did well to feed the soldiers. The men frequently had trouble identifying which part of the pig or bird they were eating mixed in, and spiced up with noodles, rice, root and leaf vegetables. The bones were never quite recognisable as bones from a bird, their provenance was questionable and much debated. Not knowing what 'bird' it was didn't bother the hungry men.

The breakfast was the same every morning, either sweet or savoury 'rice pudding' as Brad referred to it. Mr. Chan would ask him.

"Congee, Mr. Brad, congee."

"Rice pudding please Mr. Chan?"

Mr. Chan would murmur quietly to his son, pick up the meat chopper in his right hand to then bring it down onto the butchers chopping board.

"Congee, Mr. Brad. Congee."

"Okay, Mr Chan, congee. If you say so."

Smiles would break out. The pantomime back and forth would be over. Observing Czech soldiers would wonder what the hell had been going on. Mr. Chan would smile, his son would smile and nod, repeating, 'Congee Mr Brad. Congee.'

Brad would smile whilst being passed a generous bowl of 'rice pudding' with a spoonful of chopped spring onions on top. Arthur liked the sweet dough sticks and Frank would season his with a little salt and sometimes add some savoury pickles. Clear and invigorating Chinese green tea drunk without milk, or sweet Indian tea and coffee were always on tap. Milk was sometimes available.

The men had agreed to meet at the quayside later in the morning to see the Rappoports and Malevich's off on their voyage to America. Frank was joining them at the old German embassy to help them with the little luggage they had. The women had been provided with some additional clothes by the friendly wives of the White Russian generals that were still in the city. They would be unable to take their extensive wardrobes with them if they did manage to arrange an escape abroad from the advancing Bolsheviks.

The families had to have their luggage on the ship by 10am, all physically on board for 11, with a 1pm departure. Arthur and Brad went down to the quayside. The families were already on board, the last preparations were being made for the United States Ship (USS) Dorsey to slip out of the Golden Horn Bay on schedule. About a hundred yards long, this destroyer had been launched in April 1918 and named after John Sword Dorsey, an American midshipmen killed on the brig, Siren in the First Barbary War off the coast of Tripoli in August 1804. The US was allied with Sweden to suppress the activities of pirates from north Africa harassing merchant vessels, taking, enslaving and ransoming prisoners.

When Arthur and Brad walked toward the bustle surrounding the USS Dorsey they could see in the distance Frank on the quayside with Amelia. The others were on board except the Doctor who was trying to arbitrate a dispute between a family promised a berth, but now being denied by the ship's Purser. When they got there Amelia spoke in effusive, enthusiastic tones in her educated English accent.

"It's just so brilliant that we are now able to put this all behind us. I know it's terrible for the people still here, but we're praying for them every day. And the Doctor and his family have been offered sanctuary in Canada. The Canadian Red Cross have been so grateful for the work he's been doing with them. I must tell you also that Irena and Simona were very emotional at getting back the Sedan Chair. It was the last piece of work that Julias had completed. He was so proud of it."

Amelia became a little emotional and dabbed a white lace hankie on her eyes as a few tears emerged.

"I'd taken Isak to see his grandfather at the jewellery workshop one day. Julias showed him the Sedan Chair and told him it was the first thing he'd ever created when he was a boy, a little older than Isak and would be the last thing he'd make. His childhood model had been left with his parents. He'd been working on the idea in his head all his life. He knew things were changing too. The life of the old aristocracy in Russia was at an end."

More tears being wiped away.

"On that visit he said to me that Faberge had the design approved by the Tsar himself, who had commissioned it as a gift for his sister, the

Grand Duchess Olga. The Tsar is dead of course, but in all this turmoil, no one knows what has happened to his sister."

Frank asked, somewhat dubiously.

"Are the family planning to give it to her?"

"I have no idea how these things work Frank. I know it is worth an awful lot of money, but whether anyone had actually paid Julias for it, I don't know. It may be the only thing of value the family has right now. Isak's dad, Mikhail was a clever man though. He'd been warning for some time that the war would destroy Russia. His officer friends in the army had spoken many times of the difficulties they had, not just fighting the enemy, but with hostility from their own men. It was never explicit, but an undercurrent of threat. Field officers dying in unexpected accidents. That kind of thing. When the revolution started, I think he knew there would be great change. That's why he went to London; to plan for the family's escape. They'd come a long way from poverty and pogroms. Julias said he'd never leave Russia. Mikhail knew they were going to have to."

At this moment the family history lesson was interrupted by calls from sailor's on the quayside to board the USS Dorsey. It was 10.45am. At the same time Dr Malevich reappeared, told Amelia she now had to say her goodbyes.

Starting with Brad, she rather formally shook his hand and thanked him for being so supportive to the refugees generally and them in particular. Then to Arthur.

"It's a shame that Taffy isn't here also, please give him our love and thanks. And of course so very sad what happened to your very good friend Eric. You called him 'Aims'. I never understood why that was, although he did try to explain to me it was something to do with aiming a gun. He told me how you shared all your letters with him during the war and took him home with you after to meet your mum.

Looking at Frank as well.

"You two became his family. I expect you know that. Thank you Arthur......... for getting us to a safe place."

"Oh, and who was your friend Arthur, that Frank told me about? He said he worked Parliament. Is that right?"

"It's nothing Amelia. Just a crazy thought."

"No tell me. I must know. I insist."

When Amelia insisted, she normally got her way.

"Saffer. David Saffer. He works for the Loughborough MP. It's my home town, David's too."

Amelia nodded, happy that she knew.

She then moved to stand in front of Frank and looked up into his face. He was more than a head taller than her. He had a smile on his, it was fairly obvious that she could barely contain her own emotions. She lifted both her arms with her palms facing upwards in a 'I don't know what to say' gesture. Stepping forward she then hugged him like a child burying her face into his chest. Unsurprisingly, Frank looked uncomfortable with this display of feminine emotion. Unexpectedly accessing his personal space, that he no longer controlled. A breach of the castle wall. He wasn't quite sure what to do with his own arms, so he rather self-consciously put his hands together across Amelia's back.

She leant her face up to the side of his and whispered something into his ear. For the first time since he'd met him, Arthur saw Frank blush.

"We must go now Amelia." Said the Doctor.

She then planted the lightest peck of a kiss on Frank's cheek and released her grip.

"Promise you will Frank."

"I promise."

"And remember, Garrard's, Albemarle Steet in London.

"I know where it is Amelia, remember, I lived there."

"Of course Frank. Just don't forget."

*

With the 1pm departure they had time for Arthur to take them to meet the two English gentlemen on the SS Hamburg further along the docks. Arthur hadn't recalled the steamer's name. Brad and Frank both laughed when they saw their transport out of Russia was a German boat. Mr. Armstrong and Taylor were both on board, as was the skipper, Captain Felix Krull. He'd expressed serious doubts when told his small crew would be made up of three British soldiers. His concerns disappeared once he'd met them. They were shown around the steamer and where they would sleep, a cabin with only two bunks.

"There will only ever be two of you off duty, at the most. So plenty room to sleep." Explained Krull. They would be leaving on the 24th January. He told them to be on board by 6pm on the 23rd."

The three men returned to an American YMCA canteen on the quayside opposite the USS Dorsey. Drinking tea they watched servicemen and civilians of different nationalities come and go. Mainly American sailors from the other ships in the bay. They saw British uniforms being worn by soldiers, but none spoke English. As agreed with Amelia, they stepped back onto the quayside and the cold, grey, overcast day. Standing on the deck at the stern of the ship there were few people waving to the equally few waving back. They could clearly see Irena, Simona and Isak waving because next to them was Amelia jumping up and down waving both arms in the air. The Doctor was next to them with his right arm raised moving it slowly from side to side above his head.

Arthur could no longer resist the question.

"What mustn't you forget Frank?"

Initially there was no response, as if he was having to suppress some sudden thought. After waiting for a minute, Arthur took another angle.

"So who are Garrard's in London?"

Frank could deal with this one.

"It's the Royal jewellers. Apparently it's where Mikhail Rappoport is basing himself. If and when I can, Amelia asked me to message her via Mikhail, details of our return passage."

He couldn't look Arthur in the face though, as he waved up at the American warship drifting slowly out of the well-sheltered bay.

Two days later they were on their own, less impressive German built tramp steamer heading away from the turbulence of Russia and the city of Vladivostok. It would take them another three months to get home.

5.   Return to Britain.
February – April 1920

True to their word, Armstrong and Taylor had been able to secure a passage back to Britain from Hong Kong. Through the network of trading relationships the Matheson companies had, they'd arranged for the men to work their passage to Bombay on a cargo ship full of cotton yarn, groundnuts, vegetable oil, tea and silks. From there it would be a passenger liner, with the tickets paid for by the two English bankers from Hong Kong. Over the three weeks it took to get to Hong Kong on the Hamburg they'd listened to the gunners tell their tales from the war and their Russian adventure.

They learnt all about Henry Budge and his decision to stay on with the Bolsheviks, not to support the revolution, but to run the field kitchen with his mate, Arvo, the giant Finn. The alternative for him back home was just unattractive. And Taffy Davis, beyond brave in rescuing his men from a collapsed sap in the war, and now unable to step into a cellar or face the confines of a boat back to Britain. His motivation for joining the missionaries going into China was discussed a lot. Not understood but admired and respected in the sense that for anyone to still believe in a higher being despite what he'd seen over the years proved real faith and commitment. They got to know Eric too. Here they quickly recognised that Eric was a special man to both Arthur and Frank. They could only talk about him when they chose.

Most importantly Armstrong and Taylor were convinced these men really were British soldiers who, despite all odds had been able to navigate their way across the largest country in the world in the midst of a violent revolution and a lawless civil war. When they reached Hong Kong, Andy Armstrong sent a telegram to the War Office in London addressed 'To whom it may concern'. It said in its limited words that three British soldiers called Raybury, Walton and Abraham were in HK on their way home to Britain. They'd been in Russia since June 1919 as part of the NRRF.

The response was a few days in coming.

"Men with these names were posted as missing in action, presumed dead in Aug 1919. Their families were notified. They were not part of the East Russian expedition. You can assume they are imposters."

They would have to get back to Britain and plead their case to convince the authorities themselves.

During their brief stay in Hong Kong, Arthur had written to Alice and his mum, Betty. Short letters that basically said he was alive and well. In an expression of great understatement, he said they caught a train across Russia as if it were the scheduled 9.10am. service from Loughborough to Leicester. The letters would be sent through the Matheson mail system which would get them home well before the men arrived on their slow Indian Ocean/Suez Canal freight and passenger liner route. Never mind what the military and political authorities thought, they would both recognise his neat, individual letter spaced writing.

He also wrote a brief note to his friend David Saffer stating he was on his way back to England. Amelia's quayside comments on Isak's treasure had reopened his ridiculous thoughts. All he remembered was the oddity of the item on the mantelpiece and the now familiar term; pogrom, a word he'd first heard from David and the family tales he told in the chemist's stockroom. Arthur had mentioned this only once more to Frank on the Hamburg steamer after several German beers from the Tsingtao brewery as the Matheson steamer traded its way along the Chinese coast.

The NRRF had embarked in the middle of May 1919, almost a year ago. For most of that time the three men had known nothing of the changes in the rest of the world. In Bombay they boarded the Peninsular and Orient Branch Service Steam Ship, the 'Beltana', on its return trip from delivering new immigrants from London to Sydney, Australia. They were dressed in the uniforms of the British army, issued to them by their Czech benefactors when the ragged, potentially typhus infected ones were removed for burning. Marek Sedlak had arranged for a second set of kit by hectoring his officers. Every day they were in quarantine he was on their case.

"These men are our friends. They helped get a train with forty Czech soldiers and several hundred refugees to safety. The least they deserve are their own nation's uniforms. We have them in the stores. Issue them now."

When this was conceded, he did the same for them to be paid for the time they'd been with him on the train. He won that concession too.

*

The world had moved on in the twelve months they'd been away. The Versailles Peace Treaty had been signed on 28th June 1919, shortly after they'd been taken as prisoners by Privakov and his men. The Treaty was monumental in scope and consequence, changing European borders based on nationalism and self-determination, but in some places leaving large ethnic minorities to be governed by others in these new countries. Liberty and equality was delivered to many uneducated people through the introduction of new constitutions with universal suffrage for both sexes and proportional representation as a voting system.

In new Eastern European economies, under-development limited capital for investment and industrialisation. Agricultural economies to the east of the Elbe remained relatively poor and subject to the vagaries of the weather and unstable demand for food produce.

The immediate postwar environment across the European continent was fragile. The United States walked away from the war and Woodrow Wilson's carefully crafted peace by failing to ratify the Treaty. The Americans retreated into a foreign policy of isolationism. Many of the newly created Balkan countries and others had to deal with extreme politics of nationalism and socialism in delicate democracies.

In early 1919 a socialist uprising in Germany led by Bolshevik influenced 'Spartacists' failed, leading to the brutal murder of the leaders, Karl Liebknecht and Rosa Luxemburg. Marx and believers in his Communist Manifesto always thought the workers of the world would unite behind the working classes of one of the most industrialised nations in Western Europe. Britain and Germany were the favourite candidates. Poverty, starvation, widespread economic dislocation and deprivation created by the war gave rise to revolutionary socialism and extreme right-wing parties like Mussolini's Fascists in Italy. This international environment of economic and political turmoil threatened new and slightly older democracies with revolution and instability.

In December 1918 a British election held in an atmosphere of victorious, patriotic fervour returned a coalition government. The governing coalition under Lloyd George needed a mandate to deliver the peace, policies for rebuilding the country and legitimacy in power. Candidates supporting the coalition were issued a letter of support known as the 'Coalition Coupon'. They won in a landslide with many Liberals not supporting the coalition, including the former Prime Minister, Henry Asquith, losing their seats. All men over the age of 21 could vote and women over the age of 30 with certain property rights. Even by December 1918 Arthur could not have voted, not reaching the qualifying age until February 1919. The result was an overwhelming win for the Coalition, the main beneficiaries being the Conservatives and Liberals with the Coupon. Revolutionary Socialism was represented by the first women elected to Westminster. Constance Markievicz (nee Gore-Booth), an Irish Nationalist representing Sinn Fein. She never took her seat.

The election meant things had changed for David Saffer in London. Sir Maurice Levy MP for Loughborough and David's employer for the duration of the war decided not to stand for re-election. David loved his job at Westminster being at the beating heart of Britain and the Empire. There was so much going on that every day was different and he'd built up an immense book of contacts both professionally and socially, in London and Loughborough. He had a short period of thinking this would all end and he'd have to find a new job. However, the candidate to replace Sir Maurice recognised the need for continuity and when introduced to David took to him immediately. Few people didn't.

Oscar Guest won with 11,918 votes and a majority over the only other candidate, his Labour rival Herbert Hallam, of 5,537. Guest had been a pilot in the RAF during the war. He was tall and slim with a dark brush moustache. He was also the first cousin of Winston Churchill; someone David had seen many times when he sat in and took notes at meetings attended by Sir Maurice. A new working relationship was quickly established with the new MP and life in London continued.

The new government faced immense social and economic challenges in transitioning the country from war to peace. The revolution in Russia and the collapse of a vast Empire instilled fear and anxiety into British politicians. Combined with the millions of returning soldiers looking for work in low paid jobs with few rights and poor conditions, society was brittle. Soldiers had marched on Downing Street, the police, miners and many others went on strike. Coal production was crucial for the wider economy and the well-being of all households as the primary source of domestic heating and cooking. There were race riots in the port cities of Cardiff, Newport and Liverpool where the local population feared jobs were being taken by foreign men for less pay.

On 27th January 1919 in Glasgow, a meeting organised by the Scottish Trade Union Congress and the Clyde Worker's Committee led to large crowds in support of the workers. The government feared a 'Bolshevik' uprising and a few days later deployed thousands of troops and six tanks in response, resulting in disorder and bloodshed. Rioting persisted for several weeks, but the deployment of soldiers in Glasgow and elsewhere quelled the violence and potential for further conflict. Social discontent hadn't gone away, it had been suppressed temporarily.

In March 1920 The Ruhr Red Army; German left wing workers and members of the Communist Party had risen up against the elected government. Some 50,000 plus men were supported by another 300,000 miners and took over the cities of Essen, Dusseldorf and Elberfeld. They soon controlled the important economic industrial area of the Ruhr. The German government fearing the spread of revolution, sent in regular and right wing Friekorps paramilitary troops to regain control. The workers had over 1,000 men killed in the subsequent fighting before they were defeated. Within a few days France occupied the area as the Germans had failed to withdraw its men and to secure future reparation payments as agreed in the Versailles Peace Treaty.

On April 9th, 1920, railway worker's strikes in America closed down the cities of New York, Chicago, Detroit, Kansas and the whole of California. On the 13th a general strike was called for by workers in Ireland. Two days later police arrested more than 100 left wing Republican agitators.

An immediate post-war economic boom in Britain and elsewhere was created by the desire to replenish stock. Shops, larders and wardrobes needed to be refilled, purchasing power had built up and the government was slow to reduce its wartime expenditure. Global demand for commodities and manufactured goods increased prices and created jobs filled by demobilised soldiers. In early 1920 world shipping had recovered, supply of raw materials and foodstuffs flooded back to Europe and Britain and the impact of increased interest rates to curb price inflation started to bite. Prices began to fall in March 1920, demand collapsed and millions of men lost their jobs; the economic future looked grim.

*

It was into this environment of global political and social turmoil and economic collapse that the SS Beltana sailed into Bristol with the three returning gunners on board. Most of the conventional passengers, those who were part of the constant flow of diplomats, military officers and British civil administrators, had been landed and moved on to see families or report to their Imperial Service offices. From Bristol to London, where these people were headed would take another day. Most would stay in Bristol for a day on land to re-acquaint their legs with terra-firma before travelling on.

Brad, Arthur and Frank were refused permission to land. It was unclear why and there was little explanation from the ship's captain who was 'too busy' to discuss this with them. They were told their landing had been prevented by the War Office and military authorities who wanted to question them and didn't have the right facilities in Bristol. Further confusion arose from being stopped from sending telegrams and letters ashore. The men knew they were being fobbed off by excuses from embarrassed ship's officers who they'd come to know on the voyage home. The truth was, the sailors didn't know what was happening either, or why the soldiers were being prevented from leaving the boat.

The remaining few passengers seeking to get to the north of England and Scotland and a small cargo of tea, calico, hardwood timber and mahogany were taken up the Irish Channel to Liverpool, the ships final destination. They sailed along the River Mersey and arrived to tether up within the Wellington half-tide dock at 8.20pm. on the 17th April. From here they would be towed by tugs into the adjacent Bramley Moore Dock the following morning. The tug was active before 7am., taking one of the regular coal ships that were the main users of Bramley Moore and the high level railway connecting the dock to the Lancashire and Yorkshire rail network bringing in the cargos of coal. The Beltana was pulled in to replace the coal ship.

The gunners were told to assemble with their kit in the Captain's office on the bridge at 8.30 am. They were waiting for the Captain to arrive on the assumption he would be informing them they could land when six burly police officers arrived led by a sergeant. It was wholly unexpected and met with the calmness now ingrained into Brad, Arthur and Frank. With the years of Brad's military experience and having dealt with the uncertainties of daily life in unpredictable Bolshevik captivity, the sight of six big, carefully chosen, scouse coppers barely raised an eyebrow. The police sergeant entered the office with the others crowding the small passageway outside. The gunners remained seated on the comfortable red leather office chairs opposite the captain's desk. With no preamble the darkly bearded copper went straight into his pitch.

"You're to accompany me and my officers to the carriage waiting on the dockside."

Brad answered.

"Okay. Where are we going? Have we been arrested?"

The sergeant was a little surprised at the apparent immediate compliance.

"You haven't been arrested. My understanding is you are to be questioned by the right authorities. We don't want any trouble from you men."

Frank started laughing and mischievously asked,

"Were you expecting trouble?"

The sergeant stepped nervously from foot to foot. He was clearly out of his depth in dealing with these unperturbed men he was trying to secure on behalf of the British State. Behind the hirsute face there was a young looking set of anxious eyes. A great many police had served in the army during the war and by April 1920 most of the three common medals, known affectionately as 'Pip', 'Squeak', and 'Wilfred', had been issued with the ribbons worn above the left chest pocket of service uniforms, police included. There was no flash of colour on this young police sergeant's chest. This was also true of the tunics the gunners now wore. Brad and Frank's Military Medal flashes being surrendered with their train tunics sent for burning.

"I wasn't sure what to expect, but as you can see I've come prepared with my men to deal with all eventualities. I was told you would be armed. Two of my men are."

Frank laughed again and asked with a chuckling look.

"Do we need to be armed? Is there a war taking place on the streets of Liverpool?"

He then teasingly added.

"Which ones of your men have weapons sergeant?"

Brad interrupted.

"Stop ribbing him Frank. The young man is only trying to do his job."

"Of course. We're not armed sergeant, we didn't think we'd need to be."

He smiled, to himself mainly.

"Our trusted friends, our British army issued Lee Enfield rifles are locked in the Captain's armoury. Presented to him when we boarded and they've been there ever since. I'm sure he'll surrender them to you and you're men if you ask him nicely."

The copper was getting visibly agitated.

"Well I'll deal with that after. I need to escort you to the transport. There's to be no trouble."

Arthur now.

"You'll have no problems with us sergeant. I think we've had enough of fighting other men......... at least for a few minutes."

Now he was teasing the policemen. Frank knew it and laughed again.

Brad then spoke.

"Ignore them sergeant. You and your men have nothing to fear from us. But can you tell us what this is all about."

"I'm afraid not. I just have my instructions Mr?"

"Sergeant. Sergeant Raybury. Royal Field Artillery."

The policeman eyed him scornfully.

"You have no badge of rank. No insignia."

Brad conceded, shaking his head ruefully.

"I guess not. I guess not. I could explain, but it might take a while."

"I don't think it'll get us very far Brad." Said Arthur.

"No, you're right. Let's get going then."

The three stood up.

The copper again. "I'll need to put you in handcuffs."

Frank laughed as if he was enjoying the ridiculousness of it all and Brad said.

"Is that really necessary?"

"I'm afraid so, strict instructions from the County Police Commissioner. He got his instructions from London."

Brad just shook his head ruefully. It certainly wasn't the reception committee they'd been expecting.

*

The police sergeant waved in two constables to cuff Arthur first. One then led him along the passage whilst another picked up his haversack and followed behind. They were taken off the ship with comments and questions being thrown at them and the police by the crew, all of whom they'd come to know and had heard their story. Perhaps it wasn't true after all. There was no sign of the captain who the gunners thought might vouch for them.

They were loaded into the back of a motorised prisoner carriage waiting on the quayside. There was a police vehicle to the front and rear of the prison wagon. The police were gracious enough to remove the cuffs as they reached the steps at the back of the van. A black windowless box with four small air grill's just below the roof. Inside there were wooden bench seats running the length of each side, screwed solidly onto the wooden floor. The police barely engaged with them, only to say they had no idea what this was about. Several of them had medal ribbons, one of whom said we shouldn't be locking up returning soldiers wherever they've come from. He quietly apologised for what he was doing to Arthur who replied that this was a misunderstanding that would be overcome. They'd had to deal with far trickier challenges than a night in the cells of a British police station.

It took less than fifteen minutes to reach their destination. Their conversation was focussed on just dealing with the unexpected. They'd been here enough times to know that whatever was going on would be resolved. They were back in Britain, back home. It didn't quite feel like it at this moment. Despite their situation these unarmed and a little confused Liverpool Bobbies taking into custody British soldiers weren't murderous Bolshevik mutineers, nervous and armed railway panjandrums, or lawless Cossack warlords. The three artillerymen knew they had nothing to fear in this latest act of men in uniform.

The van slowed down to a halt. They could hear shouts and through the grills managed to see high walls and large, very heavy looking black gates being opened. This was no ordinary police station. Coming to a halt in a yard, the gates were then pushed back to close with a loud low toned thud. There was then a metallic rattling of more gates and the van moved forward another few yards to stop again. After a few minutes the door was unlocked, opened and a booming Irish accented voice hollered into the back of the van. This man was not in a police uniform as the gunners had expected.

"Okay, out you get you three. Welcome to Walton Gaol. This'll be your home until someone decides what to do with you. One at a time. When you step out you'll go with the two prison officers to a cell and be issued with prison uniforms. What you're wearing will be taken for safekeeping. Although, from what I hear you'll not be seeing any civvy clothes for a while. First one then."

Arthur had never heard of Walton Gaol, but he was quite impressed that the British Government had not only named a prison after him, but they'd chosen his own prison to now lock him up in. Still inside the van Frank commented.

"Who would have thought Wally, you're very own nick."

"Shut up Mr. You don't want to get off on the wrong foot do you."

The situation was bemusing for the soldiers, and when Brad stepped out of the van with his bag, the prison warders standing in the yard to receive them seemed equally baffled. The Irishman again.

"Disguising yourself in British army uniforms then. Not a very smart idea."

Brad was about to say something when the warden's truncheon was placed firmly on top of his right shoulder.

"No comments from you Mr. You'll have the chance to speak when the time is right. Same goes for you two in the back there. No talking. Right take him away. Next one out."

Brad was led off.

Arthur was the next out. With a quick look around him he could see he was in a small courtyard surrounded by mock castellated buildings several story's high. He had a flashback to the tower at the entrance to the Honourable Artillery Company on City Road in London on the day he enlisted. He was joined by two warders and marched off. As he went he saw two men standing with their sides to him in a guardroom doorway. One in a warder's uniform with three silver stripes on his tunic epaulette indicating some prison officer seniority. Probably in his late 50's, shorter than Arthur's six foot by at least six inches, he looked self-assured and military. The other, taller, similar age with a kind looking face wore a smart, dark grey, civilian suit. They were watching the unloading of the latest inmates with curiosity.

Next to them was a prisoner with two piles of prison uniforms laid on a bench with three pairs of clogs. He took in Arthur's height and build as he walked passed and started rummaging through the trousers and tunics. He wore one himself. A faded grey tunic and flapping pyjama style trousers, the broad arrows randomly spread within the material. Arthur was familiar with the arrow denoting government property. It appeared on all the boxes of shells delivered to the gun positions in France. It was on the labels of British army uniforms, boxes of rifles and ammunition. It was almost certainly on the label of the tunic he was wearing, issued by the Czechs. So now he was going to be labelled government property on the outside.

He was taken into an office and through another door to a corridor with about ten cells on either side. Loud angry shouts were coming from several of these with hands visibly gripping a very small, barred window in the black painted doors. Ahead he could see Brad being taken into one at the end with his bag left outside.

"Leave your kit in the corridor, you won't be needing that."

Dropping the bag, Arthur was sent into the second on the left, Frank somewhere behind. The strangely narrow door was slammed with a metallic thud as it connected with the reinforced metal frame. The jangle of keys turned in the lock. The white room was about four foot wide, about seven foot long, a small, barred window at the far end, set too high to see out of. To the right was a blue painted wooden shelf, eighteen inches wide, doubling as a seat and an uncomfortable looking bed with no bedding and inch thick iron legs bolted to the stone floor. In the corner between the end of the bench and the window was a metal bucket.

He'd hardly taken in the bare room when the keys turned again and the door opened. The guard stepped aside and the prisoner with the uniforms from the entrance yard appeared, a sly, pointed faced man with small piggy eyes. He threw in the two prison uniform items, a pair of wooden clogs that clattered on the floor and a pill-box style, soft prisoners hat. As Arthur picked these up he noticed a small hatch at the bottom of the cell door and a naked electric bulb providing most of the light to the cell set in the wall above the door.

"These'll fit yer." The uniform selector called.

"Shut up weasel, no talking to these prisoners. I'll do the talking."

Said the guard in a guttural scouse accent.

"Strip off, everything. Underwear too. Boots and socks. Leave them in a neat pile on the bench. You have two minutes. Anything in your pockets in here." A rough wooden box about a foot long was tossed onto the bench. The door slammed shut again but wasn't locked this time.

Arthur picked up the prison greys that smelt disgustingly musty. Having no choice, he stripped off, folding his kit and laying it on the bench in a neat military fashion. His tunic pockets had various items in them; a mixture of foreign, now useless coins, handkerchief, the transit papers and the black indecipherable booklet he'd been given by Privakov; black handled, war issued penknife with handy tool for removing stones from horse-shoes, cigarettes and lighter. These last two items he removed. He put on the prison pyjamas. The sleeves were too short, as were the legs. The waist was too big, the trousers had no belt or draw string so had to be held up by hand.

If this process was designed to be undignified, it had no impact on Arthur. Either that or 'weasel' was as useless as he looked. He'd seen prisoners of war being treated in the same way. Dressed to look and feel stupid. He felt neither, smiling to himself, understanding this was part of a game being played, whatever the game was. It was nothing personal toward him, Frank and Brad, who he assumed were going through the same process. Somebody, somewhere in the system was controlling this. It would reach a conclusion and no one's life was at risk.

The door clattered open again.

"Is that everything?"

Holding his trousers up with his left hand, he held the lighter and cigarettes up in his right.

"Sorry pal, those too. We can't have you setting fire to your smart new kit now can we?"

Arthur realised the pointlessness of answering before a last comment from the guard.

"Piss and shit in the bucket. If you need a crap, and the warder's not asleep, he may shove some newspaper in the window. Don't depend on it though. Hang on ……. Give me the watch as well. We dictate the time in here, not the rotation of the earth."

6. Walton Gaol, Liverpool
21st April 1920

Arthur sat down so as to remove the watch on his left wrist with his right hand and stop his trousers falling down. The door slammed shut, this time being locked. He remained on the bench, his mind now trying to work out what was going on. They had made efforts to notify their families. He knew Frank had written to his parents in Bethnal Green from Hong Kong. Two of his three brothers had died in the war, the third had lost a leg. It was important they knew he was heading home. His three sisters and extended family in the area would know within minutes of the letter reaching his parents.

A message to Amelia via Mikhail Rappoport via Garrard's in Albemarle Street had also been sent by Frank from Bombay. "Don't forget Frank." Arthur had reminded him of Amelia's quayside request a number of times. He'd told her the ship name, the P&O S.S. Beltana.

Since leaving for Russia last May Arthur had written to Alice twice from the training camp outside Archangel. He'd received no letters back. He knew she would have written something; her letters just hadn't reached him before their Bolshevik capture. Whilst she'd been deeply upset that he volunteered for the NRRF, there was no sense that their relationship wouldn't survive him being away again. After all, it had suffered the four years of the war, he couldn't imagine she wouldn't be there for him now he was home again. He had then sent that short letter from Hong Kong, plus one to his mother and David. They wouldn't know anything about when he'd arrive back, or where he'd land, so there was no expectation of anyone being there to meet them. Brad had no family, or certainly had never mentioned any relatives and he'd sent no messages.

Then the authoritarian response to their arrival from the ship was odd. Instant incarceration hadn't been expected. On the boat they'd discussed administrative hurdles they might have to jump with the army to explain the missing time from the attacks on Topsa on the 19th June the previous year and the mutiny of the men they'd trained in Dyer's battalion. They didn't know it, but the mutiny had been much broader than just the artillery section of the Russian volunteers. The British military hierarchy must have known that, as they'd already seen other Russian and indeed the British men of the Royal Marines refuse to fight in north Russia.

A thought came into Arthur's head, that somehow they'd been reported as responsible for the mutiny of the Russian men they'd trained and the loss of the four 18 pounder guns they'd lugged through the Ural forests to Vyatka. Or perhaps worse, were now considered deserters in the face of the enemy. The army always needed scapegoats for defeats, the loss of expensive kit and unnecessary death of men. Yet soldier's general experience of the carnage on the western front seemed to indicate that the third of these issues, the terrible waste of lives, was frequently placed with, often dead junior or field officers on the ground rather than the chateau based General Staff and politicians in London.

The six missing Royal Artillery gunners, the four missing 18 pounders and ammunition unused in the Topsa debacle could easily be blamed on those unable to provide any account in the immediate aftermath. It now started to make some sense. The army had concluded the six men of the training section under Raybury's command, now reduced to just these three, had deserted, stole the guns and joined the enemy. Having reached this conclusion Arthur closed his eyes, satisfied that once their story had been told, they would be released.

*

It was probably a couple of hours later when he heard boot steps in the passage. The floor level door hatch was lifted with a clatter. The familiar scouse voice called out.

"Sweet tea from the governor."

A white enamelled mug appeared.

"He must have gone mad treating prisoners like this."

The hatch closed again. Over the shouting din from other cells he heard the same call twice more. He assumed it was for Frank and Brad. They were being treated differently. Well that was something. Perhaps half an hour later the hatch opened with the demand, "Mug!" It sounded like 'Weasel'. Arthur passed it through.

Time then dragged into another indefinite period of a few hours until more noise from the passage. The sound of a hatch in the first cell to his right, a squeaking of wheels, then his hatch opened. A metal plate appeared with two slices of barely buttered bread, a small lump of cheese and the enamel mug again, this time with water in it. Along the corridor shouts in anticipation of what Arthur assumed was lunch.

Another short period passed, the hatch opened and Weasel again,

"Plate and mug." Arthur tried to engage with him.

"Hey, do you know why we're here?"

"It's a gaol pal. Its where they put scallys. Ask yourself what you've done."

It didn't help.

The rest of the day dragged by in a similar manner. Sweet tea, again delivered by the scouse prison warder, 'From the Governor.' Later on, a small metal bowl of beef stew, as Weasel described it as he passed it in. Arthur's had been served without beef, just potato and carrot in a watery gravy. He smiled thinking of similar meatless 'chicken stew' the battery cooks sometimes delivered to the gun position back in France.

The light outside started fading. He knew, in April, this would be around 7.30 pm. Keys rattled next door, he heard some dialogue and the door there slammed shut. Now his door. A different warder, similar accent, shorter in height, dark brown eyes and poorly shaven, square face with an untidy, almost black moustache.

"Bedding for the night."

He threw in a blanket and what barely passed for a pillow.

"I'll collect it at six o'clock in the morning."

"I'd like to lie in a bit later than that if you wouldn't mind officer."

The guard stopped, not knowing what to say. The comment wasn't threatening. It was polite and respectful. Arthur himself was a lot taller than this guard but he was sitting on the bench. The man tightened his eyes a little, lacking understanding, repeated

"Six o'clock in the morning", and slammed the door shut.

The electric light stayed on all night. Sleep on the solid wooden bench barely wide enough to lie down on for an average man was more difficult for a big man like Arthur. However, soldiers were good at sleeping wherever they could and he was well practiced at making the best of the available conditions. It was still dark and now raining heavily when the bedding was collected. It was the same short warder. Arthur tried again.

"Any news for me this morning officer?."

The man refused to answer, he just stared at Arthur suspiciously. Breakfast was sweet tea with one piece of unbuttered bread with a red smear of something with a slightly sweet taste. It must be jam. Then, several hours of nothing apart from men in the other holding cells shouting, until keys jangled in his door. It flew open with the Irish warder who'd received them and another man standing in the passage.

"Right Walton, or whatever you call yourself, come with us."

"Can you tell us why we're here?"

"No questions. Just come with us."

He was led away sandwiched between the two guards clutching his too short, fat man's prison trousers with his left hand, and placing the one-size fits all, too small hat on his head. As he walked the corridors leading somewhere, up two flights of stairs, they passed through two metal air-lock gates and then a door that led into carpeted, wooden panelled passage. They entered the first door on the right which took them into a sparsely furnished room, heavy with a plush bottle green carpet and curtains. There was a long, highly polished, oak table with one chair on one side with its back to the tall sash window and a single chair facing it. The walls had large portraits of eminent Victorian gentlemen. Some in the military uniforms of senior officers, only one picture that Arthur recognised. Perhaps the most famous Liverpudlian of all, the unmistakable, bewhiskered, William Ewart Gladstone. The room had the feel of a dining room cleared of all furniture.

"Take a seat there."

The Irishman said, indicating the seat facing the window.

"Principal Officer Myers will be with you soon."

Arthur took the seat and waited whilst the two guards left the room closing the door after them. Looking around the room Arthur spotted there was one other chair immediately behind the door as it opened. Several minutes later the door flew open and two men walked in. One in a dark suit carried a bureaucrat's briefcase and wore a black, felt trilby hat which he removed as he walked in. The second he recognised as the senior warder with the three epaulette stripes he'd seen in the yard doorway the day before. This must be the Principal Officer Myers. Arthur had stood as a matter of courtesy. The suited man walked around the table to the chair opposite Arthur. Myers, Arthur could now see, had several coloured medal ribbons on his tunic indicating his military history. In a quiet growling voice he said.

"Sit down."

The warder sat on the seat behind the door.

Arthur sat. The suit sat opposite him, said nothing, rummaged in his bag, pulled out a sheaf of papers which he placed on the table, extracted a pen from an inside jacket pocket and placed it on top of the papers. He then spoke.

"Dobro pozhalovat v Angliyu. Ya nadeyus', chto vy smozhete skazat' mne svoye imya I pochemu vy zdes?"[25]

Arthur looked at him and gently shook his head.

"I'm afraid I have no idea what you're talking about."

"Ya uveren vy delayeteda mister, nazyvayete sebya Uoltonom. No my ne dumayem chto eto tvoye imya. Rasskazhite pozaluysta, chto eto takoye?"[26]

Arthur raised both his hands, shrugged his shoulders and shook his head again.

"I recognise you're speaking Russian but despite my time there I know almost nothing of the language. Another question was directed at Arthur. He turned to look at the warder sat by the door. Myers said nothing, shaking his head from side to side as if to say no and with his right hand stretched out pointed back to the suit.

---

[25] Welcome to England. I'm hoping you can tell me your name and why you are here?

[26] I'm sure you do Mr. Walton. But we don't think it's your name. Please tell us what it is?

The questions kept coming....... in Russian. Arthur shrugged, repeated his initial comments of not knowing what he was saying and added that he could ask as many questions as he wished, he was wasting his time. The suit persisted without emotion. Arthur remained calm and courteous but couldn't answer as he didn't understand. After about fifteen minutes of this the rough voice spoke.

"Enough Mr. Kowalski, enough. This is going nowhere."

Kowalski replied in accentless, educated English.

"I have many more questions to ask the prisoner. We believe this man is the leader of these three men."

Arthur stared at the suit.

"What on earth are you talking about?"

Myers stopped him.

"Quiet Walton. This interview is over. You'll be taken back to your cell."

Arthur tried to speak but Myers raised his hand to stop him. He spoke in a more conciliatory way, his hazel brown eyes were not hostile, he nodded a little and there was a hint of a smile, but it couldn't be called a smile as such.

"Not now Walton. You'll have your chance later."

A few minutes later he was back in his cell. Back to think again what was going on. As his door was locked he heard another opening further along. Guards talking and wooden clogs on the stone floor. As the clogs approached his door he heard Frank.

"We'll be sorted soon Arthur. As Brad said, this is just a process."

A guard barked at Frank. "Quiet, no talking."

Arthur called back. "Enjoy your chat Frank."

"Shut up in there, no collusion."

From the guard who banged his truncheon on the door.

A short while later Frank could be heard coming back. Arthur called out.

"How was that Frank?"

"Shut up, before I come in and shut you up."

"They think we're spies Wally!"

"You be quiet too."

"I'll let Brad know." finished Frank.

"Shut up!"

The guard was sounding frantic as if he didn't know what to do with these men who disregarded his orders not to speak, complied with his instructions, seemed to pose no aggressive threat and spoke to each other in a confident, open way as if he wasn't there.

Before Brad went up, their lunch arrived. Several hard crackers, two raw carrots and another lump of cheese. It filled a small hole, not much more. Brad was then collected and as he passed called out.

"You okay Wally?"

"Quiet!" Said the guard.

"All good Brad!"

"Shut up in there."

Arthur couldn't resist it, so just to wind up the guard a little more.

"Enjoy your chat Brad."

"Shut up in there!" Screamed the increasingly irritated guard. Arthur chuckled; this was just too easy.

*

The rest of the day was a repetition of the first, as was the following morning. It was timeless, nothingness and solitary. Arthur was able to play chess in his head and created a game with his lost friend Eric as his opponent. It kept his mind busy in a place somewhere else and kept the memory of 'Aims' Amos clear and alive. He relived some events from the last five years, trying to remember each detail as he went. Knowing when he'd missed something and working out what it was, stuff from the war and Russia. He walked the streets of Loughborough in his head. Selecting different routes to get from the family terraced house on Clarence Street to Martins in Market Place. He reckoned there were eight routes that could get you there within fifteen minutes, three of which took him past Taylor's Bell Foundry where he'd ridden his first horse. Sam Wallace, his boyhood friend who arranged it, also now dead. Was Sam's dad still at Taylor's, he pondered.

He thought more and more about Alice and feared for the immediate future when they'd overcome this first hurdle that Brad had referred to on the ship. Would Alice still be there for him. He tried to suppress these thoughts but it rarely worked when they were firmly lodged in the front of his head.

7. 'B' Wing, Walton Gaol, Liverpool.
22nd April 1920

It was late morning when things changed. The keys rattled in the corridor and his door was unlocked. He was told to move out and wait. It was the Irish warder on the day shift. Stepping out he looked to his left to see the guard walk along the passage to open another door. Out stepped Frank with a smile on his face looking ridiculous in his similarly too small prison greys. Arthur realised he would look the same and perhaps it was this that Frank found amusing. The guard had let Brad out as well. He wasn't a big man and they both saw that his dress overwhelmed his body. He'd had to roll the trouser legs and sleeves up. All three were holding the pyjama style pants up. The undignified, ill-fitting uniforms being that calculated act of humiliation.

"Follow me."

Called the Irishman. So they rattled along the stone floors in the wooden clogs out of this reception wing across the yard the van brought them into and through a large wooden door into the main part of the gaol. There were five floors of mid-Victorian, red brick prison architecture to observe. As they walked they talked, but this time the guard said nothing to stop them. Taken into one of these buildings and up two flights of stairs they were, much to their surprise, now given some information.

"You're being moved onto a regular prison section, 'B' wing. You know, a place where ordinary common criminals are kept."

He added with an ugly toothless grin they'd not seen before.

"This section is run by 'The Boss'. Principal Officer Myers. He was the man watching your interviews yesterday. You'll have no trouble from other hard men on his wing. The Prison Governor brought him in from Brixton in London to instil some control. There's no top-dog, prison lag running things here. When P.O. Myers says jump, the guards and scally's ask how high. You'll get the idea."

The three gunners were well aware of the other man in the room for their bizarre interaction with the Russian speaking suit. His presence had been both authoritative and reassuring. He'd terminated all three interviews early despite the protests of the bureaucrat.

As an ex Regimental Sergeant Major, in the Grenadier Guards, P.O. Colin Myers had been the only man the prison governor, Sir Stephen A. Mitchell, trusted to deal with the political hot-potato thrown at Walton Gaol. Small in stature, Myers exuded authority and control. Twenty three years in the army and another twelve in the Prison Service, he'd spent his life in uniform dealing with difficult men in challenging places. He was an enigma to the prisoners and warders alike. Hard men knew his reputation before they arrived at the goal, there was never trouble on 'B' wing.

No one was ever quite sure how this reputation arose. It was rumoured he had underworld connections himself that could be called upon if there was ever a need. Or perhaps his mysterious allusions to military service incidents and survival in unwinnable actions along the River Nile and at Khartoum with General Gordon's forces created enough mystique to unnerve other men. Aside from Governor Mitchell, Myers was the only man from the south of England at Walton Gaol. Every other guard was a scouse or a paddy. Myers was originally from Stratford, East London, enlisting at the age of eighteen in 1880. Providing leadership for younger prison officers through a firm, fair approach to prisoners and never needing to prove his disciplinary effectiveness, the prisoners complied. Myers always ran an ordered shop.

The three men were walked passed some locked cells, but mainly open. There was a floor exercise session taking place outside in the open yard. Those remaining in their cells were either under sanction or didn't wish to participate. Myers saw no point in trying to force them to do so. It created friction and resentfulness. Allowing prisoners to have a very small amount of control of their daily routine gave them some self-respect which was repaid with cooperation. The open door revealed rooms a bit wider than the cell they'd come from, each one containing bunk-beds for two inmates.

At the end of the landing were three adjacent cells with open doors. The Irishman told them not to enter and stand outside the door. Arthur looked over the banister surrounding the large atrium. There were two floors below and two above with various prisoners and guards moving about being escorted to and from other places, or trustees wheeling trollies carrying urns and metal mugs, one loaded with books for those who could read. The clang of doors slamming shut, keys clinking, warders and men shouting filled the air. After a few minutes Arthur saw Myers walking along the opposite landing on the floor below. He climbed the metal stairs at the centre of the wing, crossed the bridge and headed toward the gunners.

His uniform was impeccable. Sharply creased trousers and tunic, highly polished black shoes and a prison uniform cap with the peak adjusted to cut down 'guards style' to almost hide his eyes. From an array of ribbons, Brad could identify the blue and white striped Egypt medal, the plain blue Khedive's Star, the yellow and black split with a thin crimson stripe Queen's Sudan medal and the yellow with blue centre stripe representing the Nile River, Khedive's Sudan medal. The last on was the crimson striped meritorious service medal only awarded to senior NCO's.

A long standing army veteran of irreproachable service. As he got to them he removed his hat and spoke in his low toned gruff voice.

"Gentlemen, you men are a problem for Sir Stephen, the prison governor. His problems become my problems which is not a good thing."

Myers paused and smiled.

"Let me explain a little of what I know has been a puzzling few days for you. Several days ago we received a message from The War Office signed by The Secretary of State for War, Winston Churchill. We were told to expect three men arriving from India on the SS Beltana, described as a danger to the British nation and democracy. You, apparently, are those men."

He smiled again.

"The memo stated that you were posing as artillerymen reported missing, presumed dead in August last year. This was recorded after a mutiny in northern Russia where deserting Bolsheviks killed a number of British officers and their instructors. Does this make any sense to you?"

The three of them nodded. He continued.

"Good, because it doesn't make a lot of sense to me."

Myers paused to let this sink in.

"In Eastern Russia, where you next appeared, The War Office had two battalions of infantry. Something I do know about, as well as engineers, logistics, administrators and Staff Officers. There were no Royal Artillery soldiers in Siberia. Churchill and the Prime Minister are aware of a number of British military personnel still held as prisoners by the Bolsheviks. Your appearance is inconsistent with the evacuation of British troops from Archangel, Murmansk and Vladivostok. What was known to have happened and what is still going on. The politicians have concluded you are likely to be some of Lenin's revolutionaries posing as British soldiers sent here to ferment a socialist revolution. In other words, spies and insurrectionists."

Brad tried to interrupt but Myers held up his hand to stop him. Looking straight at him he said.

"Not yet Sarn't Raybury."

Raybury's eyebrows lifted in surprise at being addressed by his rank. Arthur and Frank looked on, also recognising the change in tone. Myers continued.

"Our instructions were to separate you until you'd been interviewed by a linguist from the War Office. You met Mr. Kowalski yesterday. I sat in at the governor's request."

Brad then got a word in.

"But you stopped my interview with him after only five minutes. The man looked furious."

Frank added. "Mine after ten."

For completeness Arthur had to contribute. "Mine seemed longer than that."

Myers held up his right hand to stop them speaking.

"I needed to gauge the response of each of you to the questioning. Kowalski had told me he would only speak in Russian. His aim, to trip you up to speak in your 'mother tongue'. It was fairly clear in Walton's interview that you had no clue as to what he was saying. Abraham and Sgt. Raybury's confirmed this to me."

He then offered them each a cigarette to which he raised a light. They all enjoyed a pull and sucked in the nicotine.

"As you can see, I'm an ex-army man. Your behaviour when you arrived in the yard told me and Sir Stephen there was more to this than the War Office and Churchill's paranoia. His foreign policy adventure against Lenin and friends hasn't quite worked out the way he planned. I could tell you were British soldiers. I don't know what your story is, maybe we'll find out one day. However, right now you are still our problem, so I shall tell you what's going to happen. Or at least what is in our control."

He went on explain The War Office had instructed to keep them in separate cells away from other prisoners. The process needed to run its course. Kowalski had taken the Russian papers they'd carried in their tunics for translation into English. He'll be back tomorrow for another interview. He said they'd each carried a similar one with various stamps. Walton had another one. At this point Arthur recalled the booklet he'd been given by Privakov. And then dismissed it as irrelevant. Myers had given a verbal report to the governor and he and Sir Stephen did not see them as a threat or risk so the cell doors would be left open. They would have to comply with the prison routine. At night the doors would be closed. Underclothes, a clean prison uniform, and with a smile said, "this one should fit," and prison boots were in the room. There was a towel, a bar of soap and bathing facilities at the other end of the landing. He advised them to clean up and get out of the smelly kit they were in. All the prison officers on this wing have been briefed on the situation. He finished his words to them by saying.

"The other prisoners have been told not to speak to you. I'd like you to respect that too. I'm sure you will. This is my wing and we need to move you on from being a problem for me and the governor as soon as possible. We don't need any of these scoundrels and petty criminals screwing up that process.................. Okay. I hope that's a little clearer."

Without giving them an opportunity to ask questions, he then raised his right hand with palm facing to indicate their new cells, turned sharply to his left and walked, or rather swaggered in a Regimental Sergeant Major's way to other business elsewhere in his domain.

8. Amelia's quest
London, April 1920

The Rappoport's journey

On the 1st April 1920, Amelia and the Rappoports had sailed from New York to Southampton on the luxury, White Star Line ship, The Olympic. A sister ship to the great and tragic Titanic, they were in first class accommodation; back to a semblance of the luxury they'd enjoyed in Moscow and circulating with similar aristocratic friends. This was a long way from the chicken pox and typhus infested plague train that took them across Siberia to safety. Not a day went by that she didn't think about the men who'd saved them. Brad with his calm, mature professionalism that no unexpected event could rattle. Arthur and Eric, intimate friends that could only be seen by close, unspoken observation. And of course Frank, the apparent aloof, disconnected enigma who ambushed her with his Yiddish.

Arriving on the 9th, the family were met by Mikhail at Southampton docks in a joyous reunion, saddened by his news that his father Julias had been confirmed as murdered in Moscow by Bolshevik thugs as far back as December 1917. Irena was deeply upset by the not unexpected news, but it made it no less difficult. After one night in London, Amelia took the train from London Bridge to Hastings to spend some time with her parents at the family home, Iden Park. She shared her amazing story to an incredulous audience of her parents and the one brother and his fiancée.

But she had things to do; she had people to find. After a couple of days she returned to rejoin her Russian 'family', Irena, Simona and Isak in an unfamiliar city where they needed her help to negotiate new challenges. Mikhail was busy every day at Garrard's trying to establish a new role. Isak's Sedan Chair treasure had been passed to his father and now sat on a shelf in a tiny office provided for him. A showcase piece to display the Rappoports design capability, it shared the shelf with many other sample items by different jewellers. Garrard's were happy to provide the office space free of charge. They were very familiar with the Rappoport family workshop and Julias's designs for Faberge.

The family had taken a small suite on the third floor of the Flemings Mayfair Hotel on Half Moon Street. A short walk from Albemarle Street and Green Park where Isak could be taken every day to burn off some energy. The hotel was tucked away from the very busy Piccadilly. Extremely smart, with attentive yet unobtrusive staff, an ideal place for the Rappoports to start to build a new life. In the rush of getting to see her own family, Mikhail hadn't passed on the letter he'd received for Amelia's attention. He did so a few days after she returned from home, with profuse apologies for forgetting.

It read:

Dear Amelia,

Arthur, Brad and I have made it to Bombay, via Hong Kong. We helped crew a small freight steamer and then as stewards and porters on the second leg to India. From the generosity of two British Bankers, who paid for tickets on the P&O SS Beltana. It arrives in the middle of April at the port of Bristol.

The other two are both well.

I hope to see you soon back in England.

Frank x

It was very, Frank. Short, precise and screamingly uncertain as to how to sign off. A 'x' would do just fine. She was thrilled, smiled broadly and clutched it to her chest. Simona saw her reaction, enquiring what it was. It's from Frank. He's on his way home.

*

Leadenhall Market, The City of London. 20th April 1920.

Not really knowing what to do with this information, the following day she made the short walk along Curzon Street and Davies Street to the Bond Street Underground station to catch a Central London Railway train to Bank Station in the City of London. From there she walked past the Royal Exchange and the many bowler hatted, stockbroking gentlemen rushing about, along Cornhill to arrive at the Peninsular and Orient shipping company offices at 122 Leadenhall Street. The receptionists and clerks working in the high ceilinged, open offices on the ground floor were not able to tell her exactly when the SS Beltana was due to arrive. Another few days, maybe a week.

Seeing this confident young women refusing to be fobbed off by one of the junior clerks, an older man invited her into his office and asked his secretary to fetch some tea. She calmed down a little and he explained the numerous reasons for ship delays. With her charm now engaged, Amelia persuaded him to send a message to her at the hotel when the Beltana had arrived at Bristol. She left the man the names of the passengers she was looking for.

Two days later she received a note that had been hand delivered to Flemings hotel dated the 21st April.

Dear Miss Redron,
The Beltana arrived in Bristol yesterday. The three passengers whose names were left with me were not on board. I'm afraid P&O are unable to help you any further.
Yours sincerely.
D. Rathbone

From elation a few days ago to despair now. This had to be wrong. The letter was blunt and really didn't seem to be from the kindly gentleman she'd met. She'd go and see him again that afternoon.

When she arrived at the P&O offices the same bustle of clerical activity was humming across the ground floor. Amelia strode directly to Mr. Rathbone's office. The door was closed. The same secretary who'd made her tea stepped in front of her to stop her entry.

"I'm afraid he's on an urgent call Miss. He won't be able to meet with you until its finished. Please take a seat."

There were two chairs outside the office door, but before she sat down Mr. Rathbone had caught sight of her through the glass pane in the door. Clutching the bulky, black phone handset to his left ear and writing on a pad on his desk with his right hand they made eye-to-eye contact. He nodded with a forced smile in recognition of her presence. When the call ended he immediately walked to a coat stand. Amelia could now see he walked with a severe limp. He pulled out a hazelwood walking stick with a round polished handle, put on a bowler hat and made for the office door.

"Follow me please Miss Redron."

He walked surprisingly briskly with his limp, heading straight for the front door onto Leadenhall Street with Amelia trailing behind. As soon as they left the building, turning right, Amelia managed to catch up.

"Where are we going Mr Rathbone? I just wanted to ask about your note."

"Just around the corner here, I can explain then."

A little further on they crossed the road to walk down Whittington Avenue, named after the first Lord Mayor of London, and as they did so the noise from the iron framed, glass covered Leadenhall Market grew. Now forty years old, the building's two floors of plum red painted walls and gold pillars and the many stalls with the same green facia's and window frames were truly impressive. The poulterers, game dealers and butchers were shouting their prices, trying to draw the attention of the now, mainly retail customers; the hotel, restaurant and other trade buyers having passed through before 8 o'clock in the morning. At this time, many stall holders were beginning to pack up.

Amelia had to stare up at the huge arched glass arcade they entered leading along to the cathedral like dome over the central crossroads. Porters were loading hand carts with produce to run to the waiting motor vans parked on the streets outside, excluded from the market passages after 8am. For a while it was the beauty of the building that held her attention. Mr. Rathbone continued walking, past The Lamb Tavern in the centre; some labourers and suited City men crowding around the doors enjoying their first after work pint of porter ale, or the end of a long lunch glass of ruby port. They walked past the crowded Leaky Cauldron Café and popped out of the south end of the market into Lime Street Passage. Rathbone headed straight into a Lyon's Tea shop on the corner.

A blonde Lyons waitress collectively nicknamed 'Gladys', said.

"You're usual table is free Mr. Rathbone."

They followed her to a table against the side wall that had a good view across the room. The table sat four. Plenty of room. Rathbone spoke.

"I'm sorry to rush across here like this Miss Redron. I come here often to meet investors, underwriters, Lloyds syndicate managers, ship and insurance brokers. It's a good place to have tea and conduct business …… Without alcohol."

The 'Gladys' knew Mr. Rathbone's order and looked at Amelia with a make-up free face, fake smile and big teeth.

"And what would Madam like?"

"A pot of your strongest tea, no milk thank you."

There was sugar on the table.

'Gladys' gave her an odd look and in a sarcastic tone said.

"No milk Madam?"

Amelia's slight annoyance could not be suppressed.

"No milk. And its Miss."

"Sorry Miss, of course."

The waitress nipped off.

Rathbone looked at her curiously.

"No milk is a little unusual Miss Redron."

She sighed. "That's how I now like my tea. It's a long story Mr. Rathbone. Perhaps another time."

"Of course, of course."

She was keen to get on with the questions.

"So why did we need to rush out of your office Mr. Rathbone?"

"Yes, I'm sorry about that. So for a couple of reasons. One of which I don't understand. Firstly, I must apologise for the curtness of my note. But it had my intended effect. I was hoping you wouldn't leave it at that. You don't seem the kind of young lady that would accept 'no' for an answer. I'm glad you've come back."

Amelia's face softened and her frown fell away.

"Well you have me correct there Mr. Rathbone."

"So my first reason is that I usually come here between three and three thirty in the afternoon. So your appearance now; its ten minutes past three, fits in with my daily routine. My absence from the office for meetings with brokers would be expected by our Directors. My second is because as we sit here, some gentlemen from The War Office are on the sixth floor of the Peninsular and Orient Building making enquiries amongst the board of our company. Our receptionists on the ground floor gossip terribly with my secretary who tells me everything. She's a gem."

Amelia had listened and was puzzled. She noted the patronising but well-intentioned old school 'gem' comment. Her heart told her to react. Her sensible rational head told her to let it go..

The tray of tea arrived. 'Gladys' made a point of announcing Amelia's delivered pot.

"Strong tea, without milk." She smiled in an ingratiating way.

Completely ignoring her Amelia said with uncharacteristic brevity.

"Thank you. We're okay now. You can go."

It really wasn't what she would normally do, but she needed some answers.

Rathbone nodded to the waitress who scurried off with a look of thunder.

"So, Mr Rathbone, there was another reason?"

" Yes……. There was. When the Beltana arrived I messaged the Captain, an old friend of mine, Jonathan Milson. We'd been young ensign's together until my leg was wrecked many years ago. We kept in touch. He sailed. I ended up with a job that made sure he did. We are good friends Miss Redron. A man I trust."

"So you messaged Captain Milson?"

"I did. His response was not like Jon at all. He rang me up from the harbour office and said they'd docked in Bristol. They had trade cargo to take to Liverpool, but the ship had been boarded by government men. Not harbour or customs officials. Serious, suit wearing, inadequate looking men with pens. As he described them. We all know the type. Grifting Civil Service box-tickers determined to make commerce and life in general difficult or impossible."

"I'm really sorry Mr. Rathbone. I was hoping you might be able to tell me where Frank and his two friends are."

"Of course, Miss Redron. So when I enquired, Jon replied the men you mentioned were being monitored and investigated by the War Office. He'd been instructed to keep them on board, they were to be met in Liverpool when the Ministry had prepared their approach. He could tell me no more. He couldn't put this in writing. You need to understand that Britain has many enemies. My friend Jon sees this wherever he is. In particular when returning from Asia. He believes these men have something to do with the Bolsheviks."

Amelia's hackles were up.

"But these are British soldiers returning from Russia."

"Well of course. That's who they say they are. But with socialist revolutionary fervour everywhere, who really knows this? Jon told me the War Office had been expecting them and had arranged for them to be incarcerated in Liverpool, with the Prison officials qualified to deal with them. At the moment, your friend Frank and his pals don't seem to exist as far as the Government are concerned."

Amelia was speechless. She sipped her tea taking the time to think for a few moments. What she'd just been told didn't make sense. Rathbone then added.

"The War Office men have come to check the passenger manifests from Bombay. If they knew I'd made enquiries on your behalf, they'd want to speak with me, and probably you as well. I'm sure Captain Milson will have said nothing if he'd been asked."

"So the men will now be somewhere in Liverpool Mr. Rathbone?"

"That's correct. As Jon said, they were due to be met there and taken into custody."

Amelia finished her tea and went into her small black leather handbag to get her purse."

"No need for that Miss Redron. I'll be here for some time. I'll take care of the tea."

"Thank you Mr. Rathbone. I'm most grateful for your assistance. I'm not sure what I'll do now though."

She stood to leave as he did to say goodbye, and gently shake her hand.

"It's my pleasure. I'm sure things will sort themselves out. Your friends are lucky men to have you on their side."

*

Amelia walked back into Leadenhall Market her head full of confusion. The question she kept asking was why Britain hadn't lauded her returning soldiers instead of seeming to have treated them as traitors. Because that's what was now happening. She was trying to work out who could help her with this challenge as the doors on the underground train from Bank station were closing. From the most curved platform on the underground railway system, the shouts from the platform guards of "mind the gap" echoed in her head as it headed west.

The solution came to her as she sat at the next station, Post Office. She would write a letter. Arthur's friend worked in Parliament. She couldn't remember his name; Saller? Sapper? Snapper? She grinned, surely not Snapper! But she then remembered, Loughborough, where Arthur came from. His friend worked for the MP for Loughborough. She'd find out who he was and write to him. That was it. Decision made on what to do next, a letter to Parliament. She whispered to herself, 'thank you for the inspiration Post Office', and her heart was lighter.

When she returned to Fleming's Hotel at about 5pm she spoke with the duty manager in his lobby office. Could he find out the name of the MP for Loughborough? Within a couple of hours she had the name, Oscar Guest. Over dinner that evening Mikhail Rappoport, seeing an opportunity and keen to make contacts and showcase his ornamental design work, suggested if she got a response from the MP, she might invite him to Garrard's store to meet. He might find a nice item as a present for his wife. In the short letter she explained that one of Mr. Guest's constituents, Arthur Walton had been mistaken for a Russian and was locked up somewhere in Liverpool. She believed Mr. Walton was known to Mr. Guest's assistant. It crossed her mind to add the name 'Snapper', but then thought better of it. By 9pm Amelia had dropped off her letter at the front desk and a messenger would run this to the Parliament post room in the morning. The hotel had frequent visitors staying who were MP's or their families so delivering correspondence this way was familiar to them.

*

Parker Street, The City of Westminster. 22nd April 1920. 9.10am.

The post for Mr Guest was delivered, sorted in the Houses of Parliament and then taken to an office shared with several other Liberal Party MP's in Parker Street opposite His Majesty's Stationary Office. David was handed the pouch tipping the contents of the usual forty or so letters onto his desk. He flicked through the pile of stamped white envelopes, some with typed addresses naming Mr Guest, others hand written. The pale blue, unstamped envelope with the neatly sloping, 'Mr. O. Guest. MP., Houses of Parliament, Westminster' stood out. He flicked it over and saw the green embossed logo reading 'Flemings, Mayfair'. Intrigued he sliced it open with his ivory handled letter knife and read the letter.

Flemings Hotel, Mayfair.   **21st April 1920**

Dear Mr. Guest,

I am hoping you might be able to help. It's with regards to a man called Arthur Walton and two fellow soldiers. I believe Mr. Walton comes from Loughborough.

At reading this first line David's mouth dropped open and he had to sit down.

My name is Amelia Redron and I work for a family of Russians by the name of Rappoport who have fled from the terrible events there. We're now in safely in London. Our escape from Russia was only possible with help from Mr. Walton and two colleagues Mr. Frank Abraham and Sergeant Bradly Raybury.

These men were on the train we'd boarded to travel east to Vladivostok on the Trans-Siberian Railway. I understand they were part of a British military force that had landed in the north of Russia. They were able to protect us during a series of difficult and violent events. Sadly one of their colleagues, Mr. Eric Amos died protecting us and bravely doing his duty.

They have recently arrived on the SS Beltana in Liverpool. However, I understand there may be some confusion as to their identification and they have been taken into custody. I know we live in turbulent times, but these are British soldiers who fought bravely for our country during the war. Sgt. Raybury has been in the army for many years.

I do hope you are able to help end this unfairness. To help free these men and let them get on with their lives. I am sure their families would be most grateful to you, as I would.

I can be contacted through my employer, Mr. Mikhail Rappoport, Garrard's Albemarle Street.
Thank you for your time.
Yours sincerely,
Amelia Redron.

The letter writer's name meant nothing to David. He felt he had to go and see her. He knew where Garrard's were, a few roads along from Drones, his club on Dover Street. He'd done the walk from the office to his club so many times; across the park, up St. James Street, eleven and a half minutes. He wouldn't be missed. Mr. Guest was in a meeting at the Treasury with Mr Maynard Keynes that would last all morning. The Gold Standard was becoming a hotly debated subject.

9. Kowalski returns. Walton Gaol.
22nd April 1920. 9.30am.

As David was reading the letter in London, at Walton Gaol, the three cell doors on the landing housing the gunners were being slammed shut and locked. This was for the first time since the Governor, Sir Stephen and Principal Officer Myers had agreed they would enjoy an open regime. They weren't there to be punished, just temporarily detained. The man from the Ministry was returning. The Bolshevik papers written in Cyrillic script they'd brought back to England, considered by them to be souvenirs, had been translated. Kowalski had called and would come up by train on the evening of the 21st April. He would be at the gaol in the morning. Sir Stephen assumed all three would be re-interviewed and asked Myers to attend again.

On arrival at ten o'clock Kowalski said it was only Walton he wanted to see. He was collected and marched down to the same dining room as before. Kowalski was already sat with his back to the window. Myers was smoking a cigarette, looking up at the picture of Gladstone. When Arthur arrived Myers took his seat by the door. Today was bright and sunny so Arthur's view was more silhouette than bureaucrat. The questioner opened his briefcase and placed some documents on the table. He slid one of these across the table.

"Do you recognise this?"

"Yes I do." Arthur pushed it back to Kowalski.

"Please read it to me." It was pushed back to Arthur.

"It's written in Russian. It's not even in our letters. I'm afraid I can't read Russian."

He pushed it back to Kowalski. Myers had extinguished his smoke and had to cover his mouth with his hand to hide a grin that he was trying to suppress. Kowalski had tried the language bit before. It didn't work then; he was sure it wouldn't work now. Arthur then added.

"I can tell you what I was told it was, and when we presented it to Russian officials they seemed to accept this explanation."

"Tell me then please, Mr. Walton, or whoever you really are."

The papers crossed back to Arthur again. He picked them up and without looking at them said.

"These papers, duly stamped with …….. stamps. I guess to make them look official, were given to us to assist our passage from the Bolshevik controlled area to the White Russian and Allied controlled areas in central Russia. Roughly between Perm and Omsk. Look them up on a map, you'll find them. A Red Commissar by the name of Privakov, the leader of the mutinous Bolsheviks who'd taken us prisoner, gave them to me and the others. Abraham and Sarn't Raybury should have identical copies."

Holding up a couple of sheets of type written notes Kowalski said.

"We've translated these documents and they do appear to be travel permits and licences to allow you to move freely and without hindrance. They imply you are ordinary soldiers from the working class of Britain forced to go to Russia as part of a capitalist plot to undermine the Bolshevik revolution."

Myers snorted. He'd never heard so much rubbish. He knew Arthur was a British soldier, as were the others. But this time he let Kowalski continue. He was beginning to enjoy the back and forth ping-pong.

The suit leant down to his bag on the floor to pull out a small, black leather item a little larger than a packet of cigarettes. He placed this on the table in front of him wearing a self-satisfied smirk. He then poured himself a glass of water from a jug on a tray on the table. There was only one glass. He'd removed the other one earlier on and placed it under his seat so it couldn't be seen by Arthur or Myers.

"Do you recognise this item." He slid it across.

Without picking it up Arthur replied. "Yes I do."

"Can you tell me what it is?"

"It was given to me by the same Privakov I mentioned earlier."

"The Bolshevik commissar.

"Yes."

"Can you read it to me please?"

Arthur didn't answer straight away. He just stared at the man opposite him for an uncomfortable length of time. Myers enjoyed the tension. Arthur then said.

"Haven't we been through this before Mr Kowalski? I know you can speak Russian; I've heard you. I heard enough Russian to know what it was. I'm just wondering whether you actually understand English."

Kowalski shifted a little uneasily in his seat. The warm sun shone through the window onto his dark suit. A bead of sweat coalesced on his forehead and trickled down to his right eyebrow where it stopped.

"Okay Mr. Walton. I'll tell you what it is, as you claim not to know. We've had it translated in full, the sheet as well. I'm sure you were aware of the small flyer page folded inside?"

Arthur wasn't but chose not to say. He'd not paid attention to the book since being given it and realised he'd never be able to read it.

"The printed book is by Lenin, the Bolshevik revolutionary leader. It's called 'Imperialism, The latest stage of Capitalism. Popular outline'. It was published in Paris in 1917. But I expect you knew that."

"Of course I know who Lenin is, I lived in his war in Russia for six months. But as I can't read the script, nor speak Russian. I had no idea what it said."

"And the leaflet Mr. Walton. Perhaps you could read a little of the translation." He then added sarcastically.

"If you can read English that is."

Arthur ignored the last comment, picked up the leaflet and started reading.

"To the workers of the Entente. A protest against the Russian blockade and support of the counter revolution.

The workers and peasants of Russia, the first to free themselves from the yoke of capitalism call to you to be on your guard and not to desist from bringing pressure to bear on your government to prevent them from throttling the revolution in Russia.

On the contrary they are preparing a new attack and continue to gather all their strength to enslave us.

More than a year has passed since the Allied troops entered our territory to crush the Russian Revolution and turn Russia into a slave colony of the Great Capitalist countries. Japanese and English troops invaded Vladivostok at the beginning of April last year and soon after the English and French troops refused to leave Murmansk.

A new expedition was sent to their aid which at once began to march into Russia. Allied troops occupied Archangel and from there, attempted to pierce into the very heart of Russia. The Czechoslovak Counter Revolutionary rebels were declared to be allied troops under the protection of the Entente, and Allied hordes hastened to their aid through Siberia. Insurrections supported by Allied money, Allied officers and white guards broke out, and Allied agents prepared plots against the Soviet authority."

Arthur read confidently. A man who was at ease with himself, keeping Brad's comments in mind that there would be hurdles to overcome and this was one of them. And besides he knew this kind of literature from the leaflets his brother Wilfred used to bring home from the Brittania Iron and Steel mill before the war.

"That'll do Mr. Walton. I'm sure you get the picture. This is a Bolshevik propaganda leaflet that you've brought back from your adventures, hidden in a book you claim was given to you as a gift by a revolutionary extremist holding you and your friends prisoner. Doesn't that seem a little far-fetched to you? A little implausible? Do you think we should believe that you haven't been convinced by the cause of these international terrorists trying to promote global revolution?"

Arthur again made point that he couldn't read it as it was written in the Russian script. He therefore didn't know what it said. The dialogue continued between the two of them for another half an hour or so. Kowalski trying different lines of questioning and occasionally dropping into Russian in mid-sentence to try, in his mind, trip Arthur up. All pointless and Myers could see it. At noon Kowalski said they should stop and re-convene at 2pm. He needed to contact his office in London for further instructions.

10. Garrard's Jewellers, Albemarle Street, London.
22nd April 10.05am.

David was slightly detained by another political assistant as he left the Parker Street office so he didn't get to Garrard's in the less than 12 minutes he thought he could. On the ground floor he asked to see Mr. Mikhail Rappoport and Amelia Redron. After the blank looks and scratching of heads and a couple of calls by the receptionist, they worked out it was the affable Russian man who was always so polite and jovial. They called his office and David heard the lady saying.

"Of course Mr Rappoport, we can send a messenger to the Flemings Hotel to fetch Miss Redron."

One of them took David to an elevator at the back of the store. Made by the German company Siemens and having broken down in 1917, it had only recently been restored through the lack of access to mechanical parts. With only enough room for two at a squeeze, it rattled up to the third floor. They walked across the room with numerous craftsmen tinkering, hammering and melting metal with gas torches on the workshop benches.

On the far wall were two small glass partitioned offices. David could see a dark haired, jacketless man with silver sleeve cuffs just above his elbows. He wore a fashionable black and yellow tie, diagonally striped like a bumble bee, tucked into the waistcoat of his dark blue suit. The man stood as he saw them approaching the office door.

"Hello Sir. Mr. Guest I assume? How good of you come to see us so quickly. Miss Redron only sent the letter last night. She will be overjoyed to know that we can start sorting this thing out. My name is Mikhail Rappoport from Moscow. Miss Redron............"

David lifted his right hand with palm toward Rappoport to stop him speaking and interrupted.

"No, no Mr Rappoport. I'm not Mr. Guest. My name's Saffer. David Saffer. I work for Mr. Guest the MP for Loughborough. I'm his personal assistant, bag carrier, speech writer, letter opener. You know the kind of general dogsbody that every MP needs."

David was full of smiles in his ever-effusive way and the Russian replied holding his arm out to shake hands.

"I see Mr. Saffer. The letter opener. It's a great pleasure to meet with you."

"David, please call me David."

"Thank you, and I'm Mikhail. Michael if it's easier for you."

They stood in the office for a couple of minutes exchanging pleasantries. Mikhail explained a little about his family. Him travelling to Britain in February 1919 to arrange to get his family out of the increasingly unstable country, and not being able to do so. Amelia taking the initiative to travel east with Irena his mother, wife Simona and their son Isak. They were speaking when Mikhail suddenly said.

"Ah. Miss Redron is here."

She was alone, not needing to be shown to the office she'd visited many times in the last few weeks with Isak. Amelia bustled through the workshop exchanging greetings with some of the men she'd come to know. Her boater hat with flowers on the brim was moving at pace. Her eyes were fixed on the office and she was surprised at how young looking the Loughborough MP was. She also stretched out her gloved hand as she got there.

"Hello Mr. Guest. How very good of you to come."

Amelia was bursting with happiness.

David held a broad grin. Mikhail now interrupted

"Amelia, Amelia, this isn't Mr. Guest."

She instantly looked crestfallen. David spoke.

"No I'm not Miss Redron. My name's David Saffer."

Amelia ignited like an electric lamp.

"David Saffer, David Saffer that was it. Saffer. Not Sapper or Snapper. Saffer."

Amelia held her hand to her mouth to stifle a giggle. David laughed.

"I'm sorry Mr Saffer. It was your name I couldn't remember. It was you I really wanted to contact. You who Arthur talked about. You worked with him before the war, at a chemist or pharmacy. He told me you were in London, at Parliament with your local MP from Loughborough. I remembered that but not your name. He told me about the mercury too. It was a very funny story."

David was now getting a little confused. The letter had referred to Arthur as a constituent. Business for the boss, but Amilia was now saying it was David she'd needed to contact. Mikhail saw what was happening and suggested Amelia slow down a bit. He asked the receptionist to arrange for some tea from the manager's dining room to which he had access. He retrieved a chair from the office next door and the three of them sat in the small space he had. Him on one side of the desk, the other two facing each other on the opposite side as Amelia launched into the story of her meeting the British soldiers and their escape from Russia.

The tea arrived, Mikhail poured, Amelia continued. It was a one way verbal rush until after about twenty minutes she got to her final sentence.

"I now know from a kind man at P&O that when they arrived back in England, Liverpool I'm told, they were taken into custody. I think somebody thinks they are Russian revolutionaries, or perhaps British revolutionaries, traitors to Britain. I'm just not sure. But these are our men and they're being treated atrociously."

It was clear that whoever had decided to lock them up had made a mistake. David immediately recognised this and knew what he had to do. Mr. Guest was Mr. Churchill's cousin. It was Churchill's initiative to send men to Russia, to raise the North Russian Relief Force of which Arthur, Frank and Sgt. Raybury were part. Churchill was the Secretary of State for War and Air. Oscar Guest would have to call him, explain the situation and put an end to this injustice.

David told Amelia and Mikhail what he would do, their meeting now drawing to a close. He stood to say good bye, the others doing the same, Mikhail moving from behind the desk to shake David's hand and thank him for agreeing to help Amelia. As he did so he stopped obscuring the view of Isak's treasure sitting on a low shelf behind his back. It drew David's eyes like a magnet. Amelia noticed the stare and the sudden shock on his face.

"What is it David?"

She got no response. He continued staring.

"David, David, what is it?"

"I don't know. It looks odd. It looks familiar. Similar but very different. Very beautiful, not like I've seen before."

It then came to her.

"Arthur thought so too. He said he'd seen something like it before."

"The Report Box. That's it. The Report Box. Report. Rappoport. That's it. That's it."

He sat down again staring at the ornately jewelled sedan chair ornament. Mikhail then said.

"David you'll have to explain what you mean. Please explain."

David then told the family story of Ezra, his grandfather fleeing Lithuania when other families chose to remain, with Adam, his dad as a very young boy. It would have been about fifty years ago. The Saffer name had been adopted sometime after they'd arrived in England. He described the strange item, the box on wheels that looked like it had been made by someone as a design experiment or sample. It had been given to Ezra to look after. As he spoke Mikhail picked up the Sedan Chair, passed it to David and listened quietly without interruption. As David carefully moved the ornament in his hands he said.

"I think this is the finished item from that very first idea."

He had a tear rolling down his cheek.

Mikhail spoke. "So your family were originally from Kovno David?"

"My dad would know the name. It was never widely discussed. My grandfather died many years ago. I'll tell Adam, my father, what's happened. He always said that one day the Report Box, as we call it, would be collected. He'll come to London with it I'm sure. Or perhaps we could get you to Tynte House, where we live, in Loughborough."

11. Churchill's Intervention.

<u>Whitehall, The City of Westminster. 22nd April, after 11.25am.</u>

David returned to the Parker Street offices with his head swimming. He tried to concentrate, to deal with the rest of the morning's mail, prioritising those that would need the MP's attention, those he would respond to and invitations to Loughborough town events, openings and dinners that his boss liked to decide on himself. The Treasury meeting would finish at midday, Oscar Guest would not be available until then. David would be at the door to meet him.

It was seven minutes to the Treasury Buildings on Whitehall. It was about 12.15 when Mr Guest emerged with several colleagues in deep conversation. David had to let them finish before he could speak. Guest had seen him and that only ever meant something urgent. He trusted David's experience enough to know when his attention was required so he broke off from the Treasury Mandarins. The events of the morning were explained to him. He listened thoughtfully, asking pertinent questions, but with a thought on why the men might have been detained in the first place. Eventually he asked.

"David, I accept everything you have told me, but are you absolutely sure this man Arthur, really is your friend. Might he actually be someone else?"

"No Sir, it's definitely Arthur. I met a lady he helped escape from Russia, and she knew things only Arthur could know."

The two men left the Treasury Buildings on Whitehall taking two black Civil Service umbrellas that were propped in a packed stand by the door. Similar 'communal' rain protection lay in offices all over Westminster. It was now drizzling heavily. The umbrellas unfurled; they turned right to the Houses of Parliament where Guest had a small cupboard office shared with another MP. The dialogue continued between them. Guest probing to make sure that David couldn't possibly be mistaken. By the time they'd reached the House of Commons and he'd heard about the mercury accident, he was convinced. He would make a personal call to his cousin to discuss it. David returned to the Parker Street offices.

<u>Walton Gaol, Liverpool. 22nd April 13.55 pm.</u>

Sir Stephen, there's a call for you.

"I'm a little busy right now Johnson."

"I think you should take this one sir, it's a Miss Boylan calling from Mr. Churchill's office."

The Governor looked up questioningly over his reading glasses.

"Mr. Churchill's office? Do we know this Miss Boylan?"

"We do Sir Stephen, his personal assistant. She keeps his diary and cleared it for him to attend the governors dinner last year. It's that Mr. Churchill."

"Ah, that Mr. Churchill."

There was only one 'Mr. Churchill', but the call was wholly unexpected.

"I think you're right; I should take the call. Put him through Johnson."

He put the call through. The phone on the governor's desk rang. He picked up the heavy Bakelite hand piece. Miss Boylan confirmed it was Sir Stephen and connected him with Churchill. Out of respect and deference to the caller and without really thinking, he stood up. In a familiar and friendly voice Winston Churchill spoke.

"Sir Stephen. I know you are a busy man, as I am too, so I won't take up much time. I haven't forgotten our conversation at the Prison Governor's dinner last November at the United Services Institute. It was kind of the governors to invite me. The venison was excellent....... And so was the port .... as I recall. But I digress. You told me we need to put more money into the education and occupational training of prisoners. So they are better equipped for release and don't re-offend. I've given it more thought and I think it would work. However, this is not what the call is about, I haven't forgotten our dinner conversation though."

"Thank you Mr. Churchill. It will be important to help men get back to being good members of society."

"It will, it will. Now to the issue in hand. I'm told that instructions from well-meaning colleagues here in the War Office have resulted in you holding three men in custody; currently being questioned. Soldiers. Recently returned from Russia. From the east. Vladivostok I think?"

"We are Mr. Churchill."

"My colleagues had concerns as to their identity. No longer. I now have absolute confirmation these men are, who they say they are. Irrefutable proof from someone who knows them. They are to be released tomorrow. They are no longer to be treated as anything other than honourable British soldiers. Guests of your hostelry, if you like. I will arrange for them to be provided with the correct attire. My people here will sort that out with your administration."

"Mr. Churchill there is a Mr. Kowalski here currently questioning one of the men. Arthur Walton. He believes him to be the ringleader."

"Nonsense. He's a constituent of my cousin, Oscar Guest. Walton is by all accounts a good soldier who volunteered to go to Russia. Tell Kowalski to return to London, his mission is over."

"I'll do that Mr. Churchill."

"Thank you Sir Stephen. Tell these men they can leave Walton Gaol with their heads held high and a personal thanks from me for their war service. ...... And for that in the frozen wastes of Russia. Goodbye now."

...... And the phone went dead.

*

At 14.05pm there was a loud rap on the interview room door. Without waiting for an answer it opened immediately just as Kowalski was angrily saying.

"I said there must be no interruptions Mr. Myers."

As the Principal Officer was behind the door as it swung open he couldn't see at first who it was. Then he recognised the back of Sir Stephen. He stood and bellowed out in his parade ground voice.

"Stand up for the Governor!"

Arthur and Kowalski stood, the latter looking flustered.

"Thank you Mr. Myers."

He nodded, acknowledging the other two.

"Mr Kowalski, Gunner Walton."

The Governor had a broad smile on his face as he looked at Arthur. Arthur suddenly realised that Brad's hurdle they'd have to cross .... had been crossed.

"I have just taken a call Mr. Kowalski. You are to stop this interview process with immediate effect and return to London. Gunner Walton and his two colleagues have been identified and verified as British soldiers who'd been part of the North Russian Relief Force sent to Murmansk in May of last year."

Kowalski bristled with annoyance.

"I'm afraid, Sir Stephen my authority is from the Military Secretary, Brigadier Chetwode in the War Office. I'm sure you'll find that his position will trump whichever minion has called you up with some mis-identification and this preposterous news. We do know what we are doing in our military intelligence services you know."

Mitchell now enjoyed the bear trap he'd set.

"I'm sure the brigadier is a very capable and senior man, Mr Kowalski, but I think you'll find Mr. Winston Churchill has a little more authority. If you feel you need to, you should contact your office to confirm. You may use the phone in my assistants room upstairs."

The Civil Service man from the ministry's body now seem to involuntarily twitch and jerk with indignation inside the ill-fitting suit. He swept his carefully prepared papers and translations into his briefcase and leant over the table to pick up the black leather book gifted to Arthur by Privakov. Arthur got there first.

"I think I'll keep this Mr. Kowalski."

Resulting in more head and upper body shuddering as he strode out of the room.

Sir Stephen commented.

"Keep it Gunner Walton. He won't be needing it now."

Then turning to the door where his principal officer looked totally satisfied with proceedings, he said.

"Mr. Myers, please arrange for Sergeant Raybury, Gunners Walton and Abraham to be in my office at three pm. We have some things to discuss. And as we did before, unlock their doors when you return to the wing."

The governor nodded again to Arthur. "Three pm. Gunner Walton."

Oscar Guest's office, House of Commons. 22nd April 14.25pm.

After lunch David had to brief the MP on a dinner he was attending that evening at Mansion House in the City. There would be much discussion on the trade implications of the division of the Turkish Petroleum Company that had been signed earlier that day at the San Remo conference. David had appraised himself on what he knew, wrote up some brief notes in his neat hand-writing, talked the MP through them and left the papers with him. At the end of this meeting Guest said.

"I have spoken with Mr. Churchill, David. He agreed with me that your information and that of Miss Redron and Mr. Rappoport is conclusive. His office have now confirmed the men will be released tomorrow at 2pm. There are some things that need to be arranged by the War Office beforehand. I'll now be staying in London this weekend; Kathleen will be joining me. I won't be needing the car. So you are welcome to make use of it if you wish."

For David this was a gift. He'd been trying to work out how he could organise his weekend. He desperately wanted to alert Alice as to what was happening but hadn't had the chance to even tell her the amazing news that Arthur was now safely home. A plan began to formulate in his mind.

Guest added.

"Thank you for these notes David. I think you might have some things to do now. So go, have a good weekend and I'll see you on Monday morning."

"Thank you Mr. Guest. I appreciate the time and your generosity."

The Governor's office, Walton Gaol, Liverpool. 22nd April 3pm.

Arthur, Brad and Frank had been brought up to the governor's office for five to three At precisely 3 o'clock Myers knocked on the door.

"Come." Was the call from inside and they were marched in military style. There were normally no chairs on the room side of the great oak desk. Today Johnson had arranged three.

Sir Stephen came around the desk to shake their hands and offered them a seat. He was a fairly tall man, not quite the six foot of Arthur, but not far off it. Around sixty years of age he retained a head full of fair, to slightly greying hair that appeared to cling to his head. Blue-grey eyes, an easy smile and warm face. He had a positive view of all prisoners, believing they could be rehabilitated in most circumstances. He'd brought his Principal Officer, Colin Myers with him to create a firm, but fair regime at Walton gaol.

Johnson, his assistant delivered some tea which despite Myers offering, the governor poured himself. 'All with sugar I presume?', he asked. He then explained why they had been detained, although they'd probably worked it out themselves. Their appearance out of Vladivostok in the east of Russia several months after their disappearance during Dyer's Battalion mutiny in Troika was inconceivable to the military. So the conclusion was they must be imposters. When the men arrived a few days ago it was immediately clear to Sir Stephen and Myers they were unmistakably soldiers. They had to let the Ministry investigation run its course. Terminated by the call from Winston Churchill earlier in the day.

They would stay in the gaol for one more night. Mr. Churchill and the War Office were arranging for them to be correctly dressed and he understood there was someone on the way with some kit, arriving in the morning. A tailor had been engaged to be here at ten. Their doors would not be locked again.

"You have some useful friends in high places Gunner Walton."

"It appears so Sir Stephen." Arthur smiled.

The governor asked them to tell their story. He had a meeting at four and was clear until then. Between the three of them they covered the adventure. Occasionally correcting a place name when one got it wrong and details of particular events. Arthur tried to talk about Eric's death but got too emotional. Brad finished that by describing the view across Amur Bay.

Sir Stephen found the story fascinating, an unusual tale.

"Perhaps worthy of a book one day."

<u>Accounts Office, Hart and Levy factory, Loughborough.</u>
<u>22nd April 4.09pm.</u>

Alice was focussed on finding the missing entry to balance the customer's account. She suspected it had been mis-applied to someone else. It was an odd amount, 16 pounds, 2 shillings and 6 pence. She knew she'd get to it and was determined to do that before she finished for the day. Her attention to the problem meant she missed the shout. Her friend, Agnes on the next desk called over.

"Alice, Alice. It's something for you."

The clerical staff had gotten used to telegram's coming into the office during the war years when it was mainly women there. More recently they were very unusual, and this one in particular.

"Telegram for Miss Baker. Urgent telegram for Miss Baker from the House of Commons. It's got the portcullis stamp on it."

People stopped what they were doing. Alice became very anxious. Arthur's mum had been notified back in September 1919 that he was 'missing, presumed dead'. There'd been tears and grief, upset and anguish for six months. Then the message from Hong Kong. They'd then been told by the military authorities when they enquired that it wasn't possible for Arthur to have been in Vladivostok. But she knew they were wrong. She had the evidence. Arthur's letter, Arthur's amazingly neat writing. Then another one from Bombay. But why a telegram from Parliament? Something dreadful must have happened with the ship. She'd seen David a few weeks ago, one weekend when he was visiting his family. They both knew Arthur was coming home, but now this.

The people in the office stopped what they were doing as the slip was passed to Alice.

"Agnes. I can't read it. You must and tell me quietly what is says."

Her friend opened it and read.

"It's from David. You probably knew that. It reads. *'Small hiccup, now overcome. Arthur is in Walton gaol, Liverpool. Release at 2pm Friday. I'll pick you up tomorrow at 9am. I have Mr. Guest's car. All cleared with Sir Maurice Levy for your day off.'*"

Alice burst into tears. Agnes hugged her. Everyone looked concerned.

"It's okay, it's okay," said Agnes. "Arthur's home. He's in Liverpool. Alice will see him tomorrow."

A loud cheer went around the room and a few from the adjacent office came through to hear the news. Alice was laughing and crying at the same time. It was suddenly true. Arthur was coming home and she hoped this time for good.

12.   Release.
23rd April 1920.

<u>Oscar Guest's Hispano Suiza H6.</u>
<u>London to Liverpool, via Loughborough.</u>
<u>Departing 5.30am, 23rd April</u>

David knew Brian Halladay, Guest's driver well. It was a long drive from London to Liverpool and they needed to start early as they had to pick Alice up from her home in Craddock Square, Loughborough. They would share the driving as they had done many times in the frequent journeys from London to the constituency. The car was luxurious, reliable and incredibly well engineered. After collecting David it would then spin by the Flemings Hotel to pick up Amelia.

As he wasn't sure what the soldiers might want to do after their release; he didn't know Brad and had only met Frank briefly before he left with Arthur for Russia. So to give everyone options he'd booked six rooms at the premier hotel in Liverpool, the Adelphi on Ranelagh Place, for the Friday and Saturday nights.

They made good time along the A6 through the southern counties to Loughborough. Brian liked to test the cars speed capability when alone. With today's passengers he would need to be more cautious. On the second leg there were some delays where a delivery lorry had broken down and was blocking a lane of the road near Stoke.

Amelia and Alice hit it off straight away. Amelia able to tell Alice about the amazing rail journey, across Russia, Eric's bravery and very sad death so close to safety. She also spoke of the many times Arthur talked about Alice and David, bringing a warmth to them both. They planned to stop before they reached Liverpool for something to eat.

<u>'B' Wing, Walton Gaol, Liverpool. 23rd April 1pm.</u>

The story of the three soldiers wrongly imprisoned on B Wing had spread across the landings and subsequently the whole prison. In a closed institutional environment this was inevitable. Even the planned time of their exit through the gates onto Hornby Road was known. And if all the prison officers and the lags knew it, you could guarantee the Liverpool Echo and other newspapers did too.

At one o'clock the men were once again marched to the interview room, now converted back to a dining room in their better fitting prison greys. When they got there Myers was waiting with a proud smile as if his men were going on parade. A spread of cold meat pies, salad, cheeses and cold meats were on the table with pitchers of beer. The British issue tunics and breeches they'd been given in Vladivostok by the Czechs had been laundered with the left hand breast pocket obscured by medals. Arthur's tunic had the 1914/15 star, war medal and victory medal, Frank the same preceded by his military medal. The War Office, no doubt under Churchill's direction, had obviously gone back into Brad's records as his tunic had his full set. The newly issued three hidden behind the Queen and King's Boer War pair and tailed by his Long Service and Good Conduct gong. All the buttons on the tunics had been replaced by the Field Artillery embossed official uniform buttons. Arthur and Frank's jackets had the single chevron, lance bombardier's stripe they had both relinquished when they'd volunteered for Russia. Brad had his three sergeant chevrons back.

They would indeed be properly dressed. At Myers 'request', several ex-soldiers in the prison had spent the night with tins of black Cherry Blossom polish bulling the toe-caps of three pairs of prison boots to create a deep glassy shine. Any Regimental Sergeant Major would have appreciated the results. Peaked caps with the artillery cap badges were sitting on chairs beneath the tunics. Several other senior prison officers joined them after they'd changed into their freshly prepared, Churchill organised, 'correct attire'.

Sir Stephen Mitchell came in for the last ten minutes before they left with Myers to the main gate. He wished them luck, thanked them for their cooperation, noting with a smile that after their journey to get to Walton Gaol, the previous few nights can't have been too arduous. He also warned them that there were a number of press photographers and journalists on Hornby Road, and a small crowd of onlookers. There had been a request from a reporter to be let in to interview them which was rejected. Another claiming to be a friend acting in a personal capacity but this was also turned down. News had spread locally of their mistaken incarceration and now release. People wanted to see who these 'Russian' men were.

The gates of Walton Gaol, Hornby Road 23rd April 1.45 pm

David, Amelia and Alice had stopped at the Halfway House Inn on the Woolton Road in Wavertree before skirting the east of the city of Liverpool to get to Walton Gaol. As they drove along Hornby Road from the east toward the main gates; the mock, square castle towers and gatehouse with arched entrance, they could see perhaps a hundred people gathered outside. There was no notorious criminal being freed today and besides, the gaol's gates opened at 11 am. on release days. So they had to be here for the soldiers.

David thought it a good idea to stop a short way from the gates. The arrival of the car drew the attention of some of the crowd. The Spanish Hispano-Suiza was a rare, impressive vehicle designed by a Swiss aviation engineer, Marc Birkigt and assembled at the companies factory in Paris. Two press photographers and a man with a notebook, presumably a journalist, walked along to take some pictures.

David and Brian Halladay stepped onto the pavement and suddenly found themselves answering questions about what it was, its engine, where it was made and who owned it. Oddly, there were no enquiries as to who they were and why they were there. With the unexpected interest from local people and the papers; one photographer was from the Liverpool Echo, the other from the Manchester Guardian, David suggested Alice and Amelia remain where they were and stayed in the car for a short while to let the public spectators get over their excitement. As it was, they were currently busy laughing at Amelia's story as to how she shocked Arthur and Frank for the first time …….. just by saying 'its chicken pox' in English.

The gatehouse, Walton Gaol, 23rd April 1.55 pm

Three soldiers were now impeccably dressed in their Royal Field Artillery uniforms, peaked caps and highly polished boots. The last time the two bombardiers presented in this manner was at their training passing out parade on the square at Woolwich. They walked with principal officer Myers down to the main gates. As they did so a strange noise started rising in volume. It began behind them in 'B' Wing, a clash of metal against metal or stone. Tin mugs or plates being bashed on bed frames, floors, cell window bars and doors. It spread across the prison getting louder. Brad asked the question of Myers.

"Why are they making this racket Mr. Myers?"

"Well, all the lags know what's happened with you men. They know some of your story too. These things spread quickly and it's their way of showing you three the respect you deserve. In contrast to your reception back in the country by the military. It's also to offer their goodwill. The men here have little voice but they can really make a racket when they want to."

The artillerymen could now appreciate the short walk to their freedom with the cacophony of noise coming from the cell windows.

At the external gate Myers shook their hands and repeated the sentiments already expressed by the governor. Their three canvas holdalls which they'd arrived with were lined up for them to collect, labelled accordingly. The twelve foot black gates were pushed open. Some barriers had been erected to keep people back to the footpath and four policemen were the gate side of the barrier. A cheer rose up and several newspaper cameras popped to capture the moment of release. There were broad smiles everywhere. They were enjoying the moment. The process of securing their freedom; initiated by Amelia several days before, taken up by Mikhail and David, elevated to Oscar Guest MP, and the final stroke of luck, Guest having immediate access to one of the most important government ministers in the right job, Winston Churchill, was all unknown to Arthur, Frank and Brad. They were just free.

Behind the railings the faces were anonymous, the cheers and claps were heart-felt and the hands were waving in the air. A façade of unrecognisable, happy, congratulatory, faces. The gunners were not expecting to see anyone they knew and were thoroughly enjoying the surprise of the adulation. Arthur then saw it. A waving hand above the heads of, and behind the people at the front of the barriers. He couldn't see who it belonged to, but he knew it. A hand like no other, David's left, with the two missing fingers. Unmistakably his.

He walked toward the gap in the railings where the photographers stood, their cameras still popping once they'd reloaded the film. The others followed him on the basis that they had to go somewhere and without knowing Arthur had a purpose.

"Wally, Wally, over here."

David's voice was now clear.

Arthur pushed through the crowd to get to his friend. The people about them moved out of the way to let him through. They embraced like brothers and the clapping of the crowd filled their ears. Both Frank and Brad were engaged in conversation trying to answer the questions being thrown at them. There were pats on the back all around. After a few minutes the crowd quietened and started thinning, the onlookers having seen what they'd come for.

"I have a car and I've arranged accommodation for you and your friends. Come with me, this way, it's over here."

David led the men alongside the dispersing people walking away from the prison gates in both directions along Hornby Road. The car could be seen through gaps in the crowd. A man in a black chauffeurs uniform and cap stood to the front. As he saw David wave at him he moved to a rear door to open it. A women in a long, bottle green dress, black jacket and matching green pill-box hat emerged. At first Arthur didn't recognise her in the fashionable, sophisticated clothes and then realised it was Amelia. He looked at David, but before he could say anything David said.

"It's a long story Wally, and to be honest almost unbelievable. We'll have time to explain it all later."

Frank had seen Amelia; his face was beaming. She was walking toward him, more quickly now. They met and embraced. Halladay had walked around the back of the Suiza and was now opening the other door. Arthur was only vaguely aware of this as he was enjoying Frank and Amelia's reunion, an uncharacteristically public display of emotion from a very private man.

A second women was stepping out with the aid of the driver. All in white with a wide brimmed hat tipped down, hiding her face as she watched her step onto the pavement. She looked up straight into Arthur's eyes. Alice. Her grin was broad, she was dabbing her eyes.

"It's Alice!"

Arthur called to no one in particular as his step quickened for the last twenty paces.

"Alice, Alice." He repeated.

She was laughing and crying with happiness. They hugged. An unrestrained, passionate squeeze. Brad was looking at the two young couples with paternalistic pride.

"Welcome home Arthur. You look wonderful."

"And you look like a dream, a perfect vision."

"Thank you Arthur. You say the nicest things. "

They kissed each other and hugged again. She stood on tip-toe to speak into his ear.

"No more wars now."

Arthur leant back and laughed, then shook his head.

"No more wars Alice, no more wars."

Epilogue.
Tynte House, Loughborough.
Sunday 20th June 1920.

The organisation had taken a while for the garden party arranged by Adam and Naomi Saffer to honour the pledge made by his parents, Ezra and Miriam in Kovno, Lithuania, almost fifty years ago. What to do and where to do it with David acting as the go-between amongst the interested parties. Most importantly it was a day the Rappoports could get to Loughborough. Everyone agreed that the 'Report Box' should be collected as Adam always believed it would. He remembered nothing of the traumas of that time; he was too small for those bad things to create a permanent imprint. The day chosen turned out to be a beautiful, clear blue summer's day with his front drive roses in their prime.

Garrard's had arranged a car for Mikhail, his mother Irena, Simona and son Isak. Amelia was coming by train with Frank, now engaged to be married. They were staying as guests with Alice Baker and her mother. Alice had persuaded her friend, Madge, who'd got to know Eric over the few weeks he'd stayed at Arthur's to come as well. Her and Eric had got on so well and she was deeply upset that he never made it back. Alice wanted Frank and Arthur to talk about Eric and how important he was to them, Madge needed to hear this.

Arthur and Betty would walk to David's house on a day like this. Betty had made some wonderful cakes to recipes shared with her by Naomi Saffer. These had been collected in the morning by Adam's driver.

Sir Maurice and Lady Levy would attend with two of their daughters, as would Oscar Guest and Kathleen his wife. There were many other family and local friends of the Saffer's and Walton's present. Sgt. Brad Raybury was not able to make it. His fascination with the night-sky, planets and stars had taken him to the Shetland Isles to try to see the Northern Lights. The Loughborough Echo had sent a reporter and photographer.

Until this day, Adam had not seen the jewelled Sedan Chair. David and his brother Ben had organised proceedings. They'd set up a trestle table on the back lawn and between them they would tell a little of the early story of the 'Report Box' – the Saffer story, the one they knew. Mikhail would pay tribute to his father Julias, and his last piece of work, something he'd been nurturing his whole life.

Amelia and Frank had worked out some words about the train journey, but no upsetting detail. It was to be a day of celebration. 'Budgie' Baker and 'Taffy' Davies would be mentioned, along with the missing Brad. Frank had a short monologue on each of them. Good, inspiring men who took their own paths. Frank had words to say on Eric too.

As Arthur had declined the offer from David to tell how, back in Vladivostok, he'd made the link between the two items, Frank would also do this. Arthur wanted no credit for the outcome of events, David thought it was about time he got some.

At the end of the speeches that tied together the incredible parallel journeys of the two items, the locally made lace covers were lifted by Ben and David Saffer to display them side-by-side for the first time. United over continents, unpredictable events and coincidences. It was an afternoon for all to look to a more positive and peaceful future.

Notes.

This story is threaded through real, but largely unknown history. I hope this brings more of it to light. See the further reading list below for some of the limited number, but comprehensive historical study books available. To my knowledge there is no other imaginative English literature of these events.

The political and military narrative is factual, as are the politicians, senior military leaders of the North Russian Relief Force and elsewhere in the story. Errors of fact and interpretation are purely mine. My defence will always be a novel is not a history book, but I hope you enjoy the factual detail as well.

After publishing the first book inspired by Arthur I was advised to set up a Face Book page to let people know about the writing. Some old faces and many new friends have emerged. In particular I discovered a page on the North Russian Relief Force (The North Russian Relief Force (NRRF) - 1919 | Facebook) People from around the world with an interest in this hidden corner of history. There are some amazing pictures contributed by members of this group and fantastic to know we are part of a community with this link in time.

I've referenced books and papers I've used in my research below.

Literary 'Easter Eggs?' – Who can resist these?

Thanks and acknowledgements.

Arthur Walton, my Grandad, and his friends. This story evolved from tiny seeds planted with me before he died in 1972. I was 11 years old. Those anecdotes and further research strongly indicate he was there. His friends are purely fictional characters, but I hope they represent men and women of the time.

*

My wife, Diane, who has tolerated the mess of books spread about as I researched and wrote over the last few years, and the ideas we've discussed on what to do with the outcome.

Olivia, Tom and Sam, my children and their partners, **Steve and Ashley** who've put up with me talking about the books, telling them details and their patience and encouragement along the way.

*

My Dad, **Roderick Royal Stuart**. (1938-2024). Arthur's son-in-law and also a 30 year professional soldier. It was probably because of my dad's service we heard the stories as many WW1 veterans spoke little of their experiences. Dad was around long enough to enjoy me reading passages from the books and sharing some of my favourite chapters. I miss him.

*

My good friend **Steve Mitchell** of c50 years, who has been as intrigued as me about Arthur's tales. He read every chapter as it was written. His lifelong friendship and feedback has been invaluable and spurred me on. Further acknowledged by his cameo role in Churchill's Intervention.

*

Some characters are based on living people. Thanks to the **'Boss'**, who does what it says on the tin! **'The Trial' lawyer**, a fine young man building a public service career. And two **'Hong Kong Bankers'**. One of whom I always enjoyed working with back in the day, and in memory of the other.

*

My army friends **Brian Payne, David Lowles, Paul Everett and Jerry Compton**, for ideas, friendship, company and levelling up and down conversation. Important to have people like this about.

*

Catherine Boylan for responding to a 'cold' email from some unknown bloke enquiring after her dissertation on *'The North Russian Relief Force. A Study of Military Motivation in the Aftermath of the First World War'*.

I'm most grateful to Catherine for sending this original and fascinating work to me for reference.

*

A profound apology to Captain Savory (p226). A real and brave soldier, wrongly portrayed in this book as an insensitive administrator, for creative purposes only.

Captain, later Lieutenant General Sir Richard Arthur Savory was a British Indian Army Officer with a long and distinguished service in both World Wars. In Gallipoli and Mesopotamia as a young officer in WW1 earning a Military Cross.

As a Staff Captain in Vladivostok he wrote an incredible first hand account of the military and civilian turmoil in 1919-20. After Staff College in Camberley ('27/'28) he returned as an instructor to the Indian Military Academy and then Commanding Officer of the 11th Sikh Regiment.

In WW2 he commanded Indian Brigades and Divisions in the Western Desert, East Africa and Burma. He was appointed the General Officer Commanding Iraq in 1945. After retiring in 1948 he became a deputy lieutenant of Somerset and a Justice of the Peace.

In truth a man of great honour with a lifetime of military service.

Page 81.

A special thanks to Sarah Nicols from The Sacramento Valley in California and her amazing website **World War Knits,** recreating an array of real WW1 kit items so vital for the warmth and wellbeing of soldiers from different nations. Her work enabled me to accurately describe the balaclava in 'Is This Forever.' A must visit for re-enactors and historical accuracy.

About - HANDMADE HISTORICAL KNITS (worldwarknits.com)

Thank you Sarah!

Cover Picture. Churchill and Lloyd-George. Budget Day, 1910. Reuter.

References and Further Reading.
Isaac Babel. *Collected Stories.* 1926. Penguin.

David Baddiel. *Jews don't count.* TLS Books. 202.

Robert Cushman Baldwin. *The Allied Military Expedition to North Russia. 1918-1919.* FCAS. American University Masters Dissertation 1969

Catherine Boylan PhD Thesis. 2016.
The North Russian Relief Force. A Study of Military Motivation in the Aftermath of the First World War.

Antony Beevor. *Russia: Revolution and Civil War, 1917-1921.* Viking Press. 2022.

Ray Bradbury. *The Martian Chronicles, 1950, The Illustrated Man, 1951.* Doubleday.

Toby Faber. *Faberge's Eggs. One Man's Masterpieces and the end of an Empire.* Pan Books 2009.

'Never give in'. The Best of Winston Churchill's Speeches. Selected by Winston S. Churchill (Grandson) Pimlico 2003.

Winston Churchill. *The River War. 1899.*

Franz Kafka. *The Trial.* 1925.   *The Castle.* 1926.

Clifford Kinvig. *"Churchill's Crusade: The British Invasion of Russia 1918-1920."* Hambledon Continuum 2006.

John Morse. *An Englishman in the Russian Ranks. 1915.* Nonsuch Publishing.

Henry Pelling. *A History of British Trade Unionism.* Pelican 1963

Harvey Pitcher. *When Miss Emmie was in Russia. English Governesses before, during and after the October Revolution.* Eland Publishing 1977.

Anna Reid. *A Nasty Little War. The West's Fight to Reverse the Russian Revolution.*
Recently published (Nov 2023), after I'd finished the manuscript.

G.R. Singleton-Gates. *Bolos and Barishynas: Being an account of the doings of the Sadlier-Jackson, and Altham flotilla, on the North Dvina during the summer 1919.* Originally published 1920 as a private publication.
My version by Lightning Source UK Ltd.

Rupert Wieloch. *Churchill's Abandoned Prisoners: The British soldiers deceived in the Russian Civil War.* Casement Publishers 2019

Robert Tressell. *The Ragged Trousered Philanthropists.* 1914

ACS Savory. *Vladivostok, 1919-1920; From the Journal of Captain R.C.S. Savory of the British Military Mission.*
Published in the Journal of the Society for Army Historical Research Vol. 71 No. 285 (Spring 1993)

Klaus Wagenbach. *Kafka.* Haus Publishing. 2003.

Joanne Wheatley. *A Passion for Baking 2012.*

Emile Zola. La Bete Humaine (The Beast Within). 1890.

Manifesto of the Communist Party. Karl Marx and Frederick Engels. 1848.
Imperialism, the Highest Stage of Capitalism. V.I. Lenin 1917.
Socialism: Utopian and Scientific. Frederick Engels.1892.
The State and Revolution. V.I. Lenin 1918.
All by Progress Publishers, Moscow.

The Evacuation of North Russia, 1919. HMSO 1920.

About the author.

I was born in Malaysia in 1960 to Roderick (Ricky) Stuart and Lucy Walton, Arthur's eldest daughter. We came back to Britain a year later.

My dad was a regular soldier, volunteering as a young man in 1957. As he lived in Ripon, North Yorkshire he joined the Royal Engineers, with whom he saw service with the Gurkha Engineers in Malaysia and learnt Gurkhali. He transferred to the Royal Corps of Transport in the early 1960's, so as a family, with my two sisters, we moved between the UK and Germany several times.

Between moves we stayed with my grandparents, Arthur and Clare O'Connor from Ballinasloe, Ireland. They'd married in 1932 and lived near Aldershot.

My secondary education was stabilised at Crown Woods Comprehensive School in Eltham, South East London. Close to Woolwich, which is why I ended up in the Royal Artillery for a short army Commission prior to University. Although the 'Colonel of the Regiment' at the time told me at an initial interview, my chosen path was not meant for 'boys like me'. No doubt from the wrong kind of school.

Three years later after studying Economics at Warwick, and getting an army sponsorship, I rejoined the army. After the 7 month Officer Training Course at Sandhurst I spent time in Germany, Canada, Northern Ireland and Thirsk in North Yorkshire with 27 Field Regiment, Royal Artillery.

In 1986 I started a career in the City: securities markets and banking, most of which with Robert Fleming and travelling regularly to Hong Kong, Tokyo and New York. I left finance in 2008 to co-found a technology development business.

This book and the previous two in the chronological series came out of a 'lockdown' project that spiralled when I sat down to capture the stories Arthur Walton told. Books weren't originally planned, but his inspiration created new stories too.

Once these are complete and available, I plan another novel about fraud and scams in the financial sector, set in the 1920's/30's.

Andy Stuart.   August 2024   andystuart@andystuart.net

Printed in Great Britain
by Amazon

58331326R00165